# Ever Sin[...]

**Sara James** studied at St Martin's School of Art and went on to write for national papers and women's magazines. She also has an MA in creative writing from Sussex University. She is the director of Blue Pencil Agency, an editorial consultancy working with both published and unpublished authors. She has four children and lives in London and Wiltshire.

*Also by Sara James*
Mothering Sunday

# Ever Since That Day

## Sara James

ORION

An Orion paperback

Previously published as Christmas Day in
Great Britain in 2021 by Orion Books,
This edition published in 2022 by Orion Fiction,
an imprint of The Orion Publishing Group Ltd
Carmelite House, 50 Victoria Embankment
London EC4Y 0DZ

An Hachette UK company

1 3 5 7 9 10 8 6 4 2

A CIP catalogue record for this book is
available from the British Library.

ISBN (Mass Market Paperback) 978 1 3987 1171 6
ISBN (eBook) 978 1 3987 1175 4

Typeset by Born Group
Printed and bound in Great Britain by Clays Ltd, Elcograf S.p.A.

MIX
Paper from
responsible sources
FSC® C104740
FSC
www.fsc.org

www.orionbooks.co.uk

'I understand more and more how true Daddy's words were when he said: "All children must look after their own upbringing." Parents can only give good advice or put them on the right paths, but the final forming of a person's character lies in their own hands.'

Anne Frank, *Diary of a Young Girl*

For Alex

# PART ONE

—

## Good Friday
### 2019

# ONE

## Ceri

Ceri watched as the man with the ginger curly hair and scuffed leather jacket inched his way past a group of young girls outside on the terrace, indifferent to their flirtatious banter and perky Easter bonnets. He nodded as they lurched forward to give him an Easter kiss, laughing politely as he slipped in through the door. He was an intense, bone-thin middle-aged man who seemed edgy even when he smiled. He was dressed in a red jumper, reminding her of her custom to wear red on her birthday at Christmas, a tradition that went back to the day she was born.

He'd been in a few times and always looked tired. His five o'clock shadow and unruly hair made him appear younger than he was up close. He rarely ate anything, although he was always cheerful. Instead he sat slumped over the bar, his body like a sack of chiselled stones, talking to Jack the barman. Recently, he'd been in the bar three times and each time she'd caught him smiling at her, as if they were already acquainted. She felt as if she should know who he was, but couldn't place him. He was too old for this place, she thought.

It was Saturday, Bar South's busiest night. She cleared two tables and went back to collect some napkins at the bar. She was covering ten places that night.

3

'Couple at number four are paying by card,' she said to Jack. Jack bent down to look for the card machine.

The café, with its rustic chic and scrubbed wood and view to the beach, had always felt familiar, she'd seen versions of it all over: Bali, Thailand, Vietnam. The clientele varied, though. In Bar South entitlement rang in the air, inducing a lot of eye-rolling among the staff. The oscillation of voices, the rise and fall of emotions, matched the pitch and roll of the waves of the Pacific outside – the constant throb of life.

The girls outside were getting rowdy. The summer was over and it was Easter. To Ceri, the idea of Easter felt incongruous against the air of late summer, the smell of suntan oil and the approach of autumn. But in Australia everything was reversed, winter was summer, night was day, even the water went down the plughole anticlockwise. She didn't miss England, though. Not yet. She didn't miss London or her high-powered job as a lawyer. She missed her family, that was all. She realised then that the chiselled redhead was talking with an English accent.

'Christ, why are they so bloody cheerful.' He was perched on a stool next to where she was standing.

'Nothing a few days in Bangladesh wouldn't knock out of them,' Jack said, laughing, his blond salt-sprayed hair dropping over his eyes as he handed the card machine to Ceri.

Either that or their thirtieth birthday, Ceri thought as she swivelled on her heel and went to take table four's bill. She was thirty-four. Turning thirty had been life-changing.

She wiped down table number six, a pile of dirty plates balanced on the other arm, the cutlery rattling. The restaurant was a cacophony of celebration, not just Easter but somebody's twenty-first birthday party, and the buzz

4

propelled Ceri through. A group of students were waiting to sit down and were blocking the doorway. She could see her boss, Tim, was getting impatient, knew she had to be quick with the clean-up, signalling to him that the table was ready. She'd almost forgotten the redhead until she met his eyes as she walked back to the bar.

She was so focused on his kind smile she didn't notice a customer's handbag which was hanging on the back of a chair, its handle unbuckled so that it trailed across her path. She tripped, tried to steady herself but failed and the plates came tumbling down, cascading onto the floor, food spinning off in all directions like splashed paint, the crockery smashing together with the cutlery in a sonata of tinkling china. The smell of ketchup, burger and fried fish wafting up towards her.

The room went silent.

Then the students applauded and a cheer rang throughout the café as Tim blundered across the room, knocking into chairs, weaving in and out of the overcrowded tables, sidestepping oblivious customers in his path, arms stretched out like he was playing blind man's bluff.

Ceri felt tears sting her eyes.

'What happened?'

'I'm fine, thank you,' she snapped.

'You'd better get a plastic bag and a mop.'

'Hey, it was an accident, mate.' The redhead was beside her. 'You okay?'

Tim fired a glance at them both. 'She's fine.'

Ceri patted the guy's arm and rolled her eyes. Tim turned on the woman whose handbag caused her to fall.

'Could you place your handbag *under* the table, please?'

The young woman did as she was told, apologetic, but Tim wasn't interested. Ceri went to fetch the mop as Tim bent down to pick up the pieces of broken china and everyone settled back into their evening, the event quickly forgotten. She noticed the redhead picking up a stray broken plate, his mop of hair dropping over his eyes, before going back to the bar.

Ceri returned and Tim threw everything into the bag along with the remnants of food. He snatched the broom and mop out of her hand and told her to get back to work, but she was curious. 'Do you know that man?'

'Who, Jude the dude?' he said gesturing towards the redhead.

She nodded. 'Why Jude the dude?'

'Some name Jack came up with. His name is Jude. You know what Jack's like, has a name for everyone. Calls me slim Tim.' He laughed at the irony. Tim was a barrel of a man.

She dug out her electronic pad to take the drink orders from the group of students, then handed out the menus before going to see Jack.

'Four Coronas, one Sauvignon – large – a gin and tonic and peppermint tea,' she said.

Jack nodded, looked at Jude and then her.

'No boyfriend with you tonight?' Jude said. Ceri felt anxiety run like hot metal through her body. A spark fired up in her chest. The restaurant was crowded and hot. Her boyfriend, Pepe, worked in the kitchen, but he was off that night.

'How do you even know I have a boyfriend?' she said. 'Have we met before?'

'Kind of. When you were very little. I'm a friend of your parents.'

'Oh, I didn't realise. Sorry, I just can't place you.'

'We drifted apart, your parents and I. I've been working

here, in Sydney, and realised you were living here after seeing one of your mum's Facebook posts.'

She was trying to piece it together. So they were connected on social media, she thought, deciding to pay closer attention to her mother's Facebook page in future. Tim came up to the bar. 'Sorry to interrupt the get-together but I think table six are waiting.'

'Sorry.' As she went to leave Jude grabbed her hand.

'Any chance we could meet afterwards?'

Ceri felt unsure. There was something about this man that made her feel uncomfortable. She looked down at her hand and he let go. 'I don't finish until late. I need to get back, Pepe will worry.'

'Sure, but this won't take long.'

'Maybe another time,' she said.

An hour later, the café was thinning out yet still the high-pitched sound of celebration resounded outside, girls in short dresses and yellow feather boas, a long weekend ahead. Ceri was taking an order for desserts when she caught Jude looking at her again. He had a beer in his hand. The dragging sensation that had settled in her chest fired up. She found him unnerving, although he'd been perfectly polite.

Twenty minutes later she arrived at the bar with the last bill.

'Just one more drink,' Jude said to Jack.

'Nah mate. You've had enough.'

'One won't hurt.' He turned to Ceri, looked at her with watery eyes.

'Ceri, tell him.'

Ceri's heart pounded. Had she told him her name? She retreated behind the bar, dipping down to check her mobile, trying to figure out if they'd met before.

'Do you know him?' she mouthed to Jack.

Jack beckoned her to his side. 'Not really, he talks a lot but I don't *know* him,' he whispered. 'He's always pissed.'

As she walked past, Jude laid his hand on her elbow. She could smell stale alcohol on his skin. Jack was right, he was a drunk. Behind Jude, she could see Jack talking to Tim in the kitchen through the round window of the swing door. Tim was angry. She could tell that much.

'Listen, I need to talk to you,' Jude said. His face broke open into a smile, as if it was perfectly normal to express a need to discuss something with a stranger.

'About what exactly?'

'You don't know me, but I know you.' He kept smiling, revealing grey teeth. Ceri felt a prickle of sweat on the back of her neck. He wasn't the kind of friend her parents usually hung out with.

'Name's Jude. Your parents and I were friends, once. Good friends.' He tried to hold her gaze, but was unable to stay focused. He slipped a hand in his pocket, as if to steady himself. 'Ceri's a great name. Means love.' He'd let go of her hand and was drawing on the wooden surface with the moisture left by his glass. 'It's Welsh.'

Ceri was making herself busy but she was running out of things to do. 'Why are you telling me this?'

'Because there are things you need to know that your mother hasn't told you.'

She felt her stomach knot up. Ceri started to sweep the floor.

'We're closing, you need to get moving,' Tim said, suddenly appearing at Jude's side.

'Sure.' Jude stood up. She was glad to see Jack return, swinging the kitchen door so that it ricocheted, the rubber seal drawing it to a close.

8

'Listen, dude, you're not welcome in this bar, okay?' Tim said. 'I've been watching you and you can't seem to keep your eyes off Ceri. If anything happens to her, I know who you are.' He grabbed hold of Jude's arm and guided him out of the bar.

'No, it's nothing sinister, I promise,' Jude said.

'Tim, it's fine. He's a friend of my parents,' Ceri said.

'Well, he's still drunk.'

Once at the door, Jude wrenched his arm away and turned back to speak to her.

'Ask your mother about me. Ask her where those luscious curls come from *and* the green eyes!'

She looked into *his* green eyes; hers were mostly hazel but green sometimes, depending on the light, but it was true about her curly hair. Nobody in her family except for her great aunt had curly hair.

'You were born on Christmas Day. I know because I was there!'

And then he was gone.

Ceri felt tears prick her eyes. 'I don't think he was being offensive,' she said. 'He was a bit drunk, but not threatening.' She wasn't sure why she was defending him.

'Sorry, but he's not coming in this bar again. He drinks too much and he's always trying to distract the staff.'

But Ceri wasn't listening. She was thinking about her curly hair and the colour of her eyes. There was no doubt in her mind. He was implying he was her father.

# TWO

## Ceri

Ten minutes later Ceri was making her way home. The night air was balmy despite it being well past midnight. There was a brutality to the heat in Australia – dry and unforgiving – forcing everyone towards the shade, but she liked it. Now she could feel the season retreating, a mellowing in the air. Her mother had wanted her to go back for an Easter family holiday, kept nagging that she'd already missed Christmas and her birthday, but Ceri hadn't wanted to end this journey, nor did she want to leave Pepe. They'd not been together long – eight months after meeting a year ago – and she didn't want to upset the rhythm of their new life.

She could smell a sweetness in the air of ripened fruit, sea salt and beer. She walked up the tree-lined avenue towards the apartment, keys in her hand. This man, Jude, had left her feeling uneasy. She found distraction in the Victorian terraces with their iron balustraded balconies, squat palm trees poking out of tiny front patios. In style, Sydney's Surry Hills was part British, part French, part American and finally, Australian. A mish-mash, she thought. She crossed the road feeling another stirring of fear, the adrenaline coursing through her veins. She was completely alone. The only sound was the heavy sigh of her own breath. She had a feeling someone was watching and turned abruptly, half expecting to come face to face with him again.

A dog trotted down the road, the foliage rustled with other life and she jumped. There wasn't a soul to be seen and yet still she felt as if she were being followed. She jogged up the street, saw the yellow VW campervan that belonged to a friend and felt comforted by its proximity. Pepe had arranged to borrow it for their camping trip for a small fee. A soft breeze stirred her skirt and she relaxed a little knowing it was only a short distance until she reached home. She arrived at the gate, opened the door to the block of flats, ran down the hallway towards their condo, her feet echoing on the wooden floor. A bulb flickered up ahead, blinking light onto the grubby skirting. She went straight upstairs to their bedroom and tried to shake the feeling off like a cat would rain.

Pepe was in bed, the tangled sheet barely covering his naked body. Still breathing heavily after jogging up the hill, she crossed the room to open the French windows to let in some air. They'd filled their small terrace with potted plants and a cutting of jasmine which had begun to climb, its tendrils clinging to the lattice fencing. She closed her eyes, felt a wash of peace just listening to the sound of night. The cicadas had gone quiet, but in the darkness she could sense the restlessness of the dying heat. She walked back to Pepe, crouched down, watched as he slept. He looked sad, even in his sleep. His dark hair was swept back off his face, the stubble on his chin, black. She kissed his forehead. His eyes opened.

'Estás triste?' she asked.

Pepe smiled. 'I missed you,' he said. 'You're late.'

'Some guy was giving me grief.' Just the warmth of Pepe's eyes was enough. She let the tears slip down her cheeks.

'Cariño. Que pasa?' Ceri felt herself break open. There was something so direct about Pepe, open and calm. His father was English and his mother Spanish, so his English was impeccable without a trace of an accent, but it was Spanish that came to him in moments of emotion.

'He said he was a friend of my parents, and this sounds crazy, but he implied he could be my father. That he was the reason I had curly hair, he said. Okay, he was pissed, but it was very strange.'

'Do you believe him?' Pepe held her face.

'No.' She turned away, could barely speak. Her mouth was dry with shock. 'I can't bear the idea that my dad isn't my dad. It just seems ridiculous to even say such a thing.' Hot tears pricked her eyes. 'But, if I'm honest, I've always wondered why I'm different from my brothers and sister – you've seen the pictures – and Jude was very convincing. So a part of me wonders, you know?' She gulped back tears. A trickle of sweat rolled down her back. She felt a desperate need to talk to her father, have him reassure her, but he was still recovering from his operation and this was the last thing he needed.

He waited, holding her close until her shoulders stopped shaking and she was still. 'You need to speak to your mother.' He kissed her, unclipping her hair so that it fell over her shoulders onto his. 'Breathe. In for five, out for six.'

She did as she was told, feeling calmer instantly.

'Hold me,' she said and quickly slipped off her clothes, climbing into the bed, pulling the cool sheet over them both. His body was hot and sticky and she felt safe. She held onto his face as if it were there to steady her, and he pulled her to the side so that she was beneath him, stroking her face, her neck. When he looked at her, she felt as if every part of her belonged.

'Let's not use a condom,' she said.

Pepe raised his eyebrows.

'I won't get pregnant. I tried for two years, remember?'

'This is very bad. To say this now when you know I won't resist you.' He shook his head but he was smiling.

'I know,' she said. 'Very bad.'

They kissed and Ceri felt a part of herself fall away, so that she was just her body: flesh and bones and blood.

As they lay side by side she told Pepe about Jude, how he'd come up to help her when she dropped the plates. Pepe pulled back the sheet.

'Where are you going?'

'To get some water. We need to sleep. We have a long day tomorrow. In case you've forgotten, we're going on holiday. You should speak to your mum before we leave.'

She blew him a kiss.

Pepe went back to sleep immediately, his hand resting on her stomach. But Ceri couldn't settle. She kept thinking about Jude, how he'd talked about her mother. Inevitably she thought of her father. He'd just had an operation on his heart. She felt a stab of guilt at not going to see him, but she wasn't ready to go back, not yet.

She slept fitfully that night. Drifting in and out of sleep, thinking of Jude and the way his mouth stretched around his words and spittle flew from his mouth as Tim hauled him out. She remembered her mother's response when she'd told her she was leaving to go travelling. Her mother had been sitting at her table in her studio in the garden, putting together some sketching she'd done on the computer. She always wore an apron when she was working, even if she wasn't painting. Ceri had always loved her mother's sketches, which were loose and colourful. There was something more urgent about her paintings though, they were darker.

'What's up?' she'd said, as Ceri opened the door and leaned into the room. Her mother had always had the ability to read her face, especially when she was anxious. Ceri's mouth was dry like sandpaper; her mother had that effect on her at times like this. She'd been glad her mother had picked up one of her oil pastels and started to give texture to one of her paintings. She was poised at her art desk that spread the width of the studio.

'I'm leaving Fitzgerald and Williamson,' she'd said, her heart bloated inside her chest. 'I handed in my notice today. And I'm leaving Carl as well.' There had been such an air of determination about her that she realised instantly that she'd sounded aggressive and regretted it.

Her mother stopped crayoning and looked up sharply. 'Whatever for?' She looked back down at the painting. 'Bugger.' She got down from her stool and went to put the kettle on. 'Don't stand in the doorway, you're letting the cold in.' Ceri closed the door, feeling immediately trapped. 'If I've learned one thing in life, Ceri, it's not to make rash decisions,' she said. 'And it seems you've made a rash decision. This is quite obviously a reaction to stress. Does Carl know about this?'

'Of course, Mum, and it's not rash. I've felt like this for a few years and I can't not act on it.'

'Tea?'

Ceri shook her head.

'And how is Carl taking it?'

'Not very well.'

Her mother threw up her arms. 'Of course he isn't, poor man. And why give up such a prestigious job, where you were earning so much money? You loved it.'

'I hated it.'

'Ceri, this whole thing with getting pregnant has gone too far, you can't give up your life just like that.' She was fumbling with a packet of peppermint tea. Ceri noticed her hands were shaking.

'It's not a life I wanted, Mum. It's a life you chose for me.'

Her mother had a way of frowning that induced both fear and pity, her lips puckered and wobbled. Ceri could see something register, a thought that her mother put to one side.

'Oh Ceri. How can you say that? You're a successful lawyer, well respected in a male world, an inspiration. We're so proud of you. How can you just give that up? Throw your marriage away at the first hurdle.' All the while she was talking she was busying herself with arranging cups, then washing her paintbrushes that didn't look like they'd seen a lick of paint, until finally she broke down crying, her hands, reddened by fervent washing, planted in the basin, her body shuddering. This was the moment Ceri had been dreading, the moment of emotional tugging when normally she'd back down.

'I need to rethink my life, Mum,' she flopped onto the garden sofa, buried her head in her hands. 'I have one life and I'm as miserable as hell, and yes I know I should be happy but I'm not.' She forced herself to look her mother in the eye. 'Surely that means something to you.'

'What is there to rethink for Christ's sake?' her mother said. 'This is about having a baby, not your job.'

Ceri breathed deeply, as her therapist had taught her to do. 'I'm unhappy.'

Finally, her mother looked up, turned. 'Ceri, happiness is something that comes and goes, it's a fleeting feeling, not something you can aspire towards on an everyday basis. Most of us settle for contentment.'

'Well, I'm not content, either. And I don't agree with you about happiness. I've ploughed my way through hundreds of self-help books, not that you would know, and apparently happiness is more likely to be achieved with a healthy work–life balance and less likely to be achieved if you're in the wrong relationship. I work twelve hours a day, and have very little connection with Carl. His idea of connection is watching the "footy" together. I hate football. We have nothing in common.'

Lori rolled her eyes. 'You're both lawyers.'

'Mum, you don't realise this, but I can't talk to you anymore. I find myself tiptoeing around your expectations. In the end I can't tell you whether I'm happy, or sad, or depressed.' Her voice had risen to the point of hysteria.

'That's not fair. I've been with you every step of the way with this whole fertility treatment thing. Her mother now had her back to the sink. She looked at Ceri with wide round eyes. 'Maybe you just need a holiday.'

'Well, that's just it. I'm going travelling.'

'For fuck's sake, Ceri. What are you, nineteen? What about adoption? I thought that was the plan.'

'It was Carl's plan. It was your plan. It wasn't mine.' She looked at her mother and felt something tight in her gut, wrenching her insides into a knot. 'I just don't want to end up like you, Mum.'

She watched as the insult reached into her, this woman who she knew loved her. But love wasn't always a comfort. The emotion exploded across her face so that she was all wrinkles and cheeks. 'What do you mean?'

'You think you're happy, Mum, but you're not,' Ceri said.

Her mother threw her peppermint tea into the sink so that it smashed. Before slamming the door, she said. 'This is an act of self-sabotage! Believe me, I of all people would know.'

Ceri got up from the sofa and picked out the broken bits of bone china, stained green with flecks of tea. Nothing was going to get in her way, not even her mum.

Ceri found herself weeping quietly into the pillow, hot tears that slid across the bridge of her nose. She heard the rustle of sheets as Pepe's arm reached out to find her.

'Que pasa?' he said.

'I was remembering a time when I was mean to my mother,' she said. 'Just before I left to go travelling. I was hateful, and cruel.'

'Cariño, tranquila. We are made to hurt each other, sometimes. That's part of being human.' He pulled her closer, stroked her hair with his big fleshy hands. 'We're going on holiday,' he said. 'You just need to rest.'

Ceri had been needing to rest since forever.

She woke up the next morning to find the bed empty. Pepe's pillow was scrunched tight, a dip where his head had been. On the bedside table was a wrapped present and a cup of tea. He pushed the door open just as she was untying the ribbon. Inside the box was a thin gold tree of life bracelet.

'It's beautiful, Pepe, I love it. But it's not my birthday,' she said.

'It's our eight-month anniversary.'

She smiled as he stood holding a plate, the contents hidden by his hand.

'Happy Easter,' he said, and revealed a bread roll covered in hundreds and thousands with a painted boiled egg beside it.

'For breakfast?'

'No, we have scrambled eggs and salmon for breakfast.'
He picked out the boiled egg he'd painted a bright green,
held it in the tips of his forefinger and thumb. 'For lunch.'
He bent down to kiss her. 'It's called La Mona de Pascua.
Try some, you'll like it.'

'But I haven't given you anything,' she said.

'Da igual. You've given me you,' he said, striding out of
the door with a spring in his step. She watched the back
of his calves, the muscles pronounced.

Ceri was sitting at the breakfast bar drinking her coffee, the
heat already creeping into the kitchen so that her thighs
stuck together and thin strands of her hair clung to the back
of her neck. Pepe was washing up the breakfast things so
she was free to call her mother. A feeling of unease was
settling in her stomach. She didn't like speaking to her
mother at the best of times. It was the disapproval.

Outside, the day was shimmering. A sliver of light cut
into the kitchen, slicing the terrace in half with shadow.
She opened up her computer and waited while it hummed
into life. The parakeets were making a racket in next
door's fig tree and the sound of them seemed to echo an
internal excitement. The bracelet looked delicate against her
bronzed skin and although she felt vulnerable receiving all
of Pepe's gifts, she also felt loved. She realised the feeling
was new to her, not the love, but the vulnerability that
went with it.

'Darling,' her mother said. Ceri winced, grateful that
Pepe couldn't see her mother's exuberant greeting.

'Hi Mum. Is everyone around?'

Her mother shook her head, tucking her hair behind
her ears. 'They're all on the beach playing Frisbee.'

'What are they, twelve?'

'It's a serious sport in some places, Ceri.' Her mother was uncorking a bottle of wine. It was evening in Europe. Ceri thought she could hear the waves breaking against the shore.

'Where are you?' she asked.

'We got a house on a cliff, next to a beach in Paxos. It's baking here.' As if to illustrate the point she flapped her brushed silk blouse. 'I really wish you'd come, Ceri. We miss you. Your poor father, especially. Promise me you'll be back for Christmas. I couldn't bear to miss another birthday.'

Ceri didn't want to make promises she wasn't sure she could keep. She'd enjoyed an Australian Christmas. A barbecue on the beach with friends. As was tradition, she'd worn red.

'How's Dad?'

'Oh you know, refusing to be an invalid. Been swimming every morning. He's with the others, taking photographs.' And then on cue, her mother said:

'I wish you'd come home soon, Ceri. A year's sabbatical has turned into two.' Her mother ruffled her hair, pushing it in one direction then another. It was cut into a loose semi-curled bob. Her hair had got lighter over the years. It was once dark brown.

Ceri wasn't sure if she was up to a conversation about how travelling wasn't really relevant at her age. She remembered her mother at Heathrow Airport all that time ago, eyes filled with tears, probably knowing deep down that she was part of the reason for Ceri leaving. She was grateful that Pepe was over by the sink, unable to see her mother flitting around, nervous and awkward, which Ceri felt had something to do with her.

'Mum, something pretty bloody weird happened to me last night.'

Her mother was preoccupied with making a salad, her fingers tearing at a lettuce. 'Really, what?'

'This guy kept chatting to me. He said he was a friend of yours.'

Her mother frowned. 'Who? I don't have any Australian friends.'

'He's not Australian, he's English. He's been coming in over the past few days. He has red curly hair.'

This got her mother's attention. She stopped attacking the lettuce and stared into the camera. Even though the screen was blurred, Ceri sensed her anxiety.

'Last night he said he wanted to meet up, but he was so drunk Tim threw him out. That's when he started pleading with me. Said there were things you hadn't told me, implying in some roundabout way that, well, he was my father. That he was there on the day I was born. He completely freaked me out.'

Her mother's face had fallen. Her eyes were wide, her voice shaky. 'Go on.'

'He had green eyes. I mean like mine, but more so.' Ceri was tapping her fingers on the laminate worktop so hard that Pepe turned round to see what was wrong.

'Your eyes are hazel.'

'They're green sometimes.'

'It would help if I knew who he was, Ceri.' Her mother seemed edgy, she tore at a piece of skin on her finger, then gulped down a swig of her wine, the salad forgotten. 'What was his name?' her mother said, curtly.

'Jude.' The feeling of anxiety returned, washing over her so that she felt weak. Pepe had come to stand close to her. 'I'm fine,' she whispered and squeezed his hand.

Her mother's face was as still as stone.

'It's not true, is it – he's not my father?'

'Of course not, darling,' her mother said but there was something odd about her tone. Her voice was shaky. She sucked at her finger where she'd torn the skin.

Ceri could feel Pepe's impatience. 'I'm here with Pepe, so I can't talk long.'

Pepe was five years younger than Ceri, and she knew her mother would disapprove. Disapproval was her mother's profession. Despite her art and her hip circle of friends, there was another side to her that was less free.

'Come and say hello,' she said, holding her hand out to him.

'Voy,' he said, wiping his hands on a tea towel in a rapid swift movement. 'I'm coming.' Pepe raised his eyebrows. He had a habit of doing this, so much so he already had two deep frown lines on his forehead.

Her mother scrunched up her nose, flapped her hands up and down shaking her head, but as Pepe came into view she snapped into a smile. 'Hello,' Pepe said putting on a Spanish accent, which was an in-joke between them. This made Ceri want to wrap her arms around his neck.

'It is very good to meet you,' Pepe said.

For once her mother didn't say a word. She just smiled, nodding her head up and down. She reminded Ceri of a colourful toy bird with a nodding head she'd been given as a child. Her great aunt Marie-Claude had given it to her after a trip to Mexico. Ceri could read the surprise on her mother's face, the way her mouth stayed clenched in a smile while her brain was figuring out who Pepe was. She hadn't introduced them before, deliberately keeping her mother at bay, but then again, she didn't usually chat to her mum when he was around.

Her mother's face was like an electrocardiogram, measuring her emotions rather than her heartbeat, her eyes getting bigger and rounder.

'You are pretty, like your daughter,' Pepe said.

Ceri could have kissed him. He knew exactly how to charm her mother after meeting her for two seconds. Her mother blushed.

'Oh,' she said.

'I can see the likeness,' Pepe continued. 'How is your holiday?'

'We're having a lovely time, thank you.' Her mother's posture relaxed a little, she'd managed to pour more wine and was holding the stem of the glass, twisting it around. 'We needed some sun so we came to Greece.'

'Yes, it is just beginning to get warmer in Spain also. Here summer is ending.'

'Yes, Ceri told me how hot it is, still.'

'Okay, well I had better get back to preparing for our trip. Today we're going camping. I have to prepare the food.'

Her mother offered a finger wave. 'Lovely to meet you,' she said. When Pepe had stepped away, she made a funny face to suggest she was surprised. Just then Ollie and Jake tumbled into the room, their faces over each of her mother's shoulders. They weren't identical, but they both had dark blond hair and their father's bluish-grey eyes. Her mum sighed, her shoulders dropping.

'Ceri!' Ollie cried. 'Babe, how's things?' Ollie was the dominant twin.

'All good, come and meet Pepe.'

Pepe threw his hands up in the air, then stabbed his watch.

Twenty minutes later, her father was saying his goodbyes.

'Make sure you don't overdo it, Dad,' she said.

'Lori!' Her mother arrived and everyone else jumped into the screen and waved, leaving her alone with her mum. 'Finally! Can we chat about what happened last night?' her mother said, her voice hushed. Ceri looked at Pepe, who had packed all the food, sorted the bedding and was now leaning against the kitchen worktop, arms folded, legs crossed, looking fed up. 'Mum, I have to go, sorry.'

'But we didn't get a minute, Ceri.'

'I know. Next time.' She blew her mother a kiss.

'I'm worried. This man, Jude . . .'

'Yeah, I know. He said he wanted to get to know me. It was so invasive.' Just talking about him set her off again. She'd been trying to push the feeling of anxiety away.

Her mother's face visibly tensed.

'Stay away from him, Ceri. He's trouble.' Her voice was so strained, Ceri felt a sense of terror, a deep burning in her sternum, and then a bolt of anger aimed at her mother.

Her mum turned sharply as if someone was behind her, anxiety ringing in the way her eyes darted about and her mouth wobbled. 'I have to go.' There was something about the pitch of her voice, a strained edginess which left Ceri feeling shaky. Suddenly the screen was achingly empty. Pepe was staring at her, arms folded, eyes full of concern.

'Did you hear that?'

'Yep, and I think you should try to see this guy, Jude,' he said. 'It sounds to me as if your mother is hiding something.'

'For sure,' Ceri said. 'For sure.'

# PART TWO

—

Easter
1984

# THREE

## Lori

Lori hovered inside the foyer of Saint Martin's, pulling her leather jacket tightly around her, more as a protection from the onslaught of ordinary life than the cold. The musty second-hand smell of it was unavoidable. She gave the portly doorman her usual greeting: a flirtatious shrug of the shoulders. The boys on her fine-art course called him 'Piss Marks', because he always complained to them about men urinating inside the doorway.

'All right, luv,' he said, which was his standard form of salutation.

'It's my birthday today,' she said. She had to tell somebody.

'Well, have a good one.'

Outside, the late afternoon sun was veiled by gossamer clouds floating like threads of silk. The sky was washed out. The light was bright and she fumbled in her pocket for her sunglasses as she walked down Charing Cross Road in a fatigued daze, glad to hide behind them. A fire engine came whistling past, its siren loud and intrusive, sending her pulse soaring. She'd worked through the night, managing to get a few hours' sleep that morning in her flat in Highbury, which she shared with her friend, Anna, before going straight back into the art studio. She was working on her final year show. On the desk were bulging notebooks, preliminary sketches, pages of different colourways and techniques. She had a month to go, but Lori wanted a first. For her dissertation she was writing about the history of female artists and their impact on the world of art. None of it felt good enough. She felt like an imposter, but that was a feeling that trailed behind her like a deflated balloon.

It was her twenty-third birthday, the end of term and the start of the Easter holidays. She was due to meet her parents to celebrate. She could see her mother standing with her arms folded at the outer edge of the art-school building. Her father was referring to his A–Z.

'Oh Lorraine, there you are,' her mother said, checking out Lori's outfit. Lori had managed to change out of her art-school uniform of dungarees or torn jeans into something her mother would approve of: a pair of black trousers and a little black cardigan. The leather biker jacket would not meet her mother's approval but there were limits. She'd smoothed her hair into something less dramatic than her usual backcombed tangle.

'Hi, Mum, Dad.'

'Happy birthday,' they said in unison.

They kissed, awkwardly, her mother nervous of people passing in that hurried manner Londoners had.

'Can we come up and see your work?' her father asked.

'You'll see it in June,' Lori said, embarrassed at the thought of her parents mincing through the art studio. 'We don't want to be late for Roland.' Her boyfriend, Roland, was at home revising. He'd promised to meet them for lunch, but she needed to call him to say where.

'It won't take a minute,' her father said. 'We'd like to see what you've been up to these past three years.'

Her father guided her mother towards the entrance, his hand in the small of her back. Lori trailed behind them, all of a sudden twelve again. The sense of shame; her father had worn a suit, giving her an extremely premature hot flush. They knew nothing about art and had been horrified at the idea of art college. 'Isn't it all sex, drugs and rock and roll?' her mother had said when Lori had told her she'd got a place at Saint Martin's. It wasn't, but Lori had allowed the idea to fester.

'Well, we'll need to be quick,' she said. 'Roland will be waiting.'

'Yes, we're looking forward to meeting your young man,' her mother said.

Her parents tentatively entered the main building. 'Piss Marks' nodded as they made their way to the lift, which was one of those old-style elevators with bars you had to draw to a close before it worked. It always took Lori a couple of goes to get it to click into place.

Once inside, her mother said, 'It's very tired-looking, isn't it?'

'Well, it's government funded,' her father said, as if that explained everything.

Lori was anxious. She didn't want any of her contemporaries to see her dressed up like a schoolgirl. She'd explained to Roland, but her fellow art students weren't so forgiving. The three of them entered the art studio. Her mother clung to her father as if the more violent paintings might jump out and bite her. Lori's contemporaries were mostly men and everything they did seemed to fill the room with a political voice, a masculine self-centredness that made Lori recoil further into a world obsessed with the abstract juxtaposition of colour. These boys, who painted large canvases big enough to cover an entire wall with scrawled artwork of disconcerting images, seemed to be able to politicise everything. Lori's work was equally vibrant and chaotic. Her tutor had told her she had a talent for colour and that her work was very saleable. Lori wasn't sure if this was meant as a compliment.

Lori guided them to her little spot tucked into the corner at the back of the studio. Her mother was visibly relieved to be confronted by five paintings of kitchen objects: jugs, bowls, a knife, fork and plate, an arrangement of pears.

'Oh, they're very pretty,' her mother said.

'They're not mine,' Lori said. The work belonged to another female artist who was even more of an outsider than she was. She gestured towards an easel where her most recent abstract painting stood, splashed with red on turquoise, greens, indigo and small dots of orange. If you stepped further back, you could see the vague outline of a section of the female body scratched in red. There were scratches of blood red across it. The painting was called *The Voyeur*.

Her father nodded, peering to get a closer look, then stood back and cocked his head. 'Are you expecting to make money?' he asked.

Lori hadn't thought about money, she'd been too preoccupied with the show to think of the practicalities, but her father was a pragmatist – he didn't believe there was fiscal reward to be had within the arts.

'I haven't really thought that far ahead, Dad.'

'Well, you'll need a job of some kind.' He turned his eyes on her. 'Otherwise, you'll have to return home. We certainly can't afford to support a life in London.'

All the while her mother cocked her head and stared at Lori's work. Lori could tell she didn't understand, she was visually illiterate for one thing, but she was saddened to see her disappointment.

'I knew you wouldn't like it,' she said.

'I like the colours,' her mother said, looking now at the paintings on the wall, all abstract with traces of imagery in charcoal that Lori had painted over and scratched out.

'Have you thought about teaching?' her father said.

It was clear to Lori that they'd rehearsed this conversation just by the way her mother clutched her handbag, staring straight ahead giving her father the odd sideways glance, as one would a man in a prompt box.

'Well, I might find a gallery,' she said. 'My tutor said my work is very saleable.'

Her father nodded. 'I don't suppose that will fund a lifestyle in this city, will it?'

'We thought we'd treat you to lunch at The Spaghetti House,' her mother said. 'We have a little present for you.'

Lori forced herself to smile. She'd call Roland from the telephone box near Berwick Street Market. She dreaded them all meeting, but Roland had insisted. It was time, he'd said, although she was yet to meet his parents. It was just a few hours she told herself. Then they would meet Anna and Jude at the French House.

Roland was waiting for them outside The Spaghetti House. He must have flagged a taxi, she thought. She was grateful to see he'd made an effort. His hair was presentable – normally it was a shambles – and he'd worn a black polo-neck jumper under his long expensive overcoat. He stuck out his hand as they approached.

'How do you do?' he said. 'Roland.' Lori watched her father take him in, a ripple of confusion running across his face before he smiled.

'Graham. And this is Lori's mother, Helen.'

Lori managed to roll her eyes at Roland before they

went into the restaurant; he winked and patted her bottom as they followed her parents inside. 'Happy birthday,' he whispered into her neck.

Once seated they all sat and stared at the menus, an awkward silence forming, so that every sniff and cough was amplified. She could see that Roland wasn't what her parents had expected. For once she'd managed to please them. A part of her revelled in their surprise, but now she could see they were both rather daunted by his public-school accent and his impeccable manners.

After they'd decided on their food, which Lori knew, despite the deliberation, would be lasagne, things eased a little. Roland ordered the same, which she assumed was an attempt to fit in.

'So, what are you studying, Roland?' her father asked. Another sniff punctuated the question.

'English and French,' Roland said. 'I'm doing a law conversion degree straight after.' He broke off a bit of a breadstick and passed it to Lori. Lori watched her mother observe every small detail, offering Lori an 'ever so slightly' raised eyebrow.

'Sensible,' her father said. 'I'm in insurance. I wished I'd had the opportunity to study law.'

Lori felt herself redden. She hadn't seen her parents in months and their very presence was stifling. She longed to get back to her painting. She'd spent the last week working into the nights and had loved the way the building felt dense and forbidding when it was empty of people. She'd done her best work with her headphones on full blast, listening to the Pointer Sisters and Eurythmics. Talk Talk's *It's My Life* she played over and over. She'd done well to slip out of her parents' grasp, and the idea of her returning to Sussex to live with them was unthinkable.

She realised she'd missed a chunk of conversation. Her mother was twiddling her napkin as Roland spoke.

'My father's in property,' he said. 'I'm going to specialise in property law.'

'Is that so. Is he a developer?'

Roland shrugged. 'Industrial, mostly, although he's recently embarked on a big domestic project.'

This sparked an interest. Helen's mouth twitched.

'You might know him,' Lori said to her father.

'LBS Properties,' Roland said. 'I'm going to work for him afterwards. My father wants me to get a handle on our legal department.'

'Sounds like you have a clear idea of your future,' her father said. Her mother had hardly spoken. Lori knew it was because she was slightly baffled, out of her depth. Her father held his own, though. Roland was everything her mother dreamed of for Lori, to the point that Lori worried that her attraction was based on a need for parental approval. But it was more than that. For a start, he wasn't in awe of her like so many of her earlier boyfriends, and they'd hit it off immediately, talked into the night. She didn't go home for two days after that first date.

'We're slightly concerned about Lori's future. It's not easy to earn money as an artist,' her mother said.

Lori tensed her jaw. 'Mum . . .'

'Lori's going to do brilliantly, I assure you. Apart from the fact that she's talented,' Roland rested his hand on her knee, 'she's ambitious.'

Her mother gave a nod of agreement. That's when the carafe of wine arrived.

'Almost forgot,' her mother dug into her handbag and proffered a long thin present wrapped in silver paper. Lori slowly unwrapped it, knowing that she was probably going to have to pretend.

Inside was a watch with a classic black strap and a small gold face. Inoffensive, tasteful even.

'It's lovely,' she said. 'Thank you.' Roland helped her to put it on, although she was perfectly capable of doing so herself. 'I love it.' She leaned forward and gave both her parents a kiss.

As they went to leave the restaurant, she saw Roland catch her father's arm, holding him back from going outside. Her mother was busying herself with getting her ticket ready for the tube. She'd bought an 'away day' to include the underground. Lori wondered if Roland was offering to pay the bill.

'He's not what we expected,' her mother said, applying some lip gloss.

Lori could see the two men talking through the window. Her father chuckling, while Roland was serious.

'What *did* you expect?' Lori asked.

Her mother looked up from a little hand mirror and pinned her down with her brown eyes. 'Someone wilder. Someone more like you.'

'Well, maybe opposites attract,' Lori said. Her mother just smiled knowingly, leaving Lori feeling uncomfortable, as if she didn't quite understand what had been said.

Then Roland and her father came out engaged in conversation. Roland spotted a taxi and flung out his hand. 'I have a small errand,' he said. 'Can I offer anyone a lift?'

'Oh no,' her mother said. 'We like the tube.'

Roland gave them a hearty wave and thanked them for lunch, kissing her goodbye and whispering into her ear. 'See you later.'

34

After she'd seen her parents off at Oxford Circus station, she turned back to walk to Saint Martin's, keen to get herself dressed, backcomb her dark hair, blacken her eyes with eyeliner and slip neatly into a persona that had taken years to perfect. She undid the watch and tucked it into her jacket pocket. Her parents' visit had left her feeling discombobulated.

Faced with her work, she realised that painting would sooth her nerves, bring her back to herself more effectively than any sartorial shift. She needed art in the same way other people needed a warm bath. She picked up her brushes and a bottle of turps and watered down some red oil paint so that it was transparent, pushing the brush into the canvas and letting it dribble. She immediately felt calm, watching how the red ran over the other marks, fanning out into little rivulets, spreading across the surface, bleeding into the turquoise like tiny veins. She had worked hard to give the painting depth and texture. Over the past few weeks she'd grown to love painting, despite it being raw and painful sometimes, bringing up conflicting feelings of sadness and joy. When she worked, she felt as if she were fully formed and whole, so much so she felt lost without it.

It was when she was washing her brushes and tidying up her desk that she saw a business card that had been left on her table. It was from a well-known gallery.

Scrawled across the top was a message: Please call.

# FOUR

## Lori

By eight o'clock, she was ready. Unlike the goths who frequented Saint Martin's, Lori wore torn jeans, a paint-spattered T-shirt and a black ribbon in her backcombed hair. She turned off at Moor Street, heading into the depths of Soho, past the women loitering in short skirts outside the sex club and the French patisserie that was usually filled with first-year students getting their taste of cosmopolitan London. She breathed in the dense smell of exhaust fumes. She felt as if she belonged to the metropolis with its throbbing beat that never stopped, the constant blur of activity and socialising, the continuous onslaught of traffic and people, like blood running through a body. She couldn't possibly contemplate leaving it, she thought. The years had passed too quickly.

She'd met Anna in the first year at halls in Camden. It was Anna who took her to a party at the University College London bar and introduced Lori to her boyfriend, Jude, and in turn to Roland. They were both clever men who would rattle off an essay on deconstructionism or some other '-ism' that mattered. They'd both read Marx, Foucault, Lacan, Sartre, but Jude revelled in his brilliance whereas Roland appeared indifferent. She'd been drawn to his relaxed stance, his quiet generosity and the way he seemed to look after

36

everyone, but what she admired most was his ability to listen. He wasn't like other boys of his age who clambered over each other's egos. Roland was happy to be invisible. He didn't just listen to what she said, he listened to the stuff she didn't say as well. She'd had other boyfriends but with Roland it felt as if she'd always known him. He admired her art, talked about the boldness of her work in a way she didn't wholly understand when she took him to her studio. Roland and she became lovers that same night.

That year, her second and his third, they'd formed an impenetrable group. The four of them would sit in the French House and conduct long intellectual discussions over bottles of red, Roland often ranting in French when he was drunk enough. Sometimes lecturers from Saint Martin's would join them. They were always at the centre of every argument, mostly justifying a life of debauchery and discussing the virtues of existentialism. Jude, with his stylish curly red hair and velvet jackets, would perform at the small stained tables ringed with years of use, his intellect a shining beacon. Roland would provide the steady flow of alcohol and an argument for Jude to push against, Anna the beauty with her blonde hair loosely pinned up, and Lori the rebellious artistic element. When she'd first met Roland, the two boys had just returned from a year at the Sorbonne through some exchange system organised by UCL. They were close, but in their fourth year, they'd become more competitive.

Walking through Soho, she realised she'd miss it. By night, it was all neon and sex, a clandestine underworld, which by the next day was obscured by the buzz of daily life: people dashing about, either with cans of film or reels of fabric samples, and then there was Berwick Street Market where men hollered the price of their produce in indecipherable bursts. She'd miss being in the heart of things.

She turned down Dean Street and seconds later arrived at the French House. She walked into a wall of voices, the usual racket of people shouting orders, arguing points, making jokes. The place was packed to the brim. Roland and Jude were holding court in the far corner. Anna was at the bar clutching a bottle of wine.

'Happy birthday!' Anna looped her arms around Lori's neck. 'How was lunch?'

'Excruciating!'

Lori followed Anna back to their table. The bench that ran down the side of the pub was already crammed, throbbing with end-of-term celebrations. Lori watched as Anna squeezed in next to Jude and Roland. Her long blonde hair was backcombed into a bun, and her eyes slanted upwards, accentuated by some kohl. Roland smiled his lazy slow smile that suggested he was already inebriated. He'd had a couple of glasses at lunchtime, although she couldn't blame him. When she looked at Roland and Jude, she thought of Roland as polished sandstone, and Jude as a piece of flint freshly hewn from the Sussex Downs.

'Babe,' Roland said. 'Happy birthday! How come it took you so long? I've been waiting.' He patted his knee, offering her a seat on his lap.

'I've been painting.' Lori perched on Roland's lap, slipping her legs either side of his.

He pressed his mouth into her hair. 'I love how you work. It's as if you're in dialogue with a missing part of you.'

Lori pressed her nose into his hair, liking his smell.

'Thatcher is evil I'm telling you,' Jude was saying.

'Oh who cares?' Roland said in his slow assured voice. 'So, did I do well?'

'They loved you,' Lori said.

38

Roland turned to address Jude's political rant. 'The miners won't win.' Roland nuzzled into her neck. 'I want you,' he whispered, running his hand down her leg.

'Yep. They don't stand a chance against the bloody elite. Why take a right-wing stance?'

'I'm just a realist,' Roland said, turning back to Jude.

'Haven't got a socialist bone in your body,' Jude said, pointing aggressively at Roland who smiled his big wide-mouthed smile and shook his head.

Lori caught the eye of a girl opposite, who seemed to be enthralled by Jude holding court once again, a Gauloise wedged in between his fingers.

Roland kissed her roughly on the cheek. She'd never questioned the sex, but occasionally she wondered if they weren't very good at it. Anna boasted about Jude and her own capacity for multiple orgasms, which of course Jude expertly facilitated. Lori mostly felt out of her depth, inexperienced.

Jude was now arguing with a guy she hadn't seen before, the sleeves of his velvet jacket pushed up to expose his muscly arms. 'Derrida invented deconstruction,' he was saying before taking a drag on his cigarette.

Anna rolled her eyes. 'Give it a rest, darling.' She was talking to the girl who seemed enchanted with Jude and had stopped mid-sentence. 'You spend your life jostling for superiority armed with mere opinion. Relax, school's over now. While the rest of us go home and revise, you can sit here and have your rant.'

'I'm revising.'

'Oh, yeah, like you have to.'

Lori looked at Jude, noticing for the first time the way his jaw was pronounced enough to form a shadow down his neck. He was clearly wounded by Anna's harsh tone.

He smiled into his lap, eyes glazed. His red hair seemed to have a life of its own, the ringlets falling over one eye.

'You need a drink,' Roland said and squeezed her waist, getting up to go to the bar. Jude turned to acknowledge Lori for the first time. She was expecting some cynical remark, but instead he fixed her with his green eyes, holding her still with the intensity of his gaze. He squinted, his stare rooting her to the chair as if he'd seen something she'd hidden inside herself. 'You look anxious,' he said. 'What's the matter?'

Lori was taken aback. 'I've just spent the afternoon with my parents,' she said. 'I don't know who I am or what I'm going to do with my life. All I want to do is paint but they want me to get a job as a teacher.'

Jude smiled. There was a kindness to his expression. 'I love your raw honesty,' he said, and he pinched her chin. 'Here, I got you a present.' He handed her a parcel wrapped in brown paper.

'Gosh, that's sweet of you.' He nodded at the package. 'Well open it then,' he said, before turning back to the guy opposite to resume his discussion on the French philosophers.

She unpicked the package without ceremony, and slid out a book. It was a copy of *The Old Man and the Sea* by Ernest Hemingway. A first edition.

'Thank you,' she said.

Jude turned to her. 'I thought you'd like the cover. The colours, the fish. It's a great novel too.'

There was a tenderness to Jude's words and she was grateful. She caught Anna's eye, saw a glint of unease. She was worried that Anna, who was often keen to take offence and thought nothing of showing her disapproval, would accuse her or him of some act of disloyalty, but

Anna quickly brushed away whatever doubt was preying on her mind with a wide confident smile.

'Glad you like it,' she said. 'We found it in that second-hand bookshop in Bloomsbury.' Anna had given her a beautiful pair of earrings that morning, which Lori was already wearing. She felt a wash of gratitude.

Roland came back with two bottles of ice-cold champagne gripped between his fingers. He made a huge act of placing them on the table so that everyone was forced to acknowledge the gesture, cheering and clapping. 'Happy birthday, darling,' he said, digging into his pocket and chucking her a box. 'Let's celebrate.'

While Roland poured them all champagne, Lori tentatively opened the box. It took her a while. The paper was wrapped around the box so tightly she had no choice but to tear at it. Nobody was watching when she opened it, they were all too busy having their fill of champagne.

Inside was a man's watch, a Longines exactly the same as the one Roland wore. He'd shown no signs at lunchtime that his present clashed with the watch her parents had given her, still in her jacket pocket. She caught Jude's eye, who was staring at her, a frown creasing his face.

'Rather outshines my first-edition Hemingway,' he said.

'Not at all,' she said.

Roland punched him on the arm. Jude caught his hand and they tussled playfully.

'It's beautiful,' she said, and she meant it, but she felt guilty thinking of her parents as she held out her wrist for Roland to do up the strap.

Two hours later Lori was happily drunk, standing on the table and dancing while everyone clapped. Anna tried to pull her down but Jude encouraged her to continue.

'It's her birthday,' he said.

She scanned her audience and couldn't see Roland until she caught him shaking his head disapprovingly in the corner. She pouted and beckoned him to join her.

'It's my birthday!' she protested and twirled around and around, somehow managing not to break a single glass, grateful for every ballet class her mother had forced her to go to.

She caught Roland's eye and blew him an ostentatious kiss. He smiled slowly, shaking his head. And she had a feeling she'd caught him, and he had caught her too.

# FIVE

## Anna

Anna was watching Lori throw up in the doorway of a high-street shoe shop on Oxford Street. She was furious with Jude who never seemed to know when to stop and had ignored Lori's pleas for food. He was ignoring them both now as he danced around a lamppost singing at the top of his voice. *She'll be coming round the mountain when she comes,* only he'd started his own version of it. *She'll be puking in the shoe shop when she comes.* Anna watched as bile trickled across in the direction of her feet, stepping aside as it dribbled towards the gutter. Lori was watching its progress with great concentration.

'Some poor sod will have to wash that away tomorrow,' she said.

Anna spotted the watch. 'That was a generous gift.'

'My parents bought me a watch as well.' Lori was still bent over, leaning against the shop window. 'Not a Longines, though.'

'I guess if you have the money.' Anna was digging around in her bag until finally she handed Lori a tissue. She was the practical one of the two of them.

'My parents were scared of him, especially my mother. The watch will make them feel inadequate.' Lori heaved again.

'Well don't show it to them. Why does he hang around with us, anyway? Hasn't he got a whole load of debutantes to court?' Anna said.

Lori started to laugh. Anna rarely got drunk. She couldn't bear losing control. Lori was less careful.

'He's not like anybody else I know. He doesn't seem to be influenced by anyone or anything.'

'Oh my God, you're in love with him, aren't you?'

'I don't fucking know,' Lori said.

Lori staggered out of the doorway and stopped to lean on a lamppost. Anna followed. The boys were weaving their way up Oxford Street. A snail could have made better progress. Jude was whistling, hopping on and off the pavement, his arms outstretched, a lit cigarette burning between his lips, the odd black cab tooting at him as he carried on regardless. Roland joined Jude, their arms wrapped around each other, the two of them whistling in harmony.

'Perhaps it's because he's such a bear of a man,' Lori started to giggle.

Anna watched as Roland traipsed alongside Jude, lolloping almost, happy to be Jude's sidekick. She was beginning to see there was more to Roland than his loyalty towards Jude, though. He was ambitious in a quiet sort of way. That watch was a statement of intent. You don't spend that much unless you're serious.

'Bit of a dark horse our Roland,' she said. Anna knew she was too serious to be attractive to someone like Roland. Lori just knew how to play the game. Anyway, Anna's mother, who taught English at Cambridge, would be horrified if she'd turned up with Roland. She admitted to herself that Jude fitted her mother's ideal as well as her own, with his sharp intellect and cynicism.

'Aren't *you* in love?' Lori asked.

'It's not the same with Jude. He's prickly and difficult, which I suppose is what attracts me to him. He's not romantic but he's good in bed,' she said.

'So you keep telling me,' Lori said.

'What do you want?' Anna asked, stopping. 'I mean from your life.'

Lori carried on marching towards Tottenham Court Road as if her life depended on it. She stopped. 'Christ, Anna. You pick your moments.' She pushed back a rogue strand of hair. 'I suppose I could tell you what you want to hear: I want to be a famous painter, make my mark on the world, but I'm not sure I've got what it takes. I suppose I want to have kids, live in some big old bohemian country house with children running naked in the garden and the place filled with the smell of freshly baked bread.'

'Wow! Ambitious after all,' Anna said, aware of her own mocking tone, but they both fell about laughing, 'Well of course, to be ambitious is to court failure, isn't it?' Anna said, fishing a chewing gum out of a packet she had in her pocket. 'Here, this will freshen your mouth.'

Lori took it. 'Do they teach you this stuff at your psychology classes?' Anna was used to sparring with Jude. Sniping at each other was part of their foreplay. But Lori took things deeply.

'I grew up with two academic parents. I have a whole load of idioms to hand, it was part of my parents' verbal arsenal. Roland's parents have a gun room, my parents had a library.'

'Mine shored themselves up with insurance and paint-by-number artwork,' Lori said, and they started laughing again.

'What about you?' Lori asked.

'I suppose I want to make my mark in the world of psychology. Maybe write a couple of books, do my bit in terms of research,' Anna said. 'I've applied to do an MA.'

'Anna, that's great.' Lori wrapped her leather jacket tightly around herself. 'Christ it's cold.'

'Is it great?'

'Yes, it is. At least you have a plan. I think painting was just a way not to be like my parents, and I love it, but now I don't know where to start. A gallery left a card on my desk today. I'm terrified.'

'But that's brilliant,' Anna said.

They finally caught up with the boys. Roland was standing with his hands deeply wedged in his pockets, nodding ever so slightly. He was drunk in a very different way to Jude who became exuberant when inebriated. Roland became solid, like an ancient tree trunk. Lori reached for his hand to steady herself and they both marched ahead. Jude stopped outside the Hundred Club and started to descend the stairs.

'Jude, please,' Anna said, holding onto his arm, pulling the sleeve of his jacket.

'God, you can be a bore sometimes,' he said.

'You're coming with me,' she said.

His lovely velvet jacket looked crumpled. His hair all messed up. He looked malleable. She had to admit there was something endearing about him when he was drunk.

'Love it when you get all dominatrix,' he said, slurring.

'I'll remember that.' They followed the other two, swinging their hands between them like two children at kindergarten. Lori was singing 'Happy Birthday' to herself. Anna wasn't sure who was worse – Jude or Lori. They were both inclined to make an exhibition of themselves.

'Do you think they'll get married?' she asked Jude, watching Roland and Lori's backs hunched over in an embrace. They seemed to have melded into one.

'He's twenty-three for fuck's sake!'

Centre Point towered above them. Jude looked up. Its ugly pronounced window frames and thwarted bow structure seemed to appeal to him. He was grinning stupidly. 'I bloody love this town,' he said.

'What about me?' Anna asked. 'Do you love me?' She didn't know why but she was filled with self-doubt.

Jude looked at her with those green wounded eyes that seemed able to pin anybody to the ground. 'What do you think?' he said, grinning. He was swaying. He reached out for her and she caught his hand. This, she realised, was how Jude was. Zig-zagging his way through life and somehow collecting admiration from all and sundry. The tutors adored him, awarded him a first for an essay he wrote in one morning. God, she loved his brilliance. When she'd told her mother about Jude, her mother had said, 'You do realise academics are often alcoholics.' Anna knew she was referring to her father, but Jude was different. He wanted to change the world.

'What do you want from life, Jude?' she asked.

'Sex with you,' he said.

They caught up with the others. Roland was grinning.

Lori was spinning, her favourite party trick, screaming out. 'We're going to Paris. We're going to Paris.'

Roland caught her and reeled her into an embrace. 'We've decided to go to Paris. Celebrate end of term, Lori's birthday and anything else we feel like celebrating. Coming?'

'Great, we can go to Les Bains Douches instead of the Hundred Club,' Jude said.

'What about revision?' Anna said. 'Lori, what about your dissertation?'

'Roland said he'd help me. I'll take some reading.'

'A few days off will do us good,' Jude said, and winked at Roland.

Anna had an inkling that the boys were up to something, that this discussion had been planned. 'That's all right for you to say, you'll get a first whatever you do. The rest of us have to work for it.'

'It's just a few days,' Roland said.

Anna felt unsure. She wasn't renowned for her spontaneity.

'Come on, stop being a party pooper,' Jude said.

'Okay, let's do it!' But Anna had a feeling of foreboding she was finding hard to shift.

# SIX

## Lori

They headed to Paris the next day. Lori had to pick up
her passport from her parents en route. Luckily she'd
drunk enough water to ward off a headache. She handed
her battered road map to Anna to work out the way to
Dover from her parents' house in West Sussex. Desperate
to nurse their hangovers, both boys dozed off in the back
of the car. Forty minutes later they reached suburbia. The
day had dulled off, a heavy blanket of grey cloud pressed
down on them and the traffic was infuriatingly slow. Lori
felt tense at the prospect of introducing her friends to her
parents, but at least she'd broken the ice with Roland. She
was ashamed of them, which made her feel even more
dismayed at her own prejudice. She'd hesitated in front of
the mirror not knowing which 'Lori' to present.

She was tailing some man in a BMW, her foot flat
down, changing through the gears, nipping in and out of
lanes, sailing past cars twice the size of her own. The Fiat
Uno was actually shuddering with the effort. She looked
at her wrist. She was wearing the watch her parents had
given her. Roland had said nothing when she'd taken off
his watch that morning and popped it back in the box and
replaced it with their gift.

'I don't want to upset them.'

Roland had raised his eyebrows. 'Of course not.'

She'd left the box on the bedside table but Roland had pocketed it. As she locked the door she said, 'Did you offer to pay for lunch yesterday?'

'Of course not, that would be rude.'

'So what were you talking to my father about?'

'Business.'

Who else talks business at his age? she thought.

An hour and a half later, they turned right at a roundabout on the A24 and dipped down into a valley surrounded by fields of sheep. The hills either side of them were steep and lush. The ploughed fields, a dark peaty brown, were spotted with seagulls. They passed an old folly with a miniature tower, and then a large farmhouse. She wished for a second she could pull into some old rangy estate and surprise her friends. She imagined Anna already had an inkling of her background but Lori had been careful not to reveal too much to Roland. Now she felt exposed.

'I *have* been to France before,' she said as they came up to a junction. 'Went once with my parents to Nice.'

'We always went to Devon for our holidays,' Anna said, wincing as they cut in front of a Mini.

'We have a house in the Dordogne,' Roland said.

'Of course you bloody do,' Jude said.

'You're both awake then!' Anna said.

Ten minutes later, Lori parked up outside her parent's newly built detached house, her heart hammering away at the prospect of introductions. She didn't want any of them to see her dull family home, meet her mother who thought imagination was as scary and unpredictable as an earthquake, or her father whose punctuality was seen as a contributing factor to his minimal success. It was her art teacher who'd seen she had talent, not her parents, who had acquiesced begrudgingly when Lori's art teacher explained how hard it was to achieve a place in Saint Martin's.

Opposite the family home was a row of shops: a wool shop, a pet shop, a junk shop and an estate agent. Everywhere was eerily quiet.

'Welcome to the heartland of suburbia,' Lori said.

'Nothing wrong with the suburbs,' Jude said. 'Not sure by its very nature you can name it the heartland, though.'

'You know what she means,' Anna said, rolling her eyes as she climbed out of the car.

'We can't stop for long because of the ferry. Hopefully my father will be working,' Lori said.

'You're nervous,' Anna said.

'They're very prudish, that's all. And parsimonious.' She felt herself redden. 'This trip to Paris is going to be seen as reckless. They objected to the car, which I paid for with my own money. They disapproved of art college. Basically they negate everything I do.'

'Don't worry about it, babe. We've got this,' Jude said.

Roland smiled kindly in the rear-view mirror. They knew very little about each other's family and yet they'd been together for almost two years. Their relationship had centred around the four of them. She checked out both boys. Jude with his velvet jacket, albeit on the crumpled side, looked reasonable, but Roland looked a shambles, unshaven still, in his long expensive crumpled overcoat and unwashed hair, his camera hanging around his neck. A different man to the one she'd presented yesterday.

The front door, painted a glossy navy blue, opened. Her mum, wearing a lilac M&S twin set – Lori wanted the world to swallow her up – was standing in the doorway, arms folded. Looking at her mother as a stranger would, her face revealed a continuous diet of disappointment.

'Hi, Mum.'

'Lorraine, what *has* happened to your hair?'

'This is Anna, my friend who's studying psychology, and Jude, her boyfriend.'

'Hello, Helen,' Roland said, offering her a peck on the cheek. Her mother actually blushed.

Jude sauntered in behind him. Lori rolled her eyes. 'This is going to be painful,' she said to Anna as they all jammed into the tiny hallway.

They were shown into the living room. A faux Regency fireplace took centre stage, a gas fire flickering inside it. The wallpaper was a green and white Liberty print. Lori squirmed as she saw the house from her friends' point of view. There were landscape paintings on the wall, the type you could buy in a department store.

They all squeezed onto the green Dralon sofa while her mum brought in tea. Lori's passport was sitting on the table. She quickly pocketed it.

'Your father's on his way,' her mum said, putting down a plate of cakes, along with a teapot.

'Oh, he didn't need to come home early.' Lori squirmed again, twisting her hair around her index finger. Roland looked like he hadn't seen a bed in weeks, and yet that coat was from Jermyn Street. Jude sat there, as colourful as a child's drawing. He was already chomping his way through a cake, hadn't waited to be served. Lori's mum handed him a plate and a paper napkin. Lori noticed she was wearing several gold bracelets. She'd made an effort.

'Are you going to do a law conversion degree as well?' her mother asked Jude, preoccupied with the business of handing out cake forks. It was too late for Jude, who was halfway through a slice of lemon drizzle.

'God, no.'

'It's just me,' Roland said.

Jude choked on a piece of cake. 'You kept that quiet.'

Roland had mentioned the law conversion degree to Lori a few weeks back. She understood why he hadn't told Jude, who was bound to tease him.

'Can I help with the pouring?' Anna said.

'You could hand the cups out,' her mother said. It wasn't so much a smile that Lori could see, but something close to curiosity forming in her eyes when she looked at Roland then Jude.

'It was my idea to take us all to Paris,' Roland was saying.

'Did you tell your mother about the gallery, Lori?' Jude said, eyeing up a Bakewell tart.

Lori frowned. 'No.'

Jude flashed a smile. Lori could see the sly look in his eye, his quick mind weaving up some tale. 'I've got a friend who owns a gallery in Paris. He's going to sell Lori's paintings,' he said.

Lori felt her cheeks grow hot. 'Actually, a gallery in Covent Garden asked me to call.'

'Why didn't you mention this yesterday, Lorraine?' Lori's mother said. She had, by this point, introduced herself to the others as Helen.

'Found their card after lunch. I'll call them when I get back from Paris,' Lori said, winding her legs into a tight coil. She should have called them today, she thought. But she didn't want to appear too keen.

'Well, that is a turn-up for the books,' Lori's mother said. 'And a gallery in Paris too.'

They were all sitting with a plate balanced on their lap. Her mum kept smiling at Roland and Jude as if they were two prize-winning trout she'd been asked to cook.

Just then her father arrived with a bulging briefcase, which he promptly dropped with a thud so that Anna jumped. Roland stood up, holding out his hand, revealing his education. Jude was forced to tentatively follow, a self-assured smile on his face from years of being admired. Anna was composed, apparently enjoying the spectacle.

Her mother gave her father a little peck on the cheek. 'You've missed all the excitement, Graham,' she said. 'Jude here has managed to put Lorraine in touch with a gallery in Paris, which is why they're all going. And a London gallery want Lorraine to get in touch.' Lori felt herself redden. It was as if no one else was in the room. Her mother's excitement left her father nodding like one of those felt dogs you found on a parcel shelf of an old car, eyeing up the selection of cakes, probably wondering if he could indulge himself. Lori noticed her mother fussing over Jude. She clearly liked him. She practically ignored Anna.

'Roland mentioned the idea of Paris yesterday,' he said, smiling at Roland.

'Oh,' her mother said. 'Nobody said anything to me.'

Twenty minutes later they were all packed into the car laden with sandwiches, cake and a flask of tea. No one spoke until they were safely on the motorway. Roland, who was now in the front seat with Lori, wound down the window. Lori screamed then put the music on full blast.

'God, that was painful,' she said.

'I think your mum liked us,' Jude said.

'She liked you,' Anna said, turning to Jude.

'Yes, there's another side to my mother. I found a photograph of her taken in the sixties. She was a real wild child,' Lori said, pressing her foot flat to the ground.

'I'm not sure I like where this conversation is going,' Jude said.

'Me neither,' Roland said. 'Maybe she's just a poor judge of character.'

Jude playfully clipped him round the ear. But Lori had been surprised by her mother's obvious favouritism. She'd thought Roland would have been her favourite, but then she remembered her mother's words yesterday:

*Someone wilder. Someone more like you.*

# SEVEN

## Anna

They docked in Calais at seven o'clock in the evening, French time, all of them sitting in silence in the belly of the ferry, waiting for their turn to leave, listening to the heavy thud of cars exiting the ramp and the sound of the French officials bellowing orders. *Vite! Vite! A gauche. To the left.* Anna rather liked the hollow sounds of the port, the clanging of iron, the thump and roar of engines in water, the holler of hungry birds. She already felt as if they'd entered another world, the last few months of intense study fading. Lori didn't seem to mind driving on the opposite side of the road, and as they zipped through the port she appeared to have an enviable innate sense of direction. Anna had always admired Lori's gutsy approach.

'Hey,' Lori said, catching her attention in the rear-view mirror. 'You okay?'

'Yeah, just thinking, you know, about life.'

'Always dangerous,' Lori said, indicating to go into the fast lane. A sign for Paris hung above the road, sending a thrill through Anna's body.

'Your mother seemed to approve of the boys, although I'm not sure she liked me much,' Anna said, thinking of her own mother and how hard it had been to get her attention. As only children, Jude and Lori would never understand what it was to be brought up in a family of four girls and one son, how you had to work hard to get noticed. She'd been told by an aunt that she was the prettiest daughter, but that put her at a disadvantage as far as her family was concerned. Her mother had been an emotional butterfly, flitting from one child to the next, but most often she resided in her own world of academia. Her father was more attentive but careful not to show favouritism. She wondered how Roland was with *his* brother and sister. She didn't know much about his family life. None of them did, except perhaps for Jude. Jude adored Roland, was possessive of him sometimes.

'They approve of Roland, and for all the wrong reasons,' Lori was saying. Roland was slumped at her side, probably still recovering from his session in the bar with Jude.

'Doesn't she approve of me?' Anna asked.

'I could see your beauty put her on edge,' Lori said. 'She's always been critical of women who are naturally confident, especially if they're blonde.'

'But I'm not confident.'

'Well, my mother would have perceived you as such, and anyway, what do you mean? You'll probably get a first, you've already been accepted on an MA course, and you're beautiful.'

'Am I? My mother always used to say my nose rather spoiled my face.'

Lori took a quick glance in the mirror. 'You're kidding, right?'

The headlights of the cars seemed to blind Anna. If she squinted, there was nothing but red, yellow and white lights floating in a sea of darkness. 'My nose is a little squishy.'

'Anna, I'd kill to have your looks.'

'Well, you're pretty stunning yourself.'

'I'm attractive. It's not quite the same.'

'Will you two stop talking about yourselves. I'm suffering from an onslaught of narcissism,' Jude said, who had been hunched against the window in a drunk or hung-over torpor.

'What are you talking about? You make narcissism a competitive sport,' Anna said. She was still mesmerised by the constant rhythm of passing cars, the spangled headlights and the clunk, clunk, clunk of the surface of the road.

The car was filled with a dense silence for a few moments before Jude piped up again. 'People are frightened of beauty, that's all.'

'I'm not,' Roland said, lifting his head just a little. 'Ultimately, people are only truly beautiful if they have something raw inside them.'

'True,' Anna said, knowing he was talking about Lori.

Two hours later they arrived at the Boulevard Périphérique to find themselves in a constant flow of fast-moving traffic, vehicles overtaking on both sides. Anna peered inside the cars as they passed. The people were like city-dwellers everywhere: a sense of purpose and belonging about them. She caught the eye of a passing young guy who saluted her, a toddler in the back chewing an indecipherable toy.

'I feel conspicuous with the GB number plate,' she said.

'Well, Parisians in particular find the English unpalatable,' Roland said.

Everyone seemed to know where they were going and if Anna didn't know any better, so did Lori. There was a constant sense of movement that was unnerving, but Lori seemed to respond to it without fear.

'Do we have enough petrol?' Roland asked.

'Quarter of a tank,' Lori said with an air of buoyancy that suggested she rather liked the risk involved.

Anna was reading the directions in the back with a torch. 'You need to come off at Porte de le Chappelle and then go left around to Porte d'Italie.'

'Okay, well give me a bit of warning, I feel like I've been involuntarily entered for a slot in *Wacky Races*. It's hard to determine which is the slow lane.'

'There isn't one,' Roland said. 'Here, give me that.' He turned round and snatched the map from Anna's lap. 'You've been demoted.'

Anna thought what an odd bunch they were. Roland, she knew, avoided talking about his family but there was money there for sure. Jude made scathing remarks about his mother and her poor attempts at poetry, but it was the things he didn't talk about that worried her most. Lori appeared to have reinvented herself completely. It made Anna feel quite ordinary.

'Okay, you want to start indicating. It's not the next turn-off, but the one after.' Roland wound down his window and stuck his head out, waving for the car behind to let them in. 'Now!'

Lori did as she was told. Anna was quietly impressed by the way the two of them worked as a team getting them safely off the Périphérique and down into the unknown territory of Paris suburbia. Lori raced down side streets at great speed, undeterred by the cobbled roads and the occasional tooting from an irate driver.

'Pull over, there's a petrol station,' Roland said.

Jude was now asleep, his head lolling from side to side. Anna was beginning to see that Lori's attraction to Roland was based on a steadiness and capability. Jude was brilliant, but Anna began to wonder what was at the root of her attraction to him; perhaps she liked his sharp intelligence because it was a reflection of her own. She pulled him towards her, the pulse of her anger conflicting with a deep longing. He looked up at her.

'You know I love you, don't you?' he whispered.

She didn't know, not really. Don't overanalyse, she told herself. But analysis was what she knew.

# EIGHT

## Lori

Lori woke up in Paris the next day to the low hum of a boat's horn blaring. They were on the fifth floor in an apartment not far from the Seine and she could already feel her senses attuning to the different sounds and smells of a new city. She sat up, pulled back the blind and looked out of the window to see an endless pattern of grey Parisian rooftops along with rows of tall windows, each one with a Juliet balcony. There were stacks of terracotta chimneys against a blue silky sky. Roland had been blasé about the apartment, but its proximity to the Seine verged on the ridiculous. It belonged to a friend of his family who taught at the Sorbonne. Roland was beside her, his breathing steady, his hand resting in the dent her head had left on the pillow. She watched him for a while until he opened his eyes and then she stroked his face.

'Mon cherie,' he said. He looked rather pleased with himself. They'd made love clumsily the night before, Lori apprehensive about the sheets and Roland concerned about Lori's lack of enthusiasm until they were able to let go, fall into each other with abandon. Roland had surprised her.

For a second they were locked into each other's eyes. 'I'm not sure I know you,' she said.

'Nor I, you. You drive like a demon for one thing.'

'You knew that!' She picked up her pillow and playfully bopped him on the head. Despite the ease she felt with Roland, there was something about the meeting with her parents that had left her unsettled. He lifted up her hand like it was a sample of silk and, reaching for the box with the watch in it with his other hand, he plucked out the watch. 'I want you to wear this,' he said.

'That sounds like ownership,' she said. She was aware she sounded ungrateful, but sometimes his generosity left her feeling uncomfortable. She forced herself to smile. She hadn't woken up in the best of moods, didn't know what her problem was. Anna had once said she had commitment issues.

'Why do you make it hard for me?' he said.

Lori shifted along the bed, lying flat on her stomach, head propped up on one elbow, legs kicking up behind her. A patch of sunlight shone on the bedstead.

'I'm afraid that's who I am.'

'I don't think that's who you really are, is it?' Roland said. He ran his hand along her back, observing her body as he came to the base of her spine. She thought they might make love again, but he gently took hold of her foot and kissed it, looking at her with steady eyes. 'Incorrigible.' There was an unexpected edge to his voice.

'Well, we're never one person, are we?' she said, biting his finger gently. 'I'd like to see where you lived with Jude. Is that when you two got close?' Roland and Jude had both done a four-year BA course to accommodate a year abroad. Lori had met Roland after his time in Paris.

He seemed to think about her question. He was always careful when responding, especially when it came to Jude. The flat they shared was mostly paid for by Roland but that didn't seem to matter to either of them.

'I suppose living in Paris drew us closer, yes. But it was when he defended me in a squabble outside a nightclub against two bouncers that we became friends. Besides, I've always been grateful that Jude's never judged me.'

'Judged you for what?'

'Nothing, it's just . . .' He was distracted by some pigeons outside squabbling over some piece of territory on the opposite roof, cooing and flapping, pecking at each other. She could hear neighbouring voices below and then the slamming of windows being closed. 'He's been a good friend, that's all. Supportive in a way that's surprised me.'

'Yeah, I get that. But why would he judge you? You practically pay for his living accommodation. He's lucky.'

'I'd rather live with someone I like than split something fifty-fifty with someone I don't get on with. Besides, what does it matter, it's only money and it's not even mine.'

'Well, I know nothing about your family,' she said. 'Just that they're rich.'

Roland laughed, opened his arms and she curled into them. 'You met my brother.'

'Yeah, but he's fifteen and gauche.'

'We could visit my aunt if you like. She lives not far from here,' he said. 'I told you, I'm closer to her than anyone.' Lori knew his mother was a twin, and that she favoured her daughter, that was all. She still felt he was being deliberately reticent.

'But tell me about your parents. Every time I ask you, you avoid talking about them. I want to know why. It doesn't feel fair that you've met my parents and I barely know if yours exist.'

'Hold on a sec. I only met them yesterday!'

She sat up, pulled her knees to her chin, wrapping her arms tightly around her legs. 'Well, now it's your turn.'

'What's to know? They live separate lives. My father in London mostly, my mother in the Cotswolds, sometimes they're in one home, but rarely. They're happier apart. Part of the reason you've never met them is because I rarely see them myself.'

'You're hiding something.'

Roland shifted onto his back, avoiding eye contact. 'My mother suffers from depression and my father is very controlling, what else do you want to know?' His voice had an edge to it, brittle and disconcerting. His usual easygoing persona suddenly gone. He stood up and went to the bathroom. She sat, watching her toes wriggle as if they had a mind of their own, thinking,

'It's hard, that's all. I know we discussed the possibility that we might be together long term, but after you met my parents I realised I knew so little about you. You seem to be deliberately elusive,' she said.

Roland walked back into the room. He sat down facing her, stroking her leg. 'Why is it so important to you? Sometimes I get the feeling that you're not happy unless everything is under your control.'

Lori felt herself contract. 'What do you mean?'

'Why can't you accept I have my reasons for keeping my parents at bay.'

She stood up, threw a T-shirt that was on the floor over her head and went and stood by the window.

'I'm just curious, that's all,' she said, leaning against the glass and watching the birds squabble.

'Your parents seemed nice.'

Lori turned to him and rolled her eyes. 'What does that mean?'

'Well, at least they get on,' he said. He picked up his boxer shorts and started to dress. She could feel him closing down, his mouth tight, but then he said, 'An ex once told me that the best relationships are when one partner or the other sacrifices their life. I think it worked for my parents for a bit, until we grew up.'

'Who sacrificed their life?'

'My mother. She was a brilliant pianist once.'

'That's sad,' Lori said.

They had a late breakfast in a café in Rue des Saint-Pères off Saint-Germain. The café seemed to pride itself on its basic presentation: red chairs, Formica tables, Coca-Cola posters. The sparse décor amplified the echo of foreign voices, of people arguing emphatically or calling out orders, the sound of plates and cutlery in the kitchen adding to the general hum. Even the steam released from the espresso machine sounded alien to Lori. Roland and Jude ordered eggs. Anna and Lori had a croissant and a café crème. She was glad that Anna, like her, had only a smattering of schoolgirl French.

Roland sat with his arm resting possessively across her chair, his long grey woollen coat thrown to the side on a neighbouring table. His hair was messy, his beard unshaven. He still seemed ruffled by the intimacy of their conversation.

'Encore du café,' he said as the waiter walked by.

'Pernod, s'il vous plaît,' Jude added.

'You might have to concede on this one, Jude,' Anna was saying, referring to Roland's perfect French.

'At least I learned the hard way,' Jude said.

'And what's the hard way?' Roland said, tapping the table with the menu. It was unlike him to rise to the challenge, but Lori realised there was another side to Roland surfacing recently.

'Well let's put it this way: French exchange for me was never an option,' Jude said.

'Commendable,' Roland said. 'But it's not a competition.'

Lori felt a shot of apprehension. Roland's eyes settled on Jude's, a hidden power behind them, and then he smiled, his face softening, his dimples marking either side of his mouth as he slapped Jude on the arm, leaning across the table.

Opposite the café a grocer was manning his vegetables. The tomatoes were heaped together, a mound of misshapen fruit, different shades of red and yellow. Lettuces sprouted out of wooden crates, there were stacks of onions of differing sizes and colour, a pyramid of new potatoes and strings of garlic, all of it too neat and gentrified. Lori felt restless. She was missing painting and felt lost without the smell of turps and linseed oil. She remembered a tutor saying to her, his face serious as he rubbed his beard, 'You have to *be* the work, live it so that without it, you are no one.' She had, she believed, become her work. Recently she was only happy when she was there, in front of it, inside it.

'L'addition s'il vous plaît,' Jude said, having downed the Pernod. When it came to paying, they all realised they hadn't any francs. Roland went in search of a cash machine. Anna needed some cash, so she tagged along, which left Lori feeling obliged to stay with Jude.

'Want something?' he asked. Jude ordered another Pernod.

'Hot chocolate,' she said.

'Exciting,' he said.

Lori felt awkward being alone with Jude. He kept looking at her and smiling and she wasn't in the mood to smile back. Finally, he picked up her hand and looked at the watch.

'You're lucky,' he said.

'I know,' she said, withdrawing her hand. His green eyes reflected a frightening intelligence.

'He's a good man.'

'Why are you telling me this? I know,' she said. She shifted in her seat, anxious to see if the others were coming back.

'I can tell you're having doubts.'

Lori felt a prickle of sweat under her arms. 'Doubts about what?'

'Sorry, that was out of line.'

'It's just that I'm missing my work, that's all. I was at a crucial stage with a particular painting and I shouldn't have come.' He nodded, expecting more. She'd always admired his insight. She breathed in, trying to relax. 'You know me, I get drunk, make an impulsive decision and regret it.'

'And . . .'

'It's just that sometimes, Roland feels like a stranger and at other times the exact opposite. Does that ever happen to you?'

Jude shrugged. 'We're all strangers to each other.' He sipped his Pernod.

'I suppose so.'

'I wasn't joking about the gallery, you know. I *do* have a friend. Met him during my year at the Sorbonne. Roland knows him too. Surprised he hasn't mentioned it, actually. I could introduce you.' He looked at her with his serious green eyes, his hair flopping over one of them. Lori felt her heart race, the sensation like a rabble of butterflies invading her insides . . . climbing up towards her throat. His attention felt wrong, or was it her?

'That's kind,' she said.

Jude tapped a cigarette out of a box of Marlboro Reds, leaned back. 'It's funny about Roland; I sometimes wonder if to him marriage is just something he wants to tick off.' He gave her a coy look, took another swig of his Pernod then lit the cigarette, inhaling deeply.

'Why do you say that? We're not married.'

Jude smirked. 'Just saying . . .'

'Lori. You have to come and see this sweet little clothes shop.' Anna was calling from inside the doorway, waving. Roland was at the bar, paying the bill. Anna frowned at Jude as she called out to Lori, her eyes hopping back and forth, clearly trying to fathom the mood. Lori hated it when Anna showed signs of anxiety around Jude. She went to stand up, but Jude clasped her hand.

'I care about Roland,' he said. 'You're a free spirit, and Roland isn't. He's damaged.'

# NINE

## Anna

Anna was shaking when they reached the little boutique. She couldn't help noticing the way Jude had grabbed Lori's hand and pulled her closer to him across the table. It was an intimate gesture and Lori had looked surprised, a wildness in her eye. She wondered if she should say something, but even as they entered the shop Lori was talking non-stop.

'Paris is such a vibrant city. I think as an artist you have to keep looking, if that makes sense, and familiarity stops us from really "seeing",' she made air quotes. 'Travelling is so important don't you think?'

'We all need holidays,' Anna said.

Lori had walked up to the nearest clothes rail. 'Yes, but it's not just that, is it?'

'You seem nervous, Lori. What is it?' Anna pressed her nose to a silky shirt, inhaling the sharp new smell of it.

'Oh, you know . . .' But she didn't finish her sentence. She started rifling through the rails of clothes; pulling out a green silk blouse, holding it up to her face to see how it looked.

'That's so you, why don't you try it on?' Anna said.

Anna could see the attendant, a neatly dressed young girl with a sleek bob, revving herself up for a sale.

69

'It's a bit conventional don't you think? Anyway I'm totally broke,' Lori said. 'I'm missing painting. Can you believe that?'

'It's just a few days, Lori. I thought you wanted to come.'

'It was Roland's idea.'

The attendant spoke to them in French. Lori shook her head, smiling brightly. 'Sorry,' she said. The girl switched off her smile, drifting off to gaze out of the window, leaning forward to get a view of the street, her arms crossed.

Lori was frowning, her eyes on the clothes, her mind somewhere else. 'Do you think Jude is jealous of my relationship with Roland?'

'I don't think so, no,' Anna said, feeling her stomach lurch, as if a train had stopped sharply. She wondered what had gone on with her and Jude. 'Why would he be jealous?'

'I don't know. It's just a feeling that's all,' Lori shrugged. 'I need to get a few francs myself pretty soon or Roland will end up paying for everything.' Lori was still rummaging through the clothes, pushing and pulling each item to get a better look. She hadn't looked her in the eye once.

'Don't overthink things,' Anna said.

Then Lori turned to her, looking at her directly, her eyes large and full of feeling. 'I'm not you, Anna. I'm visceral, I feel here.' She patted her stomach. 'And I get the feeling that Jude is possessive of Roland.'

'He's protective sometimes, but I'm not sure . . .'

'Maybe I just woke up on the wrong side of the bed. That drive was exhausting.' Lori picked up a T-shirt with a picture of Blondie on it. 'This is so cool. I'm going to try it.' She waved it at the assistant and headed towards the changing rooms. Seconds later she yanked back the curtain. 'What do you think?'

'Looks great, I mean it's a T-shirt.' Anna was still churning over Lori's accusations, like change in her pocket, her mind trying to unravel their conversation. Lori went back to change, handing the T-shirt to Anna through the curtain who passed it on to the girl to bag up.

'I can put it on a credit card, I've got just enough on that.'

'You're great together, you know that, right?' Anna said as Lori came out of the dressing room.

'We come from such different backgrounds.' Lori looked out of the shop window, smiled with a closed mouth as the girl came to straighten up the rail after she'd attacked it, handing her the bag.

They walked out of the shop. 'Sometimes, I feel out of my depth, that's all.'

Roland and Jude were standing opposite, sharing a cigarette, laughing, Jude jumping on and off the kerb, as always unable to stay still. She pulled Lori to a standstill, peeling off her coat, her back to the boys. 'Did Jude have another Pernod while you were waiting?'

Lori frowned, flicking an apprehensive glance Jude's way. 'Yes, why?'

'Oh, nothing. I worry about his drinking sometimes.'

'Girls, we challenge you to a game of dare double dare,' Jude said, bowing in a theatrical manner, his arm outstretched, the jacket hanging limply from one finger, his other arm tucked into his belly. He wore an impish grin. 'If you don't accept, you'll have to forfeit something or another.' He had a twinkle in his eye as he lunged forward and planted a kiss on Anna's neck, pulling her closer, an air of mischievousness about him that made her skin prickle.

71

'I smell trouble,' she said, as they traipsed down the road to the cashpoint. A scooter flew past them, tooting. A café was spilling people onto the pavement, giving off a constant hum of voices. Paris sounded different to London, less dense somehow. Even the drone of traffic coming off Boulevard Saint-Germain was distinct, lighter.

'I love this city,' Anna said.

'Why don't we go for a walk by the Seine?' Lori said, as she pulled out her bank card and inserted it into the ATM.

Jude yawned ostentatiously. 'If we must.'

Roland put a protective arm on Lori's shoulder. 'Yes, we must.'

When they got to the Seine, with its slow green stately girth, more expansive somehow than the Thames, they slowed down in time with its passage through the city. The Musée d'Orsay had an imperial presence, the trees were spread wide, even the barges felt heftier than the boats that floated on the river in London. The symmetry of Pont Royal added to the sense of tranquillity despite being rammed with traffic. The sun bounced off the water, a plane flew overhead leaving its feathering mark on a clear sky. Anna thought about Lori's comment on travelling and wondered at what point the eye grows complacent. Jude was talking animatedly to Lori and Roland, wedged in between them, his shoulders swinging, his jacket pendulous, still hooked over his finger, as he walked. She watched as he patted Lori's back, then arm. He didn't seem to stop touching her. She slipped in between, grabbing hold of Jude's hand and folding her fingers through his.

'Why don't we go the market? We could buy some bread and brie, find a park to have lunch,' she said.

'We've only just had breakfast,' Jude said.

'If you count two Pernods and an espresso as breakfast,' Anna said.

'We're on holiday!'

'We could go to Parc Montsouris,' Roland offered a gaping open smile, 'and you can see where we used to live,' he said to Lori. 'If we buy food there, it'll be half the price.'

'I'd love that,' Lori said. She seemed to have cheered up since her manic episode in the boutique. Jude had stopped and was rocking on his heels. Of course they all came to a halt. People behaved like sheep around Jude.

'Okay, so here's my first dare. Lori, you have to flag down a scooter and ask for a lift just for the fun of it.' Jude grinned at Lori, his eyes caught in the sun so he had to shade them with his hand.

Anna wondered why he'd asked Lori. She grabbed Jude's arm and towed him along. 'You know full well Lori doesn't speak bloody French, so how is she going to do that?' she said.

'I'll do it,' Lori said.

'Don't worry about the French, I'll ask for you,' Jude said to Lori.

'Fine, but Roland does the asking. I trust him more than you,' Lori said, winking.

Jude made a theatrical protestation. 'I'm gutted.'

'But we're taking the Metro first,' Anna said. She loved his crazy ideas most of the time, his sense of fun, and she loved Lori's impulsiveness, but sometimes his need for entertainment and Lori's eagerness to supply it felt relentless. She watched how they both pouted at each other. Perhaps, she thought, I should flirt with Roland.

# TEN

## Lori

They took the Metro to the south of Paris. Lori loved the whine and sing-song sound of the underground. It seemed more tranquil than the Tube back in London and smelled of rubber and steel rather than grime. During their year in Paris, Roland and Jude had lived in the 13th arrondissement.

'We went to Parc Montsouris most weekends. Sometimes we'd meet my aunt over in the 8th, or we'd go and hang out at Les Halles, watch the dancing and mime artists outside the Pompidou.' Roland was animated, making an effort to share a part of his life. Lori wrapped her arms around his waist, feeling the silk on the lining of his coat soft against her arms. 'If we get off at Tolbiac we can show you where we used to live. It means we have to walk further, but we're not in a hurry,' he said.

'Yes we are,' Jude said, who was sitting with his arms folded while Roland spouted details of their shared past. 'You forget that Anna has already seen this.'

'You're being an irritant,' Anna said.

Jude jumped up off the seat and strutted down the carriage, plonking himself next to an old woman bent over her shopping basket.

'What about your maternal grandparents?' Lori asked.

'They live further south. In Provence.'

Lori could see Jude talking to the old woman, his legs crossed, leaning in to her slightly, nodding his head as she chatted away. He was such a performer, and most of the time she enjoyed this aspect of his character, but today he seemed to deliberately highlight something lacking in Roland. Lori thought about her mother's comment: *someone wilder.* The exchange in the café had left her feeling unsettled.

As they got further south the train thinned out, so Jude swaggered back to join the others, winking at Lori as he did so.

'Did your father speak French?' Lori asked Roland, ignoring Jude.

'God, no. He never came away with us and the few times he did, we'd all speak English. He was always working, a specialist at being unavailable,' Roland said, retying a shoe lace.

Lori wondered if this was what Jude had meant when he said Roland was damaged.

'At least you had a father,' Jude said, who had his arms folded and was sitting with his knee jutting out. 'Mine had a PhD in unavailability.'

Anna wrapped her arm around his neck. 'It's not a competition.'

The Metro station at Tolbiac spat them out into a wide tree-lined boulevard, but Roland quickly led them into a warren of back streets. The 13th arrondissement had a completely different atmosphere from the Left Bank. Less affluent, for one thing. There was a mix of new and old architecture. Tall blocks of apartments could be seen up on the horizon, pushed together, the walls covered in graffiti, and then the further away from the main drag they went, the more the roads narrowed, until they came to a spot where all the roads were cobbled. They stopped by a small shop with a tatty display of vegetables outside and a battered sign in both French and Arabic.

'Let's buy some fruit,' Lori said. She picked up a couple of apples and some grapes, pulled out some francs and went into the shop. Jude followed her in, picking up a packet of chewing gum for her to buy at the same time. Inside there was a cheese counter and a basket of bread, so the others were called in. All the time Jude was hovering restlessly until he decided to engage in a conversation with the shopkeeper. Lori felt on edge around him. He kept pointing out various cheeses, and asking to taste each one, making the whole process lengthy and laborious.

'Merci,' Lori said, feeling conspicuous with her basic French as the shopkeeper packed everything into a paper bag, smiling to reveal a prominent gold tooth.

'Wine goes with cheese,' Jude said, grabbing a bottle without even checking the price. He asked the man to open it. Then they had to wait while he found a corkscrew from the storeroom. Lori wandered around the narrow little shop with its warren of shopping aisles to get away from Jude – she could feel Anna's resentment growing and she didn't want to feed it. Each aisle was stacked to the ceiling with products piled on flimsy plywood shelves. Finally, the shopkeeper returned from his storeroom with a corkscrew. Then Jude asked where they could buy a knife to cut the cheese and apple. Of course the man ended up giving them one of his own knives – a victim to Jude's charm.

They dawdled on aimlessly, Jude pointing out his favourite bar, holding his bottle of red in its plastic bag. They came across little streets filled with small houses, overblown trees spurting from their tiny front gardens.

'This is le quartier des Peupliers, which means the poplar district,' Roland said.

'As in the trees?' Lori said.

Roland nodded, tucking Lori's arm under his.

'We used to live there,' Jude said, pointing to a small flat on the first floor, the windows crammed with pot plants. Roland lifted his camera up to his eye and took a photograph, then he took snaps of them all posing: Jude with a cigarette in his mouth, Anna and Lori with their arms around each other laughing. Then all four of them lined up and Roland put the camera on the roof of a car, flicking onto self-timer and rushing to join them. In that moment, Lori felt a wave of elation, happy to be part of their quirky group, to belong. Nothing felt forced. The restlessness had finally ebbed away and her feelings towards Roland were restored.

# ELEVEN

## Anna

Anna heard a scooter and turned to see it wobbling down the road, weaving in and out of double-parked cars and vans, the driver fluid and easy as water. She was hoping Lori wouldn't see it, but then she jumped out into the road and flagged it down.

Anna swivelled sharply, yanking her back from the kerb. 'You're not serious, are you?'

'It's just a bit of fun,' Lori said, pulling away.

'You don't know this man. He could be a serial rapist.'

Lori laughed. 'Don't be silly.'

The rider had slowed down and finally stopped. Lori turned to Jude whose eyes were wide open, a grin shaping his mouth into a curve, a series of commas punctuating his cheeks.

'I suggest you're honest and tell him I want a spin around the block as part of a game. Roland, I'd also appreciate it if you mentioned that I don't speak French.'

They waited while the two boys chatted to the young Moroccan. There was lots of laughing, hand slapping, patting of backs, the usual male camaraderie. Lori was clearly revelling in the surprise she'd caused.

Anna stepped closer to the scooter. 'I'm going,' she said.

Lori tried to grab her, but Anna, feeling nimble and

light, ducked out of reach. 'I want to feel the wind on my face,' she said.

'I thought you were nervous?' Lori asked.

'I know. Everyone thinks I'm incapable of being impulsive, don't they? Poor old boring Anna, but I can do *wild* too, you know.' She shrugged Lori off.

Roland took hold of Lori's hand. 'Let Anna do this,' he said, his voice overly soft and patient, which Anna could see left Lori feeling like a chastised child. 'You don't always need to be in the limelight.'

Lori snatched her hand back. 'Sure,' she said, her voice short and bruised. Anna felt guilt pressing. But it was true what Roland had said, it was important to swap roles. 'Thanks, Roland.'

Jude pulled Anna closer and she felt his body hard and determined pressing against hers. He whispered into her ear: 'You're so bloody sexy and I want you.'

'There's a price to pay,' she said, poking him gently in the chest until, laughing, he jumped up on a small bollard, his jacket falling to the floor. Then Anna hoisted her skirt and climbed on behind the young boy, smiling as she wrapped her arms around his waist.

'I need a helmet,' Anna said. 'Roland, ask him if he has another helmet.'

It was Jude who spoke to the boy, who pointed to the box behind. Sure enough there was a spare, which Jude lifted out and handed to her.

'What's his name?' she asked.

'Karim,' Roland said. She put the helmet on, and then before she could properly secure herself she was whisked away. She turned and waved. Roland was taking snaps. Jude scooped up his jacket and started to run after her, blowing her kisses. She was glad to have taken them all by surprise, it gave her an odd feeling of power.

The road rushed underneath the scooter, the uneven surface of the cobbled stones rattling them both. Suddenly she felt both exhilarated and free. The streets were narrow. The houses were crowded with greenery, pot plants balanced on window ledges, ivy crawling across the façades. It was as if the plants were contagious – a rash. The restaurants were smaller, the shops darker, the bars more discreet. Many of the walls were marked with graffiti, artful and colourful. There were fewer people as well. They turned into a main road and Anna was suddenly overwhelmed by a feeling of disorientation. The change of scenery from quaint little painted shopfronts to neon-lit mainstream outlets confused her. They turned back into a street that felt bleak. They were going so fast she was unsure how far they'd come. The boy leant to the left and then to the right as he passed by cars and she found herself echoing his body movements. She was so busy trying to hold on that she was barely able to see where they were going. The feeling of uncertainty made her panic. She wondered if Jude had played a joke, asked him to take her further than she wanted. She tried to remember the word for stop but her brain was scrambled, thick with terror. Then the boy slowed down and turned right, when she was expecting him to turn left. Her mouth was dry. She felt her legs go like jelly. Anna had no idea where this boy was taking her, he turned off again into a small dark alley.

'Arrête!' she said. 'S'il vous plaît, arrête!'

The boy kept on going until he came to a stop outside a house with children skipping in the courtyard and a couple of men playing cards on wooden crates. Anna's body was flooded with fear. She jumped off the scooter and ran. She had no idea where she was. The boy caught up, grabbing her elbow, babbling away in French and when she realised he was pointing to her helmet, she pulled it off her head, so that her hair crackled with static, and shoved it in his arms.

'Sorry,' she said. She started to run again, tears dribbling down her cheeks more through embarrassment and shame than anything. It was foolish to try and be brave, to compete with Lori. Lori wouldn't have behaved like this. She arrived at the end of the small alleyway and turned back down the hill, unsure which direction they'd come in, unable to remember any landmarks. She was jogging down the road when she saw Jude and Roland running towards her, Lori straggling behind.

'Oh, thank God,' Anna said, panting, a painful stitch blooming in her chest. The boy had caught up just as Anna threw herself into Jude's arms.

'He just went so fast. I had no idea where we were going. This was such a stupid, stupid thing to do. I was so scared.' She beat his chest with her fists, and Jude laughed. He actually laughed, making her feel humiliated.

'Okay, okay, baby. Shhh.' Then Jude switched to French as Karim tried to explain himself.

Roland joined him. Lori put out her hand to touch Anna, shaking her head.

'Are you okay?' she said.

'I was an idiot. It's totally my fault.'

'Jude ran so fast we couldn't keep up. Apparently they'd agreed where to meet you,' Lori said. 'Obviously, you didn't know that.'

Jude turned to her, a small smile climbing up his face. He ran his thumb across her damp cheeks. 'He said he ran out of petrol, and just needed to get home. He's sorry.'

'And there's me thinking my number was up.'

'That's a bit extreme, darling.'

81

'Not really. I was genuinely scared and totally lost.'

Jude translated and then Karim laughed, and held out his hand. Anna shook it.

'Merci,' she said.

There was more back-patting and shaking of hands and then they all turned to walk away, the girls first, the boys following, arms wrapped around each other's shoulders.

'Merci for what?' Lori said. 'You were terrified. I told you I should have gone.'

'It's not his fault I can't speak French,' Anna said, throwing her hand up in protest. She knew she sounded brittle, short.

Jude pulled her into an embrace. 'Je t'aime,' he said. Anna sometimes wondered what love meant to Jude.

'It was a stupid idea in the first place,' Lori said.

'You were dead keen twenty minutes ago. You don't have a monopoly on impulsiveness, you know.'

'Oh Anna,' Lori said.

'What's the matter, can't I be unpredictable once in a while?'

'That's not what I'm saying and you know it!' Lori strode off, her hands swinging at her sides, silent rage propelling her forward.

Jude turned to Roland. 'She's quite sexy when she's angry, isn't she?'

'Come on guys!' Roland said.

Anna ran after Lori. 'I'm sorry,' she said, putting her arm around Lori's rigid body. They walked along, until Lori conceded, smiling, wrapping her arm around Anna. The boys ran to catch them up, and they all started singing: 'Non, Je Ne Regrette Rien'.

'I'll get you back,' Anna said to Jude, poking him. She turned to Roland.

'Doesn't he deserve it, Ro?' She winked provocatively. If Lori and Jude could flirt, so could she.

# TWELVE

## Lori

Parc Montsouris presented a familiar green city landscape: families picnicking, office workers perched on benches that formed a half-circle around the lake, groups of students from the local university lounging with bottles of beer or playing Frisbee, people walking their dogs. A spring light sharpening the edges of everything. Lori had become acutely aware of a change in Anna. That nonsense on the scooter, her sudden hysteria colouring the day, followed by a mocking tone. They sat down on the bank that sloped towards the lake. A willow drooped into the water opposite them. There was a wooden footbridge with stepping stones leading up to it. It was unusually warm for April, the general air lackadaisical – a feeling of things lifting. Roland threw his coat onto the floor and they both plonked themselves down. Anna and Jude were squeezed onto Jude's jacket. Soon after, they got into a discussion about Europe, because Jude had been asked to take part in a debate about the union. Inevitably Roland and Jude strayed into the danger zone of politics. Lori found herself drifting. The grass was lush although a little damp, the smell of it reaching her senses, the promise of summer approaching. She couldn't resist lying back and staring at the clear sky. She breathed in deeply and for a second forgot everything that had crowded her mind in the last twenty-four hours: her mother, Roland's reticence around the subject of his family, Jude's weird behaviour, Anna's moment of rebellion, her own insecurities. She found herself thinking of her work. How she wanted to add more layers and texture to it, how she could use tone and line to give the work depth. She longed for the peace painting offered, the way the world receded when she was working.

Roland flopped down beside her.

'What are you thinking?' he said.

'About my work,' she replied. But she'd started to think about Roland's comment: *you don't always have to be in the limelight* and how he'd pulled her back from the scooter. She wondered if he thought her too impulsive, too wild. She remembered the way he looked at her when she was dancing on the table. Roland leaned down and kissed her and she allowed the moment of intimacy between them to ease her fears, pushing the feeling of betrayal aside. Sometimes she wished Roland would just grab her in his arms and kiss her passionately, thrash the self-doubt out of her, but that wasn't who Roland was. That kind of response was more typical of Jude. Anna was always gloating at how expertly Jude pleased her in bed. Roland didn't please Lori exactly, he was too tentative sometimes, but he was considerate and last night had been so intimate, she'd felt something shift.

'Get a room, you two.'

'Piss off!' Roland retorted, smiling at her approvingly and tracing the line of her chin.

Jude poured them all red wine. From his pocket he produced an ashtray, as if it were a party trick.

'Where did that come from?' Anna asked.

'The café.' Jude grinned. He was sprawled loose-limbed while Anna set about making them lunch, a complacency ringing off his body that acted like a magnet to some people. 'It saves us littering the park,' he said.

'Right, so you justify stealing by conserving the environment,' Anna responded, tight-lipped.

'Who cares? It's a cheap plastic ashtray.'

Lori watched them both squabbling, her face resting on her elbow, intrigued by the way they shot each other knowing glances. She sat up, took a sip of her wine.

'To good friends, good wine, and exciting times,' Roland said.

'I'll drink to that.' Jude tipped back his glass and drank thirstily.

'Are you still thinking of applying to the BBC, Jude?' Lori asked. She was intrigued suddenly by the idea of Jude away from the safe confines of academia.

'Mate, Christ knows. The competition is stiff. Maybe I'll come and live here for a bit, teach a bit of English. Although I fancy myself as a documentary filmmaker. Something that involves thinking and travelling.'

Lori envied his certainty. It was different as an artist; of course there was teaching as her father had said, but Lori wanted painting to be at the centre of her life. She watched Anna, expecting some reaction, but there was none, she was too busy spreading ripe brie onto a baguette. There was only one knife and Anna had taken it upon herself to play mother.

'Do you want me to do that?' she asked.

'Why?' Anna said. 'I'm fine.'

'What do you think, Princess?' Jude said, lighting a cigarette. 'Fancy living here for a bit?'

'Maybe, after my MA,' Anna said, not bothering to look up.

'What about you, Roland?' Anna asked, smiling at Lori and handing her some bread and cheese. She appeared to have forgotten their row, but it often took Lori longer to shift the feeling of anxiety after a disagreement.

'I've already told you,' Roland said, making a show of popping the chunk of bread and cheese into his mouth. 'I'm doing a law conversion, then working for my father for a while, then I'll set up some business or another.'

'Thatcher's dream boy,' Jude said.

'Stop with the chirruping,' Anna said, flicking him with her hand. 'You need to give up goading everyone who chooses a different life to yours.' She turned to Roland, handing him some more food.

'Christ, I thought you hated your father,' Jude said.

Roland looked up sharply, catching her eye. Lori noticed a flicker of anxiety.

'Haven't got much choice and I'm not looking forward to it either. Eventually, though, I want to make my own money. Lots of it.' He playfully punched Jude but Lori sensed his apprehension still.

'As long as you share it around, mate, that's fine with me,' Jude said, opining to an open sky.

'When has he not shared it around?' Lori said, irritated by his manner. It occurred to Lori that Jude knew more than she did about Roland's relationship with his family, his father especially.

Jude gave an awkward shrug, still prostrate.

'What about you, Lori?' Anna asked. 'Still thinking of teaching?'

'Can you honestly see me teaching?'

'No,' they all said in unison, which made everyone laugh, and helped to lighten her mood.

'I'll probably do some temp work or find some other

way to *subsidise* my art, my parents are putting the pressure on, but I'll paint by night if I have to.'

Jude sat up and stubbed out his cigarette, pushing it down hard into the ashtray so that it disintegrated. He eyed Lori intently, a glint of amusement making his mouth twitch. 'Why don't you just marry Roland, then you won't have to work?' he said. He winked, flicked Roland a coy look.

'You can't resist it, can you?' Roland said, slowly shaking his head with a good-natured smile.

Jude tittered. 'Nope, can't help myself.'

'Pathological behaviour. Another worrying aspect of your character,' Anna said. She handed Jude his sandwich.

'When are you going to give me my dare, sweetheart?' Jude said, flopping back down, holding his baguette with two hands, his legs stretched out like the blades of scissors.

'When I'm good and ready,' Anna said, flicking her hair so that it swung into one glossy blonde swathe.

'I've got one for you,' Lori said, pulling her knees up and pushing a piece of cheese into her mouth, swallowing it down with a gulp of wine.

'I'm excited,' Jude said.

'Stop being so bloody facetious,' Anna said.

'I think you mean flirtatious,' Roland said, his voice slow and assured.

Anna spouted out a mocking laugh. Lori flicked a nervous glance towards Roland, aware that he was mirroring her friend's anxiety, but Anna had returned to her sandwich-making, deliberately engrossed in spreading another chunk of brie on a piece of baguette.

'I want you to go to the lake and walk across it,' she said nonchalantly.

'Sounds a bit lame,' Jude said.

'Fully clothed: jacket, shoes, everything.' Lori staggered the delivery as if she were lobbing the words at him like stones into the lake. 'Like Peter Sellers in *Being There* when he walks on water.'

Jude almost levitated, twisting round, screwing up his face in disbelief and throwing his head back in laughter, filling the air with mirth like the major chords struck from a church band. His response was contagious. Soon they were all chuckling, even Anna, who had given up playing mother.

'But this jacket is from Cerruti,' Jude protested.

'You got it in a second-hand shop,' Anna said, rolling her eyes.

'Harder to come up with a forfeit,' Roland said. 'Mind you, I'm sure Anna will conjure up something suitable.'

'No sex for a week,' Anna said, finally turning to face him, waggling her finger, pouting provocatively.

Jude sat up straight, feigning horror. 'Okay, okay, I'll do it.'

'Incorrigible,' Anna said. They all fell about, their bodies loose and forgiving in the bright April sun, cracking through the tension that had hovered briefly.

'Transparent as cellophane,' Lori said.

Jude took an extra-long swig of wine, refilled his paper cup and downed a bit more. He tapped a cigarette out of its box, threw the packet to Roland. 'I need it for fortitude.'

He stood up, pulled at his jacket, so that Anna, who was biting into her bread, had to lift her bottom, her back to him, feigning disinterest. A light chilly breeze snagged the air, birds were swooping down into the lake to catch insects. The scene idyllic, unsuspecting. When Jude put his jacket on he looked dashing, even though his clothes were crumpled. His joy was infectious. Lori thought then how all of them were like moths flickering around his beaming light. However hard Anna tried, her body straining with the effort of not watching, it was clear to Lori how desperate she was for his attention. He strolled down to the edge of the lake, one hand in his pocket, the other preoccupied with the act of smoking, his jacket swinging like a cape. He turned back to the three of them and gave a tentative wave. They all responded with exaggerated arm movements, encouraging him forward. He bowed, his arm arcing the air like a ballet dancer.

'Vite!' Anna hollered. 'Wait!' she screamed, and jumped up. 'He can't go in those,' she said to Roland, pointing to his shoes.

Jude must have heard because he said. 'Dear, dear Anna, so you do care after all.'

'Oh stop it,' she said. 'I care about your shoes.'

'Get on with it,' hollered Lori.

Anna shaded her eyes with her hand. 'Take your shoes off!' she screamed. 'He actually goes "brogue" shopping. He's a freak when it comes to old men's shoes.'

'How disappointing. I thought you were going to ask me to take off my clothes,' Jude shouted.

Anna sighed. 'Stop it! You're making me cross.'

'I love it when you're cross,' he said.

'The trouble with you, Jude Elliot, is that you love everyone when they're cross and therefore you go out of your way to make them so,' Anna said.

They watched as he stepped backwards further into the lake, blowing kisses, cigarette still smoking as he fell onto his back. Lori could see a woman's shocked expression as she stood up from a bench, the wrapping of her food falling to the floor. Anna and Roland were clapping. Another woman was shaking her head, hand clasped over her mouth. Roland scampered down to the lake, snapping away, using his camera as a refuge against Jude's vivacity.

'Come on,' Lori said, offering her hand to Anna who had plonked herself back down. 'We need to get back to the flat and get him changed.'

'Well, I'm sure he's capable of changing himself,' Anna said, allowing Lori to haul her up. 'He loves it when we pander to his needs.'

'I know, but we're willing volunteers, especially you.' She hadn't meant to sound accusatory and she quickly changed the subject to cover the blunder. She knew she was being difficult, but ever since Anna had made that comment about her needing to be in the limelight, she felt displaced. Knowing Anna and Jude wouldn't agree, she said. 'I don't know about you, but I feel like doing something normal, like visiting a gallery or the Eiffel Tower, being tourists.' she said.

'What do you mean, do something *normal?*' Anna lifted her fingers to illustrate the importance of the word *normal.* 'The problem is that I find tourism so bloody provincial.'

Lori felt her face flush red. She hadn't meant to sound so prudish and had expected that response but it hurt all the same. It was clear that Anna was angry because of the other thing she'd said. She felt certain Roland would be happy to go to the Musée d'Orsay. 'I'm an artist, Anna. I'd just like to see a bit of art.'

'Yes, I know, I'm sorry. I'm feeling fractious. Jude's exhausting sometimes.' Anna jumped up and stomped down the slope, her blonde swathes of hair all glossy, swishing like luxurious golden tassels. Lori watched her body flailing awkwardly, her impatience making her stiff-limbed. If she were in water, she would be close to drowning, she thought.

'Come out now!' Anna was saying, waving her arms frantically, trying to hurry Jude along. 'You're making a spectacle of yourself.'

'That, I thought, was the idea!' Jude said, flapping about in the lake, like a beetle on his back, struggling to get back up. He was laughing so much he didn't seem to be able to right himself. Roland was snapping away. Lori felt out on a limb, still fretting about being accused of being provincial until Jude looked at her with an exaggerated puzzled expression.

'What's up?' he asked, suddenly finding it within himself to stand up so that the water gushed off his clothes.

'She wants to do something normal!' Anna said.

Jude frowned playfully. 'Normal? That's not like you,' he said. He blew Lori a kiss.

Lori wished to God she hadn't used that word. It was more that she wanted space and the best way to get it was to do something the others didn't want to do. Roland let his camera fall to his chest. It felt to Lori as if they were all caught in a moment of flux, the mood hovering like the threat of incoming clouds darkening the sky: Anna hostile, hands on hips, unsmiling. Jude loose-limbed, water dribbling on his skin, his hair reddened by the damp. Roland bored and Lori unsure of herself.

'Lori wants to do something else apart from play dare.'

'I'd just like to see a bit of art, that's all,' Lori said. 'You know, go to the Musée d'Orsay. Do something . . . I've never been to Paris before.' She almost stumbled on that word again, normal, but saved herself. She'd worked so hard not be little miss average, which is what she'd felt she was at school: average grades, average at sport. The only thing she excelled at was art. Going to art school had allowed her to act the rebel. But that didn't have to exclude going to an art gallery, surely.

'Right,' said Jude. 'I get it.'

'We could go to Musée d'Orsay tomorrow,' Roland said. 'And we can see the Arc de Triomphe when we visit Aunt Claude.'

'Anna and I will go back to the flat to get changed, and see you later,' Jude said.

'No, you'll return to the flat on your own and I'll go with the others,' Anna said.

Jude's shoulders sunk, he frowned and for a split second looked vulnerable, his hair sprouting up as it dried, the afternoon light turning amber behind him. Anna rarely got angry with Jude, but today Lori could tell he had crossed some invisible line and that's why she'd snapped. Jude went to put his arm around her but she shoved him away.

'You're wet.'

'Can't argue with that.' He shrugged, adopting a goofy expression. Then he turned round and pulled Anna close anyway. Their embrace was tinged with anger, or was it passion? Lori couldn't decide. Anna finally broke away, her blouse spotted with damp patches.

'Sure, we can see some sights, but I have thought up a dare for Roland,' Jude said, as if these two things were related.

'Oh good. I can't wait,' Roland said with a fatigued sigh. He rolled his eyes at Lori, serious suddenly, his camera swung over his shoulder, redundant. 'Haven't we all had enough of dare, double dare?'

'Well it wouldn't be fair if only two of us did it, would it?' Jude said, stepping up onto the bank and brushing his trousers down, which had no effect.

'We could give them a joint dare,' Anna said, picking up the leftover food, licking her fingers clean.

'Go on then, what is it?' Roland asked.

Jude fixed his eyes on Lori, squinting against the bright light. 'I dare you both to get married,' he said, flicking his gaze back to Roland and smiling broadly. Lori felt Roland behind her, a kind of bristling energy emanating from him that left his body taut when she finally turned to observe his reaction.

'You've had that ring in your pocket for ages.' Jude spoke with a bright tone, but his expression was dark.

He had crossed the line again, with Roland this time.

'What ring? What pocket?' Lori said, confused. 'Is this some kind of joke?'

Anna scowled. 'Bit extreme, darling.'

Lori looked at both the boys and sensed the complicity between them like an electrical current. 'Guys!'

Roland went to Jude and rifled around in his pocket for a cigarette. He lit it and said, 'I think we should visit my aunt.' His eyes settled on Lori, apprehensive, but at the same time there was a steely determination about him. She turned back to Jude; a bashful smile crept across his face, clashing with a sense of unease as he caught Roland's eye.

Roland had a plan, and everyone seemed to know about it except her.

# THIRTEEN

## Anna

Anna followed Jude out of the park; he was soaked and she could tell by the way he slouched that he was depleted. She could hear the squelch of his shoes, the plonk and slap of wet soles. She'd find it funny in other circumstances, but she was tired and fractious suddenly. Roland and Lori ambled along, their arms loosely wrapped around each other's waist, Roland's coat swinging back and forth. Anna had the feeling it was probably cashmere or some such thing.

She smarted at the memory of Lori's comment about her volunteering to be Jude's stooge. Anna turned to take a last look at the park as they walked through the gate. The lake behind them was partly in shadow, a gloomy wash of muddy darkness. She watched a collie chase a ball, diving into the water to fetch it before swimming back to the shore and shaking himself dry. Pity Jude couldn't have done something as simple as shaking himself dry. But there was nothing simple about Jude.

She ran to catch up with the others. In the shade the air had sharpened, an icy prickly breeze forced her to put on her cardigan. She imagined Jude was cold, but knew he'd work hard not to show it. He took off his jacket. She could see a rash of goose pimples on his neck, his skin ashen. He was almost vibrating with the cold and looked at her with doleful eyes. She knew he wanted to mull over the stupidity of his dare but she was reluctant to indulge him. Let him live with the consequences, she thought, although she had to admit Roland didn't seem that displeased, and maybe it would put an end to the flirtations.

'Why did you do that?' she asked.

'Just thought I'd help him along, I suppose. He told me he'd been thinking about it.'

'About what?'

'About proposing.'

'I thought you said they're too young.'

'They are!' Jude said. 'But you know what Roland's like when he sets his mind on something.'

Anna saw a bin and went to dispose of the remnants of lunch, shoving it down with an unexpected spurt of anger aimed at Lori. She remembered Lori that morning, her comment about Jude being jealous of her relationship with Roland when they were in the boutique.

'Is that what this morning was all about, with Lori?'

His lips curled, a smug smile shaping his face, probably because she'd noticed. 'I was sounding her out. Worried that she might reject him.'

'She won't reject him.'

'I worry about Roland, he's a bit of a lost boy sometimes. He's been carrying that ring for days now.' He patted his pocket and took out a sodden ticket for the Metro.

If anybody is a lost boy, it's Jude, she thought.

'She's not in love with him in the way he is with her.' He shook his head in some lame attempt to dry his hair.

'You don't know that.'

'Lori's ambitious, I'll grant you that.'

'Is this you trying to protect your best mate, or is this the ever-competitive Jude who doesn't want to share his best friend, or maybe you want what he wants?'

'God, no.' He sniggered. 'I don't want to get married. It's an outmoded institution.'

Anna felt a jolt of rage, but she knew that the anger was there to protect herself from the hurt. 'You can be such a cliché sometimes,' she said.

'Marriage is the biggest cliché of them all.'

'And a cynic. It would just be nice if on one occasion you treated us seriously.'

'Don't get heavy. You know I don't do heavy.' Jude patted his jacket, clearly looking for something. He realised that Roland had what he was looking for and whistled, a piercingly loud sound that turned many heads. Roland and Lori stopped, swivelling round, joined at the hip, Lori's backcombed hair haloed by the afternoon sun.

'Mate, chuck us a fag.'

Roland threw him the packet and then they both walked quickly on, heads bowed, deep in conversation. Anna knew she'd been curt to Lori but she was used to Lori having agency, a wild party animal. That whole thing about doing ordinary things felt false somehow, some vague attempt at masking her accusation.

'She'll use him up and throw him away,' Jude was saying. 'Lori's the kind of girl who likes a challenge, and Roland is many things but he's not a player.'

'And you are?'

'You know what I mean,' he said. 'The thing is, if she says no, Roland will be devastated and I'll be left to pick up the pieces.' He looked blue with the cold, dragging on his cigarette as if the lighted end was going to warm him.

'Rather a romantic view of your role in Roland's life, don't you think? Anyway, I think you're wrong. I know he comes across as this huge loveable bear, but he knows exactly what he wants. He's tougher than you think. I think it suits you to see him as vulnerable. It makes you feel useful. Anyway, if anything, Lori is the more vulnerable one.' They were strolling at a slow pace, the city had that late-afternoon glow, a sharp dryness to the air. Lori and Roland were far ahead. Roland had stopped off to use a public telephone.

'Who's the cynic now?' Jude eyed her warily. 'Lori isn't vulnerable, she's as cunning as a cat who wants more fun out of a mouse,' he said.

'The problem with you, Jude, is that your perception of people is fashioned by your own needs.'

'But you can't deny she's fickle.'

'Imprudent, maybe. Personally, I'm more of a feminist; I don't need to be seen as rash to appear attractive to the opposite sex.' As she said this, she knotted her hair into a pleat with a pencil she'd found in her pocket. Anna knew she was emulating her mother, something she was prone to do in moments of vulnerability when she felt unformed, living in her parents' academic shadow.

'That's why I love you,' Jude said. His face twitched – a faint smile forming, as ever, reeling her back in, but she felt it was her mother he loved because it was her voice speaking, not her own. *We don't bake cakes, Anna, we're not those type of people.* Anna had been trained to be Anna Jewell, which is why, despite her recent surmising of her best friend's behaviour, she admired Lori. Lori had instructed herself, reinvented herself over and over. When she'd asked to do normal things, it occurred to Anna that Lori wasn't the wild child she pretended to be at all.

'Give me one of those,' she said, nodding at his cigarette.

'There's a lot about Roland you don't know,' Jude was saying, lighting her cigarette and handing it to her.

'Like what?'

'His father is a tyrant. He's never really got on with him.'

'Why is he working for him then?'

'He's expected to. But marrying someone like Lori will be perceived as an act of rebellion. He might have money but he doesn't have it easy. Anyway, that's why I'm so protective of him.'

'I'd say you were competitive with him.'

'That too.' He stooped down to pick up a stray rubber ball from the gutter and started to bounce it, but it hit the ground and rolled away, so he kicked it from side to side until he lost interest and let it dribble back into the road.

They said goodbye on the Metro. Roland and Lori got off to change lines. From the train, Anna watched them glide up the escalator hand in hand as their train disappeared into the tunnel. Jude was attracting attention with his sodden clothes. He was chatting to some old man who'd clearly stated his disapproval in a grumpy manner. Jude's face was alive, his eyes bright. He was gesticulating as a French man would, and the old man started to chuckle at something he'd said. He loved entertaining people, she thought, enjoyed the challenge of breaking down people's defence. As always, Jude had one leg balanced across the other, so that his knee jutted out. His trousers were wrinkled, his shirt damp in patches, his hair covered in filth, but there was something about him, a vulnerability. He caught her eye, held it. There it was, that moment she'd been waiting for: recognition. She despaired of herself.

They walked up to the apartment, hand in hand. It was better like this, just the two of them. When they arrived at the apartment, he pulled her close, pressed his body into hers. He smelt of silt, filth, freshly cut grass and stale water.

'Don't ever think I don't love you,' he said.

Anna looked into his eyes and saw the longing, and perhaps, she thought, a little regret. There was an intensity to his love she thrived on. She tried to jiggle the key into the lock, gently pushing him away while he kissed her neck. When she turned to speak, he pressed his lips onto hers, took the key out of her hand and without looking, opened the door.

'How did you do that?'

'Let's get inside, shall we?' But he pressed her against the wall and kissed her again. He tasted of tobacco.

'You're getting into the bath first,' she said.

They raced up five flights of stairs, out of breath, giggling as he tried to catch her ankle. This was how they were. This was who Jude was when it was just the two of them. He was no longer the performer, the intellectual.

He was just himself.

# FOURTEEN

## Lori

Lori held onto Roland's hand as he led her through
the labyrinth of the Metro. She was thinking about her
parents and the threadbare nature of her upbringing and in
particular a holiday she'd had with them in France. She'd
lied when she said she'd never been to Paris. She'd been
once when she was ten years old. They'd driven through
Paris on a coach. Stopped off to take photographs and
hopped on a bus. She'd been consumed by the smell of
garlic and the rough texture of the seat, unable to sit still.
She remembered very little of the city, just the odour of
foreign food on strangers' breath and her parents, alarm
when she'd asked them what the smell was. What Lori
remembered most about that holiday was the shrivelled
nature of her parents in a foreign land, not the Eiffel
Tower or the Louvre, not the country itself, but her
parents inside it.

As they reached the top step of Champs-Élysées–
Clemenceau station, a gush of warm air licked their faces.
Lori felt like running into the rush of it, but Roland turned
and pressed his hand on her chest.

'Don't look,' he said.

She obediently closed her eyes and he went and stood
behind her, clasping his hands over her eyelids, whispering

into her ear, his breath warm on her neck: 'Trust me.'
They walked the final two steps together.

'I want you to always be inspired,' he said and lifted his
hands. The Arc de Triomphe stood before them, majestic.
Its structure solid, somehow signifying optimism and stature.
The boulevard leading up to it was lined with trees and
even though the road was jammed with cars, the Arc
de Triomphe's presence was unperturbed by the rush of
modern life. For a brief second, its solid structure mirrored
Roland, who took her hand and led her towards it, through
the bustle of people and off into the back streets of the
8th arrondissement, his stride long and steady. It was as if
they'd entered a different country, everything wider and
grander. Roland seemed to respond to this environment
with renewed authority, his past jamming up against his
present like cogs knitting together. They went down into
the underpass, the rush of cars resounding above, the roaring
sound ebbing away, transformed suddenly to a solitary guitar
strumming and their own footsteps echoing against the
hollowed grey concrete. The light was sucked from their
view, graffiti in the shadows, a lamp reflected in a puddle,
and then they were out on the other side, returned to the
day, walking towards the burial site of the unknown soldier.

Lori sensed what their life could be like together, the
possibility floating before her like the smell of fresh baked
buns, the future tangible for a brief moment, a life a year
ago she wouldn't have even dreamed. Roland threaded
his way through the hundreds of tourists milling about,
guiding her to the burning flame, the presence of history,
of life and death and humanity's relationship to it, turning
her gently towards him.

'I know we're young, but I would rather be married
to you for one year, as man and wife, than live with you

in some non-committal state, drifting along.' He held her close. 'Lori Watson. Please will you marry me.'

Lori felt a galloping sensation in her chest. 'Is this for real or are we still playing dare, double dare?' she said, pulling at her hair so that its backcombed ends stuck out. 'I'm confused.'

He took hold of her hands and slid the ring onto her finger. 'It's for real,' he said.

'Shit!' She felt the weight of the ring on her finger. All around them the constant transient rush of traffic, tourists milling about oblivious, an aeroplane overhead, a vapour trail cracking the sky in two. She looked at her finger, the ring was beautiful: two square cut diamonds and a yellow square cut diamond in the middle. She saw a life ahead of her, a life she wanted, a life that would never be dull. She looked into Roland's eyes, sensed his hunger and wished she could let go, embrace the warmth he was offering, but a small part of her felt as hard as an aged knot. She didn't doubt Roland, or his love: she doubted herself.

'We're very young,' she said. 'And I still haven't met your parents.'

'I'm not going to change my mind,' he said. 'And what difference does it make, meeting them?'

Lori thought about how in the morning she'd been full of doubt, believing that after meeting her parents Roland wouldn't want her. It was just a feeling after all, ephemeral, fleeting as snow in April.

'This can't change anything about my work, you know that, right? I mean I'm not one of those women who cooks and bakes cakes and gives up her own life.'

'I know that.' He looked expectant, she could read the anguish in his eyes and felt a wave of what she supposed was love, imagining them married, living together in London.

Hadn't they talked about doing that anyway? What was the difference between living together and marriage? And then she thought of Jude and his dare.

'Shit! You planned this.'

Roland dropped his head, a slow assured smile inched across his face. 'Yep.'

'Wow!' She felt a flutter of anxiety, the idea of being trapped fleeting but there all the same. She remembered Anna saying she had commitment issues.

'Yes, Roland,' she said. 'I will marry you.'

He pulled her closer and the gesture made her feel claustrophobic. 'Let's do it here, now?'

'You're kidding,' she said; her heart seemed to grow large, her throat tight. The traffic that flowed like a raging river felt loud and intrusive.

Roland shook his head, serious suddenly. 'I'm not kidding. I want us to have a private ceremony, just the four of us. We can have a proper wedding later, if you want, but something small and secret feels more special somehow. I asked your father after lunch.' Lori remembered seeing them both, the camaraderie between them as they shook hands. She felt like a squirming animal caught in a trap and yet she couldn't help but admire Roland's conviction.

'My parents will want a white wedding.'

'We'll have a proper ceremony, later.'

Lori looked at her ring, the watch. Her hand and wrist were beginning to look like they belonged to someone else, but at the same time there was an unmistakable happiness welling up inside her. He didn't mind her wildness, wasn't put off by her parents, didn't care that she was a bit rough around the edges and not an intellectual but a painter. Didn't care that she was impulsive and tricky. In that moment she couldn't have felt more alive.

'I'll need to call my parents,' she said.

'Of course.'

Roland had telephoned his aunt, Marie-Claude, from a phone box near the Parc Montsouris and so she was expecting them for coffee and cake.

'Where does your aunt live?'

'She lives down one of these side streets. I want to take us to the house in Dordogne and Aunt Claude has the keys. You wanted to know more about me, well it's where I spent a large part of my childhood, or at least most of my summer holidays, so it felt important to share it with you. You're going to love my aunt.'

They came to a big oak-panelled door. There were three or four brass plates with names on. Roland pressed one of them and the door buzzed open. A marble staircase spiralled upwards. Everything felt more expansive than in their Left Bank pad. The doors to each apartment were a heavy mahogany, the floors polished a shiny black and white. Roland's aunt lived on the first floor. The door was ajar when they arrived. Roland pushed it open, and was greeted by a young girl dressed in a grey trouser suit who gave Roland two kisses on either cheek and held out her hand to Lori.

'Hello, I am Emilé, Marie-Claude's assistant. How do you do? Marie-Claude is on a call and has asked me to introduce myself.'

'Hi,' Lori said, unable to resist gawping at the art hanging in the hallway, the glossy side table with a huge bouquet of flowers on it and the big blue and white china pots stationed either side of the front door. Lori could see into the kitchen where someone in an apron was bustling about.

'Denise is preparing the coffee, she's made my favourite, macaroons,' Emilé told them. Roland took off his coat with one hand and handed it to Emilé.

'I need the loo,' Lori said.

'It's just there.' Emilé directed her to a door on the left with a graceful balletic gesture.

'Lori needs to make a call as well,' Roland said.

'Sure. The office is at the end of the hall,' Emilé said. 'I'll let you know when Marie-Claude is off the phone.'

The loo, which was the size of a double bedroom, was painted a dark fuchsia pink with black paintwork. A grey velvet armchair sat in the corner. There was a brass sink, and an expensive array of hand creams and a few linen hand towels. Lori wondered what her life would have been like if she'd been born into a family like this, a family that didn't count the pennies and make everything boil down to profit and loss. She tried to marshal her thoughts, make sense of what was happening, utterly overwhelmed by the opulence – she could almost feel it seeping into her skin like a perfume. Her mind was victim to a spluttering of conflicting desires: the need to step into this world and a stubborn feeling of unworthiness and panic.

After washing her hands and helping herself to a dollop of hand cream, she went back into the hallway to find Emilé alone.

'Phone is free. Follow me,' she said.

The office had a French window that was partially open, the panelled shutter folded back, but the room was starved of light, shadowed by the close proximity of the building opposite. Lori sat down at Marie-Claude's desk. A telephone, computer, a few pens and pencils with paper were arranged tidily on the surface, not a thing out of place. The books were ordered by colour. Emilé gestured gracefully towards the phone and then slipped out and closed the door.

Lori picked up the phone, her mouth pasty as if she had been chewing on a marshmallow. She dialled her parents' phone number, her hand shaking. She looked out at the building opposite, saw a woman floating about in her kitchen. Something about the way she wafted from one side to another made her seem utterly content.

'Hello, Watson residence.' Her mother's voice was clipped and unfriendly. A tone she reserved for strangers.

'Mum, it's Lori.'

'Goodness, what a surprise. Is everything okay? Did you not go to Paris?'

'Yes, yes, I'm fine. We're in Paris. Everything is marvellous.' There was a long silence. Lori could hear the soft patter of footsteps on the pavement below, the harsher squall of traffic circling the Arc de Triomphe.

'Is there anything you need?' her mother said.

Lori swallowed even though her mouth was perfectly dry. 'No, I mean . . . yes. I just wondered, what did you think of Roland?' She coiled the telephone wire tightly around her fingers. There was another silence and then her mother said.

'He seems like a perfectly nice chap.'

Lori suspected her mother of being non-committal. 'Why?'

'He's asked me to marry him.'

A few seconds passed before her mother said. 'Oh darling, that's wonderful. I had this awful feeling you were going to tell me some horror story. What fabulous news. Your father will be delighted.'

Lori was tempted to say that both of them had barely had a moment with Roland, but why fight it. Most of her younger years had been spent with her mother out of her depth, unable to rely on instinct as so many mothers seem to do. She'd seen photographs of her mother as a young woman, in short skirts that barely covered her bottom, beehive hair and false eyelashes. It was hard to correlate the two versions of the same woman.

'You don't think I'm too young?'

'Your father and I got married when I was just twenty-one.'

Lori realised in that instant that a small part of her had wanted her mother to protest, but of course they'd want her to marry someone like Roland. As far as her father was concerned, marriage meant that she was no longer their responsibility. Roland had mentioned his father's company, which even she'd heard of – they had billboards all over town – so they would know who he was. She remembered how he had talked to her father alone in the restaurant. She knew Roland well enough to know he was single-minded, resolute. She assumed that was a good thing, that she should be flattered that she was part of his long-term plan.

'He wants me to get married now, here in Paris.'

'Oh . . .'

'I'm really sorry to ask but I'll need money for a dress.'

'I see.'

'It's okay, we'll have a proper ceremony when we get home.'

There was another silence. Lori wondered if her mother was crying, then she could hear muffled voices and realised that she'd cupped her hand over the receiver. She heard their muffled discussion, the rise and fall of their voices lulling her into a dream-like state. She imagined them both shivering in the hallway. Finally, she heard her father cough, snagging against the constant low hum on the line. 'Dad here.'

'I'm assuming Mum's told you.'

'She has indeed. Although I was aware of Roland's intention. We had a little chat.' His voice quivered with a sense of importance and he sniffed, usually a sign that he was about to deliver a seriously considered comment. 'Your mother and I both feel that a proper wedding would be more appropriate.'

'I've already told Mum we'll have a proper wedding, but we're getting married here first as Roland is half French. We just thought a spontaneous informal wedding in Paris would be romantic, that's all.' She sighed. She'd hoped to unburden herself, lean on her parents a little, get some reaction that would act as guidance.

'Well, you must do what's best for you,' her father said. 'I'll send some money into your account so you can buy something nice, but you will need to pay me back if we're to contribute towards a proper wedding.'

'Of course. Is Mum okay?'

The phone crackled. 'Yes, darling. I'm here.' There was a kerfuffle – Lori imagined her parents squabbling over the phone – and then her mother came back on the line. Then she whispered. 'Out of interest, has your other friend, Jude, taken you to the gallery yet?'

Lori felt her knees weaken. She was losing the will. Why on earth was her mother bringing this up now?

'Not yet, no. Why are you whispering?'

Again there was an awkward silence, a shuffling. 'Lori, are you sure this is what you want?' her mother whispered again, vehemently this time.

She was glad to hear her mother finally question her choices but the urgency in her mother's voice made her panic. Was she sure? Not really. She didn't know what that meant. She took a deep breath.

'You know me, Mum. I'll never go the conventional route, although Roland is, at least, conventional, which I thought you of all people would approve of. Anyway, I like the idea of an impromptu wedding, there's a kind of free-spirited energy to it.'

'Yes, but . . .'

'Better go.' Lori rested the receiver back in its cradle.

Lori walked into the sitting room to hear Roland and Emilé chatting away in French. As soon as they registered her presence, they switched into English. Lori rather coveted the idea of bilingualism. There were paintings crammed on every wall, modern art mixed with classical portraits and landscapes. Lori had never seen anything like it. She'd imagined herself selling to someone like Marie-Claude, not *belonging* to a family who bought art as an investment. Just the sight of it filled her with elation. She felt in one instant she had stepped towards the self she wanted to be. Three cream sofas were arranged around a marble art nouveau fireplace, above which was a huge painting of a grey horse – not one of her favourites. Lori perched on one of the sofas, swamped by the overwhelming sense of grandeur.

'How did it go?' Roland asked.

Lori could see his apprehension in his eyes. He looked genuinely worried she'd changed her mind. She took his hand and stroked it.

'Yes, all good.'

'Mon cherie!' A tall, thin elegant woman of indeterminate age, her hair tied up in a chignon, her lips painted red, strode into the living room wearing high heels, a long grey pencil skirt and a soft pink silk blouse. Roland stood up, so Lori followed, watching as Roland and Marie-Claude brushed each other's cheeks, mobilising their mouths to imitate a kiss before Roland turned and took Lori's hand.

'Marie-Claude, I want you to meet my future wife.'

# FIFTEEN

## Anna

Anna sat opposite Jude, twisting the stem of her wine glass. That afternoon they'd made love, shared a shower, gone for a walk along the Seine, had hot chocolate in a small café not far from Notre Dame, drawing faces in the milky froth with their fingers. They'd been to the Shakespeare bookshop and bought books they could have bought for half the price back in England. Jude had been relaxed, as if he no longer felt obliged to entertain everyone. A small part of her resented the loss she experienced when he was with Roland.

They'd arranged to meet at La Coupole at seven. It was six fifty and Jude was already clock watching. Anna could feel their shared intimacy ebbing away as Jude flicked anxious glances towards the doorway. The place was alive with the buzz of conversation and it gave her the sensation that they'd reached the central point of the city. Across the room, a woman was feeding her small dog little bits of food from her plate while talking to a man opposite her. A group of male students were arguing at the neighbouring table. The waiters were brusque, rushing up and down the aisles with a sense of importance, long aprons tightly wound around their middles. Even Jude, with his perfect French, didn't seem to be able to earn their respect. They watched with disdain as he swirled the house red around his glass and nodded his approval. Anna looked around her, listening to the voices resounding like waves on a pebbled shore. It seemed as if everyone was engaged in some deep animated conversation except for them. She'd spent the last five minutes studying the menu, sensing the mood shift.

'Why are you anxious?' she asked.

'Who said I was anxious?' Jude said. He was leaning over the table, his jacket sleeves pushed up, exposing his antique watch. A present from Roland.

'It's as if you're somewhere else all of a sudden,' she said.

'Nonsense,' he said.

'You were telling me about your stepfather, but you didn't finish the story.'

'Oh yes, that.' He watched his own fingers drum the table as if they belonged to someone else. 'It's just that he turned up one day to hang out with me while she was working, as if he was an old friend and I was supposed to know who he was. Mum had already left so there was no introduction. In many ways he was great. He sat down and we played with Lego all day. Come mid-afternoon, I was quite hungry and when I told him, he jumped up and said: "Oh Christ, I forgot that bit." He went and made me some beans on toast and we ate it together. I kept waiting for Mum to turn up, but it was Dave who put me to bed that night. Nobody told me where she was and when I asked to phone my grandmother, Dave said it would be better if I didn't. I was about nine and I remember thinking that it would be really uncool to cry, but I wanted to. I had no idea where my mother was or whether she'd come back. Finally, I heard the front door open about eleven and the jangle of Mum's keys drop into the china bowl she kept by the door. I remember feeling a wash of relief. I expected her to come up and see me, but she didn't so I wandered out into the hallway. I could hear music in the sitting room. The door was ajar so I put my head round the corner. I didn't understand what I was seeing at first, as my mother was naked, writhing around on the floor and Dave was on top of her. Then I realised they were having sex.'

'So what did you do?'

Jude grinned, but he was still watching his fingers with glazed eyes as they traced the imprint on the tablecloth. 'I went straight back to bed. I spent the whole night unable to sleep, thinking about my mother. She felt different to me, somehow. After that, Dave never left. He became a permanent fixture and Mum was never the same with me. She'd been on some trial day for a job, which she got, so from that day on, Dave became my prime carer. Dave was, is, a journalist, so he could work from home, but he wasn't always the best stepfather. When things went sour with my mother, he took it out on me.'

'Why haven't you told me all this before?'

Jude shrugged. 'Dunno, never really felt relevant.'

'In what way did she change?'

'She seemed more distant, that's all. Of course I understood why as I got older, but as a child it was hard to fathom.' He smiled at her but his eyes didn't settle. He went back to looking at the door, his head bobbing about, scanning the room.

'Why do you think she withdrew?'

'Dave wanted all her attention.'

Anna put her hand on his forearm as if to hold him steady. He looked up at her with apprehensive eyes and again she felt him drift away. Finally, he said: 'You know I hate talking about this stuff.'

'Why don't we get a cocktail?' she said. It was worth suggesting just to see the smile spread up his cheeks, the freckles dip into the creases around his mouth.

Roland and Lori didn't arrive until twenty past seven. By that point, Jude had downed a Martini, gone through half a bottle of wine and four Marlboro Reds. Anna was aimlessly flicking at the breadcrumbs on the table when she felt someone touch her shoulder. Roland and Lori hovered above, a feeling of possessiveness about them in the way they wrapped their arms around each other. Anna could sense that something momentous had happened by a renewed authority they both seemed to have acquired. Lori had make-up on, and she was wearing the Blondie T-shirt she'd bought that morning. Jude stood up. He and Roland did their usual thing of patting and hugging as if they'd not seen each other in years. Lori and Anna gave each other a small kiss on the cheek.

Roland sat down next to Jude, who had beckoned a waiter to their table.

'Encore du vin, s'il vous plaît.'

As the waiter swivelled round, Roland caught his arm and added a bottle of champagne to the order. 'So, we have some news,' he said when the waiter had gone.

Jude reached for a cigarette. 'Don't tell me, you're married.'

Roland raised his eyebrows. 'Close. We're getting married the day after tomorrow.'

Anna screamed, wrapping her arms around Lori. The restaurant went quiet, but just for a few seconds. 'So, you've finally allowed yourself to be caught,' she whispered into Lori's ear. She felt the prickle of sweat breaking out on her top lip. She hadn't expected them to take Jude seriously.

Jude had rehearsed a speech about how he'd been foolish to interfere, but that was redundant now. One look at his face showed her that he was flattened by the news, his body tensed and his shoulders inched up towards his ears. He was scared of losing Roland, that much was clear.

'And there was me thinking that I'd gone a step too far,' Jude said. Anna caught Jude's eye. She could sense the disquiet inside him slipping into something more dangerous.

'You knew I was planning this,' Roland said. 'So if anything, we're grateful.'

Anna thought it strange that Roland said 'we' so naturally. It was as if he'd already stepped into a new role. It was as if Lori was a lifeboat that he was using to push himself away from his past. She wondered if Lori sensed it too.

'Even so, I didn't expect you to be so . . . so . . . impulsive,' Jude said. His laugh was hollow. He gulped down some wine.

'I prefer spontaneous,' Roland said. 'This whole trip has been fuelled by spontaneity and we both love the idea of marrying in Paris, an intimate ceremony, just us four. We're really happy.' Roland was garrulous, he reached out to touch Lori's hand. That's when Anna saw the ring. 'We're going to organise a proper wedding when we get back, but we like the idea of doing it here, don't we?'

Lori smiled, then looked off in the direction of the door as if she'd forgotten some part of herself. To Anna, Lori appeared overwhelmed. She was drowning.

Jude helped himself to more wine, then remembered to fill everyone else's glass. It was obvious there wasn't enough, so when he got to Roland and dribbled the rest of the wine into his glass — a centimetre at best — he laughed. 'Celui qui finit la bouteille va se marier dans l'année,' he said.

'What does that mean?' Anna asked.

'When the last of the wine is poured out – you'll be married by the end of the year!' Jude said.

Roland raised an eyebrow and held up the empty glass. 'Sorry mate.'

Roland leaned over and picked up Jude's full glass, pouring some of it into his own. 'No problem, *mate*.'

'Fair enough,' Jude said, raising his eyebrows. He caught Anna's eye and she shrugged, as if to say she understood his mistake had been unintentional, but then she remembered the James Joyce quote: a man of genius makes no mistakes; his errors are volitional and are the portals to discovery. Jude was testing Roland, that much was apparent.

Lori hadn't muttered a word since they'd entered. Her face was immobile like stone, not like Lori at all.

'Let's see the ring.' Anna reached out for Lori's hand. 'Bloody hell!' It was unlike Anna to make exclamations, but the ring *was* beautiful. It seemed to have changed Lori already. Her demeanour was calmer, but at the same time she appeared to have faded. Even her movements were less bold, flimsy somehow. She was dressed as a punk and yet her behaviour was incongruous.

The boys had already moved on and were talking about Hemingway and his years in Paris with Gertrude Stein, James Joyce and Fitzgerald, Jude arguing that Fitzgerald was a greater writer than Hemingway, Roland arguing that Hemingway was the original existentialist.

'Existentialism came into being much later with de Beauvoir and Sartre.' Jude was looking around for the waiter to bring the extra bottle of wine.

'He wasn't an intellectual, I'll give you that, but he lived life on his terms . . .' Roland was finally taking his coat off.

'*And* he was a sexist drunk,' Jude interjected. He caught her eye again and she realised then that he was searching for her approval. She winked. The waiter arrived with the champagne and asked for their food order, bringing the conversation to a close.

'A toast to the bride and groom,' Jude said.

Anna was grateful he was doing the right thing, honouring his role. She knew how attached he was to Roland and because of that, critical of Lori, but if anything it was Lori who had been undermined. Anna wondered what had happened to them that afternoon that had left Lori diminished. They clinked their glasses. Anna watched as the bubbles raced to the top of the glass. She drank, felt the pop of bubbles on the roof of her mouth, the tingle of it as it reached the back of her throat.

'Let's go to Les Bains Douches,' Jude said. There was nothing Jude liked better than a night of heavy decadence in a state of oblivion. But a little tremor of fear flooded Anna's chest. It was the dark way Jude looked at Lori. She could see that underneath the veneer of joy, something else hovered, jealousy perhaps, or was it menace.

# SIXTEEN

## Lori

They arrived at Les Bains Douche to find a long queue of people slumped against the wall – mostly goths and punks, as if Saint Martin's had emptied itself into the belly of Paris. It was going to take them an hour to get inside. Lori was glad she'd worn her torn jeans and the new Blondie T-shirt and leather jacket; she felt as if she blended in, as did Anna dressed in an oversized men's dinner jacket and black trousers. Lori felt rather overshadowed by Anna's glamour. She kept looking at her engagement ring, not quite believing it was hers. Somehow it didn't quite go with everything else. While they stood in the queue Roland sauntered up to the door to talk to one of the bouncers, his head cocked to the side. Two minutes later, he waved them forward and they strutted past everyone, swooping into the club like a flight of swallows.

'How the fuck did you manage that?' Jude rubbed his hands together gleefully, a habit she'd noticed before.

'My aunt knows the owner,' Roland said. Normally she'd offer Roland a pout, but she felt shy suddenly, unsure.

'Of course she bloody does,' Jude said, shaking his head, smiling at the floor. He had a gift for veiling statements in an air of condescension, which Lori had rather admired before, but now she couldn't help take his slight personally.

'Why are you complaining?' Anna asked.

'I'm not. I just don't understand why Roland's aunt wasn't so useful when we lived here, that's all. Or is this some vain attempt to impress your fiancée,' Jude said, a spiteful edge to his voice.

Roland patted him on the back in a friendly attempt to still his anger. 'This is a special occasion,' he said, winking at Anna. 'Don't spoil it.'

Jude was shaking his head, putting a cigarette up to his lips, his mouth pinched into a smile.

'What does it matter? We're in the here and now. Stop with your chirruping,' Anna said.

Lori kept quiet. She had a feeling something close to envy was bubbling up in Jude. He'd been petulant ever since Roland announced their marriage. Roland had hardly paid her any attention over supper, preferring to banter with Jude, keep the mood buoyant. She'd noticed him smiling at Anna as well in that slow assured way that he had, leaving Lori feeling displaced, outside the group.

They ordered cocktails and wandered through the labyrinth of rooms, trying their hardest to look unimpressed. Lori had the feeling Roland wasn't at all enthralled, but she and Anna were both gawping at the spectacle: people dressed in suits with exaggeratedly wide shoulders and narrow trousers. It seemed to Lori as if everyone was one step away from fame. Hot sweaty bodies were pushed together, dancing to Grace Jones's 'Nightclubbing'. The light was red and orange, making everyone glow. Lori began to relax. She loved the anonymity clubs provided, bodies pressed together, music so loud it was impossible to talk or think. In a strange way it offered privacy. All that life, the events of the day, Anna on the scooter, Jude walking into the lake, Roland's proposal, had made Lori feel giddy, as if she was teetering on the edge of a wave, her life moving forward so fast she could feel it rushing past her. She couldn't wait to get back to her painting so that she could commit the feeling of elation to canvas. She kept thinking about Anna fighting to get on that scooter. *You don't have a monopoly on impulsiveness, you know.* And now here she was, getting married.

They danced together at first, the four of them in a tight knot, their hips rolling from side to side. Roland had drunk as much as she had but he was sober still and his dancing stiff. But she loved him for it. Sylvester's 'You Make Me Feel (Mighty Real)' came on. Lori felt the music enter her, the buzz of the alcohol opening her up, everything falling away. She caught Roland's eye and sensed his intolerance, but she needed to let go. Lori turned and turned, dancing with strangers, allowing her body to take the lead. Then suddenly the track was over and she was unable to locate the others. She looked from side to side but couldn't see either Anna or Roland. Jude moved closer, his angular body touching hers, his face shiny with sweat. Another track started up: Spandau Ballet, 'Only When You Leave'.

'Dance with me.' Jude pressed his body close to hers, mouthing the lyrics, *Only When You Leave I Need to Love You,* gyrating from side to side in an exaggerated manner, looking at her in a way he wasn't supposed to. She could feel his hot breath on her neck. Then he said: 'It's a pity you're getting married.'

'Why?' She had to shout to be heard. A trickle of sweat ran down her back making her shiver.

'You know I've always liked you, don't you?'

Lori felt a flush of shame, as if she'd invited the compliment.

'I don't think we should be doing this,' she said.

'But we are,' he said.

She turned her back to Jude, scanning the crowd, searching for the others, but all she could see was a collection of bodies shattered by the strobe, the whole place swamped in a blood-red light. Then she spotted them both by the bar. Roland had his lips pressed against Anna's ear, his hand resting on her hip. Anna laughed, put her finger up to his cheek. Lori felt a hot flush of panic. Was Roland playing her for a fool? When she was facing Jude again, she danced energetically, drawing him towards her, she had to admit she was flattered by his attention. The movement helped to calm her. Then they spun and spun and the strobe light took her away and she was just her body. She felt his lips on her neck and jolted back, almost falling over a man in a suit.

'I'd better go and find Roland,' she said.

'Why are you marrying him?'

She leaned forward and whispered into his ear: 'Because I want to.'

Jude grabbed her hand: 'I can feel you slipping away. Don't change who you are, ever.'

The next day they got up late, hung-over. Everyone, that is except for Roland, who'd gone over to his aunt Marie-Claude's. Emilé was helping him with the paperwork necessary for the wedding. Anna and Lori sat hunched over the breakfast bar drinking freshly squeezed juice that Anna had prepared, last night's antics forgotten after a night of love-making. Sun poured in through the window, so that motes of dust danced into the kitchen – the room instantly hazy – the air filled with pollen and something like hope. Anna opened the window and the sound of a moped roaring down the road made them both wince, but it was the sound of summer approaching and it made Lori smile.

Roland had bought croissants from the local bakers and left them in a bag. They stuffed them into their mouths while making a list of things to buy for the wedding.

'I have no idea what I'm going to wear,' Lori said.

'We could revisit the boutique, see if they have any floaty white dresses,' Anna said. She didn't seem filled with enthusiasm but that was probably down to her headache.

'I'm not wearing white or anything floaty, nor anything with puffed-up sleeves and frills. Not even for the church do. I'm keeping it simple.'

Jude staggered in, his hair sticking up on end, his chin peppered with a ginger beard.

'Darling, you look awful,' Anna said.

'Cheers, babe.' Jude tore at the paper bag and snatched up a croissant.

'Are you meeting Roland later?' Lori asked.

'Yep, what's it to you?'

'Unnecessary!' Anna said without looking at him. Lori could tell that something was wrong and that Anna had already had words with him. A sticky silence fell in the room as Jude stomped around the kitchen and poured himself a coffee.

'Why is it your hangovers are ten times worse than anyone else's?' Anna asked.

But Lori knew it wasn't the hangover making him grouchy, it was something deeper and more resonant. He sloped off, not bothering to explain himself.

Lori found a green silk vintage dress in a second-hand shop in Les Halles along with some 1930s shoes. They both got their hair done and Lori bought some lily of the valley in an exquisite florist on the Left Bank as a bouquet. Anna bought a black dress in the boutique opposite their apartment. On the surface, it had been a fun day, but Lori sensed something was troubling Anna.

The boys had gone off on an impromptu stag night on Jude's insistence. They'd booked themselves into a nearby hotel and arranged to meet at the registry office. Anna and Lori had supper in a local bistro and finished off with a glass of wine in a bar a short walk from their apartment. Anna was ploughing her way through a jaundiced copy of *Madame Bovary*, and it wasn't until Lori had started to feel restless, bored with reading about Barbara Hepworth, who was one of the artists she'd chosen to discuss for her dissertation, shifting from one side of her chair to the other, that Anna finally looked up from her book.

'What is it?' she asked, her finger resting lightly on the page.

'It's nothing, I'm okay.'

Anna put the book face down. 'You are *not* okay,' she said. 'You've been sighing and wriggling around like a worm on a hook. You are far from okay.'

Lori sighed. These past two days Lori had felt distanced from Anna, as if their foursome had finally revealed a crack. She didn't blame Anna, she blamed Jude. He'd started it, with his flirting, and then Anna started behaving in a similar way with Roland.

'What was up with Jude this morning?'

'He was hung-over, why?'

Lori shook her head. 'He's been funny with me ever since Roland announced the wedding.' She realised she was tapping her wine glass and stopped.

Anna sat with her finger still resting on the page, her eyes revealing a hidden turmoil, her face still, mouth sealed. She had the habit of licking her lips when she was thinking things through. Lori waited, and out slipped her tongue, her eyes dropping and closing, reining in her fears so that she could deliver her thoughts clearly.

'Jude just feels it's all too sudden. He hates change. Always has. He worries about you both.'

'It was his idea!'

'Actually, it was Roland's idea but Jude didn't expect you to go through with it.'

'You're kidding?' Lori wondered if Anna had seen them both dancing last night. She'd been drunk and defiant and hated herself for it, but then Anna had seemed abnormally tactile with Roland.

'Is that what you were talking to Roland about last night?'

Anna nodded, the absence of emotion making Lori shiver. 'He's manipulated this whole thing, and I wonder if you're ready, that's all.'

Lori felt a jolt of anger. Who was Anna to question Roland? Or her, for that matter? 'Maybe Jude's jealous, frightened of losing Roland.'

Anna laid the bill they had just been given between the leaves of her book before closing it, the stoicism a statement now. Anna took pleasure in control. 'Maybe it's more complex than that.'

'Go on.'

Her eyes were suddenly warmer, as if she no longer felt the need to defend herself, or maybe it was a tactic to soften the blow. 'I think he's genuinely worried that this marriage will change everything. You're very fickle sometimes, you admit that yourself, you pride yourself on your impulsivity. Are you sure you know what you're getting yourself into? I mean, Roland is quite conventional. I know everyone thinks Jude is a wild card, but he's more sensitive than people think. He's genuinely worried.'

'What's the big deal? We can always get divorced.'

'That's hardly the way to go into a marriage.'

'You're talking about it as if I don't know or love Roland. I know he's quite conventional but I need someone steady. We balance each other out, like you and Jude.'

'Why rush it, though?' Anna leaned forward, her novel forgotten.

'I want to be married. It's romantic.' Lori felt a quiver in her throat. She couldn't quite grasp what Anna was trying to say. As if her words were a physical thing, transient, just out of reach, like the bubbles she used to chase as a child. But then she remembered her mother: *Are you sure?* Doubt had wedged itself into the cracks, making her even more restless.

# SEVENTEEN

## Anna

They arrived at the Mairie du 8ᵉ arrondissement de Paris with minutes to spare. Lori's pale green dress fell just above the ankles, and her cream silk shoes were fastened with a 1930s T-bar. She'd had her hair styled so that it was sleek, and had pinned a few lily of the valley flowers in it. In twenty-four hours she'd turned into another person entirely. She looked demure, beautiful – the feisty Lori had disappeared.

'Feeling nervous?' Anna said as she tucked a stray hair behind Lori's ears. She was wearing a short black dress with shoulder pads. Power dressing, her mother called it.

'Numb, actually.'

'Oh Lori, are you sure you want to go through with this? I have no idea how I'd feel, but then I can't imagine marrying Jude. It seems he's not the marrying type.' It made her sad to think he wasn't but what could she do? She retracted her arm, sensing an unmovable rigidity in Lori. It was her fault. She knew she'd been too frank yesterday and it was hard to come back from such a candid place. It had taken her a couple of hours to coax Lori from her recoiled state last night. They'd both gone to bed red-eyed, glad that the boys had booked into a hotel for the night.

But then Lori surprised her by clasping her hand. 'I really appreciate the things you said last night. I might be fickle but I'm still here aren't I?' She laughed, quite light-heartedly, leaned forward and kissed Anna on the cheek. 'I know this is the right thing. I know it with every cell in my body.'

When Lori and Roland faced each other at the bottom of the steps of the town hall, a depth of feeling radiated from them both. Lori, demure – the nervous energy having evaporated – clutching a small bouquet of lily of the valley. Roland clearly happy. Perhaps, Anna thought, Jude had been wrong about Lori. Jude, his usual exuberant self, raised an eyebrow as she approached him.

'Looking sexy, darling,' he said as they followed Lori and Roland into the registry office.

'Any chance you could come up with something other than sexy?' she said.

'Not really, no.'

Jude had on a new suit as well, probably provided by Roland, who was wearing a velvet jacket and a white shirt unbuttoned at the neck. His hair brushed back, his face exuding goodwill. He really was imposing when he wanted to be, a mannered impenetrability she'd witnessed in men before, friends of her parents whose success was never questioned.

They climbed the stone steps and walked into the hollowed space of the town hall's reception, their voices echoing in the chamber of a domed ceiling. Looking at them all, Anna felt as if they were strangers to each other.

The wedding room had a small half-circle of gold-framed chairs. Anna and Jude made their way to the front row and stood side by side in silence as Roland and Lori faced each other by the desk where a female registrar was waiting for them. After some banter about the wedding being small, the ceremony began. Anna couldn't quite believe it was happening, it all felt so adult.

Roland and Lori repeated the words of the marriage contract in French, Lori struggling with the pronunciation so that Roland had to guide her. Anna found herself thinking about the discussion she'd had with Lori. Lori had seemed so lost at that point but now she looked as if she'd found a way back to herself. It was clear by the way they looked at each other – a stillness between them – that there was conviction behind their decision. Together they appeared stronger, that was apparent in the way they smiled and laughed through the ceremony. Anna felt that she and Jude were not on each other's team in the same way. They were two individuals orbiting each other's worlds, sparking off each other but never settling. The realisation made her feel sad. Maybe she'd been wrong to warn Lori to go with caution. Maybe it was a good thing that Roland had orchestrated the whole event. At least he knew what he wanted. Jude only seemed to know what he didn't want.

Roland had even managed to get a wedding ring. Jude handed the box to him, serious suddenly, and Roland let go of Lori's hand. Everyone waited, the air crackling, as Roland lifted the lid, took out the ring and placed it on Lori's finger, drawing her towards him so that they kissed. Jude went to reach for Anna's hand, squeezed it fleetingly. They all embraced each other and stood in an awkward huddle. To Anna, everything felt blurred and unreal as if she were watching the scene from a distance.

'Wow, that was some dare,' Jude said. They all laughed, gently breaking away, heading towards the door.

'We need to sign some papers,' Roland said. 'We'll see you guys outside.'

Ten minutes later they stepped out into the sunshine, hand in hand, both squinting against the brightness. Lori looked radiant and happy, all the anxiety from the past couple of days had fallen away. It was Anna who was anxious now. She didn't even know why. While they'd waited, Jude had smoked two cigarettes, barely acknowledging her presence.

She could see he was teetering on the edge, clearly in need of a drink, the way his fingers gripped the cuffs of his jacket. She'd witnessed Jude like this before when he appeared troubled, a darkness emanating from him. A binge-drinking session usually followed. She sensed another one coming, a bit like one senses a change in the weather, and wondered if she should be more worried about their relationship, rather than fret about Lori.

# EIGHTEEN

## Lori

Lori felt a physical explosion of happiness popping inside her chest the minute Roland put the wedding ring on her finger. Overwhelmed by a dizzying delirium when they stepped out onto the Parisian pavements hand in hand, his grip strong and at the same time careful, she allowed herself a few tears. The air was warmed by a vibrant sun. The light bounced off the pavement, the trees. Car bonnets sparkled. The cafés were filling up, tables were jammed onto the terraces, she could hear the thrum of the traffic soaring around the Arc de Triomphe. There was a flower stall on the corner, a boy serving an elegant middle-aged woman, grabbing a handful of tulips. An older man wearing a cap was manning the newspaper kiosk. There was something about the continuous sense of movement, the alchemy and pulse of a foreign city, that filled her with an unexpected feeling of joy. She felt as if she had stepped into another world. She tried to commit it all to memory, wrapping the blue cashmere shawl Anna had given her around her shoulders. She'd never felt so alive, as if the act of commitment was the very thing that had set her free.

'Let's buy today's paper,' she said.

'Why? It's not as if you can read it,' Jude said, leapfrogging over the bollards.

'To remember this day,' Lori said.

'That's nice,' Roland said, but it was Jude who bought a copy of *Le Monde* and the *Guardian*.

'Trust you to buy the lefty papers,' Roland said, folding them neatly and batting Jude on the shoulder.

'Don't tell me you wanted me to buy *Le Figaro*,' Jude said. 'I was kidding.'

'A champagne socialist,' Jude said.

'Talking of champagne . . .' Anna said. And they headed back to La Coupole for lunch, a carefree quartet, a spring in their step.

La Coupole was buzzing. People turned their heads as they walked towards their table, a flutter of clapped hands made Lori blush. The wedding had been so understated, so private, that she'd forgotten how people responded to newlyweds. And she did look like a bride.

'What about the honeymoon?' Anna said as they waited to be served.

Roland dug into his pocket and produced a large set of antique keys, jangling them under their noses. 'My aunt has given me the keys to the family home in Dordogne. It has a pool and a splendid garden.'

'Guess we need to go home tomorrow?' Jude said, churlish as usual, fidgeting and reaching into his pocket for a cigarette.

'I told you, you can stay in the flat for a couple days,' Roland said. 'My friend won't mind. Although, I feel kind of guilty that we started off on this adventure together. I mean you could join us, just for a couple of days. Why not?' Roland flicked an apologetic glance towards Lori. He knew she wouldn't be happy about it, but they had rather dumped their friends in it, she reasoned.

'Well, we don't want to impose,' Anna said, trying to catch Jude's eye. But predictably, Jude was in one of those skittish moods.

'Well it's okay with me,' Lori said, 'as long as there are no more dares.'

This eased the tension. Jude winked at Lori, smiling while picking his teeth with a toothpick.

'You could fly back to Heathrow from Bergerac,' Roland said.

Anna looked at Jude, who shrugged. He appeared to have shrunk inside his suit. Lori could tell that he wanted to join them. It was as if he didn't want them to be alone.

'Are you sure, darling?' Roland said.

'Of course,' she said, wringing her hands underneath the table. It wasn't Anna she minded, but with Jude around, she had to share Roland.

Late that same afternoon, they left. Anna drove. She insisted on allowing the two of them to be passengers in the back of the Fiat as she and Jude were both gatecrashing their honeymoon. Jude was appointed as map reader and soon they were on their way south, cutting through the streets onto the Left Bank, and then turning towards the Périphérique, all singing along to Edith Piaf's 'Non, Je Ne Regrette Rien', their favourite, which Lori had on a cassette. Jude was rifling through her collection in the glove box.

'Not a lot of contemporary stuff here,' he said.

'There's some Manhattan Transfer,' Lori said.

'I said, contemporary.' Jude was firing the cassettes so that they spun onto the floor. 'Got any Joy Division?'

'Oh please, that's so depressing.'

'Totally,' Anna said.

'Michael Jackson, Eurythmics, Marvin Gaye, what more can you want?' Lori said.

'Christ, I'm sharing a car journey with a bunch of morons.'

'I like Joy Division,' Roland said.

'That, my friend, is why I love you,' Jude said.

'I hope you're keeping track of the map,' Anna said.

Jude looked back at the open page on his lap, tracing his finger along the roads. 'Shit, we should have turned off back there.'

They all gave a collective groan.

The journey seemed to take forever. Lori fell asleep in Roland's embrace and woke up to hear Jude and Anna arguing. It was ten o'clock.

'Are you sure we're on the right road? You haven't been the most attentive co-pilot.'

'I'm waiting for signs of where we are. Any signs.'

Lori nudged Roland awake. He took a while to come to, his hair alive with static, his eyes blinking rapidly.

'What was the last town?' he asked.

'Pass,' Jude said.

Anna tentatively drove up to a crossroads. There were no other cars, the landscape hidden under the veil of night, pitch black, the moon nowhere to be seen. Lori felt the thrill of the unexpected. She loved the sense of adventure, of not knowing where they were, and for a second she forgot that she was married. In the darkness she felt the cloying presence of doubt. Unfolding herself from Roland's embrace she took a deep breath, pushing the unsettling feeling away.

'Do you know where we are?' she asked him.

'Yep, we're close. We've come off the motorway a little early, that's all. Just keep going straight.'

'Why don't you sit in the front?' Anna said. She pulled off the main road into a track running up to a farm and Jude and Roland jumped out to swap places. Outside was cold and crisp, the atmosphere leaking into the car so that Lori felt a finger of chilled air wrap around her neck. Jude winked as he slid into his seat, his eyes filled with an eager readiness for something she couldn't identify.

'Comfy back here,' he said.

Lori could sense a friction between them. Everything that came out of his mouth seemed doused in sarcasm or innuendo. Sometimes, Jude felt to her like Roland's other lover. She'd felt his tension earlier over lunch but as soon as he was drunk enough, he relaxed. At that point he turned maudlin, pawing Anna. But then she remembered what he'd said to her at the Les Bains Douche, and Anna's comment about her being impulsive. Then she thought about her mother asking her if she was sure. She looked at Roland, saw the outline of his fluffy hair as a car flashed past. For a fleeting moment he felt like a stranger to her. Had she been rash? The idea that he'd manipulated her into this marriage felt absurd, and yet the doubt flickered. She pushed it aside. But the feeling that she'd lost control of her own life made her top lip prickle with sweat, despite the cool air.

'What's up?' Jude asked.

'Car sick,' Lori said, looking out into the darkness. She thought it extraordinary how quick he was to pick up on her moods.

Ten minutes later, they turned into a lane and after another few minutes arrived at a pair of tall wrought-iron gates, with ornate curly detailing. Roland jumped out and pushed them open, waving the car through. He was smiling at them all, his face shining under the bright lights of the headlamps.

They drove up a long gravel drive, the stones crunching underneath, spitting as they gathered speed. The driveway was lined with poplars. Lori thought she saw a deer in the headlights but it disappeared into the thick inky gloom of night. A large white-stoned house with pale green shutters came into view. As they drove closer, the lights inside started to come on in the rooms downstairs. Lori could hear dogs barking, and geese honking, the place coming alive inside the dimness. As they stopped the car outside the front door, it opened. Inside stood a stout woman in a long floral dressing-gown that she was wrapping around herself, her hair pinned up into a grey bun. Lori wondered who it was, hoping it wasn't a relative. She wasn't in the mood for polite conversation.

Roland flew out of the front seat, running up the steps and kissing the woman on both cheeks. A thin wiry man of around the same age shook his hand, clambering down towards the car, clearly half asleep. Roland dipped his head back into the car.

'Everyone come and say hello to Renée and Léon. They want to greet you and go back to bed. They're normally up at five so this is completely past their bedtime. Léon will take our bags to our rooms.'

'Good God,' Jude said. 'Who lives like this? How come we didn't come here before?'

'I seem to remember inviting you and you being other-wise occupied,' Roland said.

'You didn't tell me you owned a château.'

'Well, firstly this is a manor house, secondly I don't own it.'

Lori felt a fluttering in her stomach at the thought that she'd entered a life she didn't wholly understand. Roland glanced towards her with anxious blue eyes, probably sensing her frustration at not being alone.

'Come on,' he said. She allowed Roland to take her hand as they walked into the hushed echoing hallway with its ceramic patterned tiles, so that he could introduce the housekeeper and her husband to his new wife. Léon quickly nodded and freed himself in order to attend to the luggage, ignoring both Anna and Jude who hovered outside the front door so that the housekeeper had to encourage them with frantic arms to step inside. The house was both elegant and bohemian. A large wardrobe and grandfather clock dominated the hallway and the marble stairs spiralled upwards. Renée gave Lori a reassuring nod and she understood in that moment that if she was to live this life, she would have to learn French. In the hallway she saw a painting, recognising it immediately as a Ceri Richards.

'That's my favourite painting in the house,' Roland said.
'I love his work,' she said.

A light supper of cheese, bread and salad had been prepared and left on an old pine table. The kitchen was huge with an uneven stone floor. A cat was curled up next to the range, ignoring the commotion. It looked utterly serene in amongst the cosy clutter of a house that had gathered possessions over the years so that they became part of the fabric of the building: an old pine dresser filled with china, children's drawings pinned to a board, walking sticks, boots, a butcher's block that had worn down on one side. There was something about the bohemian nature of the place that reminded her of the painters she was writing about. She imagined setting up a studio somewhere in the garden. She felt suddenly inspired, wishing she'd brought just one of her paintings so that she could add detail. Her moment of doubt forgotten amongst the serene surroundings.

Roland lit a few candles and opened the French doors. Jude headed straight for the wine, opening the bottle with a corkscrew he'd found in a drawer.

'I haven't been here in a long while,' Roland said, wrapping his arms around his middle and looking out into the obscurity that was the garden. Lori went to join him. They could hear the geese settling back down, the dripping of water, and the rustle of hidden animal life.

'I spent a lot of time here as a child with my cousins.'

'I thought Marie-Claude didn't have any children,' Lori said.

'She didn't, but there was a brother, who died. Marie-Claude was heavily involved in their upbringing.'

Lori turned to see Anna and Jude arm in arm.

'To love,' Jude said, and he looked at Lori in a way that wasn't very loving at all. She nestled closer to Roland. 'And seduction.'

'To honeymoons,' Roland said. His voice booming and assured.

Later, when they went to bed, Lori asked Roland if he'd noticed anything different about Jude.

'He's anxious that's all.'

'What about?'

'I'm not sure. I can't quite put my finger on it,' Roland said. 'It'll pass.' He ran his fingers through her hair. 'You should wear your hair like this more often,' he said. 'You looked beautiful today.'

Lori remembered Jude's words. *Don't change who you are, ever.* It seemed to Lori that Roland was eager for change, he thrived on it, as if moving forward was a marker of success. She wasn't sure if this was a good thing or not.

# NINETEEN

## Anna

Anna wasn't aware of the hour when she woke up but she suspected it was late by the raucous sound of the lawn mower and the throb of insect life batting against the shutters. It was warmer here, more like early summer at home. Jude had drunk himself silly the night before, the wedding as his excuse, and for some reason they'd all obliged him by keeping up. Now she had the most awful headache, the throbbing weighty kind that no amount of water could cure. She withdrew into the odorous protection of the bed linen but there was no way she could slip back into the shelter of sleep, so she climbed out of bed, opened the shutters, aware that the bright light would probably wake Jude up.

The garden was littered with furniture, a hammock and pot plants bursting with flowers. A discarded rake lay in the centre of the courtyard, forgotten. The swimming pool was covered by a blanket of mist. Anna wondered if it was heated – probably, she thought. The stone slabs surrounding the water were peppered with moss, like liver spots on an ageing hand. A dog was roaming around just below, burying his nose into the hedgerow and wagging his tail. She could hear the hens clucking and the flap of a pigeon's wings as it threw itself off the roof. Léon was busy digging in the vegetable garden, which was stationed behind a row of garages, his body crouched as he examined the earth with his fingers. Everything was overflowing and chaotic. Anna imagined Lori was pinching herself with the pleasure of it all. She'd been entirely convinced by their love yesterday, but Jude had worked his poisonous magic and convinced her that Lori's ambition was at the root of her longing. He had a habit of undermining her belief in people and she found it annoying. She didn't want to think ill of Lori. He'd prove it, he said, but he was drunk. She preferred it when she believed in the two of them. She liked Roland and didn't see him as gullible, which is what Jude wanted her to assume.

She turned to see Jude blink his way into consciousness, remembering their love-making the night before. It was only when they were alone and intimate that her faith in their relationship was restored. Sometimes she felt the belief required was tantamount to a belief in God. She knew that Lori thought her conviction regarding Jude's sentiments was flawed, but Lori didn't know Jude like she did; his vulnerability, which he kept for her eyes only.

'Oh God, is it breakfast time already?' Jude said. 'Why don't you come back to bed, I'm feeling horny.'

'Sometimes, darling, you are utterly predictable. Actually, always.'

'I'm glad to oblige,' he said, turning over on his stomach and grinning with one side of his face. 'Come here,' he said again. 'I want you.'

She hesitated for a second before climbing onto his back and pinning him down with her thighs, then laying herself down and whispering into his ear: 'I want you too.'

When she finally went down for breakfast, Lori and Roland were sitting outside at a small round wrought-iron table

eating croissants and drinking milky coffee from bowls. Lori
was dressed in the blouse they'd seen in the boutique opposite the café on the Left Bank, which Roland had bought
her, apparently. Anna remembered how Lori had shunned
it for being conventional. Clearly she'd had a change of
heart. She'd unbuttoned it so that you could see the lace
of her bra. Anna sat down and helped herself to coffee.

'Good morning,' Lori said, 'there's a bag of pastries and
bread on the kitchen table. The jams are all homemade.'
Lori spoke as if the 'manor' were her home and she was
hosting, not Roland. Anna knew Jude would pick up on
it. It was as if he was desperate to find Lori's Achilles' heel
and she didn't make it hard for him.

'Oh, you have settled into your new role as wife and
mistress of the manor, haven't you Mrs Hawkins?' Anna
said.

Lori blushed. Anna felt a flash of shame seeing the
anguish in her eyes, but she let the guilt and the feeling
of contempt roll around like a boiled sweet on the tongue.
She was hung-over after all.

'She's a natural,' Roland said, patting Lori like a well-
behaved poodle. 'There's hot milk on the stove.'

'Thanks. I'll wait for Jude.'

Two minutes later Jude arrived, bringing with him an
overt enthusiasm and the kind of self-assurance that comes
from lots of sex. 'God, these croissants are good, and that
coffee smells delicious.'

'I thought you wanted to go back to sleep.'

Jude was gobbling down a croissant, grinning. 'I was
worried you'd eat all the goodies. Besides, my head hurts.'

'Me too,' Lori said.

'Well, you know what they say, don't you? Hair of the
dog, nothing like it.'

'I thought I might take a swim. The pool is heated, apparently,' Lori said.

'Do you have a costume?' Anna asked.

'No, but I'll improvise.' Her tone was off, which Anna knew was her doing.

'How about a champagne breakfast?' Jude picked up a couple of the oranges in a bowl, then a third and started to juggle them. 'Or better still, a Mimosa cocktail.' He winked at Roland.

'Buck's Fizz to the likes of you,' Lori said.

'To all of us,' Anna said. 'Apart from Roland of course.'

'Good shout,' Roland said. He opened the fridge. There were several bottles of Veuve Clicquot chilling in the wine section. Anna felt a moment of panic, knowing Jude's inability to resist free booze.

'You're not serious,' Anna said, sitting down, having poured them both a coffee. 'Can't you just stay sober for one day?'

'We're supposed to be celebrating,' Jude said. 'Honestly, it's the best cure.'

'He's right,' Roland said. 'Let's face it, he's had enough practice.' Roland slapped Jude on the back. 'Here, you open this, I'll do the juice.'

As the pop of the cork opening resounded, Anna rolled her eyes at Lori, but Lori's mind was somewhere else. Anna had known it was a bad idea to come. This was supposedly their honeymoon.

# TWENTY

## Lori

Lori sat by the pool dipping her toes languidly into the water, every now and again provocatively kicking up a spray at Jude. She was feeling playful and just a little bit dangerous. Jude was sitting with his back to her. He turned round, a glimmer of mischief in his eyes as he lazily flicked some water back.

'Little Miss Trouble,' he said.

'Mrs Trouble, actually.'

Anna stretched out, tight-lipped, a sour expression forming as she lay down, arms up, spreading herself out like a piece of pastry ready for a rolling pin, but there was something about her body language: she looked as if with one slight touch, she'd recoil.

Half an hour later, Roland cracked open a second bottle and got the cards out and they sat cross-legged in a circle and played Black Maria, a game that involved passing the queen of spades around and if you were left with it, you'd lost. They were shouting and swearing as the damn queen was sneakily handed back and forth, cigarettes burning, the April sun scorching their skin. Of course it got nasty as soon as Jude lost and he snuffled around looking for trouble, poking fun at Lori, then Anna. As host, Roland relinquished the role of stooge.

'Don't you think we ought to eat something?' Anna said, feeding herself and then Jude a bit of leftover croissant.

'We need to go shopping, there's no food,' Roland said, flopping back down and trailing his hand into the pool.

'Love it, a fridge full of champagne but no snacks. That's my kind of house,' Jude said.

Lori turned onto her stomach and cradled her head in her arm, watching as Anna slowly peeled off a layer of clothing in that demure way that she had. Underneath, she was wearing a little vest top that ended just at the curve of her breast. Lori had always envied Anna's ample bosom. Her stomach was flat with one mole by her navel. Her olive skin was already honey-coloured. She ran her hands through her hair, shaking it so that it settled across her shoulders. Roland seemed to enjoy the spectacle, a cigarette planted between his fingers forgotten as he watched Anna settle herself in the sun. He was wearing his sunglasses but she could sense his eyes on Anna. He exhaled a plume of smoke and smiled to himself as if some private thought had amused him.

'I'm bored,' Lori said. Finally, Roland turned to her lazily.

'Why don't we have a swim,' Jude said, glazed and distant. Lori was feeling a little sloshed herself. At least a swim would sober them up and prompt Roland to move. She was tired of their collective indolence and the menace that simmered underneath.

'What about costumes?' Anna said.

'Who needs costumes? Let's swim nude,' Jude said.

'I don't think Renée and Léon need to be confronted with us lot prancing about naked,' Lori said. She didn't like the idea of Léon leering at them all but she knew as soon as she opened her mouth that this would be interpreted as prudish. That visit to her parents had allowed a certain insight, armed Jude in particular with an arsenal of insults. But it was Anna who pursed her lips.

'How would you know? They might.'

Lori was beginning to wonder what was wrong. The way Anna kept snapping out sardonic remarks. She glanced at Roland for support but he didn't seem to notice Anna's spitefulness. Instead, he offered a wide, people-pleasing smile to no one in particular.

'It's okay. I've given them the afternoon off as Renée's going to cook for us later. They'll be tucked up in their cottage,' he said.

Irritated by his inability to recognise Anna's sniping and his own gawking, Lori stood up and removed her clothes unabashed, impatient to get in the water. She set the bar by not removing her knickers, though.

'Wow! That didn't take much prompting,' Jude said. 'Look at her go.'

Lori knew she had one of those bodies that was lean and muscular, whereas Anna was curvy and feminine. Roland was already stripping down to his Y fronts, and so was Jude, leaner than Roland. Anna though, was more tentative. Lori could see how reluctant she was by the slow way she unclipped her bra.

Lori slipped into the pool, her skin suddenly tingling with the cool after the hot sun. Jude made a spectacle of jumping in, knees tucked into his chest, an arc of water spraying her face and causing the water to slosh about. They started to splash each other, jostling and writhing and making a racket until Lori caught sight of Anna sitting on her haunches, sullen. Roland went and knelt beside her, knees jutting out as he looped his arm across her shoulder. Anna shook her head and he bent down to whisper something in her ear. It reminded Lori of how they were in Les Bains Douches the other night – an intimacy that didn't seem proper – then he took hold of Anna's hand and said something, which made Anna smile sweetly. After a while, they jumped in together, Anna squealing in an overly girly manner.

Jude was floating on his back, oblivious.

Lori started to swim, determined to show Roland that she didn't care, her mind still turning over the way he hadn't taken his eyes off Anna and how he'd gently taken hold of her hand, and how coy Anna had looked when she spoke to him, holding onto him even after they'd entered the water. In comparison to Lori, Anna *was* sweet. She'd learned at some point to use her femininity as a weapon, whereas Lori had always been a tomboy, been teased mercilessly as a child for it. Art school had allowed her to use that aspect of her character to her advantage.

Roland found a ball and threw it to her. She caught it and punched it back to Jude, making a show of jumping up athletically and arcing the ball towards him.

Anna ducked under so that her hair swept back, clean off her face. She looked like Bo Derek.

'Let's play water polo,' she said, swimming over to Roland. 'Ro and me against you two.'

'I've got a better idea,' Roland said. 'Here, Anna, climb up. Chicken fights. I used to love this game as a kid.'

Anna started to scramble onto Roland's back. She got one leg over his shoulder, but then she slipped back into the water. Roland caught her and hoisted her onto his back, his hands on her bottom. From there she climbed onto his shoulders, her breasts squashed into his ear as she did so. She seemed to have lost all inhibitions.

The second Lori was on Jude's shoulders, aware of her crotch pressed into the back of his head, Roland charged towards them, growling, which made them all laugh until they tumbled over again. Lori tried to let go of the way Roland had watched Anna in what he thought was a private moment, the way he held her buttocks to help her onto his back. But it was the way he whispered into her ear that had got to her most. It was the same intimacy they'd displayed the other night in the club. She began to wonder what was going on, why Roland had married her when he was so clearly attached to Anna. Then she remembered Anna trying to put her off marrying Roland.

They scrambled about trying to get on the boys' shoulders. Jude ducked, making it easier for her but Anna was trying to mount Roland from the edge of the pool. She watched as Roland reached up to take hold of Anna's hand. Anna flicked back her hair.

Lori stood staring at them both until Jude said. 'Get a move on!'

Once stationed on Jude's shoulders, Lori flicked a glance at Roland and noticed how his hands squeezed Anna's legs, then he growled again and pretended to bite her inner thigh, which made Anna writhe about with laughter. Lori felt hot tears well up. It all felt so wrong.

It was Jude who did the charging this time. Lori gripped Anna's arms and they started to wrestle, hurling their bodies from side to side, tossing their heads back. They were lunging at each other, snorting and grunting, mocking the wrestlers they'd seen on television, but then Anna shoved Lori a little too hard. Jude began to topple as Lori took a swing at Anna, grabbing her wrist and pulling her down with them until they all tumbled over. Lori tightened her grip around Anna's wrist just as they all went under. Anna screamed.

'That hurt!' She lashed out at Lori, catching her face.

'What the fuck!'

'Calm down!' Roland said.

'Oh right, so it's okay for Anna to play dirty but not me.'

'I wasn't playing dirty,' Anna said. Lori held her hand to her cheek. She could feel the heat on her skin where Anna had slapped her.

'It wasn't intentional,' Roland said, frowning, his eyes solemn.

'Girlies,' Jude said, laughing. 'Stop fighting, it's too much of a turn-on.'

Roland took Anna's wrist. 'Are you okay?'

Lori swam to the side, hauling herself out of the pool in one swift move.

'Sweetheart,' Roland said, turning to Lori.

'Don't you bloody sweetheart me,' she said, grabbing her T-shirt and running into the house.

'I think this has got out of control,' she heard Roland say.

'Hardly surprising,' Anna said. 'We've done nothing but drink for two days.'

Lori could feel the hot tears running down her cooled skin as she ran into the kitchen, through the hallway and upstairs. She'd felt Anna's antagonism ever since she'd come down for breakfast and then that whole act of being helpless to gain Roland's attention. She scrabbled about, peeling off her knickers, finding a fresh pair and rubbing her hair with a towel.

Roland came bolting into the room. He'd managed to put a pair of shorts on and a shirt which was covered in wet patches. He padded around the room, picking up their clothes from the night before, shaking them out like an irate nanny chastising her charges.

'What the fuck has got into you?'

'Oh what, you think I didn't notice you flirting with Anna?' Lori was looking for something to wear, throwing

148

clothes onto the floor from the suitcase in an attempt to find her Blondie T-shirt.

'What are you talking about?' He stood stock still, one of his shirts scrunched tight inside his fisted hand.

'I saw you, Roland. You couldn't take your eyes off her, you bit her inner thigh! You sided with her, not me. We've been married for a day. We're supposed to be on our honeymoon!' She pulled on her T-shirt.

Roland was still staring at her, his sunglasses perched on the crown of his head, frowning, as if she were some difficult equation he couldn't make head or tail of. 'Lori, it was just a bit of fun. You really are taking this too far.' She hated the switch of tone, the false concern.

'Oh, so if I bit Jude around the crotch you'd like it would you?'

'Jesus you can be difficult sometimes!'

Lori's head was swimming. Ever since the night of her birthday, Roland had been tugging at the reins of her life.

'Fuck you!' She flicked the damp towel at him so that it cracked the air like a whip. They stood staring at each other, the air between them thick, cluttered with emotion forming an invisible wall that neither of them could break through.

'Anna and Jude have to sort out their flights. We need food, so when I get back from the supermarket in a couple of hours, I expect you to be in a better mood!' Roland said in that manner he had as if he were the only adult. He walked out of the room, picking up some more laundry on the way out.

Lori wanted to run after him but her limbs didn't respond. She wondered if all three of them would go shopping without her. A feeling of abandonment made her throat tighten. She stuck her head out of the window to see Anna trailing after Roland. She ran down the stairs not knowing what to do next, a feeling of recklessness consuming every cell, which mutated into an ugly need for revenge as soon as she saw them step into the car together.

# TWENTY-ONE

## Anna

Anna and Roland climbed into a Citroën Deux Chevaux that apparently belonged to the house. As they chugged down the driveway, the gravel spitting out from under the car, she noticed Lori striding out into the grounds, a towel over her shoulder.

'Lori still looks pissed off,' she said. 'Is everything all right?'

'Oh you know Lori. She's being oversensitive.'

'Yes, she can be explosive at times.' Anna thought his response rather tactful. 'Maybe she should have come instead of me.'

'I thought you needed to sort your flights out.'

Anna felt the redness spread across her cheeks. They really shouldn't have come. 'I feel awful that Jude and I have gatecrashed your honeymoon. I think I should book a flight for tomorrow if possible?'

'Hardly seems worth you coming.'

'I get the feeling that's what's upset Lori. It's a big thing you've both done and you need time alone.'

Léon was waiting by the gates so that when they drove through, he was there to close them. Roland gave a little wave as the car jolted over the cattle grid which she hadn't remembered noticing before.

'If anything, it's thanks to you two Lori and I are married. Anyway, a row was inevitable. It's been an intense few days.' Roland pushed the gears through, the engine purring. It sounded more like a lawn mower than a car. She felt rather vulnerable in it, although she was quite impressed by his ability to adapt. He seemed at ease with the clunky gear stick that protruded from the dashboard. Roland wasn't an anxious person, and yet she felt a tension emanating from him and wondered if it was anything to do with leaving Jude and Lori behind, but this was probably her own neurosis, not his.

'It *was* a bit of a surprise, the wedding, wasn't it? I didn't think Lori would say yes,' she said. 'But Lori is nothing if not unpredictable.'

'On the surface, yes,' he said, staring ahead.

Anna found herself fiddling with the hem of her denim jacket. It was unravelling, and she picked at the threads in need of a distraction, feeling that if Roland suspected she was wholly attentive, he wouldn't be quite so forthcoming.

'She likes to present herself that way. As if being normal won't make her an artist. But for all of her wildness, she's quite vulnerable.' He was driving with one hand on the wheel. She saw his aquiline nose and thought about his aristocratic roots. France seemed to have brought out the indomitable side to him. 'What made Lori so cross?'

'I think we all got carried away.'

'Yes, I agree.'

'We used to play that game as kids,' he said, a childhood memory dancing across his face. 'It was always such fun. I thought she'd like it.'

'Most of us didn't grow up with swimming pools,' she said.

Roland was somewhere else. She could see him churning over his thoughts, his face alight, mobile. 'Lori was lost, I knew that. I'm more observant than she realises. She had no idea what she was going to do, and her parents aren't exactly supportive. I knew I wasn't going to change my mind about her, so I decided to act.'

'In quite a cunning way though.'

He chuckled.

'Anyway, I don't think Lori was lost,' she said, in the mood to play devil's advocate, the feminist in her making her feel prickly and difficult. 'Tell me, you seem pretty decided on *your* feelings, but what about hers?'

Roland turned sharply to look at her, the car veered off to the middle of the road, an approaching truck tooted and he righted the steering. 'What do you mean?' he asked once the crisis had passed.

Anna's heart was thumping hard. There was a fleeting moment of panic when she'd believed he'd lost control of the car. 'I think you have this image of Lori that's all. It's dangerous to make assumptions. How people see us can change the way we perceive ourselves.'

Roland didn't answer straight away. He seemed to take on board what she'd said, before talking about the supermarket, and how one was overpriced and dependent on tourists, and how the market was the best way to shop but it wasn't the right day. They chatted about the weather, about surface matter, until much to her surprise he said, 'I'm not making assumptions.' He turned towards her again but she pretended not to notice so that his attention went back to the road.

'It's just that you sound like someone determined to get her off the market.'

He laughed. 'We both know that both Lori and Jude have commitment issues and are deeply insecure but we shouldn't pander to them.' He turned briefly and smiled, as if he'd delivered a hot pie, or a birthday cake.

Anna wasn't sure how to respond. Like many men she'd known, Jude avoided conversational intimacy but Roland seemed unusually mature yet at the same time immutable. She wanted to confide in him, explain she was worried about leaving the other two alone, that she hoped that one day Jude would recognise what they had, that she was waiting for Jude to love her in the same way as she loved him. It seemed to her that Roland had the measure of life. She found herself feeling maudlin and gazed out at the landscape hoping to find solace in the unfamiliarity of it, but even the turreted château and lush trees sprouting from the hillside wasn't enough to distract her from her own internal storm.

'You're worried about Jude, aren't you?'

Roland's prescience took her unawares. She turned to see he was smiling knowingly. 'How did you know?'

He rolled his eyes.

'Oh God.' A wave of shame made her sink further into the seat.

'As I said when we were by the pool, Jude is all mouth and no trousers. He flirts with everyone, even me. He's a bit of a game player but harmless enough, you know that.'

They passed a bicycle with a long stick of bread strapped across the back. The grass was flattened by the breeze, turning silver; she admired a line of birch trees leading towards another château with a turret and a luscious arc of wisteria that was just beginning to flower, running under the guttering of the roof.

'A part of me suspects Jude is jealous of Lori as much as anything,' she said, thinking out loud. She believed Jude was envious of Roland too, not just of his wealth, but his unfaltering ambition, his steady approach to real life. Jude was all about experience, living in the moment.

Roland flicked the window up, stuck his elbow out. 'I think Jude suspects Lori isn't so taken with him,' he said, 'but we all know really, don't we?'

'I suppose we do, although I'm not sure we listen to that visceral knowledge,' she said. She was wrangling with exactly that feeling now. Sensing Lori and Jude would get up to no good. That argument had left them all on edge, except for Jude, who grabbed her before she ran after Lori and told her not to interfere.

'You're very tolerant of him,' she said.

He indicated to turn left and the car shuddered and whined as they slowed down. 'Well, he's generous in his own way too. He makes us all feel better about ourselves, don't you think?'

'Yes, but he's aware of the power that gives him.'

'If you're that concerned about leaving them alone, why did you come?'

She'd been frustrated by her own passivity. There was something fiendishly cunning about the way Roland had manipulated her into going shopping, even if she did need to sort their flights. She wondered if he'd orchestrated the whole outing so that Jude and Lori were alone. He could've telephoned about the flights, surely.

'They were pretty flirtatious in the pool,' she said.

'So were we! Lori's furious.'

'Shit, really? Oh that's out of line. Lori's overtly flirtatious at times.' She found herself scanning the skyline, noticing an eagle hovering above the road, probably eyeing up its prey. In the distance, she saw the sign for the supermarket looming, its cylindrical neon façade brash on the horizon. She didn't want the conversation to end, she felt the candid nature of it was rare. She wiggled her finger into a hole in the seat. Roland was tapping the steering wheel, patiently waiting, his sleeves rolled up. They swung across the road towards the car park.

'It's not easy being Jude's girlfriend,' she said finally.

He looked at her, frowning. 'It wouldn't hurt to be a little more unavailable sometimes. Let him fret.'

Anna knew he was right. She wondered if this visit to the supermarket had been orchestrated by Roland in order to make Lori jealous. Jude was wrong about Roland; he was a player.

'Anyway, nothing's going to happen,' he said.

Anna wasn't so convinced. She found it impossible to ignore her dry mouth and racing heart.

# TWENTY-TWO

## Lori

Lori didn't so much see Jude looking at her, as sense his eyes on her body eyeing her up like one does an aperitif. His attention was tangible. She ignored him. She had more important things on her mind. She was furious with Roland for one thing. He'd been an idiot to suggest that game, although he'd so obviously enjoyed Anna's attention, then he'd refused to stick up for her when it was bloody obvious Anna was being deliberately vicious. Lori was in the hammock, swinging back and forth, trying to read about Barbara Hepworth — not easy while on the move — several times she had to reread passages. It was hard to concentrate. Her mind kept flitting back and forth, thinking about her argument with Roland, his look of disbelief, as if she were a recalcitrant teenager. She kept reliving the last twenty-four hours, wondering if she'd been too impulsive. She couldn't let go of the idea that Roland had orchestrated the whole thing: the trip to Paris, the marriage, the four of them going on the honeymoon and then the bloody wrestling game. She remembered reading about a divided self. That was exactly how she felt: one part flattered that he'd gone to that much effort, the other half feeling like a butterfly caught in a net.

There was a pleasant hum of insects, the swallows kept swooping down to drink the water in the pool, chattering away. Lori could hear the rattle of a lawn mower in the distance. The clanging of pans in the kitchen. Renée was back in the kitchen making onion soup – and the plop, plop, plop of Jude swimming. Then the plopping stopped. Through the netting of the hammock, she spotted Jude resting his head on his elbows, watching her.

'Not so warm this pool is it?' he said.

'Cold water swimming is supposed to be very good for you.' She smiled, a feeling of generosity catching her by surprise. She'd hated them all minutes ago. 'People swim in the pond in Hampstead all year round.'

'Admirable. This pool is heated, though, which just takes the edge off.'

'Could have fooled me. I thought it was bloody freezing.'

He dipped back down underwater, turning elegantly and kicking off to do another length, deliberately showing off, having found an audience. His swimming style was perfect, breaking the water with a twisted flattened hand, turning his head every couple of strokes to fill his lungs effortlessly. She went back to her book, although from the corner of her eye she could see him going back and forth, his arms slapping rhythmically into the water. He had the shoulders of a good swimmer.

When he'd finished, he came up to her, a towel wrapped around his waist, his red hair still wet, falling in ringlets around his face.

'What are you reading?' he asked.

'I'm not, I'm browsing. I can't concentrate after that row. I'm supposed to be writing my dissertation.'

He smiled approvingly, picked up a small pile of books she'd left on the table nearby. 'I see you have one of my favourite artists here, Bridget Riley.'

'I'm not a fan but she was the queen of Op Art. She's

theoretically rigorous, which is the absolute opposite to me.'

'Yes, she was far from spontaneous. Don't read this. It'll give you nightmares.' He held up William Burrough's *Naked Lunch.'*

'I just picked them at random. I'm trying to get my head in the right space. I told you, I'm not really reading, I'm pretending.'

He threw back his head, coughed out another laugh. 'Yes, you're good at pretending, aren't you?'

She glanced at him nonchalantly. 'What's that supposed to mean?'

Jude laughed. 'Nothing. I'm goading you.'

'Well don't. I'm not in the mood. I think we've all had enough of goading each other for now.'

'Yes, I do think Roland and Anna were flirting outrageously.'

'Do you? So it wasn't just me.'

'Roland's not a saint, you know.'

'What's that supposed to mean?'

'Well everyone has a past, darling.' He winked.

'Oh stop it!' she said, laughing.

There was something predatory about his proximity, the way he was leaning into the hammock, his arms brushing against her legs, his wet hair dripping onto her shins.

'You do realise that there's an original Ceri Richards in the hallway, don't you?' she said. She wasn't sure why she said it, perhaps just to change the subject. 'Roland's favourite painter and one of mine too.'

'Never heard of him.'

'It's all right. I only know who he is because my art teacher was named after him. Ceri with a C. She's Welsh, like him.'

'I'm Welsh.'

'Are you?'

'Half Welsh and half God knows what,' he said, 'seeing as my mother has failed to tell me who my father is.' He put his weight onto the hammock and she heard the rope creak. 'I thought Ceri with a C was a boy's name,' he said.

'It is, mostly.'

'Of course the Welsh side is the only side I know. My mother comes from a rather progressive Welsh family, hence the hippy commune where I was conceived.'

'How exciting,' she said. She watched as he digested her response. 'I was probably conceived on the first night of my parents' honeymoon in some desperately unglamorous bed and breakfast in Cornwall,' she said.

He tittered, genuinely amused.

'Do you want to see the Ceri Richards painting?' she asked.

'Sure.' He held out his hand. She gripped it tightly to steady herself as the hammock lurched away from under her.

'Do you find it exciting?' he asked.

'What?'

'Being around this money.'

Lori blushed, glad that they'd walked into the cool obscurity of the hallway where she floundered, suddenly blinded by the gloominess. Jude's feet were wet and slopped against the terracotta tiles. 'Perhaps you ought to get dressed,' she said.

'I will, but I want to see this painting first.'

The painting was an abstract, oil on wood. Simple shapes in blue hues, typical of its period: 1963. It looked to her as if it belonged in the Tate Gallery, the way it was framed in heavy gold.

'It's extraordinary,' he said. 'Quite incredible the amount of art there is in this place. I think there's even a Picasso upstairs.'

'Really?'

She turned to find him standing so close to her that their bodies touched. He held her gaze and she felt the unexpected stirrings of desire and something else. The thing with Jude was when he looked at you, it was as if you'd been touched by God, that well of love, of life, that spilled out of him and reflected onto them all. She'd never understood this until now – how his attention made her feel special.

'It hasn't gone away just because you got married,' he said.

'What hasn't?'

'You know perfectly well what.' He straightened the collar of her shirt, running his fingers down her chest.

Lori felt herself redden.

'It wasn't just Roland and Anna flirting. We were having a good time out there, weren't we?' He cocked his head. 'This will probably be your last opportunity to know what it is to be loved by someone else.'

'Stop confusing sex with love.' She sighed, turned her head, stepping away so that his hand fell limply to his side. She could sense the crushing undercurrent of hostility – the shadow side of his light – although on the surface Jude was perfectly mannered. She wondered what he was up to but when he smiled, it felt so genuine she felt foolish for thinking him inimical. Her confusion left her feeling defensive.

'I know you find it hard to believe, but I love Roland,' she said, picking at a thread on her cut-off denim skirt. 'I'm just cross with him now, that's all.'

'I don't blame you. To love is to enter muddy waters,' he said. 'It's so tangled up in need, that's what makes it messy. That and sex.' He didn't look at her. He was too busy twisting his towel to keep it hanging on his waist.

'The problem with you, Jude, is that you think sex is tantamount to love but it's something else entirely.'

'You're right. Of course you're right. Let me show you the Picasso.'

He turned on his heel, reaching out his hand behind him for her to hold but she ignored it. 'Why don't you get changed. I'll come up and see it later,' she said, nonchalantly walking back to her spot in the garden, leaving him with a half-baked smile. She felt an exquisite moment of pleasure leaving him like that.

'Sure,' he said to her back.

Lori returned to the garden, blinking wildly, blinded by the sharp light after being in the darkness. As she stepped out onto the patio, she nervously scanned the garden and then the kitchen for Renée, in case the woman had witnessed the awkward exchange. The smell of onion soup was tantalising but Lori was restless and at the same time sleepy, thanks to the mix of champagne and swimming. She was beginning to understand that one factor of adulthood that was both menacing and irritating was the presence of conflicting emotions: at the moment the need to eat, the desire to sleep, the contemplation of her marriage – she couldn't quite believe she'd married Roland – and then Anna and the row and what had just taken place in the darkened hallway with Jude and the idea that Roland thought it was perfectly acceptable to bite the inside of Anna's leg. And now he and Anna were together in the supermarket on *their* honeymoon. It was exhausting.

The place felt suddenly empty of life, a silence humming except for the lackadaisical presence of insects and bees feeding off the common comfrey. She hopped back into the safety of the hammock and picked up her book, but the words merged together and she found herself gazing out onto the pool watching the light move on the water. Everything felt light and the fluttery feeling inside her continued to dance. A feeling of abandon overcame her. The inexorable presence of Jude's desire filling the space like an unwanted guest. She thought of Roland, how he'd readily helped Anna onto his shoulders, invited her even. It was Roland who suggested the game. Of course, now she was Mrs Hawkins – God, she was furious when Anna had called her that – Roland was already complacent.

The problem with Jude, she thought, was that he had this enormous appetite for life and he needed everyone to admire him. She wasn't too dissimilar. His flirting wasn't about love, she knew that, it was about conquering, but it felt good to be worthy of his attention. What was Jude talking about earlier, about Roland not being a saint? She disregarded the nagging doubt that Jude was provoking her into an act of infidelity for a reason. Instead she allowed herself to imagine making love with him, the sun, the unfamiliar setting opening her up like a flower. The pull of his desire was beginning to feel non-negotiable against the backdrop of Anna and Roland's cosy enterprise in the supermarket. She let her leg drop over the edge of the hammock, looked up into the endless blue of the sky feeling herself physically unravel. She missed painting, she missed the solace it offered. As she began to focus she saw Jude hanging out of the bedroom window. He waved, as if he had been watching her contemplate the possibility all this time.

He didn't come down straight away. But she waited, expecting him, a thrill sliding around her system like something warm and arousing. Damn him, she thought.

He came to her with a glass of crisp white wine.

'Haven't we had enough?'

'It's never enough.' He offered her a chunk of goat's cheese which he pushed into her mouth, holding down her tongue for the briefest moment before handing her the wine without ceremony, as if she'd been expecting it and he was late.

'What shall we do?' he said.

'Have you seen Renée?'

He took a gulp of wine — it was always a gulp — and shook his head. 'Are you going to come up and see this painting or not?' He flashed a sideways glance, then gawked at his glass, holding it up to the light. 'Some blasted insect is helping himself to my wine,' he said. He stood watching the tiny fly flap about, drowning. Jude frowned as if he were tussling with some inner demon before pressing the creature onto the side of the glass with the tip of his thumb, scowling as he scraped it out.

A feeling of anxiety clashed with a growing ache. If she went upstairs, they both knew they were crossing a bridge. A part of her hoped that if she had sex with him, that would be it. They would both be free. She didn't want him in the way she wanted to be with Roland. She wanted something else: an exchange of power. For some reason, Roland's orchestration of the marriage, his orchestration of the wrestling match that morning, his flirting with Anna, left her with a need to push against him.

'It had better be worth it,' she said.

'It's a Picasso. How can it not?'

# TWENTY-THREE

**Anna**

Anna watched Roland chatting to the man behind the fish counter. He was laughing and joking, totally at ease in this environment, pointing to various open-mouthed specimens behind the glass. The fishmonger obliged him by scooping up each piece of fish to give Roland a closer look. Finally, he settled on dorade, happy as a lark as he waited for it to be wrapped up. She wished she could be so carefree, but she had a weighty feeling of trouble looming. She'd completed her list – she was buying dry goods and Roland was on fresh food – and found herself floating down the aisles imagining what it would be like to live here, to have a life far from London, to speak French, to *be* French. To be a provincial housewife with children to feed and chores to do. No, this wasn't a life for her.

The possibility of being someone new must have passed through Lori's mind. By marrying Roland, she was not only stepping into a different life but more importantly she was walking away from the rather dowdy presence of her past, but she'd been doing a pretty good job of that anyway. Anna didn't feel the need to leave her past behind. She loved the eccentricity of her family, the academic excellence she'd been brought up to follow, the assumption that she would do well. The chaotic way they circled each other when she went home, each knowing which pile of papers belonged to whom. She assumed Roland and she were quite similar in many respects. They both had siblings, whereas Jude and Lori didn't. Lori was always talking about how utterly oppressive her mother was – neurotic, she'd said. Anna's own mother was the opposite. It wasn't that she took little interest, it was just that there was no questioning her children's ability to achieve success and no questioning the authority of each parent.

While she waited, she ambled up the cereal aisle noting the French brands, the cartoon characters advertising various versions of grain. She arrived at Roland's side just as he was referring to his list.

'I'm done. What about you?'

'For some reason I forgot the strawberries when I was in the fruit aisle,' he said.

'Good. I think we need to get back.'

'Why the hurry?' He smiled, a compassionate glint in his eye. She understood then that he pitied her and felt a stab of impatience at her own disconcerted state. She envied his cool calmness, which if she didn't know him better, could be perceived as indifference.

'I was hoping to stop at the local bar for a spot of lunch,' he said. 'The travel agent is next door as well. You could pop in and enquire about flights.'

Anna ignored the anxiety wheeling around her stomach, a part of her reasoning that she was being ridiculous. Jude often forced her towards outlandish thinking and it was clear that Roland considered her to be a victim. But Jude was often provoked into rash behaviour by his own insecurities, and she, like a dog on an invisible leash, was implicated.

'I thought you'd be in a hurry to get back,' she said as they meandered through the aisles of the supermarket, its brash lights a comfort, somehow, the music indecipherable. 'It is your honeymoon after all.'

'Plenty of time, yet. I think if anything, Lori needs space to calm down.'

Anna felt herself tense. What was really going on between them? 'Well, Jude and I are probably leaving tomorrow. I'd like to get back to enjoy the house.'

Roland stopped dead. 'Anna. Why don't you let him miss you? It won't hurt him.'

Anna understood then how Roland, and probably Lori too, perceived her. The acquiescent girlfriend. Reliable. Boring. For all her supposed glamour she was incapable of game playing. She doted on him, just as her mother did her father. She wondered if this underlying trait to always be there for Jude was the very thing that undermined her confidence.

'You're right,' she said. Was that what Roland was doing, making Lori wait? She thought about how he'd made that wedding happen, appear spontaneous, part of a game. She hadn't realised until now how Machiavellian Roland was. She'd seen him as this cuddly bear type. No wonder Jude enjoyed his company.

The travel agent told her that there were two flights the next day and another the day after. Anna promised to call first thing to confirm one. The bar was spitting distance from the house, on a strip of road dotted with the occasional shop: a butcher, a baker, all empty of people. There were five old men spotted about in the bar, either leaning against the counter, or playing dominoes on a cheap Formica table. A young girl was serving, her shoulders exposed in a ruched black blouse. As soon as the girl registered Roland, she came running from behind the bar, dousing him in kisses and exclamations Anna couldn't quite catch. Roland smiled and waved, still with his laissez-faire stance. One of the men playing dominoes stood up and shook his hand with boisterous energetic force. The bar echoed with celebration before the quiet of concentration settled back around the table playing dominoes. Anna had a sudden vision of Lori's future life. Her own future seemed murky in comparison. Jude was a living example of her need to make her life complicated, to follow in her mother's footsteps.

They sat down outside in the sun. Roland ordered a glass of red wine and so she ordered a Campari. Something about the sun, the slowness of the village, allowed her to relax. Roland's steadiness was calming. She understood why Lori had married him and wondered why the prospect of stability had never appealed to her in the same way. She had to admit there was a vanity to her choosing someone like Jude, as if his brilliance was a reflection of her own. As she stared out into the clear blue of a spring day, she understood what it was that had fed her anxiety about Jude over the past few days. For Jude, Lori was a challenge, she belonged to Roland, whereas Anna was a dead cert.

# TWENTY-FOUR

## Lori

The painting, which was above the bed, was an ink drawing of several half sketches of bulls, drawn on what appeared to be a torn paper napkin, so not really a painting at all. It was framed in a thick ornate gold frame. The signature was unmistakable, though. There was something about the presence of that painting, the fact that all of this had never been mentioned by Roland, that made her feel very distant from him. Jude stood behind her, pressed close, his chin resting on her shoulder. There was a camaraderie in their shared discovery.

'Has Anna seen this?'

He shook his head. 'There are many things Anna fails to observe.'

She could feel his breath on her neck, her breasts tingling. His hand wrapped around her stomach, lifting her blouse, his fingers moving towards her breast. She could smell the lavender of his soap, the mint on his breath and underneath that, an oily masculine odour. She turned round, the wine shook in her hand and she let it fall. It didn't break. They both turned to watch the glass roll into the skirting.

Then he kissed her.

Lori kissed Jude back. The taste of him: alcohol and toothpaste was unfamiliar but his kiss was just as she'd imagined. He slipped his hand up her skirt, pulled her pants to the side and slipped his fingers deep inside her. She pushed him back towards the wall and pressed her lips onto his. She wanted to be the one with the power here.

'Is this what you want?' she said.

'You're so wet,' he said.

They began to tear at each other's clothes, a renewed sense of urgency about them. One part of Lori was preoccupied with Roland and Anna's return, but she was getting closer to a feeling of complete abandon.

'So this is what all the fuss is about,' Lori said, pushing him onto the bed.

Jude smiled, pulled her on top of him. They moved like two synchronised swimmers. Instantly Lori felt her power return as she removed his shirt, noticing the sinewy muscles on his arm. They needed to be quick, she thought, as she ran her fingers through his hair and pulled him down.

She didn't think of Roland or Anna, nor did she think much about Jude. She was responding to an inner rage, which completely took her by surprise. She was angry that Roland had left her alone. He groaned, and she put her hand over his mouth.

'Shhh!' Then she pushed his head back.

'Jesus!' he said.

She kissed him hard. Everything felt blurred as if she were playing to some inner tune, her body rising and falling, perspiration trickling down her neck. Jude kissed it away with such tenderness, she almost cried out Roland's name, a fleeting moment of guilt puncturing her like a burning-hot needle, followed by sorrow. Tears pricked her eyes and rolled down her cheeks, Jude wiped them away with his thumbs and there was something in this gesture that mirrored her vulnerability. The fury flared up again.

She didn't bite him, instead she pulled at his hair. If it hurt, Jude didn't show it. She couldn't quite understand the anger, but she knew it wasn't just directed at Roland, or Jude, but her parents and most of all herself.

She closed her eyes.

She wasn't sure how long they were lost in the act but Jude brought himself to orgasm just as they heard the door slam. The loud bang made her body go rigid. She felt a wave of panic course through her veins.

'They're back,' she said, her heart hammering like a diesel engine at the thought that they might be caught, literarily with their pants down. She leapt off him, scrambled across the bed and picked up her clothes, yanking up her pants as she made her way to the door, throwing on her T-shirt.

She turned to face him, stepping into her denim skirt. He was sitting loose-limbed on the bed, grinning. 'I hate myself right now,' she said, 'but I hate *you* more.'

Jude laughed. 'Don't be so overdramatic,' he said, flopping back down, his head cupped by his hands, his elbows sticking out like wings. 'We had fun.'

Lori stared at him, could she detect malice in his eyes? Suddenly horrified at her own stupidity. What was wrong with her? 'I've just made a huge mistake,' she said.

His eyes widened. 'Oh come on, you can't let guilt get in the way, now. It doesn't change anything. It was just one time.'

Lori thought for a second, knowing that she didn't really have a second. 'I'm not going to tell anyone about this. That would be foolish, and if you so much as spill one word,' she whispered hoarsely, pointing her finger at him, 'you're a dead man.'

Jude laughed. 'I'm not *that* stupid!'

Lori could hear voices on the stairs. She didn't have the time to argue. She could feel his sperm running down her leg. 'Oh Christ,' she said. She crossed the hallway into the shower. But she was in the wrong bathroom, so she shot out again, leaned over the banister to get a peek at what Roland and Anna were doing, realising in an instant that it was Renée who was downstairs shuffling about in their bedroom, probably making the bed. She quickly ran downstairs into the bathroom which was adjacent. She tugged at her denim skirt, her pants were all tangled and wet. Jude had seemed incredibly laid-back, she thought. He'd shown no remorse whatsoever, which was possibly the safest action, but did he honestly care so little? Whatever had just happened needed to be forgotten. It was the safest option for both of them, but she found his disregard disturbing.

She stepped into the bathroom, locking the door, pressing her back against it and taking deep breaths, trying to break free of the muddle in her head. What was wrong with her? She'd had too much to drink, that was for sure. The bathroom offered solace. The big iron bath with its clawed feet looked inviting but there was no time to luxuriate, or to analyse what had driven her to do such a thing. The best thing she could do was shower quickly and get back downstairs as soon as possible and pretend that nothing had happened. Her heart was pumping so hard, it felt too big inside her chest. She undressed, rinsing her knickers, scrubbing them with lavender soap, banging her head rhythmically against the mirror because she was so angry with herself.

In the shower she washed every inch of her skin with a creamy bar of soap she found, and managed to wash her hair as well. She didn't want one inch of her to smell of Jude. Already she was beginning to block out the memory.

She hated herself for her need to prove something. God knows what! That she didn't care? That she was in control, when she so clearly was not!

When she was dressed, she didn't bother drying her hair or going to see Jude, there simply wasn't time. The house was eerily silent. She tiptoed downstairs, slipped outside onto the patio, back into the hammock and tried to convince herself that this wouldn't change anything. It had started to cloud over. Lori shivered but she was loath to go upstairs again to retrieve her cardigan. She was hungry so she went into the kitchen and helped herself to the onion soup, sitting herself down at the table she'd shared with Roland that morning, the anticipation of his arrival making her pulse quicken. Anna didn't bear thinking about. How could she have done that to her friend? My word she was an idiot. Where had that rage come from, that muddled thinking?

She forced herself to eat just to appear normal. She noticed a blanket on the back of a kitchen chair and nabbed it, then picked up her book on Barbara Hepworth, hiding behind it in the hammock while she silently loathed herself and Jude. Her mind fizzing and popping, her own internal fireworks, the arrival of Anna and Roland looming. Lori swore she would never act impulsively again.

# TWENTY-FIVE

## Anna

Anna sensed a change in Lori immediately she saw her pretending she didn't hear them arrive. The Citroën was as noisy as a school bus. But before she got to ask Lori if everything was okay, Jude came bouncing down the stairs with his usual air of enthusiasm. He'd clearly had a shower. He looked pumped, sexy in a linen shirt over jeans, a cotton jumper slung casually over his shoulders, different from his London vibe.

'Babe, you've been an age.' He opened his arms and pulled her into an embrace that turned out to be a painfully tight squeeze. 'Where have you been?' he said, helpfully taking the shopping and walking into the kitchen, beckoning her to follow with a nod of the head. She could smell the lavender soap he'd used, but something felt off, although she couldn't put her finger on it.

She told herself her paranoia was unjust.

'What have you bought for supper?' Jude said, opening the bags.

'Dorade,' Roland said as he waltzed past carrying a box full of groceries. The kitchen smelled of onion soup. Anna saw one bowl on the side by the sink, washed up, and wondered if it belonged to Lori or Jude. Obviously they didn't lunch together. Renée appeared from nowhere and started to unpack, silently working around them, invisible, while Roland instructed her on what to do with the fish.

It was five o'clock. Late. She felt as if the hours had evaporated. She walked back out onto the patio wanting the sun on her back.

'Sorry it took so long. We stopped off at the local bar.' She had directed her apology at Lori but Lori stayed hidden behind her book. 'What are you reading that's so absorbing?' Anna said, her patience waning.

Lori peeked over the top of the open pages. Her eyes unfocused. 'Sorry, I didn't realise you were talking to me. It's about Barbara bloody Hepworth. Quite interesting actually.' She tried to sit up but the hammock made the move impossible and it swung from side to side until she gave up.

'I think I'll get into the pool.'

'It's chilly now,' Lori said, who had covered herself in a blanket. Jude came sauntering out eating an apple. He bit it right down to the core and lobbed it into the vegetable garden. Anna felt an odd rigidity between him and Lori, but then Jude slapped the hammock playfully and once again she chastised herself for being untrusting.

'Why don't you join us. You've been in that bloody hammock all day!' he said.

'I've got to do this,' she said. 'I haven't a clue what to say.'

Finally, Roland appeared, acknowledging Lori with a peck on the cheek. Lori seemed to have got over their row, at least.

Renée had laid out supper in the dining room. There were candles, a small vase of tulips, a lace tablecloth, a basket of bread and a green salad. The fire had been lit, although it was still light outside and the French doors were open, reaching out onto the patio, bringing in a cool evening breeze. Roland was reading. He looked so utterly accustomed to this lifestyle that Anna found it hard to remember the Roland before Paris: the good-natured Roland who talked about the Vikings a lot, scraped through each exam and was always seen with a beer in his hand. This version of Roland was sitting with a sherry and appeared to be at least ten years older.

'Help yourself,' he said, gesturing to the side table where there were some coloured crystal glasses laid out, a chilled white wine and a sherry waiting.

'Thank you.'

'Can't believe Renée has cooked the fish. I thought I'd be tasked with the job.'

Roland looked up from his book. 'Yes, we're lucky enough to have someone cook for us, but that luck comes at a price, belonging to a family like this one.'

'Does it?' she asked, genuinely curious.

'Sure.'

'Tell me,' she said.

He laid down his book, slipping in a bookmark, and leaned forward onto his knees. 'There is no question of whether I shall be working in the family business, for a start. I won't get any privileges either. I'm expected to start at the bottom and work my own way to the top. I don't get much choice in who I marry, although I've managed to circumvent that one. There'll be a price to pay for that, though.' He smiled wistfully, shook the thought away.

'What kind of price?'

'Nothing obvious, but the disapproval will be shown one way or another. My mother gave her blessing, so she'll be blamed as much as I will. The punishment will be psychological. I'm hoping Lori will work her magic on my father.'

'Jesus.'

'In short, I am not a free man. So you see, everyone has their woes.' He sat back, crossing his legs.

'I'm aware of that,' Anna said, thinking of the price she paid for being a child of two academics. The endless suppers, the mood swings that followed, the constant stream of students that passed through their home, her father sleeping with some of them. She loved the eccentricity of her family but it hadn't all been rosy.

Lori was the last to arrive. Over supper, she draped a possessive arm around Roland and was noticeably more attentive than usual. Obviously they'd got over their argument, but it seemed to Anna that the tension she'd observed earlier between Lori and Jude had grown. Roland noticed it too.

'Whatever is wrong with you two?' he asked when they ignored each other.

Jude said, 'Christ knows!'

Lori smiled brightly, all teeth and very little sincerity, 'Just tired, that's all.'

Of course Jude's answer was to get drunk. After pudding, they sat by the fire, drinking. Roland was back in his armchair with Lori tucked into his legs on the floor; they'd been glued together all night. Jude was on the ottoman.

'Let's play a memory game,' he said.

'Not sure we're in a fit state,' Roland said.

'Failure to remember something means a forfeit of losing a layer of clothing or drinking a shot,' Jude said.

'Let's stick with the clothes option. I think your memory will fail you all too often if we have to drink each time we forget something,' Roland said.

'Okay, okay. I'll start,' Jude said. 'What everybody wants is a glass of wine.'

'You mean what *you* want is a glass of wine,' Roland said, filling his glass. 'What everyone wants is a glass of wine and a warm bath.'

They all turned to Lori who was glassy-eyed, twisting the stem of her glass, focused on the flames in the fire. 'What everyone wants is a glass of wine, a warm bath and to be heard.'

'Oh that's profound,' Jude said.

Lori pinched her lips together, her hand reaching out for Roland's like a reflex. Anna was growing tired. She longed for her bed, but she knew Jude would protest. 'What everyone wants is a glass of wine, a warm bath, to be heard and to be recognised,' she said.

'It's not supposed to be meaningful,' Jude said, 'it's supposed to be complicated.'

'It *is* complicated,' Anna said.

Jude winked at her, then looked at Lori with a fixed clownish frown, forcing Lori to acknowledge him with a small, tight smile. She looked up, her face flushed as Jude recounted the list: 'What everyone wants is a glass of wine, a warm bath, to be heard, to be recognised and to be rescued.'

For a second, Anna thought he was being his usual humorous self but his tone was deadly serious and the intensity of his gaze was almost comical. Rescued from what? she thought. Did he believe Lori needed to be rescued, or was he referring to himself? She was just about to comment when Roland jumped in:

'What everyone wants is a glass of wine, a warm bath, to be heard, to be recognised, to be rescued and to play table tennis!' He leapt up from his armchair, startling everyone as he made his way to the door, skipping over a small chair. 'Last person to the table forfeits a layer of clothing!'

Anna jumped up and raced out behind him, jostling and giggling at the door. She wanted this evening to be fun for all of their sakes, despite the undercurrent of tension. It was obviously going to be their last, they'd clearly made a mistake in joining them. As they raced out onto the patio, she looked up to see a clear midnight blue sky peppered with stars. Lori was behind her, sullen and dark as the sky.

'Isn't it beautiful?' Anna said.

Lori looked up. 'Beautiful!' she said, overly bright.

Later, Anna would tell herself that this was the moment when she knew deep down that Lori had fucked Jude. It's the small changes in behaviour that give us away, she thought.

Jude was the last to get to the table, which was tucked into a storeroom next to the garage. He came ambling in, hand in pocket, full glass of red in the other, as if he didn't give two hoots what he had to forfeit. Anna asked him to remove his shirt. She wasn't going to leave him to decide which item of clothing to take off because knowing him, he'd choose his trousers. He was in that type of mood. She helped him take his shirt off, kissing his neck, catching Lori's sullen face.

'Christ, it's freezing,' Jude said. 'Let's get this game on the road.'

Lori teamed with Roland. Several of Jude's balls were aimed at Lori, as if to cajole her into a better mood. Anna didn't blame him; her sulky attitude was contaminating the evening. Roland was his usual laid-back self, impervious.

Jude missed another point delivered by Roland and she could see he was ready to snap by the way his jaw tensed.

He was always competitive with Roland but tonight Anna sensed an undercurrent of malice.

Roland served again, adding flourish with a backhand. Jude smashed the ball straight back to him. But Roland was sober and Jude was no match for the rally of balls Roland fired at him. Anna watched Jude's frown deepen in an effort to concentrate. At one point, it was just the two boys playing. Normally, she'd attempt some deriding remark to Lori to get her onside, but Lori wouldn't meet her eye. The more this went on, the more Anna was convinced that something had gone on while they were out that day. She was so busy weighing up the evidence that she missed another point. Jude screamed.

'For fuck's sake, Anna!' He threw the racket to the ground and stormed out, snatching the garden shears on his way into the night. They all stood still, wide-eyed, an overwhelming feeling of inertia sweeping over her. She was tired of fighting Jude's internal demons.

'I wish he wouldn't drink so much,' she said, as if this was explanation enough.

Roland walked out to fetch him.

'He needs to see someone about his drinking,' Lori said, her eyes on the middle distance.

Anna sensed that something was preying on Lori's mind. 'What happened today?' she said.

'Don't *you* start,' Lori said, storming off to follow Roland.

'Lori, wait!'

Lori stopped and slowly turned, the anxiety singing in her eyes.

'You slept with him, didn't you?' Anna said. She knew it was heavy-handed but she needed to know.

Lori sighed. 'Maybe you just have to accept that Jude is a drunk,' she said. And then she left.

Anna could hear Roland shouting, so she quickly followed them all out into the garden. Jude was dancing barefoot in the damp grass, the shears in hand. His hair flopped over his eyes, he grimaced as he caught her eye. It took her a second to understand what he was doing. He was attacking the daffodils one head at a time, tussling with Roland who was trying to seize the shears, as if they were in a pub brawl, until Jude danced out of reach, screaming like a demonised hyena. Anna stepped towards him but Lori strode past her and snatched the shears out of Jude's hand, discarding them on the grass.

'Just stop it, will you! You are so bloody destructive.' She walked past them all.

'And what about you, you little temptress,' Jude shouted, swaying.

Lori went up to Roland, her face an inch from his. 'Can't you see?' she said. 'He wants to destroy you and us. For fuck's sake, Roland. Wake up!'

'Lori!' Anna said. But Lori didn't answer. She carried on walking towards the kitchen.

'I think it's better that we leave,' Anna said to Roland.

'You're probably right,' Roland said, raking his hair with his fingers.

'Happy now?' Anna said to Jude. Jude tittered drunkenly, an air of resignation about him in the way that his shoulders drooped. He slid down onto his haunches and started rocking.

'I'm so sorry, Anna. I'm so sorry.' And that was the moment when Anna knew for certain.

# TWENTY-SIX

## Lori

Lori woke up the next morning to the sound of whispering in the hallway, followed by the clunk, clunk, clunk of a case being dragged down the stairs. Next to her, Roland was sleeping on his back so deeply she found herself staring at him to check that he was breathing. She watched as his chest rose up and down, taking in the aquiline nose. She smiled to herself at the slightly aristocratic nature of his profile, the way the soft curls of his hair fell onto the pillow, but it was his frown, which even inside the depths of sleep was etched across his forehead, that endeared him to her most of all. She found herself overwhelmed with a deep feeling of anger, frightened that she would lose him because of one mistake. One! She vowed never to get drunk again. She leant over and kissed him and he opened his eyes.

'I think Anna and Jude are leaving,' she said.

'Right. Does that bother you?'

She shook her head. 'I want us to have some time alone,' she said.

'Me too,' he said, reaching for her hand.

'I'm sorry about our row,' she said.

'Me too.'

What she wanted was to undo the damage of yesterday. The memory of them both recklessly using each other to

182

feel better about themselves disgusted her. At least she thought that was why they'd done what they'd done. Her analytical skills weren't the best. That was Anna's department. Oh God, Anna. Lori yanked back the sheets and stepped over to the window to see if she could see them outside. Renée was hanging out some washing, the tablecloth from last night. The breakfast table was laid but there was no sign of Jude or Anna.

'I guess we need to say goodbye,' Roland said, leaning on his elbow watching her.

'Jude behaved appallingly,' she said, knowing Roland didn't know the half of it.

Roland walked towards her, took hold of her face and kissed her. 'He's a troubled soul, that's all.' He tucked a lock of her hair behind her ear. 'But you would tell me if there was anything bothering you, wouldn't you?'

'Why are you so tolerant of him?' she asked as she walked away to hide her blush. She remembered her mother asking the same of her father when Lori was a difficult teenager. 'You're always so bloody forgiving,' she'd said over and over again, but he wasn't forgiving, he was controlled, and it seemed Roland was similar. She wondered if that was the reason her mother had lost her wild side, perhaps she'd been tamed. She heard the crunch of footsteps below.

'We'd better get a move on,' she said.

Roland was stepping into his chinos, pushing his bare feet into his deck shoes, raking back his hair as he grabbed the toothbrush.

'There's something wrong with him,' she said.

'Hey, Jude's my best mate. People make mistakes. Just let him be. Everyone has their reasons. He was drunk.'

Lori wondered if that included her. What was her reason? 'He's always drunk.'

A part of her despised Roland's forbearance, his measured approach, but that was guilt speaking, chewing at her insides like a hungry puppy. She wondered what he would say if she told him. Let's face it, regret is a useless emotion. It was best to forget, she thought. But then she thought of Anna. Jude had given himself away with his behaviour last night, but he would lie to her, surely. Or would he tell Anna his version of the truth? The thought hadn't occurred to her until now. Supposing he told Anna that Lori had tried to seduce him. Her brain was in a tangle of 'what ifs' and 'should haves' and definitely 'shouldn't haves'.

They went downstairs to find Jude and Anna sitting at the kitchen table writing a note. Anna was the one scribbling things down while Jude stood over her. The light was spilling in from the patio, just reaching their shoulders, dappled dark at the kitchen table. Their faces were shadowed, the sun behind them giving off a halo of light around their hair. The way they were holding onto each other as they leaned over the piece of paper, it seemed as if they were afloat, both unsteady on a stormy sea.

They tilted their heads at the same time.

'We were just writing a note,' Anna said, her voice bright and breezy. 'We didn't want to wake you.'

'I can see that,' Roland said, walking to the stove to check if there was any coffee.

'Have you managed to get a flight, already?'

'Yes and we've ordered a taxi.'

'Well cancel it,' Roland said, 'Léon can take you to the airport.' All the while he spoke, Roland preoccupied himself with the business of pouring them all a coffee. Lori was grateful for his calmness and composure. Deep in thought, she looked up to see Anna watching her. She smiled, automatically, needing to diffuse the situation, but feeling the apologetic nature of the gesture by Anna's plaintive response.

Anna turned to address Roland. 'Roland, really, it's nice of you, but Jude and I have some things we need to sort out on our own and I'd just like to hit the road straight away if you don't mind.'

Roland walked up to Anna and put his arms around her. Jude had his head bent, unable to meet anyone's eye, especially hers, which immediately suggested that he'd made that classic mistake of thinking that the truth will heal. It was written all over his face. He'd probably gone and poured it all out, guilt fuelling his tongue, hoping Anna would admonish him and then later forgive. Lori knew Anna better than that.

'Anna, it's not like you to turn a lift down,' Roland said, smiling broadly.

Outside, they heard someone hooting.

'I'm really sorry everyone, but I need to go.' Anna turned to Jude. 'Stay if you want, but I would like to go home now!'

'I'm coming,' Jude said. 'Roland, I'm sorry mate. I'm sorry about the daffodils, and about everything. I guess I'm just a total dickhead.'

Roland let Anna go as Jude took her small suitcase and they left to get into the taxi. Anna didn't bother to say goodbye to Lori, she gave a nod of the head but nothing was said. Lori could see the light had gone from her eyes, extinguished, and knew she was responsible for it. She hated herself. As she walked past the table she grabbed the note, shoving it into the pocket of her jeans. Jude offered an apologetic wave, and their eyes met for a split second.

'Anna,' Lori said. Anna turned, but the sharpness of her tone when she said 'Yes,' made Lori wobble.

'Take care.'

Anna didn't answer, and that in itself made it abundantly clear that Jude had told her. What version she had no clue.

She and Roland went and stood outside the front door, arms loosely wrapped around each other, and waved their friends off. Jude lifted his hand in salute. Anna was curled in the back seat looking in the opposite direction.

Lori understood that she had lost her best friend.

# TWENTY-SEVEN

## Anna

They didn't talk on the way to the airport. Both of them were pressed up against opposite doors of the back seat, sitting as far apart from each other as possible. Anna looked out at the French countryside, the cultivated gardens of the château with the line of birch trees looked tragically beautiful with its neatly trimmed hedging and striped lawns, all of it blurred by Anna's tears. She swore she'd never talk to Lori again.

At the airport they went through the motions, queuing to check in, Jude attempting to ask banal questions about whether she was hungry, wondering if there would be food on the plane.

Finally, Anna swung round, aware that her ponytail struck him in the face. 'I don't care about food right now. I'm in shock.'

'I know, I'm sorry.'

'Roland was your best friend, we ambushed their honeymoon and you repaid him by fucking his wife.' She wrapped her arms around her chest.

The outcry turned a few heads. She watched Jude redden. Revelled in his humiliation.

'Why?'

Jude looked churlish. He hadn't shaved that morning, they hadn't had time, and she could see his red beard breaking through his skin. His green eyes wobbled until he looked at the floor.

'Honestly, Anna, I don't know. We were drunk. Let's face it, you flirted with Roland.'

'We did not flirt! We are not insecure idiots like Lori and you.'

The queue moved up, everyone shuffling their suitcases forward to the backdrop of the loudspeaker announcing various flights in its automated staggered voice. The coming and going of people that Anna normally found exciting.

'You don't know?!'

'People make mistakes, Anna. I was just . . .'

'And there are consequences,' Anna said. 'Weirdly enough, I expected it of you — it was just a matter of time — but not Lori. If you really want to know, I'm more upset by her behaviour than yours.' She wondered why that was. Why had she expected more of Lori and not Jude? Her father she supposed, but still she couldn't fathom how Lori could do such a thing.

'I've said I'm sorry.'

'You haven't just broken me; you've broken up a beautiful friendship.'

'Well, it wasn't just me.'

'I will never speak to Lori again, or you.' Tears pricked her eyes, she wished now she'd heard Lori's side of the story, but what did it matter? It led to the same sorry act of betrayal.

'Anna, can't we just . . .'

'Fuck you!'

Anna noticed the shoulders of the woman ahead of them raise ever so slightly, imagined her wincing while her husband/partner/lover/boyfriend stifled a laugh. They all shuffled forward.

They sat apart on the plane. Anna had asked the girl at the check-in to move her as far away from Jude as possible. The only seat available was a middle seat three rows ahead. She sacrificed a window seat but it was worth it just to see his humiliation. She was aware of his eyes boring into the back of her head throughout the entire flight, but she didn't turn round, not once. She could feel his sorrow but as far as she was concerned it was self-inflicted. At Heathrow, she raced to passport control and sped off, not looking back, grateful that she only had hand luggage. She caught a train to her parents' house, went through the niceties and then locked herself in her old bedroom. It was only then, when she was confronted by her old Marc Bolan posters, that she allowed herself to cry.

Two days later, her mother tapped on her door. 'Lori on the phone,' she said.

'Tell her I'm out.'

Her mother didn't argue, but Anna was surprised when she knocked on the door ten minutes later. Anna opened it to find her mother proffering a tray of tea and shop-bought cake.

'Are you going to tell me what's happened?' she said, placing the tray on Anna's desk and perching on her single bed, running her hand over the hand-stitched quilt that had belonged to her grandmother.

'It usually helps to talk,' her mother said.

And so Anna went and sat beside her and let it all spill out, tears running down her cheeks. Her mother listened, her face immobile as Anna exclaimed she didn't care about Jude, but expected more of Lori.

'Yes,' her mother said. 'It's interesting how we expect more of our friends than our husbands.'

Anna didn't like to point out that she and Jude were

not married, and anyway she suspected that her mother was referring to her father who'd had a string of affairs and didn't do much to hide it. When Anna had finished telling her the story, she patted Anna's knee.

'People makes mistakes,' she said. And then she wiped her cheek with her thumb. 'Sometimes, the most powerful revenge is to forgive.'

# TWENTY-EIGHT

## Lori

They spent the week in the house, the ghost of their friends about them. They didn't talk about Jude and Anna's departure. If anything, it felt to Lori as if Roland was avoiding any potential conversation. They played chess or backgammon every evening, swam naked in the pool, roamed the fields picking wild flowers, cycled to the local bar and made love with the French doors open. Roland helped Lori with her dissertation, explaining how structure could help formulate an argument. Lori felt as if she was getting to know Roland for the first time. It was during that week, in the wake of the disaster, that she truly fell in love. She pushed the guilt into a corner, knowing her own feelings of insecurity had done enough damage for a lifetime. She needed to use this time to heal any potential rupture.

It wasn't until they got back to London that they heard that Jude and Anna had split up. Jude had called Roland to tell him that Anna had moved back in with her parents and had been accepted to do an MA in Oxford. She was revising at her family home and coming down just to do her exams. Lori felt overwhelmed with guilt. She heard how Jude had applied to the BBC and got a place on an apprentice scheme. Lori had tried a couple of times to call

Anna at her family's home, but she was repeatedly unavailable, so it was clear to Lori that she'd lost a friend. She told Roland that they'd spoken so as not to arouse suspicion but she kept it vague. Roland didn't ask, and Lori wondered if he knew that they weren't speaking. She didn't ask. Painting offered her a place to put the conflicting emotion and she used it day and night, sometimes working through the night.

They moved into a family-owned flat in Pimlico with a small roof terrace. Lori went into college every day and painted, and one lunch time finally plucked up the courage to call the gallery. She was invited in and told to bring photos of her work. The first thing she wanted to do was call Anna, but of course she couldn't.

Roland and Jude met up a couple of times, but Roland always returned home early, saddened that Jude had lost his spark. One night, a month after the honeymoon, he came back drunk, a trace of his old shambolic self suddenly apparent.

'Jude and I had a row,' he said.

'Oh God, what about?' Lori was vacuuming their tiny apartment dressed in a baggy T-shirt. 'Not about that awful daffodil incident, surely,' she said.

'Actually, it was. You shouldn't use that thing so late at night,' he said, pointing to the vacuum cleaner and the flat underneath.

'Oh don't worry about them, they're deaf.'

Roland laughed.

'So what was the row about?'

'I told him he had to watch his drinking and he got really cross. Then he said something about you I can't forgive. He told me why you and Anna aren't speaking.' Roland looked at Lori under a shield of hair, his eyes searching hers, making her feel hot with anxiety.

'He's jealous,' she said, suppressing the desire to find out exactly what it was Jude had said. 'And we are speaking, it's just that we're both busy. Anna's revising like you.'

'I'm not sure Jude and I will speak ever again,' Roland said.

Lori swallowed. She was careful not to show her relief. 'Well, I think we should send them both a wedding invitation – separate invites of course – I think you'll miss him if he's not there.'

'It's just that he wants me to be a lad about town again, but what he doesn't get is we're all taking work seriously now. It's not just because I'm with you.' He was having trouble untying his laces. 'Do you think Anna will come?'

'Of course,' Lori said, knowing it was unlikely, but she'd become an expert on sounding convincing. Conviction, she'd learned, was the key.

When Lori went to pack and collect her things from the flat she shared with Anna, she unlocked the front door to find boxes of Anna's things piled up in the hallway. Lori waited for Anna to return but after a while gave up. During that time, Roland was studying all hours and Lori was working on her final show. When she wasn't painting, she was busy making wedding preparations with Margot, Roland's mother, who turned out to be a rather uptight version of Marie-Claude but less vocal. She was, however, extremely determined in that quiet way people tend to underestimate, and so Lori quickly learned to agree to everything. Her own mother was happy to take a back seat, as was her way, especially as the ceremony was being paid for by Roland's family. Her mother was probably dreading the ceremony, but Lori had too many other things to worry about. A day didn't go past without her reliving that heady moment. The worst part of it was that she hated herself and had to pretend to Roland she didn't.

The day Lori was booked to see the gallery she had a crisis of confidence and was desperate to speak to Anna. Every time she picked up the phone, she was reminded of that day with Jude and would quietly lay the telephone back in its cradle, chastising herself for her betrayal.

Finally, she let it ring and was shocked when it was Anna, not Anna's mother, who picked up.

'Anna, it's Lori.' She heard Anna sigh. 'Please don't hang up.'

'Lori, I . . .'

'Anna, I miss you. I know Jude's told you his half of the story but you need to listen to mine. I was drunk, for a start, and I hate myself, but I never set out to hurt you.'

'But you did hurt me,' Anna said.

'I know, and I'm sorry. Will you forgive me?'

She heard Anna sit down. She let out another sigh. 'Does Roland know?'

Lori thought for a second. She did what she always did when on the phone, coiled the wire around her finger. She was contemplating whether to lie or not. She knew that Jude had told Roland something, she just didn't know what. She understood that if she said to Anna that Roland knew, Anna would be more likely to forgive. But that would mean another lie.

'Not yet, no,' she said.

'Well, when you've been honest, give me a call.'

Anna put the phone down. Lori didn't get to mention the gallery or the wedding but she felt more buoyant somehow, as if speaking to Anna had relieved her of a heavy weight.

The gallery was in Covent Garden. Lori absorbed the sense of hallowed space that all galleries have, which allow the viewer to observe and think about a piece of work. She spoke to the elegant woman at the desk who was dressed in white.

'Ahh, yes, we've been expecting you,' she said, standing up and offering her hand. 'Emma Turner. We both loved your work. Have you brought your portfolio?'

Lori thought for a split second. Should she introduce herself as Watson or Hawkins? 'Lori Hawkins,' she said. 'Yes, I have it here.'

The interview was brief, as there was no question of the gallery not representing Lori. It was more a question of how many pieces she could produce for a coming show in September titled 'What's New?' Lori walked out of the gallery on air, desperate to celebrate. But they were due to meet Roland's father in a restaurant in South Kensington, so instead she went to meet Roland still wearing the Blondie T-shirt and ripped jeans she'd thought appropriate for the interview.

Roland was standing outside South Kensington tube, wearing a blazer, loafers and faded jeans. He looked expensive and European. He squeezed her hand and pulled her into a kiss. The roads were jammed with cars, tourists were pouring out of the tube, alongside commuters. The day was exceptional without a trace of cloud, and she was glad she'd worn her T-shirt and shocking pink strappy sandals she'd bought in the Manolo Blahnik sale.

'How did it go?'

'I have a gallery,' she said,

'That's brilliant news.'

'And I spoke to Anna today.'

'Oh, and how is she?'

'Good.'

He took her hand and they walked towards the restaurant. She could tell Roland was nervous by the sweatiness of his palm.

'What is it?' Lori began to wonder if Anna had called him, her stomach growing tight as a clenched fist.

He stopped, pulling her face towards him. 'Just take my father with a pinch of salt, that's all.'

When they walked into San Lorenzo's, Lori immediately felt underdressed in her jeans and T-shirt. Roland had said not to dress up but to be herself, but he'd somehow managed to look casual and smart at the same time, whereas Lori felt scruffy in her torn jeans and Blondie T-shirt that had made her feel so special in the gallery and in Paris. Every woman looked like Princess Diana with flicked back hair and highlights.

'Why didn't you warn me?' she said.

'Because I wanted my father to meet the girl I fell in love with,' Roland said.

Roland's father was over six-foot-four, with broad shoulders and thick fair hair that waved back off his forehead. He stood up as they joined his table and held out his hand, smiling, although Lori could see his eyes held a note of disappointment. Lori didn't feel pretty enough, posh enough, sexy enough, or good enough.

'At last I meet my son's new bride,' Roland's father said. 'Charles.'

Roland pulled out her chair – something he had never done before – and gestured for her to sit. Lori wasn't quite sure if she could remember how to. Didn't debutantes get trained to plonk themselves down in a chair? She was expecting Roland to say something but he looked at the table with a glazed immoveable expression. She knew in that instant that Roland wasn't able to help her, that she was on her own.

'Is Margot on her way?' she said.

'Mum's in the country,' Roland said.

'Don't lie, Roland.' His father looked at Lori. 'I can see neither Margot nor Roland have told you the facts of our marital state, but Margot and I are in the middle of a rather ugly divorce.'

Lori observed the way Charles's pale blue eyes narrowed as he spoke. 'So, Roland tells me you're an artist.'

'Yes.'

'A good one, I hope. Not an easy life for a woman,' he said, leaning back as if to find a more favourable angle from which to observe her.

'Well, I don't know about "good", but I've just had an offer from a gallery in Covent Garden,' she said proudly.

'Oh, is that Marie-Claude putting her oar in again?' he asked Roland.

'No, the gallery left a card on my desk,' she said, sharply. 'I don't ask favours, and anyway, I suspect that most of the galleries Marie-Claude is connected with are from Cork Street.' Lori was surprised by her own vehemence.

Charles's sharp eyes caught her own, a vacancy to them that left her feeling uncomfortable. He was not a happy man, bitter as the rind of a lemon, but she could tell she'd earned his respect. He smiled, but there was no warmth in his face, no sincerity. 'I see you know your galleries,' he said, 'For some, art is an investment rather than a matter of taste, so you're right, Cork Street is the family stamping ground.' He clicked his fingers and a waiter scurried to their table.

Roland still hadn't uttered a word. By the end of the evening, Lori got the sense that Charles had measured her in much the same way a tailor does a man as soon as he walks through the door. She didn't feel he once addressed her in a way that made her feel welcome, but more as someone who was expected to perform her duty. When he left, having paid the bill, Roland sighed.

'He liked you,' he said.

'I didn't get that feeling at all,' she said.

'Well, let's put it this way, you would have known if he didn't like you,' Roland said. She noticed him gripping the stem of his glass as if to keep himself from falling.

It was after spending a day painting that Lori realised that the soreness of her breasts and a missed period couldn't be ignored. That day she dropped off a urine test to the doctor. A week later she got the result and was asked to make an appointment to see the doctor. She didn't tell Roland straight away. She found herself unable to broach the subject until one morning she woke up and was sick.

Roland was sleeping as she sat staring at the loo. She didn't think of Jude. She thought of her and Roland, and the idea of her carrying their child sent a thrill through her body. She was young but there was no question of an abortion. She felt as if she already knew the soul of the little life within her. She felt bonded. After she'd retched and was unable to bring anything more up, she went into the bedroom and stood at the end of the bed watching Roland sleep.

Into the darkness she said the words: 'I'm pregnant.' She didn't expect Roland to answer, it was as if she was testing how the words felt on her tongue.

He opened his eyes and they looked at each other, the silence washing around them until the sounds of London crept into their orbit: a plane overhead, the traffic down by the river, Capital Radio blasting out of someone's wireless.

'Wow,' he said. 'So much for the withdrawal method. Are you happy?'

'Yes,' she said.

'Then so am I.'

She went and sat down on the bed and leaned over to kiss him. He looked into her eyes, stroking the hair back from her face, fixing a stare. 'I love you,' he said.

'And you.'

He sat up, his hands on hers. 'Tell me,' he said, hesitating, as if he needed to tread carefully around something. 'You are sure the child is mine?'

And that is when she allowed herself to remember Jude. He hadn't used contraception and she'd been so busy worrying about Roland and Anna's imminent return from the supermarket that she'd failed to mention that she'd forgotten her pills and she and Roland had been using the withdrawal method. Roland had been careful. Jude had not. But then the horrific realisation reached her. Did Roland know what happened that day? Had he always suspected what had gone on? The thought made her cheeks burn. She turned away, willing her body to behave itself.

'Lori, answer me.'

'Sorry. Why would you ask such a thing?' She pretended to brush something off the bedspread, until finally she had no choice but to look at him squarely. She held his gaze, her breathing shallow while she did so. She could see he was waiting, expecting her to break free from his hold. This was the moment when she could be honest with him, when she could call Anna and tell her that she'd revealed the truth. She had never seen his eyes so blue. But she feared for the life of her child. It was too late. If she told the truth, everything they'd shared would be broken. She had thought over and over about that day with Jude, trying to understand what had driven her towards a moment of self-sabotage.

Roland was still watching her with a levelled curiosity. She forced herself to smile brightly.

'It's just that my father has insisted that you sign a prenuptial agreement,' he said, vaguely apologetic. 'We had a row about it actually. Basically he said if you don't, we won't get any help. And we'll need help if there's a baby.'

'But we're already married,' she said.

'Not in England.'

'Wow!' Lori felt her body give way to a hot flush of fear that started in her stomach and curdled in her throat. She stood up abruptly, glad to move away from him, marching towards the bathroom, made dizzy by the sudden movement. She turned. One look in Roland's blue eyes told her that what she said now could change everything. She thought about explaining how she'd felt vulnerable and she'd slept with Jude just to boost her own ego. How she was drunk, and reckless and angry with Roland, how she'd believed that Roland had flirted with Anna. How much she hated herself for making a mistake.

He climbed out of bed and followed her into the bathroom.

'Don't think I wasn't aware of Jude's fixation.'

She felt her face grow hot, imagined her cheeks flushed red. She didn't dare look at their reflection in the bathroom mirror. The sweat trickled down from under her arms. This was a side of Roland that rarely showed itself.

'I know full well Jude wanted to destroy us. I told you as much, but he failed. I want this child,' she said, turning her back to the mirror and looking at him straight. 'Our child.'

Roland fixed her with his soft blue eyes. She felt as if he was willing her to be honest, but she couldn't bring herself to speak the truth, there was too much at stake. She already felt protective of this baby.

And that was the beginning of the lie.

# PART THREE

---

## Present Day
## Two weeks after Easter

# TWENTY-NINE

## Lori

Lori woke up in the dead of night, the sound of the sea slapping and slurping against the rocks. She tiptoed out of bed, bathed in sweat. It was either a hot flush, too much sun or the nightmare. Jude again, invading the centre of her being. The anger she felt that he'd tracked down Ceri was palpable, so much so she wanted to pummel something soft and malleable to rid herself of the tart bile collecting in her throat. 'It was just one time,' he'd said and yet clearly he hadn't forgotten.

She went out onto the veranda via the kitchen. Looking down into the blackness that was the water, instantly soothed by the rhythm of the waves. She could see the sharp edges of the rocks lit by the moonlight, the sea glistening, the sand, silver. She remembered the last time she'd seen Jude, at a mutual friend's funeral twenty years ago when she'd been pregnant with the twins, eight years after she'd had Savannah – the children had been staggered. Lori and Anna had spoken, but Jude and Roland had barely acknowledged each other. Roland had said afterwards, 'You and Anna seemed happy to see each other. How long since you saw her last?' Lori hadn't seen Anna since Ceri was born. She'd had Savannah since but by that point they'd lost touch. When she had the boys, she thought to get in touch but didn't. That funeral had given them an opportunity to reconnect, but neither made the effort.

She thought back to that Christmas morning, the year Ceri had been born. She'd been to the supermarket on Christmas Eve, early in the morning to avoid the crowds, when the contractions started. She'd managed to get to the till and pay for the shopping, before calling Roland. It was a month before Ceri was due and Lori assumed they were Braxton Hicks. But when they'd arrived at the hospital she was told she was six centimetres dilated. Roland had called everyone, including Anna.

Anna had been the first to visit her in hospital that Christmas morning, the day Ceri was born, her arms filled with flowers and presents, all wrapped in red. Their friendship had been partially restored, courteous at least, even though it was clear that Lori hadn't told Roland the truth. Anna had come to their wedding and they'd had a couple of lunches and Anna had been gushing the day Ceri was born, giving Lori hope that they could resume some level of intimacy. Ceri had been sleeping in the bassinet beside her, sleepy because she'd been born a month early at two thirty Christmas morning.

Anna had arrived soon after breakfast, just as Lori was dozing, Roland having nipped home to shower. Lori made a show of opening Anna's gifts, seeing the anxious glance Anna gave to Ceri.

'Was it painful?' she said.

'Bearable. I kept telling myself thousands have done it before me.'

'I can't believe you're a mother already,' she said, reaching to touch Ceri's soft cheeks.

'Neither can I,' Lori said, wondering if she suspected anything, hoping that Ceri's premature birth would indicate that Roland was her father because it would have been before they went to Paris.

'I thought I'd pop in on the way to my parents'. Jude's sulking at home, refusing to go for Christmas lunch. I've had to make all kinds of excuses,' she said while balanced on the end of Lori's bed. It was usually Lori who was garrulous when nervous, but Anna seemed very tense.

'I can't believe you're back together after what happened,' Lori said.

'People make mistakes,' she said looking at Lori with solemn eyes. 'The problem is I can't seem to live with or without him.'

'Yes, no one is more aware of that than me.'

Anna laid a trembling hand on Lori's, looking so directly at Lori she was forced to find distraction in the unwrapping of the presents. 'She's not Jude's is she?' Anna said.

Lori felt a wave of fatigue. She felt hot and sore and bruised. 'No, she's not.' She made a tight fist under the sheet. 'Anna, it was the biggest mistake I've ever made and I'm sorry.'

Anna looked down at her knotted hands. 'I can't imagine having a baby to look after when I can barely look after myself,' she said. This brought closure to the matter and if Lori could have sealed the subject in a manila envelope never to be reopened, she would have.

Carols could be heard at the nurses' station where a tired string of red tinsel was looped around the desktop, and cards cluttered the surface. The cleaner mopped the floor wearing a Father Christmas hat.

'I've not known pain like it, but it was worth it,' Lori said, holding up the tiny red babygro with a white lace collar and a little red cardigan. 'Oh Anna, it's beautiful.'

'Oh good. I'm glad you like it. I went straight out to John Lewis yesterday as soon as Roland telephoned to tell me you'd gone into labour. I thought red made a change from pale blues and pinks.' She picked up the red wrapping paper and folded it neatly. Roland had called Anna because Lori had asked him to, hoping that a momentous thing such as a birth would do the trick, but she understood in that moment that what was between them was her inability to forgive herself. Anna was a reminder of her foolishness.

'I shall dress her in it as soon as she wakes up and make it a tradition to wear red every Christmas,' Lori said.

'She's a dear little thing, and I love the name,' Anna said, peering in.

'Named after my art teacher, and also mine and Roland's favourite artist.'

Anna rested her hand on Ceri's blanket.

'How are things?' Lori asked, unwrapping the small red teddy Anna had bought and placing it inside the cot.

'Oh, you know. Jude's making a huge effort. He's upset about us not spending today together, but he doesn't want to face my parents. I told him to come, that my parents aren't ones to judge. It's just one day. Ever since we split up, he's been reluctant to face them, so I come down to London to see him. We exchanged our gifts last night.' She patted Lori's arm.

'I can't say I blame him,' Lori said.

Anna stared at her, as if searching for an answer to a question and Lori wondered if she'd bring up the subject of Ceri's paternity again. But instead she offered a bright smile. 'Gosh you look well. You're positively blooming. Motherhood suits you.' The words were sharply delivered and then her gaze settled on Ceri.

'Thank you.'

'Where's Roland?' Anna was fiddling with the babygro. It was clear that Anna hadn't just come to celebrate Ceri's birth, she'd come looking for answers and hadn't got them.

'He's gone home to change, get some rest. He'll be back later.'

'I wish they'd make up,' Anna said, leaning over and brushing the top of Ceri's head. 'You never told him, did you?'

Lori felt a physical explosion pop in her sternum. She shook her head. 'I'm sorry,' she said.

Anna stared at her then, her face revealing her disappointment, an infinitesimal twitch of the mouth. 'I'd better be off. Lunch is at one, my father's a stickler as you know.' Anna stooped down to give Lori a kiss. She clutched Lori's hand. 'Call me, won't you.'

Several hours later, five minutes after Roland had again left for home, Jude turned up. He was drunk. His cheeks were ruddy, either with drink or exertion. He had that scattered energy he acquired when he was inebriated, side-stepping a nurse who tried to block his path, claiming to be a father. He walked straight up to Ceri's cot.

'Hi there,' he said as if they'd been in touch recently when the truth was they hadn't seen each other in months. He swayed as he stood over her, looking vacant and dazzled. Lori tried to stand up, her legs buckling, her hands shaking, as Jude reached down and stroked Ceri's head.

'Can I hold her?' he asked.

'She's only just dropped off,' Lori said. 'Does Anna know you're here?'

Without permission he scooped her up so easily it was as if he'd done it a million times before. Lori wondered if he'd deliberately waited until Roland had left. How did he have the nerve?

'You shouldn't be here,' she said.

'Why not? She's mine, isn't she?'

'No, Jude, she's not *yours*.' When he laid Ceri back down, he'd done so tenderly, stroking her cheek. 'I'm sorry,' Jude said. 'I'm sorry about everything.' And then he left, striding off cockily, his hands wedged deeply into his pockets.

Lori never called Anna after that. She wrote a letter thanking her for the presents, explaining that they'd decided on a christening in France, which had been partly true.

She didn't receive a reply.

Looking down into the Ionian Sea, Lori thought about Jude. He'd opened Pandora's bloody box by introducing himself to Ceri. Lori hadn't heard from her in two weeks. She turned to see Roland leaning over the balcony of their bedroom, his knuckles gripping the modern balustrading, like shining white pebbles in the moonlight.

'What is it?' he said.

'I haven't heard from Ceri in a while.'

'She's a big girl, Lori.'

Lori ran her hand through her hair, shaking out the knots tangled in the night breeze.

'Come back to bed,' he said.

She woke the second time to the low hum of the others having breakfast and the deafening throb of the cicadas on the mountain behind them. She'd been up half the night, her brain unable to shut down. An anxiety kicking in she hadn't felt in years, effervescent random thoughts plaguing her mind while Roland slept soundly beside her. Lori hadn't known what to do when Ceri spouted out Jude's name. She'd cut the call as Roland strolled back into the kitchen. Now she wished she hadn't reacted so rashly.

The room was steeped in darkness, except for a few feelers of light that broke through the slatted blinds. The bed covers had fallen onto her side of the bed. She found herself imagining a life without this ugly truth hanging over her like a trapped angry wasp. She often wondered what her life would be like if she hadn't married Roland, hadn't followed Jude up those stairs to see that painting, hadn't lied. Ceri wouldn't exist. Would she be an artist, living a bohemian life somewhere deep in the country, smoking rollies, living off-grid? Or would she have turned into her mother?

It was hard to tell what time it was. She picked up her watch. Eleven o'clock. Roland must have already been for a swim and organised breakfast. Not much got in the way of his routine, not even a heart attack, and the man could sleep though an earthquake. She thought about the complexity of her feelings for Roland. She'd thought he was going to die a few months back as she sat waiting while he had heart surgery. Nothing like a visit from death to clean out the emotional tubes.

Love is such a tangle of wires.

The villa was modern, angular and designed. Roland liked buildings that had an architectural edge to them, although he'd chosen it because of its location, but she wished they'd forfeited the sea view for something less clinical. She slid out of bed and immediately stepped into the shower. She liked the bathroom at least, with its pebbled flooring and glass wall. As the water sluiced over her tired body, she churned over the conversation with Ceri again, trying to find a way towards peace. But this was Jude. He'd already intimated he was her father and she knew it wouldn't stop there. She wondered what he'd told Roland all that time ago.

Roland walked into the bedroom just as she stepped out of the shower.

'Oh, you're up. Coffee?'

'That would be nice, thank you. I didn't have a good night.'

'I know,' he said.

'Can't stop fretting about Ceri,' she said, picking up her towel.

'Don't,' Roland said. He knew her relationship with Ceri was volatile. He didn't know about Ceri meeting Jude, though. Surely he'd put the pieces together if she told him Jude had introduced himself. Although recently he didn't let anything disturb his sense of equilibrium. He'd been having therapy.

'She's become more and more distant,' she said, patting her legs dry with the corner of the towel.

'She is on the other side of the world.' Roland was leaning against the door frame into the bedroom, his white shirt was creased, his tan just the right honeyed colour, his hair, bleached by the sun, was ruffled from his morning swim. Sun suited him. She could see he'd applied a new dressing to his wound. Once she'd offered to do it for him, but he hated her fussing and complained about her hands being covered in paint. He held the coffee percolator in one hand, rubbing his neck with the other, his eyes reproachful. She could feel his impatience, not wanting her anxiety to reach him. He needed this holiday. It was his doctor who'd suggested a break after having the stent inserted. 'He needs to take it easy,' he'd said. Clearly this doctor had no idea what Roland was like, his whole life was fast-tracked. He didn't *do* easy. So, she'd booked a three-and-a-half-week holiday over Easter.

He was frowning at her now. 'She's been through a divorce, Lori. What do you expect? You need to stop telling her she's making a mistake every five minutes. It undermines her choices. Let's face it, it was you who pushed her towards Carl in the first place, and he was wrong for her.'

Lori felt herself blush. Hot tears sprung to her eyes. 'I seem to remember you approved.' She knew she had a habit of controlling Ceri, more than the others.

'That was then, Lori.'

'But Ro, she was doing so well. She was earning a packet. It's not getting pregnant that's changed her.' She mopped her face with the towel, feeling a desperate need to curl up into a ball, but it was so hot. 'She has systematically gone all out to ruin her life.'

'Maybe the change is for the better.'

'It isn't just that . . .' She stepped up to the sink, caught his eye in the reflection of the mirror. She didn't know where to begin. In the end she said, 'I can't believe it doesn't bother you that she's a waitress. She could be so much more.'

He rolled his eyes. 'Lori, don't impose your values onto Ceri. Life's moved on.'

Lori felt the violence of his accusations. Violent only because it was true. Her values were dated, she knew that. Roland was in the process of re-evaluating his life, he'd even spoken about doing a month in a monastery, but he hadn't grown up with penny-pinching parents and his were still First-World problems. 'It's just, I think . . . I think she may have bumped into Jude,' she said, finally.

He flicked her a glance, scanned the room as a fly buzzed about until it settled on the window sill. He flicked it with a hand towel and she watched it drop dead to the floor.

'Jude?' he said. 'In Sydney? Why didn't you tell me?'

'She couldn't remember the guy's name, but by the way she described him, I'm guessing it was Jude. He introduced himself as an old friend, said he knew us well.' She picked up the toothbrush, already wanting to end the conversation.

'That's rich.' He was winding the towel around his wrist. 'Wonder why he's come out of the woodwork now?'

'We were close at one point, or have you forgotten?' she said.

'I will never forget the night of the daffodils,' he said.

Lori's head was already pounding. Her shoulders were rigid with tension. Roland turned and went back to the kitchen.

'I'm putting the coffee on,' he shouted as he padded down the hall.

Lori thought about Jude. How had he found Ceri? Her mind effervescent, popping out questions. What did he hope to gain?

She could hear Savannah and Will outside, whispering and kissing. She'd been glad that Savannah had brought her boyfriend. He fitted neatly into the fold and it meant Savannah was happy. The growing crisis had made Lori aloof. When she found Roland in the kitchen, she whispered under her breath.

'Let's not talk about Ceri in front of the children.'

Roland carried on clearing the surfaces. Loading the dishwasher with gusto to emphasise the point that he'd been alone cleaning the kitchen. He turned to face her, dishcloth in hand. 'One: they're not children. Two: Ceri *is* their sister.'

Lori bit off a chunk of leftover toast. 'You shouldn't be doing this. Why don't you go and chill?'

'I'm fine,' Roland conceded with a closed smile. 'I bought some more Greek yogurt. That raw honey is delicious,' he said, pointing to the pot. She went out onto the terrace and saw he'd made her a fruit salad. He threw her a glance as she sat down. 'Please, Lori. Let's try and enjoy this holiday. I don't mind the physical stuff, it's the stress I need to avoid. Forget Jude, he's probably just reaching out.'

Lori smiled. 'Sure.' Roland didn't need any of it. Not now, not when he was so vulnerable, *and* in the middle of a mid-life crisis. She wondered what he talked to his therapist about. She leant forward to touch his hand. 'Did you know that Damien Hirst considered pickling a human body?' Oddly enough it was the first thing that came into her head. She felt emptied out and the day hadn't even begun.

# THIRTY

## Lori

Another week passed and Lori still hadn't heard from Ceri. They were on the beach, in individual pockets of companionship: Savannah brushing sand off Will's back. Roland with the boys down by the water. While she was alone, she tried calling Ceri again. It was night-time in Sydney, but Ceri was often late back from the café and usually picked up. The phone rang and rang. Lori must have phoned ten or twenty times and still she'd heard nothing. She could see from WhatsApp Ceri hadn't been online, hadn't looked at any of her messages. She texted again, waiting for those three little dancing dots. She sat with her stomach doing its own version of Houdini. Roland was showing the twins something he'd dug up. All of them huddled over whatever it was. The boys' frames sturdy and big-shouldered, mirroring their father's.

Lori dug out her sketchbook. She looked out at the bay, at the sail boats bobbing up and down, the marine blue of the sea fading into a pale turquoise over a spattering of rocks, thought about how to transmit that sense of tranquillity into a painting. A couple of young girls in fluorescent costumes were splashing about in the water, laughing as they dove in. She remembered when the children were young how absorbed she'd been in their pleasure. She'd always felt lucky, and yet recently an emptiness had begun to grow, making space inside her chest, bringing with it a numbness. Ceri's absence had tainted Lori's very being, fragmented her sense of self.

Roland was alone now, crouched down picking at shells, his knees unnaturally large, his bare feet impervious to the sharp little stones. She watched as his hands shifted through the wreckage of the shoreline. Hands she'd loved tenderly, along with the looseness of his long limbs that even now moved with a certain eloquence, as if his body were a language. Watching him, she was reminded of a time when it had just been the two of them and the adventure had been each other. She'd learned during those first few months of his capacity to break away and retreat into boyhood activities when he was stressed. He used to whittle at a piece of wood, always frowning, focused on the sharp end of a tool, or he'd retreat behind a camera.

Roland looked up from his reverie and caught her eye, as if he knew she was observing him with the microscopic view of a familiar lover. He held her gaze, didn't look away, fixing her stare until she smiled and was forced to find distraction in a tube of sun cream. She could feel the throb of his anger, even here on the beach where he was always at his happiest. She squeezed out a blob of cream. Her skin was crisp, the tightness made worse by the hot sand. The effort of putting on more sun cream felt impossible but she rubbed with firm strokes until her skin hurt.

She thought of calling Anna, picked up her phone and punched into the Facebook App. They were 'friends' although Anna rarely posted anything, just stuff about animal welfare, climate change and endangered bees. Lori always signed her petitions, though, feeling in some way that this connected them. She flicked through Anna's photos:

Jude and Anna on some mountaintop squinting into the camera, at an Extinction Rebellion meeting near the city, and then there were quite a few photographs of them on the Brexit March, Jude wearing an EU starred top hat. They hadn't had children, but from what Lori could tell after a quick stalking session, they were still together.

Her thumb hovered above messenger. What to say? Hi Anna, how are you? Is Jude working in Australia? Of course he was working in bloody Australia. It's not as if there are hundreds of Judes who happened to know Ceri's birthday.

She deleted the message.

Hi Anna, how's things? Just wondering . . . She pressed delete. Roland is trying to track down Jude, she wrote. But that sounded wrong. Delete, delete, delete.

She watched her legs fall into shadow before she realised Roland was looking over her shoulder. She shoved her phone in her bag. He came and crouched down in front of her, grimacing in the face of the sun.

'All this,' he brushed the horizon with his hand, 'and you're looking at Facebook.'

'I just wondered what Anna was up to, that's all.'

He rolled his eyes. 'Coming for a swim?'

Lori had already done fifty laps of the pool and was exhausted. Roland stood up, shading his eyes.

'Sure, darling,' Lori said, aware that she'd been disso-ciated, in her bubble of worry that was Ceri. She didn't really want to go, she needed head space, although God knows what for, the thoughts were the same, swimming around the same troubled waters like a fairground goldfish.

They ran across the hot sand straight into the sea. The water was warm. Tiny silver fish swam from underneath their feet, barely visible as they darted quickly out of reach. Lori wallowed in the sea's embrace, swinging her arms into backstroke. She was free out in the bay where there was no barrier to nature, just salt on the tongue, her skin tingling. She turned to see Savannah on her own. The boys had nabbed William to join them fishing. She wished they wouldn't do that twin thing and leave Savannah out. She beckoned her to join them but Savannah shook her head. She knew Savannah missed Ceri. They weren't close in age, there were six years between them and then eight years later the boys had arrived, but they were all still close. Ceri had been a good sister to Savannah up until all this business with trying to pregnant with Carl's child for over three years. Finally, she resorted to fertility treatment, but it hadn't worked. That's when Ceri became unavailable to everyone. Lori had watched her youngest daughter realign to the new Ceri, the Ceri who was self-obsessed and angry, always in some process, injecting herself daily. Savannah had been bereft until Will came along.

'It's beautiful, isn't it?' Roland said. He'd been observing her, while treading water. Lori turned to see the cove with its white bleached sand, the mountain climbing up behind it, ragged and hewn by the sea, Greek mountain tea sprouting from its cracked, scarred surface. Perched on the cliff edge was their holiday home, modern and defiant.

'Yes,' Lori said, and blew him a kiss, grateful for so many things.

'You're not wearing your plaster,' she said.

'Salt water is good for the scar, apparently.'

The scar from the stent ran down the centre of his chest, purple skin stitched roughly together, protuberant and raw. Lori knew she should live in the moment: be mindful. Be grateful for every day.

'You know, I've been thinking,' Roland said. 'Did Jude bump into Ceri, or did he track her down?'

'I'm not sure,' she said.

'I am,' Roland said. 'I think he deliberately sought her out. Now why would he do that?'

He flipped onto his back, kicking his legs, propelling himself away. Lori knew that wasn't the end of it. He was putting the pieces of the puzzle together and it was only a matter of time before he saw the whole picture.

# THIRTY-ONE

## Anna

Anna was in the garden trying to tame the daffodils that appeared to have doubled in quantity since last spring. Impossible, she realised, so Jude must have planted more. Her Wellingtons flapped around her skinny jeans. She'd grown too thin and felt the cold biting into her flesh. There was only one remedy, which was hard physical labour. She didn't enjoy gardening but had to admit to a certain pleasure in getting things sorted. She'd booked herself out of the clinic for a week over Easter and was due back to work in a couple of days. She'd hoped Jude would return, but then he'd changed his plans, sent her a bleating email complaining about the impossibility of long-haul flights. Better for the planet, she thought. Sometimes, she had the feeling he was avoiding her. There was very little to determine their love, no children, no routine or mutual close friends, not even a dog. They'd talked seriously about separation, but even the practicalities of this option had been circumvented. Jude *was* an avoidant.

She dug the gardening fork into the ground and started to turn it, getting some grim satisfaction from seeing the fresh darker brown earth alive with grubs, picking out a fresh crop of stones that she'd unearthed. From the back of the garden, the cottage looked cobbled together, a part of it covered in slatted wood, and then there was the brick extension and the bathroom that jutted out with its round window as if from the hull of a ship. It had been their home for fifteen years and she felt as if they'd both melded into the very structure of it. Jude's books and piles of paper spread across his study, and her own ordered library in the smaller front room that they both called the clinic, which practically held up the wall. But something was shifting, she could feel it. She wasn't quite sure what it was yet and she couldn't tell if it was internal or external, but the feeling was like the tremors that happened just before an earthquake.

She was ready. Had been for some time.

She heard the phone ringing. She was enjoying the solace of physical work and if she stopped now, she wasn't sure she'd go back to it. But the bell was like a chiming alarm clock, persistent and intrusive, and there was the slim chance it was Jude. She hadn't heard from him in over a week, nearer two. Although this had happened before, she was beginning to worry that something else was going on, that this shift she was feeling was his doing.

She thrust the fork deep into the ground so that it was stationed in the bed, and stomped into the kitchen to pick up the phone, not even bothering to remove her Wellingtons. She was surprised the bloody thing was still ringing, but more so when she heard Lori's voice.

'Hi Anna, it's Lori.' Her tone had such a lightness to it, a gaiety, as if they'd spoken only days ago, Anna was rather taken aback. It had literarily been years since they'd spoken to each other. They sent Christmas cards, and Lori always remembered her birthday, but they hadn't actually talked in a long while. The last time they'd seen each other was at a mutual friend's funeral around the turn of the millennium. Lori had been pregnant. Again.

'This is a little unexpected,' Anna said, picking at a food stain on the kitchen surface.

'Yes, it is. I'm sorry. It's been a while.' Lori had switched from bright and breezy to strained. 'I'm actually calling to speak to Jude. Is he there?'

Anna felt herself tense, her heart thumped with renewed gravity. It was as if the ghost of their past had brushed past her, right there in the kitchen. Were they still in touch? If so, why hadn't Jude told her? She remembered him saying how appalled he was by their wealth, yet he didn't seem to mind when Roland's wealth came his way. Money often came between people, and geography also, but it wasn't something as simple as money or geography that had torn the four of them apart.

'He's not here,' she said. 'He's away. If you must know, I'm a little concerned about him. I haven't spoken to him in a week or so. He seems to have disappeared.' She heard the choke in her voice, surprised that speaking to Lori had somehow unravelled her fears. Lori was silent. Anna wondered if she'd put the phone down.

'Hello.'

'Yes, sorry. I'm here.' Lori sighed. Anna had the feeling something was wrong. She could sense the tension in Lori's voice and the switch of mood revealed her psychological state, although she'd always been a little eccentric.

'Is everything all right?' she asked.

'Yes, I mean, no, not really. It's just that apparently Jude bumped into Ceri in Sydney. At least I think it must have been him. Is he in Australia?'

Anna's heart resumed its thumping presence. 'When I last spoke to him, yes.' What was he doing speaking to Ceri? How did he even know she was in Australia? Anna certainly didn't.

'Apparently he said . . .'

She heard the tremor in Lori's voice.

'He wanted to make himself known to her.'

Anna felt the breath leave her, an emptying of more than just oxygen. 'I see,' she said. 'Well I can't help you, I'm afraid.' She knew her manner was curt, but what did Lori expect? She was about to put the phone down when Lori said, 'The thing is, Anna, Ceri's gone missing and I'm desperate.'

Anna wasn't sure how to respond. She felt angered but at the same time she had the feeling that this was the very thing she'd sensed earlier.

'Okay, I'll try and track him down and get him to call you,' she said.

When she put the phone down she realised that she was perspiring. She was sticky around the collar and felt a trickle of sweat run down her cleavage.

'Damn that woman,' she said, and threw off her jacket, discarding it on the kitchen floor, striding back to the garden, grabbing her garden fork; then looking at the daffodils she changed her mind and went to the shed, drew in the musty smell of it, which took her right back to her childhood and to her grandmother's garden. But the memories that plagued her now were those of her life in her twenties. Of the holiday spent with Lori, Roland and Jude. It was inevitable, she thought, that Lori should come back into their lives. And she felt sure that Jude had engineered it, consciously or subconsciously, it didn't matter which. She remembered going to see Lori in the hospital on Christmas Day, hours after Ceri had been born. Jude had admitted to visiting her also. But that was before their own baby was born, before the real tragedy.

She grabbed the gardening shears and went to the border where the pert daffodils shined back at her. One by one, she cut off the heads of each flower.

'Damn you. Damn you. Damn you!'

# THIRTY-TWO

## Lori

Lori tried not to look at the phone. It was the last evening of their holiday, she'd spoken to Ceri four weeks ago and since then, nothing. The others were engrossed in the film – some espionage story she'd lost track of. Roland had worked his way through half a bar of dark chocolate. He'd stopped eating sugar, but as far as he was concerned eighty per cent cocoa didn't count. She didn't have the will to chastise him and anyway, she had her own things to feel guilty about. She still hadn't told him about speaking to Anna. The twins were both sitting on the sofa, manspreading. Savannah was cuddled up with Will, who had somehow managed to get all this time off work. She had no idea what he did, something related to computers. Savannah was due to start her MA in Durham as a mature student – she'd decided to return to university after five years working in marketing – so that would mean seeing less of her now. Lori's heart ached at the idea of them all disappearing into their separate worlds. She was beginning to resent living with the constant throb of worry that was Ceri. She got up, stretched her arms to give the impression she was more relaxed than she was, and reached for the bottle of wine, pouring herself a large glass of red. She headed for the stairs.

'I ought to go finish packing,' she said, picking up her phone.

'Mum, it's just getting to the exciting bit,' Jake said. Jake and Ollie had seen the film before. She could read his disappointment, but the need to break free, tap into her phone, see if Ceri had posted anything on Facebook or Instagram, was too strong.

'OK, darling. I'll be back in two secs.'

A quick glance at social media told her nothing. She'd already folded the clothes, so it was just a matter of putting them into the case, which took her all of thirty seconds. She pulled out Roland's drawer and noticed that he'd done nothing to prepare for leaving. She quickly folded his T-shirts, all the while worrying at the thought of Ceri like a loose thread. She wondered if Ceri's best friend, Rachel, had heard anything and dug out her phone from her trouser pocket.

Where to start? She knew communication would be perceived as an act of betrayal but she had to talk to someone.

*Hi Rachel, Lori here. How are you? Just wondered if you'd heard from Ceri? Xx*

She was surprised to see the three lines skipping in response so promptly.

*Hi Lori. Good to hear from you. If I'm honest, I'm concerned. Are you around for a chat? X*

*I'll call you xx*

Lori closed the bedroom door and went into the bathroom, taking her glass of wine with her. Unable to find anywhere to put it, she placed it inside the sink. Rachel picked up immediately.

'Hi Rachel. How's things?'

'I'm okay, thanks. Ceri probably hasn't told you but I'm pregnant.'

'Oh, that is good news, congratulations.' Lori felt her stomach tighten. Rachel's pregnancy can't have helped, she thought. Maybe it had nothing to do with Jude at all.

'Thanks. We're really excited but I get the feeling Ceri's upset. I don't know what to do, Lori.'

Lori closed the lid of the loo and perched on the edge of it, pushing her feet further into her espadrilles, balling her toes, hunching over her thighs. 'Oh dear, and I thought it was just me.'

'We talked the other day, well a month ago, actually. She was so closed and every time I brought up the subject of the baby, she changed the subject.'

'Well, that's hardly surprising.'

'I know, but she has to face it. I can't not have a baby because of what's happened in her life, not if we're to remain friends. It's unreasonable.'

Lori winced. 'I know, I know,' she said. 'But these feelings aren't easy to reason with, are they?'

'The thing is, she's changed,' Rachel said. 'Ever since she's been with this new guy. Did you know she was living with him?'

'No.' Ceri hadn't mentioned that detail. Lori felt a tremor of panic. Why hadn't Ceri told her? She thought about Roland going on and on about letting Ceri make her own choices, but clearly it wasn't just Lori who felt she'd lost the plot.

'She seems so edgy. Never has time to talk,' Rachel was saying, the words falling out of her. 'And then there's this old guy she met a few weeks back in the bar who knew her name. Ceri has become obsessed with the idea that he knows something about her. That *you* know something about the past that you're not telling her. I'm really sorry for the things she's been through, really I am. I know it was tough, but I think she's overreacting by packing up and leaving everything.'

'We agree with you,' Lori said, which wasn't entirely true. Roland blamed Lori. Lori sat up, bracing herself with the help of a slug of wine as Rachel continued on.

'I feel really bad talking behind Ceri's back, but I'm genuinely worried. She's changed, and seems to have gone off on one, and doesn't have any intention of coming home, which makes me really sad. I miss her.'

This thought sat heavy in Lori's heart. Rachel began to cry. Lori felt her throat contract and didn't dare speak. She blew slowly out of pursed lips to calm herself down, picked up the glass of wine again.

'Lori, are you still there?' Rachel sniffed.

'Yes,' she said. The wine burned her throat. 'Still here. I'm just thinking.' She was remembering the conversation she'd had with Ceri, wishing now that she hadn't cut the call so abruptly. 'When did you speak to her?'

'Saturday morning over Easter weekend. They were travelling up the coast, apparently. Please don't tell her I said this,' Rachel was saying, 'but honestly, if I wasn't expecting a baby I'd fly over to Sydney just to talk some sense into her. But she's not even picking up my calls. Quite honestly, I'm worried. After reading about that traveller who murdered his girlfriend in Vietnam. I mean, Ceri doesn't really know this man, does she?'

'She's been with him a while now,' Lori said, fear bubbling away, 'and that girl's murder was after a one-night stand.' Lori didn't know if she was trying to reassure herself or Rachel.

After she put the phone down, she sat cradling it in her lap. She felt worse than she did before she spoke to Rachel. Just then, Roland pushed the bathroom door open.

227

He looked at the phone, then the empty wine glass in the sink, and noted the fact that she was sitting on the loo with the seat down with a raised eyebrow.

'What is it?' he asked. 'We've paused the film because it's getting heated. The boys are desperate for you to come and watch.'

Lori didn't give a damn about the film, but this wasn't the time. She'd have to talk to Roland once the others had gone to bed.

'Sorry,' she said. 'That was Rachel. I'll tell you about it later. Let's go.'

Roland let out a sigh. 'Lori, it's our last night, please make an effort for the sake of the others,' he said.

A well of anger erupted inside her. 'Fuck the film, Roland. Our daughter could be dead in a ditch. If you must know, Rachel is as worried as I am. She thinks something has gone terribly wrong, but you know . . .' She took a deep breath. 'You have this way of making it seem as if I'm overreacting. They say when people's behaviour changes it means they are in trouble. This isn't Ceri. This isn't who she is. She always calls back!'

Roland stood wide-eyed, rooted to the spot, arms folded, face like stone. 'You're right,' he said. 'It isn't who she is.' He opened his arms. Reluctantly, she stepped into them. 'But then again, she has just made huge life changes, so it's hard not to think it's all part of the same thing,' he said.

She looked up at him. 'She wouldn't just ignore my messages.'

'I'm going to call the café,' he said. 'Can't believe you haven't done that already.' He went downstairs and came back with his phone. She sat on the bed and watched as he slipped out onto the balcony and dialled the number. Then he started pacing back and forth. God knows why she hadn't thought to do this before now, probably because she was worried that Ceri was angry and this whole business with Jude would blow up in her face.

Lori could hear the television on downstairs, the sound of gunshots and screams snaking up the stairs. She sat on the bed curled over, waiting.

Roland pulled back the balcony glass door and came back in. 'Apparently, neither Ceri nor Pepe have been in for the past month. They're travelling around Australia.'

'Something must have happened,' she said.

'Let's not jump to conclusions just yet. I'm going to call the Foreign Office, first thing.' He stroked her hair, something he hadn't done in a while.

'We've got to leave this house *first thing*.'

'Then I'll do it when we're at the airport. They're brilliant at tracking people. They have eyes on the world.' He smiled kindly, which surprised her. She'd grown used to his intolerance.

'What a dreadful thought,' she said, but she was grateful that someone somewhere would be able to tell her if Ceri was okay. She'd gone from worrying about the truth spilling out to worrying about her daughter's welfare. She kept replaying Rachel's words: *I mean, Ceri doesn't really know this man, does she?* But then Lori wondered if we ever truly knew anybody. Ceri had suddenly become a mystery to her. Even Roland felt distant, although that was her fault – a secret does that to people, and this was the mother of all secrets.

# THIRTY-THREE

**Anna**

Anna opened the door to see her client, Janet, huddled inside the door protecting herself from the rain. Janet was the first client she was seeing after her week off. She'd enjoyed the break, loved being free of other people's problems, and the sight of Janet, a nervous introvert, standing on her doorstep left her feeling irritable. It was late afternoon. Janet worked as an administrator for a dog rescue charity. She wasn't as wealthy as some of Anna's clients but she had genuine issues. Anna had gone through her notes twice in order to prepare herself for the session, even though she was familiar with Janet's mental condition and her past. Jude's absence and this business with Lori had caused a break in concentration and she was finding it hard to switch back into therapy mode when her own life was cracking.

She took Janet's coat. Janet walked into the clinic, did her usual thing of checking the room out, brushing the sofa clean of non-existent crumbs before sitting down. Anna made a point of switching her phone off, even though it was already on silent, giving Janet time to settle. Just as she did, she saw a missed call from Jude. Her stomach lurched. It must be about three o'clock in the morning in Sydney. She was going to have to do a whole hour with that in the back of her mind. The conversation she'd had with Lori a week ago had played on a loop. She'd avoided calling Jude even though nineteen days had passed without contact because she didn't want to confront him about Ceri. Apart from her being bloody-minded, the thought that her marriage was finally over wasn't easy to digest. Janet was sitting with her legs crossed, twisting at a loose thread on her skirt. Anna smiled. She was going to have to focus to get through the next fifty minutes.

Immediately after Janet left, Anna picked up her mobile phone and dialled Jude's number but it went straight to answering machine. She threw the mobile across the room and roared with rage, curling up into a foetal ball. Almost immediately, she picked up the phone again and dialled Jude's office. Adrenaline spiked through her body. She didn't like the idea of admitting to Jude's team that all was not well, but maybe something had actually happened.

She was relieved to hear Lucy's voice on the other end of the phone. Lucy was Jude's personal assistant, not exactly one of the crew but they'd bonded at last year's Christmas office party.

'Hello, Lucy, it's Anna here.'

'Anna, how are you?'

'I'm okay.' Anna's throat closed. She coughed. Jude's Bengal cat, Colin, was curled up on one of the chairs. She wondered if he'd been there the entire time through Janet's session. As if sensing her eyes on him, he stretched out a paw.

'You're wondering about Jude, aren't you?' Lucy said. There was something in the pitch of her voice, a concerned softness which set Anna's teeth on edge.

'Yes, yes I am. It's been a while and I missed a call from him earlier, the first in some time actually. Now I can't seem to get through.'

Lucy didn't answer straight away. Anna breathed slowly, closed her eyes.

'What time did he call?' Lucy asked.

'It must have been around five. I had a patient, so I couldn't pick up.'

'Well, that's going to be about three in the morning where he is.' Lucy was hesitant. 'Look, Anna, I don't want to worry you but we're concerned for his welfare. He's been in the Outback and seems to have gone AWOL. None of his team know of his whereabouts. We did hear from the sound man. He said Jude was drinking again. Apparently they had to cancel filming because Jude was out of it. I'm really sorry, I wish I had better news.'

Anna's mouth was dry. She went to respond but the words wouldn't form.

'Anna, are you okay?'

Anna was digging her nails into the palms of her hands, half-moons patterned her skin. 'Yes. I'm fine. Can I ask why nobody called me?'

'John said there was no point. Apparently this has happened before, am I right?'

Anna thought for a moment. John was talking about a time when Jude was covering a 'behind the scenes' documentary of the Rolling Stones. It was hardly surprising Jude lost it then. 'Yes, but that was a long time ago.'

'If you do speak to him,' Lucy whispered – it was clear she'd moved to somewhere else to talk privately because there was an echo – 'tell him John's on the rampage. He needs to get his act together, sharpish.'

Anna was shaking. The first thought she had was to thank God the cottage didn't have a mortgage. The second thought was that maybe he was having an affair. 'Thank you, Lucy. I'd better go. I have another patient and I need to prepare.'

'I'm so . . .'

'Bye.'

She didn't like to cut Lucy off like that but she could feel her control slipping. She threw the phone back onto the sofa, went into the kitchen to pour herself a whiskey. She couldn't face eating. Instead, she went straight to her computer and looked up flights to Sydney, downing the alcohol, feeling the burn, the sting in her mouth, imagining Jude doing the same somewhere on the other side of the world, although maybe he was actually sleeping – probably not. When he was in this state he rarely slept more than two hours. She was surprised by the tears. She thought she was immune to Jude's antics, well mostly his drinking. She didn't think he was having an affair, not really. He'd not been unfaithful since Lori, but there are other means of betrayal, especially to the self. The phone call would have been some drunken apology he'd forget the next morning; sometimes she felt as if he used her to communicate to himself. This had been their life. This is how it was with Jude. If it *was* another woman, she was welcome to him. She'd forgiven him once and she wasn't going to again; she'd divorce him. And then the thought occurred to her: maybe it really did have something to do with Ceri. What could possibly be going on?

# THIRTY-FOUR

## Lori

Lori woke up at seven to find the bed empty. She'd drifted into a thin sleep in the early hours, her thoughts scuttling on the surface so that she was never fully unconscious, and now her eyes felt scratchy. Splintered light shone through the shutters, patterning the sheet. Normally she would turn over and allow herself the pleasure of an extra hour but they had a plane to catch. She knew it would be her that had to rally the others into action. Roland had taken a back seat since the operation. She could hear him talking on the phone in the hallway and imagined him already organising meetings for his return. She crept to the top of the stairs to see him striding back and forth, his shirt sleeves rolled up, his Rolex glinting on his wrist.

'Yes, she's never left it this long before.' He sighed. 'Honestly, I wouldn't be calling if I felt this wasn't unusual. It's not like her, this behaviour is completely out of character.'

Lori folded her arms and hugged herself. She wasn't sure if hearing him act passionately was a comfort or not. In a way his denial had allowed her some elasticity.

'No, she's not into drugs.' His pacing was getting more frantic. 'Well, if it was something as simple as losing her phone, she'd have found some other way of getting hold of me, surely.'

Lori turned to go to the bathroom and caught his eye. He nodded and she sensed an apology in the way he held her eyes.

She was packing the final bits into their cases when he marched in, a sense of purpose fizzing off his body.

'They're onto it,' he said. 'They're going to try and get hold of her. They have to talk to their man in Sydney, and it'll take a couple of days. Apparently we have to register Ceri as missing to the British police. Can you believe it? I asked him if he needed her passport details and he said he already had them. I'm not sure if that's a comfort or not.'

Lori knew that he was pleased with himself; nothing fired Roland more than gaining control. She felt her chest tighten. It was as if they'd declared war. But this *was* out of character and Rachel *had* said as much. She had to keep reminding herself that it wasn't just her being hysterical, trying to cover her own tracks, but that the possibility of something dreadful happening was a fact.

'What else did they say?'

'They asked for her email address, her telephone number, a description, although I'm guessing they know that if they have her passport details.' The timbre of his voice was deliberately calm. As he spoke, he picked up the last few things beside his bed: his books, receipts, his hand cream. 'They said they'd do their best to track her down but that ultimately we had to register her as missing before they could do anything official. They'll call if they get any news. I mean they're good. Made me proud to be British, actually. I feel better for talking to them.'

Lori preferred it when he was downstairs, striding back and forth, his bare feet slapping the ceramic flooring. She wanted an emotion that matched Jude's destructive shadow.

'Did you tell them we're about to get on a three-hour flight? And that's after the time it takes to get to the airport.'

'They said it was unlikely anything would happen today because of the time difference.'

'Yes, of course.' Lori finished stuffing her make-up into the toiletries bag. She felt numb. 'Have you finished in the bathroom?'

'Not quite.' He walked towards her, gently turned her round and wrapped his arms around her waist. 'I'm sorry I didn't listen,' he said. 'But I really believe it's going to be okay. It's probably something simple.'

She felt the rough edges of his bandage press into her skin. 'You don't know that.'

'No, but I feel comforted by the guy at the Foreign Office. Apparently this happens all the time.' He broke free and picked up his razor. 'If I know Ceri she's probably having a total ball and a part of her is punishing you because of your obsession with her returning to work as a lawyer.' He was running the shaver over his face.

'I have not got an obsession, and she's far more likely to find someone suitable if she's working in a law firm, rather than a café on a bloody beach on the other side of the world.' She watched as Roland pulled his skin this way and that. She felt old, suddenly, watching him, noticing the way his skin wrinkled around his neck, his ears.

'I'm going to pretend I didn't hear that,' Roland said as he tapped his shaver against the sink.

'This guy she's living with is a chef.'

He looked at her reflection in the mirror. His soft blue-grey eyes were steady. 'We both know that this guy, otherwise known as Pepe, isn't really the problem. This has flared up since she bumped into Jude.'

Lori felt instantly sick. He knows, she thought. Maybe he always has. In the mirror, Roland's eyes wobbled, a frown forming. A shadow crossed the window, probably a bird. 'What's really bothering you?' he said.

Lori's mouth was dry. It was too late for honesty now. 'What if she decides to stay there, forever? It's as if he's put a spell on her.'

'And what if she loves him? This is as much about you as it is Ceri.' His voice was softer now.

She hadn't been talking about Pepe, she'd been referring to Jude, but she let the idea sit there as a distraction. He turned and took hold of her hands. She wanted to pull away, withdraw into herself. She'd missed painting. She always missed it when they went away.

'You like Pepe, don't you?' she said, looking down at their entwined hands.

'I don't know him and neither do you. I just want to keep an open mind, for Ceri's sake. Let's meet the guy before we go judging him.'

She knew he was right but Roland being the voice of reason didn't make her feel better. They heard one of the boys jump into the pool. 'Blast those boys, they both know we've got to get out of here in a couple of hours.'

'Oh, let them have a last dip.'

He bent down and kissed her. She realised that she'd barely touched him during the holiday. Lori looked at the door, knowing that the day was pressing for attention.

'I need to get the other two up,' she said, 'we've a plane to catch.'

She was clearing up after breakfast, her mind churning over the conversation she'd had with Roland, the relentless hamster wheel of worry whirring away while her body moved through the chores on automatic, aware of Ollie, Jake and William puffing up and down the stairs, their footsteps echoing on the tiled flooring, along with the rattle of wheeled suitcases across the forecourt. They were running late and Ollie had lost his phone, which he'd left on silent. It was the usual family chaos and she was glad of it – anything to distract her from Ceri and Jude.

'How are we doing?' Roland asked.

'Fine, nearly there,' she said. Her phone pinged. She picked it up to see a message from Anna. She felt a shot of adrenaline run through her body.

*Any chance we can meet up? I'm worried. I can't get hold of Jude. X*

Lori flopped down on a kitchen chair. A large beetle was bashing against the mosquito netting and she could hear Ollie swearing. She punched the digits of her phone. She had the feeling that this was the beginning of something, not the end. There was not going to be a neat conclusion to this little scenario.

*Sure, back in the UK later. Will call you this evening. XX*

'Who's that?' Roland asked. He was leaning against the door frame.

'Rachel, just asking for news.' She wasn't even sure why she lied. But often one lie led to another, she knew that much. She knew also that Roland's tolerance was waning.

# THIRTY-FIVE

## Anna

Anna was hunched up over her desk stalking one of Jude's colleagues on Facebook. Her last client had just left and the evening one had cancelled, so she had the afternoon off. She looked up, unsure how long she'd been sitting staring at the screen, and saw that the light outside was the same soft grey it had been all day. The garden looked bruised from her recent outburst, the daffodil stalks shorn, limp and naked. She felt a wash of shame. The clinic was chilly and the air still. Even the cat had slunk off without her noticing. Anna sat scrolling through social media, prying into other people's lives, occasionally dipping into a jar of mixed dried fruit and nuts, her cardigan buttoned up to the collar as she grew stiff and cold. Jude didn't do social media and was proud of it, but Anna had pretty much connected to everyone on his team, netting his life like a digital predator, orbiting his world of television and politics, observing him switching from his usual intense persona to perform his role as documentary filmmaker, a stranger to her.

Jude often worked closely with a researcher during the months leading up to filming. Having covered the first reconnoitre most of the team had returned to the UK waiting for the next leg of filming. The documentary he was working on covered the history of the Aborigines and an inherent wisdom, which he believed had been lost. Jude had been obsessed by how their culture had been crushed over such a short period. He wanted to highlight the racism. Looking back, so many of his recent documentaries were about the annihilation of tribes or outsiders: people living off-grid, hippy communes, permaculture communities, gypsies, obscure religious sects. He was good at his job, good at informing people and always brought in an emotional viewpoint. His most recent researcher, Ella, was a young girl of Aboriginal origin based in Sydney who'd done a PhD in Aboriginal art. It was Ella's Facebook page that Anna was scrolling through now, having explored the rest of the team. There were a couple of photos of Jude. One taken back in January on the beach of him standing in the centre of a group of eight. His red hair had grown long and had been made stringy in the sea air. In the photograph, on the surface, he looked relaxed, happy even. The caption read: *Jude and his squad of pirates.* She recognised the cameraman, Johnny, who Jude worked with constantly, and the sound man. In another he was in a group of people of Aboriginal descent, his face painted, smiling into the camera, happy, a stranger to her. Even at sixty he was attractive, those bright green eyes, which to her showed signs of early childhood trauma.

She picked up the phone and dialled Johnny's number. He answered immediately.

'Johnny, it's . . .'

'Anna, I've been meaning to call you.'

'What's going on?' she asked, walking towards the fridge and grabbing the Sauvignon, then looking at her watch, changing her mind. It was too early.

'I don't know, Anna, but it ain't good. Haven't heard from Jude in a while and we're supposed to be scheduling the next chunk of filming. He went out to the Outback with Ella – don't worry, there's nothing going on there – and lived and breathed Aborigine for a couple of weeks.'

Anna sighed. 'Is he drinking?'

'I'd loved to say no, but I'd be lying.'

'Shit!' No wonder he hadn't called her. He would be riddled with guilt and shame.

'I didn't call because I didn't want to worry you, and I was kinda hoping it was a phase. I know he went to rehab at one point.'

'That was years ago.'

'Anyway, since then he's gone off-grid.' He sighed. 'I'm so sorry, Anna.'

'It's not your fault,' she said. 'Is he still in Sydney?'

'Apparently so. Only person who's actually spoken to him is Ella, the researcher. I'd give her a call, but the boss has tried and she's not giving anything away. She's young, so her loyalty is greater than her sense.' He chuckled. 'The boss is going bananas. I'm telling you, Jude is this close to losing his job.'

Anna imagined Johnny holding up his fingers to illustrate how close Jude was to the edge. A part of Anna wished Jude would get fired, but that would be catastrophic; without his job he'd have an identity crisis, and she would be left to pick up the pieces.

'Thanks, Johnny. I appreciate the honesty. I'm thinking of going over there myself. It's just difficult with work, you know.'

'Well, if you do, let me know. I'll point you in the right direction. Have you got Ella's number?'

'No,' she said.

'I'll ping it over.'

She went into the grey light of the kitchen and opened the fridge, plucking out a chunk of cheddar, slicing off thin portions with a vegetable knife, grabbing some out-of-date crackers she'd bought at a deli a while back. Picking up an apple, she divided it up into slim, easily edible pieces in some vague attempt to make her snack healthier. She'd lost a lot of weight recently but she didn't care. She looked better for it. It was the anxiety she resented. She felt that Jude had hurtled down an irrevocable road of destruction without considering the consequences, but what was new?

Scrolling through Lori's Facebook page, Anna had been captivated by their extravagant lifestyle. Of course she'd always known Roland was wealthy but had not realised the extent of it. She wondered, as if she were a stranger to herself, if she was jealous, but she'd never been driven by the need for money. They appeared to have homes in London and somewhere in the Cotswolds, and of course there was that place in Dordogne they'd all been to years ago. From what she could make out, the house in France had been modernised with a new pool and a gym. The gardens were cultivated, everything precise and ordered; hedges cut into round balls and a line of heather arcing around the front of the house. Lori's life was a far cry from her roots and it was that which Anna found intriguing. Anna had looked up Lori Watson, then tried Lori Hawkins. It seemed that Lori was still painting and her work was sold in a few galleries and went for a few thousand a piece. She had talent. If there was anything to envy it was that.

Anna's phone pinged. It was a message from Johnny with Ella's contact details. Just as she was replying a thank you, another message came in: Lori.

Anna felt a bubble of anxiety grow and took her plate back into the clinic, hoping to contact Ella by email so that she'd get it first thing. It was early, still, and really she should have been writing down her notes after her last session. She opened Lori's message.

*If you're around this evening, I could drop by. X*

Anna felt her body heat rise. How could she drop by? She lived in London for Christ's sake! But then she remembered it was she who had suggested they meet up.

*Could be there in an hour or so, if you're around.*

Anna felt her heart thumping like the engine of a tug boat. The thought of Lori in their shabby cottage making her skin prickle.

*Sure. You'd better bring some wine. I'll make up the spare bed. X*

She stopped herself using an emoji. She didn't want to appear too welcoming. If anything, she felt as if she was preparing for battle. She went into the living room, which was piled with artefacts, African woven plates, ethnic treasures, books, dust-covered photographs. She had just seen bits of Lori's house on Facebook: giant red ceramic jars, huge abstracts on the wall, sculptures in the garden.

Looking around her living room, her own life looked littered with various bits and bobs, there was no sense of cohesion. Sod it, she thought. This is who we are. No, this is who I am.

# THIRTY-SIX

## Lori

Lori was waiting for her suitcase in the baggage hall. Heathrow was buzzing, every luggage belt on the go, the activity bringing with it a sense of modern madness. Even in the airport the light felt brash, the cold air shocking – they hadn't even stepped outside yet – already she yearned for the softness of the warm sun and wildness of the Greek islands. She'd texted Anna as soon as they'd touched the ground, one finger hopping over the keys, knowing that the boys would chide her for not using her thumbs. But no one had been looking, they'd all been focused on retrieving their cases from the overhead locker. She was surprised when Anna answered with an affirmative. The feeling of victory took her by surprise. She'd tossed her phone into her bag without much care for the consequences, but when it came to telling Roland she'd found herself unable to broach the subject.

Everyone in Lori's small group was looking bored and listless after the flight, their individual suitcases stationed beside them. Ollie was slumped against the family luggage on the trolley, clearly playing a game on his phone. For some reason Lori's suitcase hadn't arrived. She watched other passengers luggage belt emptied, the constant rhythm of it mesmerising, her mind focused on how to break the news to Roland that she was about to visit Anna rather than go home. Roland was scrolling through his emails wearing the same vacant expression of every weary traveller unwilling to return to reality. Savannah was tucked under Will's arm, loose and willowy. They'd go back to their shared flat, Lori thought, their life and dreams still intact. The boys would come back home with them before returning to uni. It was just going to be her and Roland rattling around their home again. The art studio beckoning like a lover.

'Any news?' she asked Roland.

'Not yet. It's still the middle of the night in Australia.'

She'd had the idea of visiting Anna about an hour ago, but still hadn't managed to muster up the courage to speak to him about it. She hadn't even told him they were in touch.

A small part of her felt angry. This was as much his problem as hers, but he could so easily disassociate. But let's face it, he had the right to. He'd been through it recently. She had to constantly remind herself of that. She remembered how he was that morning. Then she remembered an incident from years ago.

Lori had been sitting in their London garden reading. Ceri was playing with her friends, marshalling them all into a line, pretending to be soldiers. Savannah was four and already the difference between them was clear. The tepee Ceri had erected earlier was base camp. Ceri's friends immediately broke ranks, aiming their water pistols at Ceri. Ceri was using her lightsaber and they were running around gleefully. Ceri pretended to die, her legs splayed, and just seeing the way she spread herself out, legs scissor wide, brought back a memory of Jude, doing exactly the same on that day by the lake in Parc Montsouris. Ceri's legs were nothing like Lori's. They were shorter, more muscular than Roland's. Ceri had Jude's legs. But it wasn't just that, it was the gestures as well.

She remembered another time after the twins had been born and they were all together in the garden. Lori was observing the three younger children, their blonde hair exactly the same tone, their long elegant bodies mimicking their father's. God, it was as if her genes hadn't got a look in. But Ceri was different. Her curly auburn hair and pale skin was nothing like the others, and her body was compact. She was the only child who had hazel eyes like Lori's. Roland had joined her, followed her gaze as he sat down with a beer.

'Ceri got them all organised again has she?' he was laughing, shaking his head. 'Sometimes I wonder,' he said.

Lori felt the moisture disappear from her mouth. It was as if he was reading her mind.

'Wonder what?'

'I don't know,' he said, picking up his bottle of beer and watching the bubbles surface. He turned to her then and she saw a flint of unrecognisable emotion in his eyes – was it anger or resentment? 'Savannah's so different – I mean to look at – that's all,' he said. He held her gaze and although desperate not to look away, she found herself unable to do anything else.

'Mum says Ceri's just like Aunt Alice. Genes are a funny thing, aren't they?' she said. 'Isn't the first one supposed to look more like the mother, to ensure its loved?' She scratched at some invisible mark on her skirt.

Roland put down the beer. 'No Lori, I think it's the other way round. They're supposed to look like the father.' He got up and walked away. He always walked away. Last word addict.

He ran around chasing the children, getting them excited by turning on the hose. He'd always treated them equally and she had no idea why he chose that moment to confront her, although he'd not explicitly done so, just used a little bit of passive aggression. She'd been in denial for years, but watching Ceri that day she had to admit that she was different. She had sharper edges to her than their other children.

Lori looked at Roland under the harsh lights of the Heathrow luggage reclaim, remembering that moment, a feeling of compassion rising up inside making her tearful. It would destroy them all if the truth came out. Roland was still scrolling, frowning at whatever it was that had caught his attention.

'Roland, I'm going to hire a car and drive down to see Anna.'

He shot her a sharp look, his hand still poised holding his phone. 'What? Anna as in Jude's Anna? Why?'

'We've been in touch. Apparently, Jude is missing as well. I didn't want to mention it because I thought it might spoil the last day of your holiday. I just thought, you know, it might be connected. I mean it's pretty bloody weird.'

'You've spoken to Anna and you haven't told me?' He was frowning, his exasperation visible, shimmering off his body.

'I didn't tell you because I knew you wouldn't approve! I just think it might help, that's all. I don't think it's a coincidence they're both missing!' She knew there was gravity to her words that he'd find difficult to ignore.

He put his phone in his pocket, stepped towards her so that he didn't have to raise his voice. 'Christ! What are you hoping to gain?'

Lori could feel the perspiration run down her back. 'I just thought she'd be able to talk to me if we were alone, you know.'

'What could she possibly do but make it worse?'

'What do you mean?'

'Lori. We both know what's going on here.'

Lori felt herself flush.

'Mum!' Ollie was struggling with her suitcase and in the process had managed to drop his phone. He let go of her case just as he was about to put it on the trolley so that everyone's luggage toppled over like dominoes, while he scuttled after his mobile.

'Is it broken?' she asked.

'No, thank God.'

Roland didn't move, didn't even help them with the cases. She had to keep reminding herself of that scar, a bruised ripple of cracked flesh.

'It'll give you some alone time with the boys,' she said as she swept past him. 'I'm going to hire a car.'

He pulled her close, grabbing her arm. She could see the anxiety in his eyes, a glint of rage. 'Lori, you need to tell me. Why involve Anna?'

'I will,' she said. 'Later.' She wriggled out of his embrace.

She hired something modest, a Polo. She knew Anna well enough to know how she'd frown upon anything other than a basic vehicle. Anna had texted her the postcode. The drive down was bearable, the early evening light casting the horizon with a soft blueish hue. She wasn't surprised by the remoteness of the village – Anna had never been one for big cities – but she was stunned by the cuteness of the cottage with its pretty little front garden. Wisteria arced over the front door. There were pansies in wooden window boxes. Lori thought about her own grey cubed boxes with white cabbage plants. Everything ordered and clinical, which is how Roland liked it.

Lori had managed to grab a couple of bottles of Merlot in a corner shop. She'd brought some cheese, grapes and biscuits. She realised she was trembling when she knocked on the door, more from nerves than the chill in the air. This was a woman she hadn't properly seen in twenty years, not since the funeral of a mutual friend just before the boys were born. A woman she'd betrayed, yet here she was standing before her looking willowy, beautiful and as fiercely intelligent as ever. She was surprised by her own tears. Anna's stoical response, the stiff way she held herself – arms folded, hands clenched – didn't surprise her.

'Anna, you look just the same.' It was the first thing that popped into her head. She smiled broadly and was going to step into the hallway but Anna didn't move. For a second they stood facing each other, eyes locked, before Lori turned away and looked back at the car parked at the front gate.

'I'm so sorry to barge in like this,' she said.

'Don't apologise. I suggested it,' Anna said, shifting back so that Lori could step inside. Lori found herself ducking, even though the doorway wasn't low.

'I've brought these,' she said, holding out the bottles.

'Let's hope we don't get through both of them,' Anna said, relieving Lori. 'I'm not up for a hangover. I have work tomorrow.' Anna walked down the hallway, which was lined with black-and-white photographed landscapes. Lori followed, not stopping to look.

'You're still doing clinical psychology?'

Anna shook her head. 'I trained as a therapist a few years

back.' Lori caught a glimpse of the packed bookshelves as she passed an open door. Years of training and reading.

'Roland's seeing a therapist,' she said. She knew she was gabbling, but couldn't help herself.

'That's what Jude and I call the clinic,' Anna said, seeing Lori's glance. 'Why don't you go into the sitting room?' Anna gestured to a room opposite. More books. The place was rammed. Roland wasn't keen on bookshelves, he liked the home to feel sparse and minimal, so Lori had bought a Kindle. Anna and Jude's living room was filled with African objects: masks, wooden sculptures, a large antelope. There were a couple of hand-quilted throws over the sofas, and art all over the walls. Photographs of Jude in Africa with an African tribe, another of him in Colombia. It was bohemian and jumbled together in a considered way. Lori had got in an interior designer to do their place in Notting Hill.

'Sit down. I'll bring in the glasses and put these cheeses out.'

Lori didn't sit. She walked up to the bookshelves and picked out a book on Peter Beard, an artist who lived in Africa and created gruesome collages which he spattered with blood. She realised that in many ways, Jude and Anna were still the same people they were when they'd hung out together as students. It was Lori and Roland who'd changed. She picked out a sketchbook that was balanced on top of a row of books and found herself flicking through a collection of drawings. After a second, she realised some of them were her own. Anna would often pose for her when she was an art student – she could barely recall those lazy afternoons they'd spent together, drawing. She turned to see Anna staring at her, still holding the empty glasses, eyes fixed on the sketchbook.

Lori held it up. 'I'd forgotten about these,' she said.

'Keep it if you want.'

'Oh, I didn't mean . . .'

'Tell me. Why you are you here, Lori? I mean, I know I invited you but . . .' Anna was opening the wine bottle, dropping the foiled lid to the table and pushing the cork-screw into the cork with a firm grasp, twisting it so that in three turns she was able to pull the cork out. 'Do you think Jude has abducted Ceri? Is that it?'

Lori felt herself flush, a prickly sweat breaking out under her arms. She went and sat down, picking up the wine Anna had poured. 'Cheers,' she said, but Anna left her wine on the table. She was waiting for Lori to respond.

'I don't know, do you?'

'I have no fucking idea,' Anna said. 'I mean why would he even introduce himself?' Her derisive tone made Lori wince.

'Yes, well it's partly that I wanted to talk to you about.'

Anna spat out a laugh. 'Better late than never.'

Lori drank the wine for fortitude, hoping it would help loosen her tongue. 'Jude has insinuated he's Ceri's father. Since then, Ceri has disappeared. She's not answering my calls.' She gulped down more wine. 'We've been in touch with the Foreign Office and registered her as missing. And since Jude has also gone "missing", I thought it might be connected.'

'Jude is more likely holed up in a bar somewhere. It's possible that they're not connected in the slightest.' Anna smiled, a tight straight line that didn't offer any warmth, but for some reason Lori felt a sense of relief. Anna wasn't the type to let her imagination run away with her, and she was strong enough to confront the worst possible scenario.

'Is Ceri Jude's?' Anna's voice wobbled. 'I mean we both know that's a possibility, don't we?'

'Oh for God's sake, sit down,' Lori said. 'You're not making this easy for me.'

Surprisingly, Anna plonked herself down next to Lori. 'I'm not sure it should be easy,' she said.

'Anna, we were friends once.'

'It was you who changed that.' Anna's gaze fell onto her wine. Her hand was shaking and she stilled it by setting the glass on the table.

'I thought it was time, that's all,' Lori said.

'For what?'

'Time I told you what happened.' She knocked back another slug of wine.

'I know what went on,' Anna said, finally conceding to the need for alcohol and taking a sip. 'What I don't understand is why you lied, why Jude and I confronted the truth and you didn't.'

'I made a mistake. Of course Jude admitted it to you, that much was clear after the attack on the daffodils, but I felt I had too much to lose. We all have different ways of dealing with our blunders and mine was to pretend it didn't happen.' Anna went to interrupt, but Lori touched her knee to stop her from talking. 'I was lost, jealous, panicked but mostly I was a fool, scared of commitment. I felt Roland had made everything happen and I was a passenger in my own life.'

'Lori, I'm a therapist, I spend my life unravelling people's failings. And I can tell you, if you want to rescue your relationship with your daughter – I mean that's why you're here isn't it? – then you're going to have to tell the truth. I told you that years ago.'

'Yes, well I wasn't ready.'

'And you are now?'

# THIRTY-SEVEN

## Anna

Anna was gloriously drunk. She could almost sense her brain cells popping. She hadn't been this smashed in years. How could she be with Jude always on the brink? She'd known him to grab a whiskey for breakfast for Christ's sake. She'd had to be the stable one for their entire marriage and she no longer wanted to play that role; she was feeling dangerously defiant.

Lori and she had talked about nothing and everything. She'd forgotten how easy things were between them, once the wine had allowed them both to relax, that is. Of course she had friends but not like Lori. Her other friends were sensible intellectuals who took themselves and their work seriously. Lori was nothing like that. Lori was fun.

Anna was in the clinic, the room wobbling as she yanked open the drawer looking for some paracetamol to ward off a hangover. All this time and she'd forgotten what it was like to feel completely without a care in the world. Therapy had turned her into such a rational thinker and she'd forgotten how to play. She'd become so bloody earnest. Of course Anna had always known about Lori and Jude, but she'd been in denial over Ceri for years for her own reasons, even though the thought occurred to her several times when she came across photographs of the girl with curly auburn hair. Somehow she'd managed to put that knowledge aside like an unwanted plate of cold porridge. Now she felt free of the need to guard herself against it.

The room was spinning. She was going to have a corker of a headache, for sure. She'd have to cancel her eleven o'clock. After grabbing the packet, she went back into the hallway, glimpsing the sofa on the way out, remembering her client, Janet.

'Bloody men,' she said, noticing the slur in her voice.

'Abso–bloody–lutely,' Lori cried out from the sitting room.

Anna walked in to find Lori sprawled out on the floor on a pile of scatter cushions, glass of wine in hand, her bobbed hair loosely falling over her shoulders. She looked flushed, yet radiant. Of course she was tanned. Anna started to giggle.

'What are you laughing at?' Lori said. 'Do I look that bad?'

'God no, you look great!'

'Oh, Anna. I've missed you,' Lori said, wildly flicking her hair back.

'Have you?'

'Yes.'

'Then why let it happen?'

Lori caught her eye, flicking a nervous glance at the window as if she were afraid of the dark. By the way she frowned, Anna could tell she was deliberating between telling the truth or sidestepping the question.

'It isn't just *you* I miss. I didn't even realise it until this evening, but it's a part of me that I miss as well.' Lori picked out a bit of cork that was floating about in her glass.

Anna plonked herself on the sofa, popping out four tablets, passing two to Lori and swallowing down two herself. 'Well, if it makes you feel any better I feel a part of me has died somewhere along the line too,' she said. 'You know I was pregnant, don't you? Twice, actually. I had two late miscarriages. After that, Jude turned to drink again, and his inability to be supportive meant that I put an end to the idea of children. He begged me to try again. But I said no. In many ways, it's no wonder he's grabbed at the possibility of a child, even though she's effectively someone else's,' she said. 'It was the only time I really felt like picking up the phone and calling you. I missed you so much during those years.'

Lori leaned forward, put her hand on her knee. 'Anna, I'm so sorry.'

Lori's phone went off, loud and intrusive. Lori pulled out a brand new gold iPhone from her pocket. 'Sorry,' she said.

'Hi Ro. Yes, I'm here with Anna.' Lori sounded sloshed. 'Sorry, I forgot.'

Anna could hear Roland's voice, measured and flat, although she couldn't make out what he was saying. She watched as Lori's face tensed up, frowning as she listened. She put the phone down looking preoccupied.

'Ro, checking up on me,' she said, apologetically.

Anna waved the explanation away. 'You know what I miss? In the same way Jude had the ability to make people feel beautiful, you made them feel free. I think that's what Roland wanted, for you to release him from his demons. He was never a free man even then.'

'Gosh, Anna. That's very profound.' They both fell about laughing.

'I didn't free him though, did I? Instead, I walked into his gilded cage.' Lori's mood flipped. Serious suddenly, she looked into her wine, went to take a sip but changed her mind.

'It's funny. I'm a therapist, I make my living from listening. People come to me to be healed but in the end, I believe we can only heal ourselves.'

'True,' Lori said. She took a long deep breath, her eyes tearing. 'You know that day I'd seen you and Roland flirting, and I felt defiant. I wanted to punish you both. But I think in retrospect I was driven by a need to gain control. Roland thinks I'm very controlling.'

'That's rich, coming from him, Lori.'

Lori laughed, and just as she had turned sullen, she switched back to her playful old self. Anna could tell she was teetering on the edge of something. We are all buccaneers when it comes to mining our hidden knowledge, she thought.

'What about Jude?' Anna said, pushing a little.

Lori put the glass down and was trying to reach for one of the throws, which she successfully extracted from a pile on the sofa and wrapped around her middle. She was leaning on her knees. 'I sometimes wonder if he wanted to prove to Roland I was unworthy.'

Anna shook her head. 'Jude liked a conquest. I didn't offer enough of a challenge.'

'You can't blame yourself.'

'At the time, I blamed you but that was because I didn't want to face up to the part I played. I'm wiser now.' She smiled knowingly. 'We're all to blame, don't you think?' It was the first time Anna had contemplated the role she'd played, and Roland too. It wasn't just Lori who was teetering on the edge, it was herself. 'I think. I became my mother in many ways, turned a blind eye to the drink, to his flirting.'

Anna leaned forward so that Lori was forced to look her in the eye. Lori didn't do a very good job of it, she couldn't maintain eye contact. 'You need to ask yourself why you felt you couldn't be open with Roland. I mean Jude risked everything to tell me, why didn't you feel free to do the same?'

Lori frowned, looked at her hands. 'Guilt, I suppose.'

'Yes, and that guilt grew, bigger and bigger. You might want to think about that.' Anna felt sharpened, a bolt of adrenaline coursing through her veins. 'You know when we were at the supermarket, I kept telling Roland I was worried, that I wanted to get back. I knew deep down you were feeling vulnerable and like all animals, it's when we feel weak that we attack, but Roland was very determined to stay away.'

Lori was still concentrating on her hands, turning them over, splaying her fingers. 'What, you think he purposely left us alone?'

'Unwittingly perhaps, but yes.'

Lori shook her head. 'I don't know about that.'

'Lori, you were a catch. You were this wild, untameable creature and that's what Roland loved about you. I think unwittingly Roland wanted you to sleep with Jude.'

'Why?'

'What better way to tame someone than use their own guilt?'

Lori was shaking, hunched. The fire was slowly dying, its embers glowing and the wood crackling softly. Anna laid her hand on Lori's forearm. 'Anyway, thank you for finally being honest.'

'It didn't help that you kept telling me how good he was in bed.' Lori laughed but the gesture was hollow.

'Well, I think *we* were good in bed, not him, and I probably boasted about the sex because there was very little else going for him,' she said.

'After you and Jude went home, all I wanted to do was make things right. I loved Roland, you see, it's just that I was scared.' She was focused on some interior detail Anna couldn't see.

'And when I found out I was pregnant with Ceri, Roland asked me, straight out. I think he suspected something had gone on that day. I think Jude must have told him. So . . . I lied. I mean, we'd been using the withdrawal method, so Ceri could have easily been his.' Lori didn't look up. Her voice was cracked with grief. Anna suspected this was the first time she'd talked to anyone in years. She was twisting the fringe of the throw around her fingers. 'I've lived with the knowledge that Ceri's Jude's child for years and it's been such a weight.'

Anna broke off a square of chocolate, popped it into her mouth, handed a piece to Lori. 'So what do you think Roland would do if you told him now?'

'God knows!'

'You need to tell him, Lori. It's the only way you're going to get yourself back, and the respect from Ceri. She needs to know as well. She has to hear it from you, not Jude.'

'I have to go to Sydney,' Lori said. 'I need Jude's number.'

Anna picked up her phone from the coffee table. 'I'm coming with you,' she said.

# THIRTY-EGHT

## Lori

Lori drove back home the next morning, her head throbbing. She was in the kitchen waiting for Roland to get off the phone, pacing around the island, the car keys still in her hand along with the set of door keys, which she kept jangling from her index finger. She liked the way those keys felt in her hands. Their live-in housekeeper, Doris, was busy cleaning the pantry. Roland was standing on the other side of the island, talking on the phone in a gruff manner. She'd rarely seen him this disgruntled. He'd started off with a verbal assault as soon as she'd walked in the door, not giving her a minute to speak, accusing her of keeping things from him, not being there, then his phone had rung and she'd been surprised when he'd picked it up. It was someone from the Foreign Office.

Lori tiptoed across the kitchen.

'Doris, would you give us a minute. Roland and I need to discuss something privately.'

Doris nodded, eyes round and startled as a hooked fish. She quickly returned the tins of tomatoes, black-eyed beans and chick peas to the cupboard. Lori could hear the boys downstairs playing on their PS4, probably slaughtering an entire digital army. She thought they'd have grown out of that by now.

Roland finished the call and looked at Lori with unwavering eyes. His hair, still streaked blond by the Greek sun, was brushed back off his face and his tan looked darker now they were back in England. For a second, she was reminded of his father. He stood watching her, his body rigid as a wooden clothes peg.

'What is it? What's happened?' she said.

'Ceri's phone has been found on a beach.'

'Oh Christ!'

'She could have just lost it. You need to stop imagining the worst, Lori.'

'Do you really believe that?' Lori said. 'She's never lost her phone. Never. She's careful.'

'Yeah, well, it seems to me a big shift is happening in Ceri land. It's a pretty major thing to walk away from a high-powered job, a husband and your mother in one go.' He was staring at the floor and he looked up and narrowed his eyes. There was his father, Charles, again. 'Tell me, why go visit Anna? You haven't given a second thought to her in Christ knows how many years!'

'I'm trying to tell you, but you won't even let me speak!'

Roland seemed to take this in. He buried his head in his hands and sighed.

'I'm scared, Lori. That's all.' Lori went to stand before him and swept his hair back off his face. He leaned against the wall and looked at her, his eyes searching hers for answers, then he let his head drop into his hands, the span of them appearing to her masculine and strong. She didn't suggest he sat down, there wasn't time.

'I need to tell you what happened thirty-five years ago,' she said.

Roland's head snapped back up. 'Christ.' He glared at her and she realised that his eyes were rimmed red. He leaned against the wall, his legs crossed, his arms folded. 'Go on.'

'Remember the day after our wedding when we played in the pool and you and I had a row and then you and Anna went to the supermarket?' Her voice was shaky. She felt raw, a permanent state of fear had left her with a blunt pain in her sternum. She pressed on.

He nodded. 'Go on.'

'Jude wanted me to see a painting after I showed him our favourite, the Ceri Richards. He wanted to show me a Picasso in the upstairs bedroom.'

'The one that paid for the repair of the roof, that Picasso?'

'What does it matter which bloody Picasso! I'm trying to tell you something important and you're asking me which bloody Picasso like we have ten of them!'

He held up his hand. 'Sorry.'

'I followed him upstairs, and when we were looking at the painting he kissed me.' A gravelly feeling in her throat made her want to swallow. 'It didn't stop there.'

'Christ,' he said. He sank down, squatting onto his haunches so that his knees cracked. She let the thought ruminate for a bit. 'So, you're telling me that Ceri's not mine?' He looked at her, a glint of anxiety forcing her to look away.

'That means you've been lying to me for thirty-four years.'

He waited for her to reply but the words were all tied in a knot inside her head. 'To all intents and purposes, she is yours, Ro.' She kept thinking about Anna's words: *What better way to tame someone than use their own guilt?* She looked down at her feet, noticing a grass stain on her trainers. 'When Jude introduced himself to Ceri as an old friend, he also implied that he was her father.'

Roland was shaking his head. 'Christ, Lori!' he said, again, standing up and throwing his arms in the air, then swivelling round to look out of the window at the wide tree-lined avenue, at the apple tree they'd planted when they'd first moved in. All that tranquillity appeared to be mocking them, and the war zone they'd created inside their home. Roland had a wild look in his eyes. 'Have you gone mad? What do you think Ceri's going to think of you? If we find her that is.'

He started pacing again. 'You know Jude told me that you'd made a play at him, and I told him if he ever dissed my wife again . . . That's why we stopped talking. Turns out, he was right.' He shook his head, grimacing.

Oddly enough, Lori didn't feel enraged, she felt totally numb. 'Tell me, why did you flirt with Anna? Why did you take so bloody long at the supermarket?'

He twisted round to look at her, his eyes deadened with fury. 'You can't turn this back on me. That's not happening.'

'Roland, we all played a part in it. It's never just one person.'

His eyes were wild and unfocused. 'It's probably completely fucked her up.' He threw his arms up again. 'I gave you the chance to tell me the truth when you first told me you were pregnant . . .'

Lori went to interrupt but Roland held up his hand.

'No, Lori, let me speak.'

Lori folded back against the kitchen island. The feeling of deadened despair finally whipping into rage, the taste of it swilling in her mouth, sour and unpleasant. Her eyes went to the window as a young couple walked past the house, hand in hand, laughing.

'Don't think I didn't know about Jude. I knew he'd push and push to prove a point. He never believed in you.'

'Then why didn't you stop him?' She raised her voice. 'It wasn't me he didn't believe in, it was us! And actually

262

he was competitive with you, and what better way to make him feel better about himself than to seduce your wife.'

Roland's eyes widened, his mouth went slack. 'Don't make this about me. Don't ever make this about me.'

Lori felt something cold enter her, deadening off any guilt she felt. It wasn't something as clear cut as anger she was feeling, but whatever it was left her feeling hardened like an old conker.

She sighed.

'Roland, I made a mistake, but I had my reasons. I was lost, I'd lost the reigns to my life, and you were good at dealing with that, weren't you? Somehow taking everything in your control, bit by bloody bit and it left me feeling powerless. The only thing I had left was my painting and even my relationship with that somehow dissipated. And Jude, well, part of his charm was that he was fucked up. You loved that about him, we all did. His difficult step-father, that made you feel better about your own father. But he made me feel powerful just for an instant, until I realised what I'd done and the guilt set in, but you knew that, didn't you?'

'I said don't make this about me!'

'But it is as much about you as me, don't you see?'

Their eyes locked, and she saw fear – it was mostly fear – and recognition. Then he slapped the table hard, gripping the edges of the surface. 'Yes,' he said.

They were still for a while, the room ringing with silence in the wake of their words.

'Anna thinks this whole thing with Ceri is most likely Jude reaching out to find the daughter he never had and Ceri's disappearance is something simple: perhaps she's angry, maybe she's just extended her camping trip,' Lori said.

'And the phone?'

'I don't know about the bloody phone.'

'I still don't understand why you didn't tell me.'

She got closer to him, looked him square in the eye. 'I was scared. I was completely lost, Roland. The money, your aunt, the wedding, the dare game, the way that you took advantage of my impulsive nature. I told you, I felt powerless. I felt you had taken control of me. I couldn't find it in me to make the right decisions anymore. Don't think I haven't analysed the whole thing over the years. I have.' It was Lori's turn to pace back and forth, the sharp edges of the keys biting into the palm of her hand. Roland folded his arms and stood by the window. The sun was shining, there was an air of summer beginning outside and yet inside they were both swamped in an invisible darkness – a winter of their own making. Anna was right, she'd been immobilised by guilt.

'I can't believe you thought sleeping with Jude would make you feel more powerful.'

Lori was running out of steam. 'Of course I regretted it immediately.'

'When were you planning on telling me?'

She sighed. 'Life got in the way, Ro. And anyway, if I told you when I was pregnant, we wouldn't have Ceri. If there was no doubt that she was Jude's, which by the way was never the case, would you have honestly brought the baby up as yours?'

Roland was leaning against the wall, his shoulder scrunched up by his ear, looking out the window. A tear tracked down his cheek. 'Probably not.'

'Exactly. Of course it became apparent pretty early on, the curly hair, certain aspects of her character. But we tell ourselves what we want to hear, don't we?'

Roland walked towards her, leaned on the island, defeated. He raked his hair. They didn't speak for a while. The sound of the birds twittering, distant traffic noises, a plane overhead, the room thickening with the unsaid. Lori was digging around in her handbag, trying to find the tissues Anna had given her. She couldn't get past the idea that Ceri wouldn't exist if she'd told the truth.

Roland spoke first. 'You're right, Ceri is *my* daughter, and no one is taking that away from me, especially Jude.' He looked up and into her eyes. 'What matters to me is that you lied. For years.'

'Jesus, Roland. Has it ever occurred to you that the whole prenuptial agreement thing undermined our marriage as well. Your father controlling you, you controlling me, me controlling Ceri. I was ashamed, confused, don't you see? I'd convinced myself she was yours, I wanted you to love her. I didn't want to destroy us before we'd even started.'

'And yet you did.'

'Come on, Roland. I think we both did.'

They stood staring at each other. Lori felt as if Roland had built an invisible wall around himself. He looked wounded, his body hunched and weary.

'I'm booking a flight to Sydney tomorrow morning. I'm taking this into my own hands,' he said, picking up his car keys from the kitchen surface and pinning her down with wounded eyes. 'You need to take the boys down to Bristol.' Lori felt as if she'd broken in two. She grabbed her bag.

'I'm getting on that flight with you. Like it or not, we're tackling this together, and don't you worry, I'll book my own flight, and, by the way, Anna's coming too. It's me that has to break this to Ceri, not you, or Jude.' She watched as Roland's face dropped.

'You're going to tell Ceri?'

'Yes. If you're so concerned about lies, then now is the time to change that.'

'But . . .'

'No, Roland, this is just another example of you undermining me. The boys can make their own way down to bloody university.' She walked out of the kitchen, instructing Doris to hand the car keys back when the hire car company came and to unpack her suitcase from the holiday and repack another with clothes suitable for autumn.

Roland had opened the kitchen door, leaning on the door frame, watching her as she turned to go upstairs. They locked eyes briefly but Lori kept going.

'Lori, I'll book the flights, one for Anna as well.'

Lori could feel Roland watching her as she turned the corner on the landing. The strain in his voice revealing an internal wrangling, unsure what was the right path to take. Welcome to my world, she thought. She went and sat on their bed and punched in the search button: Jude.

He picked up after two rings. 'Hello.'

'Jude, it's Lori.'

'I was wondering when you'd call,' he said.

# PART FOUR

—

## Present Day
## Sydney 2019

# THIRTY-NINE

## Ceri

They got back from their trip early on Saturday evening. Their flat looked sad, lifeless. A cold damp had settled in, the plants were drooping and covered in dust despite their neighbour watering them. Ceri dropped the bags and went straight to the sink to find a damp cloth to wipe the leaves and filled a bottle of water. Even the birds fighting over the fruit of next door's tree had quietened. A stack of letters was in the post box. Ceri put on a wash and worked her way through them while Pepe unpacked the kitchen stuff and washed down his surfboard in the back yard. They worked together in silence, able to read each other like synchronised swimmers.

Most of the envelopes were bills, one was a letter from her grandparents and another was from the local police station informing her that her phone had been found on a beach just up the coast. Ceri was relieved. She'd lost it while playing volleyball. They'd spent the entire evening looking for it and assumed it had been stolen. She hadn't bothered buying a new one while she was away as she'd rather enjoyed not having a phone. For one thing, it meant she didn't have to speak to her mother about this business with Jude until she'd sorted it out in her head. But now she felt a deep need for answers, sparked mostly from Pepe's belief that this was important.

They went straight to the police station to pick up the phone. She knew her mother would be worried and Rachel, her friend who was pregnant. The last conversation she'd had with Rachel had been strained, and with her mother too. The station wasn't far from the beach so they raced down to Bronte because Pepe wanted to get a look at the waves, see whether or not he could go surfing the next day. There were still swimmers in the seaside pool, probably three sixty-fivers, their arms plopping rhythmically into the green seawater, their brightly coloured swimming caps making them look like fluorescent beetles.

Ceri and Pepe plonked themselves down on a small faded rug. Pepe opened a bottle of beer for them to share. Ceri looped herself under Pepe's arm and they sat staring out at the Pacific, the wind whipping at their hair.

Bronte had become home.

'Waves look promising,' Pepe said. Ceri felt the weight of her phone in her hand, feeling her throat tighten at the thought of the messages waiting for her. She was glad that the battery was dead, that she'd have to wait until it charged before contacting everyone. She'd been careless in not letting her mother know she was well, but since the incident with Jude a part of her had simply wanted to hide.

It was Pepe who brought up Jude. It was always Pepe. 'It will be nagging at the back of your mind forever if you don't face it,' he said, continuing a conversation they'd been having on and off over the past few weeks.

'What will?'

'Jude the dude.'

'Oh, let's not go there,' she said, picking up a handful of sand, enjoying the sensation of it running through her fingers.

'Why go to that much bother, though?' he asked. The waves crashed onto the shore, the sea crackling, foaming, dribbling onto the sand. 'I mean, he tracked you down. Like I said, he could be telling the truth. He reminds me of my Tio.'

'Pepe, we've gone round in circles. Can't you see, I'm frightened?'

'Si, cariño, but fortune favours the brave.'

It seemed to her that ever since that day she'd walked away from Carl and handed in her notice, she'd continued to throw aside bits of her life: her friends, her family, her career always pressing for attention. She was angry with her mother; knew she was hiding something and could sense the rising hysteria even from on the other side of the world. She thought the trip would help, but it had been a continuous stream of conversation between them.

It was late. They had more unpacking to do. She realised Pepe had been talking.

'What were you saying?' she asked, reaching for the beer and sidling closer to Pepe for warmth.

'When I was a boy, there was this man who was always there, you know. Every family outing or holiday, he got invited. Sometimes, he'd bring his sons and we played well together, so I never questioned it. We called him Tio. He introduced us to a game called Sardines. We used to play it all the time up in the mountains.'

'I know Sardines,' she said, remembering playing it with her cousins in France.

'Tio became part of the fabric of our family and none of us questioned why. My father was often working away, but Tio was always there to take his place. I thought he was a friend of my father's but just before my father died, my older sister, Maria, told me that he was my mother's former lover. That piece of knowledge left me unsettled for months. I don't even know if my father knew or not, but he just accepted this man and I'll never know why. I wanted to ask him, but we ran out of time.'

'So, ask your sister, or your mother.'

Pepe shook his head. 'I can't.'

'Why?'

'I don't know. It just feels wrong. You know, when you get the feeling that someone doesn't want to talk about it.' He picked up a clump of sand, squeezed it into a fist. 'Knowledge isn't always a good thing when the dead are involved. But in your case, I think it's different. And there might be a time when it's too late to ask.'

Ceri was sifting the cold damp grains of sand between her fingers, allowing the rhythm of the movement to relax her a little. She thought of her mother, how she bristled her way through life, as if carrying a weight that made her intolerant. Had she always been like that?

'Was he there, at your father's funeral?'

Pepe nodded, he was drawing something with his finger, a crescent moon. 'But he and my mother didn't even acknowledge each other, it was very strange.'

'So, what's your point?'

Dusk was inking the sky darker. Ceri shivered. Pepe picked up a stone and threw it into the murkiness that was the sea, before looking at her. Up close, she could see a smear of beer on his lips, glistening. The cold damp sea air whipped around them. They had talked about this and their future while travelling, grown closer because of it. Although she couldn't see into his eyes, she could make out the faint form of his face, sense the sadness. 'Tell me,' she said.

'Your friend Jude reminds me of Tio.'

'He's not *my* friend, he's my mum's friend.'

'Exactly. That's why I think you should talk to him. I mean, he clearly believes he's your father from what he said. If it were me, I'd want to know.' He picked up another stone, tossed it from hand to hand.

'But Mum was so dead against it.'

'Yeah, and that's exactly what made me think she's hiding something.' He lifted her hand to kiss it. 'I'm sorry, babe. I know that doesn't make you feel comfortable.'

'You think he is, don't you?'

Pepe shrugged.

'But how am I going to find him?' she said.

'Jack will know. He's got his ear to the ground, knows what goes on in the bars around here. Let's ask him.'

'I don't know,' she said. It was hard to ignore the way her stomach contracted at the thought of seeing Jude. 'He might not even be here.'

'Let's find out,' Pepe said. He took out his phone and called Jack.

Jack reckoned they'd find Jude a couple of streets up in a café on Thomas Street. He knew the owner. Apparently, they'd joked about Jude and his habit of making himself known to the barman. Before going home, they took a detour and there Jude was in a café called the Blue Lagoon, propping up the bar just as Jack had predicted. When they walked in he turned round and waved, as if they were old friends and he'd been expecting them.

Ceri felt a wobble inside her chest, her breathing suddenly shallow. She stopped and forced herself to breathe deeply. She knew Pepe was right. If she didn't face this, face him, the mystery surrounding it would follow her like the smell of an old woman's perfume for the rest of her life. She needed to know.

# FORTY

## Ceri

The next day Ceri worked the breakfast shift at Bar South. She brought the pending brunch orders to the bar and instructed the new waitress. Her first shift in a month had been gruelling, people wanting pancakes, blueberry muffins and smoothies, which she'd had to prepare herself. It was time to consider more serious work. She was tired of running.

Jack had popped in and was making himself a smoothie. The whine and whirr of the food processor filled the bar.

'So, did you find him?' he asked, adding a load of blue-berries into the processor and switching it on.

'Yes.' Ceri untied her apron, folding it neatly as she spoke to him.

Jack nodded, he was strutting back and forth to the beat of the music, his blond hair flopping back and forth.

'He was exactly where you suggested. We arranged to meet today but I'm having second thoughts.' Ceri poured herself a glass of water. 'I'm not sure it matters who he is, but Pepe thinks it's important. Anyway, he's a complete lunatic and a drunk.'

'Oh, for sure, but he is charismatic. Truth is, you can't let shit like that go. It'll fuck with your head, man.'

Ceri loved the way Jack was as loose as elastic. She smiled up at him, appreciative of the care.

'I'll hear Jude out but after that, I don't want to see him again.'

'By the way, I think your father called. I mean your real father.' He smiled. 'Seemed to think you'd gone missing according to Faye.'

Ceri was untying her apron, and felt a flutter of panic. She'd read the messages from her mother. 'Oh God, when did he call?'

'Last week, I think. Ask Faye.'

'I don't know who Faye is.'

'Course not, sorry.'

She should call, she thought. Instead she was going to see a man who claimed to be her father. It felt wrong. 'I dropped him a text this morning. Lost my phone, but someone handed it in, can you believe that?' she said, feeling the need to explain her selfishness.

Jack shrugged. 'You'd do the same, wouldn't you?'

'I guess I would,' she said, her mind still on her parents. She'd have to call them this evening.

She went and changed, shoving her leg into her tight jeans knowing Pepe was pacing around impatiently outside. He'd sacrificed an afternoon of surfing to accompany her and she felt grateful, but it meant she couldn't back out. They'd arranged to meet Jude for a coffee in a small café overlooking Clovelly Beach.

After the trip, working at the café had seemed like a slog. Equally, it felt impossible to think how her life was before: up at six, in the City by eight, suited and booted. It was her mother who'd persuaded her to do the law conversion degree instead of an MA in English. She was still living at home and had talked to her mother about wanting to be a journalist. Her mother was stretched out on a yoga mat practising breathing techniques. She'd offered Ceri a sideways glance as she bent down to touch her toes.

'What's up?' her mother said, stretching her arms up this time.

'I'm thinking of doing an MA,' Ceri said. 'Journalism.'

'Really?' her mother said, taking a long deep breath, counting to five before she breathed out, her mouth in the shape of an O. 'Journalism is low paid and you'll be expected to work all hours. It's very competitive. Why not do a law conversion?' She took in another breath, trying to catch up with the instructor.

'I'm not sure it's really me,' Ceri said.

'Of course it's you. You'll earn lots of money and there's so many areas of interest,' her mother had said, 'and you'll be your own woman.'

Her mother had no idea what that law conversion degree took out of her, how little it had to do with what Ceri wanted from her life, and yet she'd obediently followed the advice. As her mother had predicted, Ceri had been so good at it she'd risen to the top in under ten years.

She'd been as miserable as hell, though.

She slammed the locker door shut. She could hear the café filling up for lunch, the clatter and snap and crunch of the kitchen. While they were away, she and Pepe had talked a lot about Jude and what happened that night but it was Pepe who was pushing for a conclusion. She'd agreed to this to please him. They'd talked about their future too. They both knew that it was time to face reality. She scooped her hair up into a knot, decided not to bother with make-up, pulled on her Converse and wrapped the laces around her ankles. Her cotton polo-neck jumper itched around the collar. Winter was on its way, but winter in Sydney wasn't like winter back home. She found Pepe waiting for her, leaning against the wall, hands wedged into his pockets, the sound of the café's kitchen resonating. He looked up and smiled, his eyes soft and welcoming. As soon as she stepped up to him, she felt calmer.

'Por fin!' he said. 'You look great. How was it?'

'Busy,' she said. 'I don't know how long I can keep this up.'

'Keep what up?'

'Blocking out real life.'

'I know, I'm dreading my next shift,' he said. 'We need to make some decisions soon.'

They walked through the park and the warren of residential streets, the houses getting more spread out and architecturally designed as they got closer to the coast. Back in London, Ceri had always liked to see how people lived, the paintings on their walls, or rows of books and ornaments, but here it was all about views, luxuriant garden furniture, and the relationship a house had to the outside world.

Although the future had been something they'd talked about on the trip, they hadn't arrived at a conclusion. Everything felt so tentative, what with the transient nature of their set-up and the fact that their real life belonged in two different countries. She couldn't go back to working as a business lawyer – she'd grown out of that world – and wondered if it was too late to retrain as a journalist. Before going away, Pepe had worked for a charity rehoming Palestinians. Maybe she could use her legal expertise in the charity sector. Pepe thought she should develop her painting, but watching her mother, nervously eyeing the red dots while circulating during her exhibitions, put her off.

As they drew closer to Clovelly, she became more unsettled. It felt wrong to be meeting Jude behind her parents' back. But she trusted Pepe. She knew he had a point. They decided on taking the coastal path. Walking allowed them time to talk and helped ease the sense of disquiet that had built up overnight. The blue sky was clear of cloud, the air crisp, the light sharp. The surf was up, the surfers bobbing about on the horizon waiting for the next big wave just short of the break. One look at the light shimmering on the water was enough to lift Ceri's heart. She squeezed Pepe's hand and he responded by kissing her fingers.

'Guapa,' he said. 'It's going to be okay.'

'I should have spoken to Mum, first,' she said, 'at least let her know.'

'If you'd spoken to your mum, you wouldn't be doing this,' he said.

He was right, but it felt wrong all the same. They fell into a steady rhythm, their footsteps padding along in unison. Ceri looked down at the pavement at the burned stains of bubble gum, at the moss peeking through the cracks in the tarmac, the patina of years giving the ground texture. She'd felt safe in Sydney, a thousand miles from her past, but now she felt a bubble of anxiety expanding in the centre of her chest.

As if sensing her angst, Pepe swung her to a halt, picking up a loose strand of hair that was caught in her lips. 'Whatever he has to say, remember he comes with his own agenda. You need to take on board what he says and then talk to your mother before making any conclusions. Ultimately, it doesn't have to change who you are. Try to stay calm.' He tapped the end of her nose. 'I'm here for you.'

The breeze swept their hair off their faces. She felt a brief moment of elation knowing she'd found someone who could read her moods, wasn't threatened by them. 'I really appreciate you coming, but I can't shift this feeling that my life is about to change. Again.'

'It already has,' he said. 'You're behind the times, mi amor.'

She smiled back at him. It was true, meeting Pepe had changed her. She looked down at the rocks, at the grey pools of sea water, life crammed into the cracks eroded by years of waves breaking across stone. Two boys were out with their nets, trousers rolled up to their knees, caps wedged on backwards to protect their necks from the sun. She realised that she'd been running from something for a long time, although she had no idea what. And for the first time she felt as if she was going to confront the very thing she'd tried to escape, not Jude exactly but an inexplicable fear that had wedged itself deep inside, about her future and who she was. Ever since Jude had said: *You were born on Christmas Day,* she'd felt some deep internal shift.

The sound of their footsteps matched the beating rhythm of her heart. She could easily change her mind, she thought, turn back, and yet she kept moving forward.

They arrived slightly out of breath, having jogged the last few hundred yards. Pepe's idea, probably to take her mind off the meeting. Jude was sitting on the terrace outside, reading. As they walked towards him, he put the book face down on the table and stood up, holding out his hand to Pepe. Ceri sat down quickly. She didn't want to shake his hand or kiss or do anything that drew her closer to him because it felt like a betrayal, more towards her father than anything.

She gave him a nod, picked up his book: *Aboriginal Myths, Fables and Legends.* Somehow, she'd got him down as a man who read thrillers.

'The land is my mother, my mother is the land,' Jude said. 'Aborigine communities were far more connected to Mother Earth than we are.'

'I don't know much about their culture,' she said.

'They're spiritual people, wise people.' Jude's words hung in the air, weighty and thick. 'For them, the concept of individualism doesn't exist. Aboriginal dreamtime,' Jude picked up his book and waved it around. 'Myths, stories, rituals connected the people to the earth. The Aborigines, or what's left of them, believe that with the death of collective dreaming we're witnessing the death of our planet. They see the degeneracy in what we call progress.' He sat forward, leaning on his elbows. 'The saddest thing about the modern world is that not only are we suffering a massive list of biological extinctions, there is even starker evidence of major cultural extinctions and with them, basically, we're losing collective wisdom.'

Ceri was surprised by Jude's passionate stance. He was an intense man, with sharp edges. She felt Pepe sit up.

'So you're making a documentary about the Aboriginal dreamtime?' Pepe asked.

Jude shook his head. 'It's as much about an inherent wisdom that has been lost due to colonialisation. People blame capitalism, the use of fossil fuels, and general human greed for the destruction of this planet, and obviously an easy solution of choosing cleaner energy would help, it's essential. But this thinking goes a long way back to Middle Eastern imperialism, colonialist destruction. We are now literarily bleeding the world dry. I believe the destruction of the indigenous people has contributed to a collective blindness towards climate change. Native American Indians had a similar inherent wisdom in regards to their relationship with this planet . . .'

Ceri turned to see where the waitress had got to, catching Jude's eye.

'I'm sorry, I'm boring you.' His face flushed red. 'I've ordered pancakes. I hope you don't mind. And some tea.'

'I'll have a smoothie,' she said. She could feel her own defences rising. She didn't want Pepe to be interested in anything Jude had to say, even if it was akin to their own thinking, when he hadn't met her real father. It felt wrong.

'I'll go for a beer, and it'll be good to eat someone else's pancakes,' Pepe said. Pepe's eyes were warm and shining. She was grateful that he was able to be open at least, because she felt the opposite, as if her body was folding in on itself. Jude's eyes danced around the café, everywhere but on her.

Her phone buzzed in her pocket. It was unlikely to be her mother as it was still the middle of the night back home. Whoever it was, it wasn't more important than this.

'So you're a documentary filmmaker? Cool,' Pepe said.

'Well, I'm on my last lap. I get the feeling this is my ultimate series,' Jude said.

'And you're from England?' Pepe said.

'Yep. Been here for a few months now, meant to go back for a few weeks but then I saw Ceri was here, and I thought why not stay and continue my research.'

Ceri felt the punch of his words, a shot of adrenaline spurred by fear belted through her body. The waitress appeared but everything felt distanced and slow, as if Ceri were seeing it all from behind a lens: Jude's lined face smiling, the half-moon creases around his mouth, Pepe's head nodding, his hair flopping over his face, his fingers clasped together as if in prayer, the waitress's polite introduction, the way her ponytail bobbed up and down.

'What can I get you guys?'

'I'll have some pancakes and a beer and Ceri will have a blueberry smoothie,' Pepe said, laying his hand on her thigh.

'I'll have a beer as well,' Jude said.

As soon as the waitress was out of earshot, Pepe said: 'You need to see how strange this whole thing is. Ceri doesn't know you, so when you talk about her as if she does, it leaves her feeling pretty shaky. I'm going to be straight with you. It's creeping her out and I'm not happy about it either.' He sat back. Up until now he'd always presented this happy-go-lucky persona, even in the kitchen when tensions were high. 'You see, you seem to know who Ceri is, but Ceri has no idea who you are.' Pepe's smile was tight-lipped, but still warm, a sparkle in his eye.

Jude leaned forward, touching Pepe's arm. 'You've got nothing to worry about, my friend. I'm not here to cause trouble.' He turned to Ceri. 'Actually, Ceri, I spoke to your mother last night. She's coming over. She wants to talk to you herself before I put my size ten feet in it.' He held up his hands. 'I feel I should respect her wishes.'

'My mum's coming here?'

'Yes. And I think it's better if we talk afterwards. You see we were friends once, your dad as well . . .'

'What, so Mum has interfered?'

Ceri felt a tight knot of anger forming in her chest. The sun was blinking on the sea, blinding her for a second. She reached into her rucksack to find her sunglasses and felt herself retreat behind them. The thought of her mum walking into *her* world made her throb with rage.

'Why now? It's a little late don't you think?'

'It was a weird coincidence, walking into the bar, seeing you in person, I mean I believe in synchronicity and . . .'

'You know what, I'm not interested,' Ceri said to Jude. 'It doesn't matter what happened back then. Firstly, I know my father, he's the man who has loved me and brought me up.' She saw a ripple of panic spread across Pepe's face. 'Secondly, this is my mother's problem, not mine.'

'Cariño, tranquila!'

'No, I will not stay calm.'

She stood up, the chair clattered to the floor, making the neighbouring table of middle-aged women jump. She heard someone knock over a cup of coffee. 'Hey!' they shouted.

'Don't you understand what this means? It means my parents have lied to me their entire life, or at least my mother has. It means my father isn't my father, or *might* not be,' standing akimbo she did a couple of air quotes. 'It means that nobody has thought about how this affects me.' She pointed at Jude. 'You, especially.'

Jude stood up. 'Listen, this isn't about what happened back then, I . . .' She saw his hands were shaking. 'I didn't mean for this to happen.'

'Oh please. This is exactly what you wanted. Well, if you think I'm going to put my arms around you and say *Daddy,* you're mistaken. You can't just walk into someone's life and tell them their whole life has been a fabrication.'

'But . . .' Jude went to speak but Ceri swivelled round and ran. She heard Pepe mutter something to Jude and felt him come running after her. She pushed past a bunch of surfers, their light-hearted banter grating against the internal war in her head. She picked up her pace, blinded by her tears, heading down the cliff path, stumbling a little at the rough nature of it, and onto the beach. She didn't want this man. She'd always believed she was her father's favourite. Had lived with a feeling of guilt because of it. And yet, that feeling of disconnection, not being one of them.

'Ceri, para!'

Ceri turned and shook her head at Pepe, who was chasing her. 'Leave me alone!'

Pepe reached out to her, grabbing her wrist. 'I'm here for you.'

'You don't understand, this changes everything. I don't even know who I am anymore.'

'You're overreacting.'

'What!' She snapped her wrist out of his grasp and ran towards the road. Pepe turned back and walked towards Jude. In her pocket, her phone buzzed. She dug down into her pocket realising then it was a phone call not a message, seeing at the same time a message from her mother, which she must have sent in the middle of the night. The phone continued to ring. The number was a local number, she answered it.

'Yes?'

'Hello, my name is Adrian, I'm calling on behalf of the UK Foreign Office. Am I speaking to Ceri Hawkins?' Ceri was tempted to say no, but then a well of nerves fluttered inside her chest. Had something happened? She was panting as she raced on.

'Yes, speaking.' Ceri's breathing made it hard for her to hear, the tremor of anxiety was growing, tightening in her chest. A dog was barking at the sea, running back and forth chasing the waves as Ceri came up to the coast road. She felt as helpless as that mutt, up against something bigger than her.

'We've had a call from a Mr Roland Hawkins, your father. He's been trying to get in touch for some time and he's concerned for your welfare.'

'I'm sorry, what did you say?' She cupped her hand over her ear so that she could hear better, turning her back to the road. The sea was crashing into the shore, the wind had picked up, parting her hair so that it flicked wildly onto her face, like thickened thread. The cars were thrusting past her, music blaring out of windows. She could see the surfers far out, bobbing up and down like crows on the horizon. The dog had stopped barking and was bolting towards the road.

'We've had a call from your father. He's reported you as missing. We were told that you'd picked up your phone from your local police station and we just wanted to check that everything was well.'

Ceri felt numb. She was so filled with rage she couldn't compute. 'Tell my father I am safe, but that I don't want to speak to him. I am now in touch with my *real* father.'

There was a moment's silence. 'I'm sorry to have disturbed you,' Adrian said. 'I will relay your message back to your . . . er father.'

When she ended the call the wash of the tide ringing in her ears, she whispered, 'But he isn't my father.' That thought spurred her forward. She rushed blindly across the road, heard the cars tooting, then the unmistakable sound of crunched metal and tarmac. She thought immediately of the dog but when she spun round on her heel, it was Jude lying flat out on the road, his arm reaching out towards her. But the real collision was the one that happened inside. Something messy and knotted, tight as a fist.

She heard someone scream, then realised it was herself.

# FORTY-ONE

## Ceri

Ceri sat outside the emergency ward waiting, her arms tightly wrapped around herself to still the growing anxiety. Jude had been rushed away for an emergency MRI. He was still unconscious as they rolled him out of the ambulance, his head cradled within padded support, his face unmoving, a bandage wrapped around the gash on his forehead, his red hair brushed off his face by the kind touch of the paramedics, thick and stiff with dried blood.

Feeling hollowed out by a mix of guilt and grief, she slumped forward. Pepe laid his hand on her back. She found herself thinking of her father, remembering the moments they'd shared. One winter he'd made her a sledge. How old was she then? She must have been six or seven because Savanah was still a baby. She found him in the shed one day planing a piece of wood, his strong forearms going back and forth see-sawing the edges, sanding it smooth and running his hands along the wooden blade to check for stray splinters. She asked him what he was doing but he said it was a surprise. He had measured, sawed and sanded for days, finally tying a piece of rope to it so that she could haul the sledge up the hill. He presented it to her and she remembered how she'd been so delighted and then upset because there was no snow. Trust me, it'll snow soon, he said. A few days later it snowed. He whistled for her one morning and told her to hurry and they went out together, his big hand wrapped around hers, tugging the sledge behind. They climbed up Parliament Hill, him in his sheepskin coat, her wearing her Christmas outfit and favourite red bobble hat and mittens. They'd gone up and down that hill for hours and she'd felt loved, lucky to have her father to herself for those few hours. Looking back, she realised he'd made the effort because he was concerned she'd feel left out after her sister was born. He *was* her father.

Ceri stood up, walked up to the nurse at reception whose head was bent over some paperwork behind a closed window, her finger tracing a line of names. She didn't look up.

'Excuse me,' Ceri said, tapping on the glass.

The nurse took her time finishing whatever it was that she was doing, then acknowledged her with a frown, pulling the glass window back just a nudge.

'I was just wondering if you had any news on a patient who came in about an hour ago?'

The nurse looked at her blankly. 'Name of the patient?'

Ceri felt a wash of hopelessness. 'Jude. I don't know his full name.'

'And you are?' Her curt tone felt like a sharp blade on skin.

Ceri was tempted to say she was his daughter but how could she be if she didn't know his name. 'I'm just a friend.'

'Then I'm afraid I can't help you.'

'Any idea who *would* be able to help? I have no idea what's going on.'

Ceri was crying, unable to control the overwhelming feeling of helplessness. The nurse finally softened.

'Let me try to find out where he is.' The nurse punched the keys on her computer, picking up the phone, covering the mouthpiece to speak to Ceri. 'Why don't you sit down, I'll tell you as soon as I find out what's going on.' She handed Ceri a wad of tissues.

Ceri mopped her face and stepped towards the pale green bucket chairs, the weight of her legs slowing her down. She kept thinking how mean she'd been and how awful he looked in the ambulance – pallid and thin.

Pepe pulled her towards him. 'Shhh, now. He's going to be fine.' He put his arm around her, and she let him cradle her head, unable to fight any longer.

'You don't know that.'

'No, I don't know for sure but gut feeling tells me that he's going to be okay.' He took her hand and squeezed it. 'I'm going to get you some tea. It will help.'

He came back five minutes later with a Styrofoam cup full of steaming hot peppermint tea. Ceri looked at him, saw the concern and warmth in his eyes.

'You should call your mother. She'd know whom to call,' he said. 'Assuming he has a family.'

Ceri, finding it hard to speak, shook her head. 'I can't face her right now.'

'Your dad?'

Ceri remembered the conversation she'd had with the man at the Foreign Office.

'I can't face him either. Besides, it's five thirty in the morning in the UK.'

Pepe nodded. 'Right, well I'll let them know what's happened at Bar South first, and then give me your mother's number and *I'll* call her after that. Six forty-five isn't unreasonable.'

'She doesn't wake up until eight.'

'Well, I think this is an exception, don't you?'

Ceri bent over her knees. 'Thank you.'

She scraped around in her bag for her mobile, scrolling to find her mother's number and handed it to him.

The woman at reception had managed to track down Jude's movements through St Vincent's Hospital, explaining that someone was on their way to escort her to ICU. Pepe was outside making the phone call to her mother. He'd been a while. Inside, the chambers of the hospital were ringing with an odd muted sound of monitors, voices, and the padded footsteps of the medical staff. The smell of illness and detergent clashing like oil and water, the sense of calm and urgency pushing up against each other in equal measure. Ceri had never liked hospitals, not since the endless rounds of fertility treatment. To Ceri, it felt as if they were all trapped in an alternate universe, floating, suspended in time.

Pepe walked through the main revolving doors, which sucked and swished as he entered the hallowed space of the hospital.

'Couldn't get through. I've had to leave your mother a message.'

'Shit, maybe they're on their way.'

'Tim said not to worry about a thing, he's got us both covered and please could you let him know how Jude is. Weird, he was actually quite nice. Nothing like an accident to bring the best out in people.'

Ceri felt empty. She hadn't thought about work, but she imagined Pepe's absence would cause chaos. 'It's all my fault. I shouldn't have lost my cool.'

'Ceri, it's not your fault. It was an accident. Jude ran out into the road, he'd downed a whiskey in the time it took me to get back to his table, and then ran off after you. I watched him, he just didn't look. The poor guy who was driving probably didn't see him until the very last minute. The police have asked for witnesses and I had to put myself forward. From where I was standing, Jude stepped out into the road without looking.'

'Well he wouldn't have been running if I hadn't shouted at him.' She felt weak, there was a permanent metallic taste in her mouth, she was starving, even though the idea of food repulsed her, and her breasts felt bruised. Her period must be due, she thought. She tried to remember when her last period was but couldn't.

Pepe crouched down in front of her chair, his knees bulging out of his jeans like two cricket balls. He forced her to look him in the eye.

'I managed to bring you some food,' he said, proffering a brown paper bag with some snacks inside. 'When I went to speak to Tim I passed the hospital café. I just thought, knowing you, you're starving.'

Ceri took the bag, looked inside. There was a healthy-looking brown bread sandwich packed with avocado, hummus and vegetables, along with a freshly squeezed orange juice and a brownie.

She thought for a minute. It was just a hunch, probably hope muddling her thinking, but what had she to lose?

'Could you do me a favour?'

'Claro que sí,' he said, biting into his own sandwich.

Ceri wanted to ask him to get her a pregnancy test, but she realised that was a mistake. She'd have to go herself. 'Can you just wait here while I go to the loo? I'm expecting someone to take me up to the ICU any minute,' she said.

'Sure.'

She picked up her bag and went to find the pharmacy. As she turned, she saw him leaning on his knees, eating his sandwich, and felt a wave of gratitude. She pushed open the swing doors, exposing the sound of a siren, and followed the signs to the pharmacy, which was on the opposite side of the courtyard.

In the pharmacy she was confronted with a few brands of pregnancy tests. She'd tried them all, believing if she switched brands the test would be positive. She grabbed the most expensive one, paid and stuffed it into her bag. She got back to find Pepe in exactly the same position as she left him.

'Where did you go? The bathroom is just there.' He pointed to the sign for the loo.

'Sorry, didn't see it,' she said.

Pepe's phone rang. He dug it out of his pocket and said, 'I have to take this.' He jumped up, phone already pressed to his ear, and walked off. As she watched him leave, one hand in his pocket like a cocky young teenager, she wondered what call could be so urgent. Then she felt a tap on her shoulder. She turned to find a male nurse standing behind her.

'Ceri?'

Ceri nodded, her stomach tightening ready for the punch of bad news. 'How is he?'

'He's in the ICU. I've been asked to come and get you. If you'd like to follow me.' The orderly started towards a different set of swing doors. Ceri followed, her mouth dry; her chest felt like an empty bag of air, hollowed out. She followed the young man down the corridor. She didn't want to ask how Jude was again. The fact that he hadn't answered directly didn't bode well. She imagined she was going to be led to an office where someone, probably a consultant, would explain Jude's condition. An awful feeling of doom trickled through her body. What if he *was* her biological father? She'd barely had a chance to know him. She felt as if she'd been running from something she didn't understand and no matter how hard she'd tried, she hadn't been able to outrun it.

She was shown into another waiting room. The hushed sound of the ICU ward left her feeling close to death. Only the sound of monitors could be heard, the purr of machines keeping patients stable. The nurses talked in low whispering voices. It was as if she'd disappeared into a vacuum.

Two minutes later a doctor arrived, bringing with him an authority that made Ceri shake. He had a thick blade of hair, not too dissimilar to Pepe's, that fell across his forehead. There was a kindness in his eyes that left Ceri wanting to cry. 'You must be Ceri Hawkins,' the doctor looked down at his notes. 'Are you his daughter?'

This time she decided to be honest. 'Yes, I think so,' she said. 'Sorry, this is going to sound really strange, but I've only just discovered the possibility that he may be my father but I'm not sure.'

Two vertical lines scored his forehead. 'Apparently they haven't managed to speak to your mother yet, but they've spoken to a work colleague.'

Ceri felt a wash of shame. She wondered if she should explain further and decided against it. This man hadn't the time to contemplate the ins and outs of her mother's chaotic sexual history. The doctor was scrolling through something on his electronic notepad.

'The first thing you need to know is that he's well and in recovery. Are you aware if he's on any medication?'

Ceri shook his head. 'I don't think so. I'm not sure if it's important but I think he's an alcoholic.'

'Good to know,' the doctor said. 'Follow me.'

'Is he going to be okay? How was his MRI?'

The doctor held the door open for her and smiled. 'He's had a heavy blow to the head and is at present sedated. The team decided against an induced coma, which would have meant his brain was effectively switched off, because we didn't feel the injuries were severe enough. So in effect, that's good news. That said, we may still need that option. The next twenty-four hours are crucial.'

Ceri went to speak, but he continued, stopping outside a door. 'It's nothing to worry about, it's pretty much normal practice when there's been a head injury. An induced coma allows us to mitigate any swelling, but the MRI scan suggested that the swelling wasn't sufficiently severe. We were divided as to the best route to take. The downside of a coma of course is that he would temporarily lose the ability to breathe without the assistance of a mechanical ventilator.'

'May I ask what *you* thought, I mean if the team was divided?'

The doctor held her with his honest brown eyes. 'I felt sedation was sufficient. The most important thing at this stage is that he's not suffering any pain. Apart from the head injury, he has a fractured fibula.' He looked at her, the concern shaping his frown. 'His right shin, basically,' he said.

'But he's going to survive?'

'We're optimistic, but we're just not sure if there's been any serious tissue damage.' He smiled, his eyes concentrated on hers. 'The good news is that Jude opened his eyes and engaged with the doctors before passing out again. He asked for you, actually, which is why I assumed you were his daughter. I certainly don't want to make any prognosis

293

quite yet but I would say the odds are in his favour.' He looked down at her clenched fists. 'Would you mind washing your hands,' he said.

Ceri hurriedly washed and scrubbed. She was utterly uncoordinated, unable to make the soap dispenser work. As soon as she returned, they travelled down the corridor, one side of which was a wall of windows looking out onto the courtyard. The doctor opened the door to Jude's room. His straightforward approach made her feel as if Jude was in safe hands, but nothing had prepared her for the paraphernalia of Jude's condition: the medical equipment, the screens monitoring every angle of his body, the oxygen tube, the sacks of saline and medicine pumping into his arm. She could see the shock of his red hair peeping out of his bandaged head. The rest of him was underneath a light sheet. She went to stand beside him, saw his face, clean now and at peace. She realised he was quite handsome when his face was stilled by sleep. His freckles mirrored her own. His hands were placed on top of the sheet, his skin pale and translucent. She laid her fingers gently on his.

'I'm here,' she said. She was following some deep internal instruction that pulled her towards him like a thread through a needle.

# FORTY-TWO

## Lori

For the last leg of the journey Roland had slept soundly beside her. He'd barely spoken to either of them throughout the entire flight, remaining unavailable behind a wall of concentration, either on his airport novel or on the screen. Although he'd been polite, he'd achieved an aloofness she barely thought him capable of. It was extraordinary how he managed to keep his distance and yet remain inoffensive, at least to Anna. She'd been embarrassed when he waved Anna's offer of payment away but then barely talked to her after that, apart from to discuss the airline's menu. Lori had been relieved when he joked at Anna's vegetarian option. At least he'd noticed.

It was clear to Lori that Anna wasn't keen on air travel by the way she'd gripped the arm of the seat as the plane lifted off. It was after supper, when the wine had loosened her tongue, that she finally told Anna about the phone call she'd had with Jude.

'Why didn't you tell me before?' Anna asked, stirring powdered milk into her decaffeinated coffee. 'I mean it must be a huge relief to know she's alive, even if she still hasn't called you.'

'I was waiting for the right moment,' Lori said, wiping her face with the flannel they'd given her to clean her hands. 'I wasn't sure if you'd talked to him so I didn't mention you were coming too.' She bent closer. 'It's just that I haven't told Roland.'

'Oh dear, you do have a habit of withholding information, Lori.' Anna frowned.

Lori felt her jaw tense. She'd forgotten how forthright her friend could be at times.

'Probably because of some childhood need to keep some part of myself hidden from my parents when I was young,' she said, in attempt to lighten the mood.

They both laughed. 'Don't try the psychobabble on me,' Anna said. 'I'm immune.'

After a pause she asked, 'So, how did he sound?'

Lori thought for a second. The conversation with Jude had been running over and over in her mind. He'd been so accommodating, sympathetic even, contrite. It had left her feeling disconcerted.

'I told him that I needed to tell Ceri myself,' she said.

'And?' Anna asked.

'He said he understood.' She bent closer and whispered in Anna's ear, making it clear why she hadn't spoken about the conversation before because of Roland's proximity. 'He asked if he was right about Ceri being his daughter. I answered truthfully. It's highly likely but you need to consider Ceri and Roland, because no matter what a DNA test reveals, he's her father. He thought about that for a moment and then said "of course"'

Lori watched as Anna's face registered the conversation. Her eyes welled up. Lori thrust her hand on Anna's, aware that Roland would detect the sudden movement, but when she turned to look his eyes were closed.

'He's not a bad man,' Anna said.

Lori wasn't sure how to respond, because it was true; he'd tried to make amends and agreed not to speak to Ceri, but equally he'd have done well to speak to Lori before he smashed into Ceri's life. She swallowed any need to spout out a complaint. She'd forgone that right.

When Anna went to the loo, she nudged Roland and tried to tell him about Jude. But he'd shaken his head, looked at her with solemn eyes.

'Not now, Lori, I haven't the mental space for it. It's just one more thing you've withheld.'

Lori sighed. What *did* he have the mental space for then? 'Well, I thought if you knew she was alive and well, you'd cancel the flights.'

'It seems we don't know each other very well,' he said and closed his eyes.

'Oh, that's not fair,' she said, but his eyes remained shut.

Anna returned from the loo. Most of the passengers were sleeping and the cabin was drenched in an unnatural murky darkness. Lori could see the dawn breaking through one oval window that someone had failed to close.

'How do you feel about seeing him?' she said to Anna.

'I don't know. I keep thinking about the time we got back together after your wedding. He's never been unfaithful since that one time,' (Anna said it as if it wasn't Lori who he'd been unfaithful with) 'and I keep wondering what it is that has made him want to reach out. I mean, we haven't been great over the last few months, but I sensed something had shifted, and I couldn't work out what it was.'

'Maybe it was meeting Ceri for the first time,' Lori said.

Then Anna whispered into her ear. 'I'm worried about Roland. He's barely said a word.'

'Me too,' she whispered back. She had an awful feeling he was going to turn Ceri against her and she didn't blame him.

# FORTY-THREE

## Anna

Anna felt a wash of relief as the plane smoothly met the runway at Sydney Airport – she really hated flying. Outside she could see a soft pink sky blushing the horizon. The foreignness of the land not as extreme as it had been when they'd landed in Doha, which was flat, the air unnaturally air-conditioned. She'd felt as if she'd been transported into the future with its consumerist universe and extreme architecture. Lori had seemed unfazed and Roland had failed to acknowledge the fact that they were back on solid ground, barely looking up from the book he was reading. It seemed they weren't talking. For the first leg of the journey she'd sat in between them like a small child between warring parents. Roland had bought the tickets – Business Class – and had waved her away when she'd asked how much. But after that he had been quite cold. She'd expected him to confront her, ask her opinion, but he'd barely uttered a word.

Lori had said, 'At least she's alive.' But Anna knew that she was dreading speaking to Ceri. It was a big lie to hide and Anna wondered how on earth Lori had managed to do it for so long.

It was late afternoon. Despite making a supreme effort to do everything recommended for long-haul travel, her body felt like it had been through a mangle – a physical rendition of Dalí's melted clock. The journey had taken a lifetime and she hadn't managed to get much sleep until the last leg of the journey, while Lori and Roland had slept soundly beside her. Anna's mind had danced athletically through all the possible outcomes of a confrontation with Jude. The fact that he'd been so amenable to Lori had taken her by surprise. She'd found herself thinking of Lori and Roland's second wedding. The ceremony had been in a small church in Chelsea. Anna had arrived late, hoping to slip in at the back and go unnoticed. An usher greeted her, whispering in her ear, 'Bride or Groom?'

'Both,' she said, and so she'd been directed to Lori's side where she had perched on the end of the pew, apologising even though she hadn't disturbed anyone.

She'd gone expecting Jude to be absent but searched for him in the congregation anyway.

Lori and Roland were just at the point of taking their vows – again. Anna couldn't help but note the irony. Maybe the fact they were spoken in English would have more impact, she'd thought. The atmosphere was solemn as people strained to hear. Sun slanted down onto pink, yellow and lilac hats on Roland's side of the church, the stained-glass windows giving off a soft blue and green hue. That's when she caught sight of Jude staring at her, his serious eyes pinning her down; a small curve of his mouth was as close as he got to a smile. Her mouth felt instantly dry because he'd told her he wouldn't go. She turned away. Her head willing her to ignore him but her body betraying good sense.

Later, when they had all thrown confetti and Roland and Lori had stood for the photographer outside the church,

Jude had sidled up to her and whispered in her ear, 'You look beautiful.'

Surprised by the sadness in his voice, she'd turned to him.

'I miss you,' he said. 'I miss being me with you. You have always made me want to be a better person.' His lips trembled, so he bit them.

It was impossible to move without causing a problem for the photographer, so she clenched her jaw, closed her eyes and tried to block out his presence. She couldn't resist her reply. 'Except when we were in the Dordogne.'

'That is the biggest regret of my life. There is no one else like you. It's always been you.'

Tears slipped down her cheek. She had wanted to hear those words so desperately, and now she was hearing them she realised how scared she was.

'You will hurt me,' she said. 'And I don't want to be hurt again.'

'I know,' he said. 'I don't want that either.' He looked at her, his face softened with emotion. Then the group dispersed and more confetti was thrown, and Jude slipped away into the back streets of Chelsea.

Anna had spent the rest of the day looking for him, an ache blossoming in his absence.

He'd called her two weeks later and she'd practically fallen on the phone when her mother told her who it was. They met in London, at their favourite restaurant in Soho. It had been a great night, until Jude muttered an apology, changing the mood.

After she'd brushed the apology aside, he'd got down on his knee and proposed. She'd known the leap he'd taken was a big one. He wasn't the marrying type.

'I thought you didn't agree with marriage,' she said, trying not to give anything away.

'That was before I lost you.'

She wondered if she'd truly forgiven him. 'Are you sure this is what you want?'

'I can't imagine a life without you.'

She had thought the same, but her mother had been right; forgiveness had empowered her, set her free. But Jude had left a hole and she felt that loss every day. Just seeing the apprehension in his eyes was enough to fill that hole. She had never stopped loving him. Forgiveness wasn't just about revenge, it was an essential part of love, surely.

'Yes, Jude Elliot, I'll marry you, but please promise me you'll never speak to Lori again.'

And he never had until now. So, really, if Anna thought about it, she had been just as responsible for the break-up of their friendship as Lori. She hadn't been honest either, and she wondered if it was too late now.

The cabin rang with the sound of overhead lockers snapping open, seatbelts clicking their release, along with the rustle of clothing and bags being collected. Anna's skin felt dry and her mouth crisp even though she'd drunk gallons of water, probably because she'd drunk the same amount of red wine. Lori had barely had a sip, apparently she was still suffering after their night of debauchery. This from the girl who could down a bottle and still stay standing. Anna on the other hand was getting a renewed taste for it.

She hadn't warned Jude she was coming – an impromptu visit to the other side of the world felt a little absurd, but here she was – her stomach was beginning to anticipate the reception. It was while they were in the queue for passport control that her phone pinged into life. Lori was scrolling through her messages at the same time.

It was Johnny the sound man. Anna picked it up.

'Hi Johnny, I'm in Sydney, in the queue for passport control, so can't really talk.'

Anna could hear Johnny's laboured breathing, as if he'd just climbed a steep flight of steps. 'Anna, thank God you're there. There's been an accident. Jude had both you and me as his point of contact in case of emergency. He's been taken into hospital.'

A flush of fear left her legs wobbly, as if the bone and muscle had vanished instantly. Of all the confrontations she'd envisaged, she hadn't imagined this one. She had to stop, her eyes blurred and watery. People stepped around her, tutting. Lori and Roland were up ahead.

'Is he okay?'

'He's alive, but apparently he's had a serious head injury. Look Anna, not sure if this anything to worry about, but he's with a woman called Ceri.'

Lori had told her about the conversation she'd had with Jude, how he'd promised not to speak to Ceri.

'No, I know Ceri,' she said, 'so nothing to worry about.' Anna imagined the worst: Jude, flat out and unconscious, Lori's daughter beside him. She was in a daze and she had to be reminded twice by strangers to move forward.

'What's the name of the hospital?' she said.

'St Vincent's.'

'Thank you, I'll go straight there.' She was in such a state of shock she forgot to say goodbye. She went through immigration to find Lori waiting for her.

'Anna, are you okay?' Lori was standing in front of her, pupils as large as two pound coins. 'I've just received a garbled message from Pepe . . .'

'Yes, I know. Jude . . .' Tears pricked her eyes.

'We'll go straight to the hospital,' Lori said, holding her hand.

'Why don't you go and sort out the hire car. I'll take a taxi,' Anna said. She needed time alone. She was suddenly overwhelmed with remorse. She didn't want to lose him, and yet she'd lost him a while back. He'd been dead even though he was alive, and she'd been dead too. But, he'd brought them both back into the land of the living by making life uncomfortable and seeking out the truth.

She loved him. She wished she didn't, but she had no choice.

# FORTY-FOUR

## Lori

Lori was perched on her oversized suitcase outside Sydney
Airport in the drop-off area. She was waiting for Roland,
who had gone to pick up the hire car. There were the
usual comings and goings of airport traffic, families spilling
out of cars to say their last farewell, taxi drivers jumping
out to unload luggage, their hands upturned, waiting for
a tip. Lori felt disconnected from the world. The anticipation of seeing her daughter, telling her the truth, was
beginning to feel impossible to negotiate. She'd talked it
through with Anna who had listened, quietly placing her
hand on hers and advising her not to think about it too
much. But how could she not?

When she listened to Pepe's message on the phone, she
was surprised by how mature and sensible he'd sounded.
He didn't appear to have a Spanish accent, either. She'd
been so convinced by his unsuitability that she felt a flush
of humility. She thought about Ceri, how she'd been
determined to move forward, away from her past. As she
stood outside the airport, aware of the distance between
her and her other children, it was clear to her what Ceri
had been running away from. She felt a wash of shame.

'It's yourself you don't trust,' Anna had said, when
Lori had talked about how Roland complained of her

overprotectiveness towards Ceri. Being next to Anna had allowed her to unravel a little. Anna's calm presence, the way she'd listened to Lori without interrupting, made her acutely aware of the looseness of her own tongue. Roland had sat with his earphones on protecting himself. She understood why, but they needed to confront what was about to happen at some point.

Instinctively she reached into her pocket to call Ceri, the reflex was something she seemed unable to stop. At the same time her phone buzzed and rang. She assumed it was Roland instructing her where to stand. Lori stood up, the case wheeled from underneath her into the road. She just managed to stop it from tipping over, the phone clamped into her ear.

'I'm right in front of you,' he was saying.

She saw Roland driving towards her in a blue four-door BMW, as ever looking in control. He pressed the horn even though she was looking straight at him. He'd parked at an angle which meant people were stuck, unable to get past. Several cars started to toot. Lori ran up to him just as he pulled out again, driving further up towards the front of the queue of people picking up passengers.

Lori piled all the suitcases on top of the big one and pushed it forward with both hands. Finally, Roland came running to help her and they both loaded the suitcases into the boot. She jumped in beside him and laid her hand on his shoulder. He bowed his head. She watched tears drop onto his chinos.

'Roland, can we have a truce, please. We're not going to get through this if we don't work together.'

'I'm sorry, Lori. If it makes you feel better, I'm not angry with you. I just don't know where to start. I've spent the last twenty-eight hours trying to work out what part I played in this whole scenario.'

'I thought you were sleeping,' she said.

'I'm a better actor than you think.' He turned and held her eyes. She saw then a younger Roland; the man she'd loved for so many years. Life can be such a distraction, she thought, from the things we love most.

'We can talk about this later, but I want you to know I love Ceri as my own, nothing has changed, how could it? You don't suddenly wake up and stop loving someone who has done you no harm, but it's because I love her, I want her to know about Jude.'

'I should have told you before,' she said.

'Yes, but you're right – there would be no Ceri if you'd told me when I was a young man. And that thought doesn't bear thinking about.' He put his hand on her knee, then lifted it to stroke her face. His touch felt tender. He hadn't touched her like that in a long while.

'Now, where to?' he said.

'St Vincent's Hospital. We can call Ceri on the way.'

Lori looked up St Vincent's Hospital as Roland indicated to pull out. The GPS instructed them towards an arterial road; Roland indicated, swiftly cutting in front of a car, crossing four lanes of traffic so that he could drive fast. She'd always admired the way he sliced through traffic, even when the city was unfamiliar to him. Their driving styles were similar, although she'd grown more cautious with age. She felt her heart breaking open, the relief that she was going to see Ceri, tell her the truth, clashing with a growing anxiety that the time was near. Anna had been right. Honesty was going to set them all free.

Lori picked up her phone to call Ceri, but it went straight to voicemail. It felt almost pleasurable to feel frustrated at her daughter's unavailability. She was dreading the next twenty-four hours but Roland's words and the way he had stroked her face, had left her with a feeling of hope.

She texted Ceri instead.

*I got Pepe's message. We're in Sydney, on our way to the hospital to see Jude. Anna (Jude's wife) should be there by now. I'm so sorry, Ceri. I've been wrong about so many things. I need to speak to you about the past. I hope you will forgive me. Dad sends his love xx*

It wasn't the best way to deliver a piece of news, but it meant that she had laid down the foundations.

There was no turning back, now.

# FORTY-FIVE

## Anna

Anna entered through the revolving doors of St Vincent's, negotiating her suitcase over a series of ridges just in time before being spat out into the vast reception area. The hospital was slick and modern, a gleaming white beacon to health. Every time Anna entered a hospital – any hospital – she was transported back instantly to the two times she'd suffered a miscarriage. Those years had been her darkest, even darker than when she'd discovered Jude had slept with Lori. Mostly she remembered the blood, the pain and look of despair on Jude's face. The first miscarriage had been medically assisted after discovering the baby was no longer alive, but the second had been classed as a still birth, she had been twenty-eight weeks pregnant. She had asked to see the baby, a girl, beautiful to Anna even in her unformed state, clotted and matted with the scum of afterbirth and blood. She had cried for months afterwards, until she'd been diagnosed with PTSD and referred to a therapist. In a way it was her little girl, Amelie, who had pushed her towards being a therapist herself.

She was told to go to the ICU, which involved a labyrinthine tour of the hospital, her suitcase making a terrible racket. Finally, she arrived on the fourth floor. The receptionist looked at Anna's suitcase before making eye contact.

'Can I help you?'

'I hope so,' Anna said, feeling suddenly foolish, as if she'd mistaken the ICU ward for the arrivals desk. 'I'm looking for Jude Elliot or Ceri Hawkins. She's not a patient, she's . . .'

'You must be Ceri's mother?'

'No, I'm Jude Elliot's wife,' Anna said.

'I see,' the nurse said. 'Your name is?'

'Anna Elliot.'

The nurse buzzed through for someone to contact the doctor.

When Ceri walked through the door, Anna was taken aback at how much like Jude she looked, the ringlets in her hair, the hint of red, the freckles, the direct way in which she looked at Anna, although the similarity seemed to disappear after a few milliseconds, and suddenly Ceri reminded her of Lori. On Facebook it hadn't been so obvious, but in real life it was clear; it was the lightness of her bone structure that was similar to Jude's, a fine chiselled body with sharp edges.

Ceri had turned and they stood staring at each other. Anna noticed the grey rings under Ceri's eyes. She had a fleeting thought she was too late. She stepped forward.

'Ceri, I'm . . .'

'I know who you are,' Ceri said, 'you're Jude's wife, aren't you? My mother said you were on the way.' She reached out and held Anna's arm. 'He's okay,' she said. 'He's okay.' And they stood like that for a while, two strangers holding each other.

'Right, well now I'm here it seems this suitcase feels a little ridiculous.' But it wasn't the suitcase that had left her feeling cumbersome. She felt like an intruder, too loud for the hush of the ward. 'You've spoken to your mother, then.'

Ceri nodded, smiling as she raked her hand through her curly hair, giving it a shake, looking at Anna with Lori's hazel eyes. It was a kind smile, Anna thought. She appeared to be utterly exhausted. 'Is he through here?' Anna pointed towards the corridor that had windows down one side, her voice wobbly with the effort of staying in control. There was an open door.

'I'll take you to him,' Ceri said. She started to walk back down the hallway.

'Wait, I'm going to ask if I can leave this here.'

The nurse on reception popped out from behind the desk. 'Here, give it to me,' she said, wheeling it back and stationing it next to her chair.

'Thank you, that's very kind,' Ceri said. She appeared to be in control, definitely her mother's daughter, Anna thought. She realised as she followed Ceri that she'd been in one huge building after another for the past thirty-six hours. The hospital, like the airport, had that air-conditioned air that left you feeling tired.

Ceri spoke as they travelled down the hallway. 'Jude has been heavily sedated, but they're reducing his meds, slowly bringing him back to the land of the living. I wanted to be here when he wakes up but I think having you here will be much better,' she said.

Anna felt herself blush. 'Well, please don't feel you have to leave. I'd like it if you stayed, actually,' she said. But nothing could prepare her for what she saw next. It felt to her as if Jude had left his body. His face pale as magnesium was turned to the side. She was used to him always being animated and cheeky, a plucky defensive spark in his eye, but his eyes were closed, the lids translucent, marbled with a tiny map of veins. There were monitors and tubes. Jude's body, like an experiment, was in the centre of all the paraphernalia. A PICC line was attached to his arm, the nuts and bolts of it grotesque against the transparency of his flesh.

She felt one tear dribble down her cheek. He looked so still and at peace. Seeing him like this made her realise how he'd been at war with himself for a very long time. She thought of Amelie, dead on the day she was born, blue, covered in mucus and blood. Jude looked as new-born as she had, an innocence to him she hadn't witnessed before.

She held his hand. He was the most troubled soul she'd ever met, but he was *her* troubled soul and she loved him still. She thought about those layers they'd all acquired. She'd always known who Jude was behind the mask he presented to the world. Isn't that what lovers were to each other? A place of refuge.

Fifteen minutes later the doctor arrived. Ceri stood back and Anna tried to take in all the information the doctor was relaying, nodding her head, dabbing her eyes. She still held Jude's wrist as if to keep him from getting up.

'Your daughter has been a trooper,' the doctor said.

Anna turned to Ceri. 'Ceri's not *my* daughter, but she's the daughter of a very dear friend of mine.' Anna watched as the doctor's eyes flitted back and forth, looking confused, and who could blame him? He stood up straight. Took a deep breath.

'Well, we're going to change his catheter and his dressing, so maybe now's a good time to go and get yourself a coffee.'

They went down in the lift in silence, until Anna decided on breaking the ice, still with her case pinned to her side.

'I gather Jude has kicked up a bit of a storm,' she said.

Ceri frowned. The lift doors pinged open. 'Well, I'm sure my mother could have prevented this from happening with a little foresight.' She held the door back while Anna tugged her suitcase out of the lift. 'Is that why she's here?' Ceri's voice was tight. Anna detected an underlying feeling of resentment and anger. She realised that she might need to defend Lori, not something she'd ever envisaged, but it was time they all moved on.

'Well, your mother has her reasons.' Anna felt a wave of fatigue. The image of Jude unresponsive, and the doctor talking about the impact replaying in her mind.

They went to the café, which was full of tempting pastries and protein bars. An Italian coffee machine whistled its way through several espressos, the two girls manning it sliding past each other nimble as children.

'Why don't you grab a seat? What would you like?' Anna said.

'I'll have a mint tea, please.' Ceri went to take Anna's case. 'I may as well take this so you can carry the tray.'

Anna hesitated, as if the suitcase was the only thing holding her upright.

'Why don't you sit down and I'll get these,' Ceri said.

'I'd rather keep busy,' Anna said. She knew her voice was shaky, her movements slow and hesitant.

Ceri took the case and found a seat next to the window. Anna watched Lori's daughter as she settled into the chair. There was something about the way she moved, her profile, the way she used her hands, how her hair curled around her ear. There was no doubt in her mind that this young woman was Jude's daughter.

# FORTY-SIX

## Ceri

Ceri sat in the café a little stunned by the day's events. She felt like an island surrounded by activity: the coffee machine whistling, the hustle and bustle of the kitchen, people coming and going outside in the courtyard. She texted Pepe trying to find out what was keeping him. She still felt sick, exhausted by the stress, remembering the pregnancy test waiting in her bag. She braced herself for her mother's arrival. Of course she was contrite, she'd been caught out. A feeling of dread welled up inside her. Her mother's words could only mean one thing: Jude was her biological father. She wanted Jude to wake up so he could tell his side of the story.

The café faced onto a courtyard with tables outside. There was a wall of windows floor to ceiling. She recognised Pepe as he pushed through the swing doors on the other side of the hospital courtyard and crossed from one side to the other, his phone clamped to his ear. He stopped, turned his back to her, his head bent down, a finger in his other ear to block out the surrounding sound. Who could he be talking to?

She turned to see Anna shuffling towards the counter. Two women were manning the coffee machine, which hissed and clunked as it produced endless Styrofoam cups of coffee. Both girls were buzzing back and forth, their black aprons wrapped tightly around their waists, taking orders, preparing food on a small metal surface, the kitchen behind them brightly lit. Ceri was desperate to get to the bathroom but she didn't want to lose their table. She didn't think for one minute she was pregnant, but she needed to discount it. A part of her wanted it to be true, but she'd learned to manage disappointment as far as having a child was concerned.

Anna nodded at Ceri as she queued up behind a man and his son, a young boy of around five who was jumping up and down with an excitement that felt incongruous, somehow. Ceri looked up to see that Pepe had travelled to the furthest corner, away from the flow of people that used the courtyard to cross from one side of the hospital to the other: a constant flow of white coats, blue overalls and clogs. He was hunched over in the corner, clearly trying to find a place quiet enough.

Finally, Anna sat down with a tray of goodies and shrugged off her raincoat, gesturing for Ceri to help herself. Ceri tucked into a Danish pastry.

'Looks like you were hungry,' Anna said.

'I just needed a sugar hit,' Ceri said. She looked at Anna. There was something about her, her blonde thick hair that was twisted into a pleat, her kind blue eyes and generous mouth, that allowed Ceri to relax a little. 'There's a small possibility I might be pregnant,' she said, the words hurtling out of her mouth before she had a chance to regret it.

Anna's eyes widened. 'Well, that's lovely news. I'm assuming you're happy.'

Ceri blushed, feeling the heat sting her face. 'It's a little early to say and I might well be wrong. It could just be stress. Before I went travelling, I spent three years trying to get pregnant and was unsuccessful, so we weren't careful. I'm not even sure how Pepe feels about it.'

'Most men still think pregnancy is a miracle. I had problems getting pregnant, so I sympathise,' Anna said.

'They couldn't explain it. They finally decided that my ex and I were incompatible. Apparently, there was a way to overcome this, but by that point I'd had enough, so I filed for divorce and went travelling instead. Mum wasn't happy,' Ceri said. 'But maybe you know about that.' And then she started to cry. 'I'm sorry. I think I'm just so tired.' She looked to see if Pepe was off the phone. 'That's my boyfriend, over there in the courtyard.' She pointed to Pepe, who was still on the phone, treading a figure of eight, his elbow cupped in his hand. She wondered for a second time who he was speaking to. 'Life is feeling pretty surreal right now.'

Anna had tears in her eyes as well.

Ceri reached over and patted her hand. 'I'm sorry. I shouldn't be talking about myself,' she said.

Anna shook her head. 'No, you should. It's just, we lost two babies, one was quite late.' Anna mopped her face. If she thought about it, those two babies were Ceri's half siblings, if what she suspected was true. 'I still can't believe this has happened. Jude looked so fragile up there, and he's usually so robust. I know he's caused you a lot of distress, your mother told me all about it – that's partly why we're here – and he hasn't been good, always, but deep down he's not a bad man, really he's not.'

Ceri wondered if 'we' included her mother. She sat back, ate a little bit more of the pastry. The coffee tasted different to the one they served in Bar South. She noticed Pepe had finally finished his call and was scrolling through his messages on his phone. He looked up, probably sensing her eyes on him in the way that lovers do, and waved. He had his hand splayed out to indicate he'd be five minutes. The breeze was pushing his black hair across his face. She watched the way he stood dead straight, his legs hip-width apart as he scrolled. There was something in his stance that told her what he was doing was important.

'The odd thing was that I was coming over to Sydney to ask Jude for a divorce,' Anna was saying. 'But seeing him like that, vulnerable and broken, and yet . . .' Anna reached down into her handbag to retrieve a pack of tissues. 'He looked more like the Jude I remember before drink took him away from me.' She glanced up from unwrapping a tissue, dabbed her eyes and then held Ceri's gaze. 'Who he becomes when he drinks isn't who he is, he becomes a monster, and for years I've been enabling him by turning a blind eye. Watching him lying up there, all these tubes attached to him, the oxygen feeding into his system,' the words dribbled out. She shook her head, 'He seemed at peace. Somehow it reminded me of the man I kept believing in, even when the spaces between him being sober got bigger and bigger.'

Ceri looked down at her plate, gathered the little crumbs with her fingers. She was still hungry. She knew it was important to listen to Anna but a part of her was wondering what Pepe was doing, waiting also for her mother to arrive like an unexploded bomb. She didn't want to hear any of it but she took a deep breath and said, 'I can imagine he was quite fun at one point.' She felt slightly out of her depth, like a child talking to an adult.

'You see, I thought perhaps he fixated on the idea of you being his daughter when he realised we'd never have one of our own.' Anna was pulling at her tissue like it was a knotted up ball of thread she had to unravel. Then she held Ceri's eyes once again. 'If you *are* his child, I think it's important you know that we all played a part, even your father.'

Ceri felt something internal break free; it was the oddest of feelings, like ice-cold liquid travelling through her body, running down her throat, across her chest and reaching into her fingers. She instinctively knew that this was the piece of knowledge she'd been running from for as long as she could remember.

'What do you mean?'

'I've already said too much, I'm sorry. I'm so utterly overwhelmed.' Anna's eyes were wide, she scrunched up the tissue. 'I think we should wait for your mother to arrive. I can imagine this has been difficult, but to understand what's been happening these past few weeks, and perhaps your entire life, you need to know what happened wasn't just your mother's fault. I believe knowledge changes things, for the better. I can tell you my side of the story, but you need to speak to your mother.'

Ceri wished Pepe was next to her. She felt wobbly and uncertain. She started to cry again, shaking her head as if the knowledge could be undone that way. Anna reached across and held her hand. 'I was angry for many years that your mum avoided me rather than tell the truth, but everyone has their reasons,' she said. 'I've learned that much. She was protecting you; actually, in a way your mother protected us all from that truth. I've had plenty of time to think about the part your father and I played in what happened.'

Ceri wasn't sure she wanted to know 'what happened'. But looking at this woman, the way she talked about her mother, Ceri realised she hadn't a clue about her mother's life before she was born.

'But when did this happen?'

'It happened in Dordogne. The four of us went away together.' Anna smiled. 'Honestly, as young people we were hedonistic, reckless and irresponsible. We drank ourselves silly and lost any sense of responsibility or morality for that matter.'

'My mother was reckless?'

Anna laughed. 'Yes, we all were.'

Ceri couldn't compute the idea of her mother being reckless – she was too uptight. She sat and listened to the details of that holiday, her mouth open, as Anna described a woman that appeared like a stranger to her.

'I can't believe you're talking about my mother,' she said.

Anna leaned forward. 'Listen, perhaps it's not my place to say, but I've learned one thing – in the end, forgiveness leaves you stronger. My mother said that it was the best revenge, but I think it's more than that, it's the most generous act of love we have to offer.'

Ceri sighed, a long exhalation of exhaustion. 'Well, I'm not angry with my mother for not telling me who my father was, believe it or not. I'm angry with her for telling me how to run my life, when clearly she'd been so lost at one point, and fucked up her own. She's never allowed me to be lost.' Ceri tore off a strip from her paper napkin. She looked up to see Pepe had disappeared. 'And actually, it took being lost to find myself.'

'Well, I'm not a parent, but I'd say it's probably the hardest job out there and we're all completely unqualified. You won't get it right either – if you get the chance to try – but like your mum, you'll try your hardest. If anything, she's probably like she is because she made those mistakes.'

Ceri was staring at the shredded paper before her, thinking about her mother. She realised that her mother had tried so hard to get it right. She saw then that Pepe was standing over the table.

'Ceri. How are things?' He looked at Anna when he spoke, concern shaping his tentative smile.

'Pepe, this is Anna, Jude's wife and an old friend of my mother's.'

Anna stood up. 'Lovely to meet you,' she said.

Pepe shook her hand, but he was focused on Ceri, and finally crouched down, the constant flow of people outside a distraction. 'You okay?'

She nodded.

'How *is* Jude?' He sat down, a protective arm on her shoulder. 'Is everything okay?'

'Well, it's hard to say just yet,' Anna said, her eyes brimming. 'He's heavily sedated. Apparently there's no damage to the frontal lobe, and the swelling isn't too serious, but I'm assuming we won't know about brain damage until he's conscious. Although my knowledge of neurology is rusty, I'd say it's unlikely. The doctor seems quite positive.' Anna had to dig out another tissue from her bag which she handed to Ceri. Ceri felt a wave of compassion. She looked grey with fatigue, but it was clear to Ceri that this woman loved Jude and her mother also.

'Well, I had better go, and I think you should get some rest,' Anna said, putting on her raincoat and rummaging around in her oversized bag, retrieving a small card, handing it to Ceri. 'Here's a card with my number on it, just in case.' Ceri read: Anna Elliot. Psychotherapist and systemic family therapist. 'Your parents are on their way.'

'We'll be up soon,' Ceri said.

They watched her walk towards the exit, her back straight, her raincoat swinging, her hands gripping her suitcase tightly. Ceri flopped back down into the seat. 'This is all so intense,' she said.

'And it's about to get more so,' he said, smiling, 'with your parents arriving.' Ceri felt a stab of anxiety. She was still trying to process the conversation she'd had with Anna before the interruption of Pepe's arrival. She looked across at the entrance to the café; a swarm of people had just entered. She remembered the test in her bag and stood up.

'I'll be back in a moment,' she said. She went to the bathroom, her heart beating a deep and steady rhythm as she glanced towards Pepe.

Inside the cubicle she fiddled with the box and peed on the stick, something she'd done a million times, it seemed. She waited, immediately feeling foolish for even thinking there was a possibility. She balanced the test on the loo roll holder and pulled herself together, feeling a sense of urgency to get back to Pepe. When she saw two lines indicating that she was pregnant, the first thing that came to her mind was that the test must be faulty. But then she saw the definite quality of two strong lines, felt the hardness of her breasts and the metallic taste that was swilling about her mouth and felt a wave of joy, quickly followed by panic. The first person she thought of was her mother. It was her mother she wanted to tell first, after Pepe.

She popped the test up her sleeve and went to wash her hands.

Pepe was staring out at the courtyard, deep in thought until he turned to see her walking towards him. She tried to make her face impossible to read.

'Everything okay?'

'Hold out your hand,' she said, which he did. She laid the stick in the palm of his hand and squeezed it, the stick digging into both of their palms. He looked down at the results, a ripple of confusion running across his face.

'It's positive,' she said.

Pepe's eyes widened, his face stretched and open

'Madre mia!' he said. He sat looking at the stick, his eyes wide, until he bent down and kissed her fingers.

'Are you happy?' she asked.

'Are you?'

Ceri nodded. 'I'm ecstatic,' she said.

'Then I am too.'

# FORTY-SEVEN

## Anna

The hospital was ringing with its usual pattern of sounds: the arrival of lifts, phones ringing, a floor-cleaning machine chugging along the pearly white corridors. As she walked through the door of Jude's room he opened his eyes, his face rippled and folded into a frown. He tried to pull himself up, and failed.

'Christ!' he said, his voice heavy and slow. 'What are you doing here?'

'Trying to save you from yourself,' she said, walking up and sitting beside him, picking up his hand. 'You're awake then.'

'I'm not entirely sure,' he said, slurring a little. 'They've put me on morphine and I'm tripping.' He tried to smile.

Anna contemplated kissing his forehead but her body wouldn't obey the command. Then the doctor entered.

'Mrs Elliot . . .'

'Anna, please.'

'We've had a busy time while you've been downstairs, haven't we, Jude?'

'Yep, no peace for the wicked in this joint,' Jude slurred, wincing. 'Got a bit of a headache, though.'

The doctor made himself busy at the computer that was on a tall trolley and was rolled from room to room. 'How are you feeling?' he asked.

Jude buried his head in his hands, shaking it back and forth. 'I kind of liked the deep sleep, Doc.'

'Does this mean there's no danger of any brain trauma?' she asked the doctor.

'Looking at the results of the MRI this morning, and looking at the patient, it appears not,' the doctor said. He smiled at Jude, clearly taken in by his charm. 'The orthopaedic doctor will be over later this morning.'

'Yeah, I'm guessing the new hardware I'm wearing means my leg is broken,' Jude said, still slurring. 'That car bumper was a little unforgiving.' His hair was dirty and hung in tight ringlets.

The doctor chuckled, continuing his routine of checking Jude's eyes and adding notes to the computer. 'So, you remember the moment of impact?'

'Sadly, yes.' Jude grinned, but Anna could see it was an effort. 'I saw the car and felt it at the same time.'

The doctor laid his hand on Jude's shoulder. 'Good to see you're on the mend.' Then, acknowledging them both, the doctor left.

Anna wasn't sure where to start, or if this was the right time, but then Jude spoke.

'Listen, Anna. I know I've been a shit, I'm no good for you, we both know that.'

Anne held his eyes, knowing that he was perceptive enough to understand what she was feeling. Even he must have worked out that she'd decided on coming before the accident. A little tremor rattled across her chest. She poured them both a glass of water.

'Well, you're not much good at looking after yourself, either.'

Jude looked away then. His eyes watery and unfocused.

'It seems you've caused quite a lot of chaos,' she said.

323

She watched as Jude tried to work out what she meant, then his face opened up a little, as if the chaos he'd caused had been a good thing. 'Oh, you mean Ceri. She's great, isn't she?'

'Yes, I mean Ceri,' Anna said, making sure to temper the sarcasm in her voice, knowing that Jude was too fragile for this type of confrontation, despite his attempt at joviality.

'Yeah, well as I said, I'm no good to anyone,' Jude said, turning away and reaching out for the water. 'I could do with a drink,' he said. 'Something a little stronger than this.'

'Jude, I know right now you're pumped on morphine, but you need to look at all of this as objectively as possible.' Anna walked across to close the door.

Jude took a large swig of water. 'Here we go, Anna the therapist, the great healer of the human condition.'

Anna swallowed back the anger. Jude had always been nasty when he was drunk but this time he was defensive for a whole new set of reasons. 'Well, I've come to hand my notice in on that front,' she said, patting his leg, feeling a tightness in her throat. 'If you want me in your life, which I have to admit you've shown no evidence of doing, then you're going to have to check yourself into a rehabilita-tion clinic. And, if you believe you have a right to play a part in your daughter's life, if she *is* your daughter, then I'd think very seriously about what I'm about to tell you.' She stood up, pulled off her raincoat, pacing in circles.

'She *is* mine, Anna. I know it.'

Anna nodded. 'Yes, I agree, it's highly likely she's your biological daughter, and let's not bother with discussing how that makes me feel.'

Jude dropped his head down onto the pillow and turned his head away. 'I know how hard it was, Anna. If that's what you mean.'

'You weren't there for me. You took your solace in drink.' She nodded at the water as if it was full of the familiar amber liquid. 'I realised then that even if we did have a child, I'd be parenting it on my own. That a child would be the end of us . . . but I was wrong, we'd already reached an end.' Anna clutched her hands together, squeezing them hard, as if wringing out a woollen jumper. 'I've known for a very long time about Lori but I think a part of me didn't want to accept that Ceri could be your child, but . . .'

Jude went to speak but Anna shook her head.

'You haven't given Ceri one thought have you? Nor Lori, or Roland.'

He held her gaze then, his green eyes sad and empty. 'I didn't tell her, in the end.'

'You told her enough the first time.'

'But Anna, Lori's lied for all this time.' But when he caught her eye he seemed to change his mind, dropping his eyes to the floor. 'Sorry,' he said, 'I told you I'm no good.'

She took a deep breath. 'Anyway, I'm here to tell you that unless you check yourself into a rehab clinic, you're going to lose your job, which you may have lost already, your wife, a potential daughter, and more. And while I'm at it, you need to think about how you're going to face Lori and Roland. They're both here in Sydney, by the way. They were extremely concerned about Ceri and you've rather forced Lori's hand. She's going to have to explain everything. Ceri's a lovely girl, well woman, really, and Lori had her reasons.' Anna was running out of steam, suddenly overwhelmed by fatigue, probably jet lag. Outside in the courtyard below, a constant flow of nurses and doctors travelled back and forth. She turned to face him.

'I just wanted to meet Ceri, that's all. I'd got to the point when I couldn't ignore it anymore. Something happened to me when I was in the Outback, a sense that I needed to put things straight, but I made a complete cock-up of it. As soon as I recognised her, I had this feeling that if I died tomorrow, I would've left something good behind other than a trail of hatred.'

'Well, at least it's all out there now.'

'I wanted to apologise to Roland, but somehow I lost my way. I did speak to Lori, though. That's a start. I suppose I thought I'd be able to offer Ceri something, but as soon as I spoke to Lori, I realised that wasn't the case.'

Anna rolled her eyes. 'Jude, you're not able to offer anything until you've dealt with your drinking habit.' Anna knew her timing wasn't great but he needed to hear all of this, or perhaps she needed to say it.

Jude was fixated at some spot on the green cotton blanket.

'This isn't about you, Jude. This is about Ceri. She needs to know the truth, but I warn you now, whatever the results, Roland will always be her father. You haven't left yourself fit to father anybody, but if you confront your problems now, you may at least have a chance to have some kind of relationship with her.' She picked up her bag and raincoat.

Jude looked up, beaten. 'Don't go, please Anna.'

Anna stood, a feeling of lightness spreading through her body. She was doing this for him, for them all. 'After you leave here, you need to sort yourself out,' she said. 'Only then will we talk.'

And then she walked swiftly out of the door.

# FORTY-EIGHT

**Lori**

Lori was perspiring with the effort of staying calm while Roland, clearly stressed, his forearm muscles tensed, pulled into the forecourt of the hospital with his usual flourish. Lori felt the adrenaline coursing through her body, spurred as much by Roland's driving, the tension spinning off him, at the prospect of confronting Ceri. After his mini break-down outside the airport, he'd barely said a word, but it was clear to her that his mind was churning over various thoughts by the way he chewed his lip.

'Are you coming in?' she said, as she opened the door.

Roland shook his head. 'I think you need to speak to Ceri alone.'

'Right, well I think Ceri has enough going on . . .'

'Don't lecture me about Ceri, please.' He pinned her down with his blueish eyes. 'You're not in a position to lecture me about Ceri's welfare, that's all.'

'Okay, okay!'

'I'll find a café, there must be one inside, and text you,' he said.

'Fine!' She went to close the door.

'Lori, wait. I need to tell you something.' He was looking ahead, not at her, his eyes focused on something neither of them could see, his brow furrowed.

'Can't it wait?'

'Not really, no.'

Lori saw the awkward angle he was parked. She got back in the car. Noticed the way he clenched the gearstick. 'Well at least park the car properly,' she said.

Roland obediently straightened the car, neatly slotting it in just behind a parked ambulance. He looked straight ahead, his hands gripping the wheel, until he let his head drop into them.

'Lori, I want to tell you the part I played in what happened that day.'

'Ro, not now, this isn't . . .'

'Please,' he said.

Lori nodded. 'I knew I was giving Anna more attention. It was deliberate. I think I hoped to make you jealous, and it seemed I managed that. Do you remember at Les Bains Douches, when I caught your eye while I was talking to Anna at the bar?'

Lori nodded. She remembered it like it was yesterday.

'That was deliberate too. I *wanted* to make you jealous because I saw the way you were dancing with Jude, or rather the way Jude was dancing with you. I was angry.'

'At me?'

He shook his head. 'I realise now I was angry with myself. I should have stood up to Jude.'

Lori wasn't sure what to say. She had been so busy preparing herself for Ceri she felt unable to process his words. She took a deep breath. She understood how hard this was for him, even if it was ill-timed.

'Why now?'

'While you were at Anna's the other night, I broke down. I mean seriously broke down. I think after the holiday, you seemed so distant and I felt you were holding something back. But it's not just what's going on now, it was the time leading up to the heart attack, the way I've hidden in my work, my inability to trust . . .' he gulped '. . . anybody.' He looked into her eyes, and there was a flicker of anxiety she hadn't seen in years. 'It's stuff like this I've been discussing with my therapist.'

'You haven't told me what you talk to Simon about.' She dropped her gaze to her lap. 'It's not just you who feels locked out.'

He nodded. 'Finally, after I broke down, I spoke to Simon and we worked through the reasons why I was . . . *am* so controlling and why I didn't trust you back then, and what part I played in the rocky beginning.' He sighed. 'I've spent the entire flight going over the conversation I had with him. I know you thought I was being sullen, but it wasn't that. I've been trying to work it all out.'

'And?' Lori was still miffed by his timing. All these years and he picked now, but at least he was communicating.

'Simon thinks it goes back to the relationship I had with my father,' he said, turning to her. 'I know I haven't been the easiest of people . . .' He looked at her, his eyes full of self-doubt.

She laid her hand on his knee. 'You've been a good provider.'

'But you couldn't get close to me, could you?'

Lori felt tears prick her eyes. She shook her head. 'I thought that was my fault,' she said.

He looked at her and shook his head, his pleading eyes resting on hers. 'It's never just one person's fault.' He picked up her hand that was still resting on his knee and kissed the fingertips, then held it to his cheek. They sat in silence for a second, until an ambulance went whistling past, its blue light flashing, echoing her own sense of urgency.

'Thank you for telling me,' she said, gently pulling away.

'I miss you, Lori. I've been missing you for a very long time and I know it's not just you. Perhaps when all this is over, we could start again.' His smile was tentative.

'I'd love that,' she said, and leaned over to kiss him. 'And I love you — always have. But now I have to go. I've spent my entire life worrying over this moment. It's time,' she said, climbing out of the car and pushing the door shut. He opened the window. 'We'll talk later,' she said. 'I heard you, and I know how hard that was for you.' She ducked down and kissed his forehead. 'It's going to be okay.'

For a second she couldn't work out where to go, the vast clinical reception was too overwhelming, the whiteness of it, until she saw the bank of elevators and a sign for the ICU. It was while she was waiting for the receptionist to get off the phone that she spotted Ceri. Looking at her as a stranger would, her curls falling over her face and onto her shoulders, she realised that she was a beautiful grown woman. Ceri was disposing of something in the rubbish bin in the corridor and had stopped to look out of the window, looking wistful and worn out. When she turned she caught sight of Lori and there was a moment when mother and daughter took each other in. Ceri strode towards her, her face taut with stress.

'Mum! Oh Mum.' And then she collided into Lori's arms. Lori was rather taken aback; she had expected rage, antagonism, but not this warm welcoming creature melting in her arms. She took her daughter's hand and they went to sit in the reception area with its bank of leatherette chairs. Mercifully the woman on the desk hadn't looked up from her telephone conversation.

'How are you?' Lori asked. 'And Jude, how is he?'

'He's not good, not good at all.'

'Where's Anna?' Lori asked.

'You've just missed her. She's gone back downstairs. She's very emotional and had to get a drink. Now Jude is beside himself because he's only just woken up and Anna has told him she's leaving. I feel so responsible.' She lifted her clenched fists and rubbed her red eyes with the heel of her fist. Lori took hold of Ceri's hands.

'You of all people are not responsible.'

Lori hadn't seen her daughter like this since she was much younger. Over the years Ceri had learned to curb her volatile nature. Studying law had made her controlled, mindful, but now it was as if the years had been reversed. But most of all Lori detected the absence of anger and she wondered why.

As the realisation settled, she said, 'I was stealing myself. Ceri, I don't know where to start, I've made so many mistakes.'

Ceri gripped her mother's arms, forcing Lori to look her in the eyes, twisting awkwardly in the line of chairs. 'Mum, I can't tell you how angry I've been. But something happened, which changed all of that. Two things, actually.'

Lori made the effort to breathe deeply. This isn't quite what she'd expected but she braced herself.

'Anna told me about a holiday you had in France, how you had all been playful and reckless, which I found hard to believe.' She was pressing her hand down on her thigh, then balling it up, a tissue scrunched inside her fist.

Lori smiled, encouraging her to continue, wanting her daughter to relax.

'She said that it wasn't just you who made the mistake, that in some way you all played a part in what happened,

331

even Dad.' Ceri looked at Lori with expectant hazel eyes. Sometimes, Lori felt she was looking at a younger version of herself, but Ceri was so different, more assured she realised.

Lori wondered if this was a generous act on Anna's behalf, or if she, like Roland, felt ready to share the blame. It had never occurred to her that Anna and Roland were complicit. 'Go on.'

'She said she could tell me her side of the story, but I needed to talk to you as well. She told me about how you worried that if you told Dad of the possibility that I was Jude's child, Dad might have left you and you would have been forced to have an abortion.' She looked down into her lap, at her balled-up tissue. 'Then I wouldn't have been here.' Ceri looked at Lori, a childlike earnestness lighting her eyes. 'Mum, it's true, isn't it? Jude is my father.'

Lori took another deep breath. She realised then that Roland had released her from a deep anguish. It had been a long time coming, and at one point she'd hoped the time would never come, but as the words collected in her throat she was glad to be able to speak them. 'Dad will always be your dad,' she said. 'But I believe that Jude is your biological father, yes.'

Ceri's eyes were huge. Lori could see the anxiety she'd caused. She thought it was all that she could manage but then she realised that she needed to say more. 'I haven't always believed that. When you were born I believed you were Dad's child, but as you grew older, it became clear. I've made some huge mistakes, Ceri. I became overprotective of you because I'd lost control of my own life. Also, I felt guilty, if that makes sense. I felt guilty that I'd deceived you.'

Ceri nodded. 'Mum, you're allowed to make mistakes, but you're right. I've been angry for a very long time. I didn't understand why you were more controlling of me than the others, and now I know.' Ceri's smile was tentative. 'Look, I just wanted to say that even if Jude *is* my biological father, I'm glad it was Dad who brought me up.'

'Well, I think the person who needs to hear that is Dad, but let's cross that bridge when we come to it. He's waiting downstairs in the café, I think.'

'I have something else to tell you,' Ceri said. Lori saw a spark of light in her daughter's eyes.

'I'm pregnant.'

The news hit her like a wrecking ball. She was expecting some revelation but not this. Her daughter had finally conceived a child. Tears of joy stung her eyes. They sat huddled together, until Ceri broke away.

'I'm coming to terms with the idea of Jude. I mean now that I'm carrying Pepe's child, I think it's important to know who I am,' she said.

'Well, you're someone who has taken the trouble to care for a stranger, you're capable of being a top business lawyer and a fun waitress, you're a brilliant daughter and I'm sure you're going to be a wonderful mother and a supportive partner.'

'Thank you.' She took a deep breath. 'You're going to love Pepe,' Ceri said.

Lori had forgotten about Pepe. 'Is Pepe happy?' she said.

Ceri nodded. 'We haven't had much chance to talk about it, but he's really happy, yes.'

'And he's a chef?'

'No, he works in the charity sector. He's taken a sabbatical after his father died.'

'I see.' Lori realised how acutely she'd misjudged the situation. 'I owe you an apology. I haven't met Pepe yet, but I can already see he's good for you. You seem to have grown into yourself. It might be the pregnancy but there's a serenity about you that I haven't seen since you were a child. I'm not sure, but I think it's because you're no longer internalising your emotions.' She realised she was sounding more like Anna. 'So, I like him already.'

Ceri's eyes filled with tears. 'You don't know what that means to me,' she said.

'I'm beginning to,' Lori said. She let go of Ceri's hand and stood up. 'Now let's go and see Jude and then I think your father also has something to say to you.'

Jude was slumped against a wall of pillows. When he looked up, Lori noted the way he smiled at Ceri, but she could see the despair in his eyes. 'Hello, Jude,' she said.

Jude held up his hand. 'So the terrible foursome is back in business,' he said, but his attempt at humour failed. He shook his head. 'Lori, as I said on the phone, I'm sorry. I'm sorry to both of you. I should have kept my mouth shut.'

Lori took his hand. 'Jude, you did what you believed was right; I'm tired of trying to juggle different versions of the truth.' Ceri went and stood by her side. 'At least this way, we're all on the same page.'

# FORTY-NINE

## Anna

It was as Anna was walking along the corridors of the hospital towards the café feeling both strong and fragile at the same time after confronting Jude, that she caught sight of Roland. She thought how Mediterranean he looked in his chinos, white shirt and navy sweater. He was way up ahead of her in a stream of people heading in the general direction of the café. He was on the phone, talking to somebody, that old sense of authority about him. He stopped in his tracks and turned round. He didn't seem to recognise her at first, but then his blue eyes settled on hers. She'd once considered his eyes to be soft and dreamy, but now they appeared harder, more direct. That plane journey had shown her another side to him. He nodded, as if they'd both agreed on something, said goodbye to whoever it was on the phone.

'Anna,' he said. 'How is he?'

'Bloody awful. I don't know where to start,' she said. 'Coffee?'

'I suppose so,' she said. 'I came down to get a drink, actually.'

Roland looked at his watch. 'We're in a hospital. We can have one when we get to the hotel.'

He took long strides as they made their way to the café. Anna found it hard to keep up with him. He was a different man to the one she remembered. He seemed to know where he was going even though he'd been in the country for just a few hours, and then she was reminded of his innate sense of direction she'd noted in Paris. They arrived to find the place was almost empty. Just one person ahead of them in the queue. Roland removed his jacket and offered to take her raincoat and threw them both over a nearby chair.

'I wanted to say how sorry I am,' he said. 'Not just about the accident, but about everything. There's nothing like a twenty-eight-hour flight to get you thinking,' he said. 'I feel like I played a part in this whole mess somehow, by staying away for too long that day in some lame attempt to make Lori jealous. I didn't listen to you and I should have,' he said. He pinned her down with his blueish eyes, and she was reminded of his younger self sitting in the armchair in the house in Dordogne.

'I think we all played a part in it one way or another,' Anna said. 'I was jealous of Lori in many ways. She had agency and I was a product of my parents. I told Jude to never speak to her again.'

'I can't say I blame you.' When he looked at her she sensed an apologetic glint in his eye. He seemed a different man to the one sitting next to her on the plane.

'Lori is with him now, I think,' he said, as if the two things were connected.

Anna nodded, catching the barista's eye who was waiting. 'Shall we order our coffee?'

They went and sat down, Roland carrying the tray, settling it down on the table and reaching for a sandwich he'd bought for himself.

'Jet lag,' he said, holding it up to explain.

A group of medical students walked up to the counter, all of them in white coats talking loudly about their morning cases.

She said, 'Ultimately these past few days have left me feeling very confused and now Jude is in this state, more so. I came here to confront him and let him know that I'm filing for divorce.' She cursed herself for tearing up. 'But seeing him so vulnerable hasn't made it easy. I've told him unless he goes to rehab, it's over.'

Roland reached out his hand and rested it on her arm, as if not knowing what else to do. 'Christ, no wonder you need a drink,' he said. 'It must be hard.' He raked his hair, looked around anxiously. 'I came with my own agenda. I wanted to get Ceri as far away from Jude as possible. It's too late for him to barge into our lives now, but then I realised it's not about me, is it? I have to keep thinking about Ceri and what's best for her.'

'Well, Ceri's up there with him now.'

'Oh God, is she?' His face had turned red with the effort of bringing up his feelings. He was sweating. She noticed the fleshy span of his hands, the long fingers, the way he rested them on the table as if he was about to play the piano. 'I don't understand why Lori didn't tell me, that's all,' Roland said. 'I mean I do, because I kept things hidden too.'

'Oh that's simple,' she said. 'She *wanted* Ceri to be yours.'

Anna saw the thought register in Roland's face, his muscles softening. 'Ceri's a lovely girl,' she said.

'That's kind, thank you.'

She saw the same group of students huddled in a corner, a rabble of white coats, shedding their medical skin and flirting with each other. This was who *they* were once, the four of them, blind to the cruelty of life, believing in their ability to ride every wave and not fall.

She wondered if Roland would agree to a DNA test, but it wasn't her place to ask. Suddenly he jumped up, knocking a chair over. Anna turned round to see Lori and Ceri.

'Dad,' Ceri said, flinging her arms around Roland. 'Dad.'

Anna saw in a flash that no DNA test was going to take away the fact that Roland was Ceri's father. Blood wasn't so thick as to annihilate the years spent parenting.

Anna stood up to embrace Lori. 'Anna, I've just seen him, he's in such a state.'

'I know, I know,' she said.

# FIFTY

**Lori**

The café was buzzing with medical students. Lori sank
into a chair, exhausted, her mind still processing the
conversation she'd had with Ceri and then Jude, but
more importantly Roland. She felt as if a wall had fallen
between them and for the first time in a long while they
were being truly honest with each other. She looked up
to see Roland and Ceri chatting and smiling. He put his
arm around her shoulders and pulled her tightly into an
embrace. He would never not be her father, whatever
the DNA results said. They'd gone to get more drinks
and she was tempted to close her eyes and let the buzz
of the café wash over her but then she realised Anna was
watching her expectantly.

'Tell me what happened?' Lori asked.

'I socked it to him when he was down. Not very noble
of me.'

'Anna, I think you're allowed to be human once in a
while.'

Anna sat forward, her face animated. 'Listen, I want to
talk to you quickly, while Ceri and Roland are away. I
was wondering about DNA tests.'

'Anna, I'm not sure Roland will agree to that,' Lori
said, feeling a spark of anxiety just when things were calm.

'But if Ceri is Jude's daughter,' Anna's voice wavered, 'it just might give him something to live for . . .'

'Stop there.' Lori sat forward, leaning onto her elbows. She looked behind her to see Roland and Ceri in the queue chatting, Ceri gesticulating wildly, reminding Lori of a young version of herself. 'Ceri is vulnerable right now. I don't want her to feel obliged to do this.' She could hear the tremor of her voice, the anger apparent, but she didn't care.

Anna stared at Lori, pinning her down with her intelligent blue eyes. Lori could sense the desperation. Anna always could outwit most people with her sharp tongue and quick aptitude, making Lori feel vulnerable.

'I've studied and worked hard to know one thing,' Anna raised her voice slightly. 'Lies are destructive and not knowing which man is her biological father will eat away at her. This is you, Lori, controlling. Ceri should at least have the choice.'

Lori felt herself shrink. She hugged her handbag, which sat bulging across her stomach. Then she remembered Ceri's words: *I think it's important to know who I am.* Anna was right – Lori was still so busy protecting herself and Roland, she hadn't considered what this meant to everyone else.

'I don't know what to say,' she said.

'It'll come to you,' Anna said curtly.

Neither of them noticed until far too late, Ceri and Roland standing above them. Roland had a tray loaded with fresh coffee.

'What's this about?' Ceri asked, sitting in between Anna and Lori.

Anna pinned Lori down with her clear eyes.

'Anna thinks we should do a DNA test,' Lori said. She knew how Roland would react but she wanted him to listen to Ceri's opinion on this.

Ceri's face broke open. 'Well, I think that's a great idea.'

'I don't,' Roland said. Placing the loaded tray down and bringing in a chair from a neighbouring table without even bothering to ask if that was okay. Lori shrugged an apology as a woman flashed an angry look at Roland. Ceri sat back, her arms wrapped around her middle, mirroring Lori.

'Then the only person who is holding this up is you,' Lori said, looking at Roland whose mouth was sealed tight. 'And in light of the conversation we've just had, you might want to think about that.' She was thinking in particular of his admission to being controlling.

Anna leaned forward, directing her gaze at Roland. 'I spend my life with people, my patients, unravelling the lies they have been told. Now I'm embroiled in a scenario I couldn't have dreamed of, so I consider this as field work.' Anna smiled, and in that moment Lori realised it was the warmest she'd seen Anna since they'd reconnected. 'Knowing the truth won't change anything, you can't undo a lifetime of parenting, but it'll bring clarity and give us all a chance to heal.' Anna batted Lori's knee under the table as a way of acknowledging what Lori had done, which was to stand up to Roland.

'I agree,' Ceri said.

'Roland, I've been thinking . . .'

Roland held up his hand, but Lori took hold of his long fingers and said, 'No, Roland, you're going to let me speak, please.'

'Yes, Dad, listen.'

Roland continued to stare at her. 'Okaaay,' he said. He held up his hands. 'You're right.'

'Thirty-four years ago I made a mistake. I allowed fear and jealousy to rule my heart. I'd love to say I regret it, but regret is a pointless emotion and if I regret anything, it's not confiding in you. However, because of that mistake we have a beautiful daughter who, I realise, has turned into the most extraordinary woman, and I can see that's partly thanks to this new man Pepe, who we haven't even met yet, so you were right about that. But it's also because we did a fine job of bringing her up together and nothing that comes from this DNA test is going to change that.'

'Oh, Mum.' Ceri grabbed her arm.

Roland's eyes widened, his leg jiggling under the table. A habit he'd always had.

'Ceri has the right to know,' Anna said.

Ceri nodded. 'It won't change how I feel about you, Dad. Nothing will change that.'

Roland's head dropped, his gaze fixed on his shoes, his eyes were shiny. Lori leaned closer. She couldn't stop herself.

'And none of this changes the fact that I have loved you and provided you with four lovely children. I've never been unfaithful, apart from that one time when I allowed myself to be flattered and seduced when I was feeling threatened. I know you've worked hard to provide, but in order to allow you that privilege – and it *is* a privilege – I gave up part of myself. Like so many women, I put your needs before mine. And sure, I never wanted for anything, but there was a price. You need to look at this woman, me, and know that I've tried hard to be the best person I can for the people I love.'

Roland appeared to absorb her words, she could feel his body gently ease. He nodded. 'As I said to you in the car, I know the part I played in this whole scenario.'

Lori sensed Ceri shift. She was grateful he'd said this in front of her. She put her hands on the table and looked into his eyes. Ceri and Anna had receded. It felt for a second as if it were just the two of them. There was a chink of light in his eyes, a hint of a smile. Roland gently took her hand in his, leaned over the table and kissed her. "Thank you for being you.'

'Mum.' Lori nodded, squeezed her daughter's hand and nodded. She knew what was coming.

'Dad. Pepe and I are expecting a baby.'

Roland looked from Lori to Ceri, a frown forming. 'Did you know this?' he asked Lori.

Lori nodded. 'Just found out.'

'You as well?' he asked Anna.

Anna shrugged. 'Not for sure, no.'

'Christ! Ceri, that's amazing news.' He stood up and Ceri did as well, and she ran around the table so that he could fold her into his arms.

'So, you see, I'd like to know what genetic make-up our child has,' she said.

Roland softened, his shoulders sinking a little. 'I see.' He looked down at his shoes. 'I'll do it for you,' he said and then he rubbed her stomach. 'And this little one.'

'Let's go and see Jude,' Ceri said, when their cups were empty.

Anna and Lori got up. Roland looked at all of them in turn, his eyes finally dropping onto the floor. 'This isn't going to be easy,' he said.

When they got to Jude's room, they stopped outside and Anna gestured to Roland to lead the way. 'I can't go back in. I've made a vow that I'll only see him if he checks into rehab.'

Roland nodded and took the step alone. 'Jude, mate,' Roland said, his voice wobbly.

'You can call me something else if you want,' Jude said.

# FIFTY-ONE

## Ceri

Ceri felt for Pepe's hand and pulled him gently towards her, spooning his back. They'd worked the late shift at the café last night and had fallen into bed exhausted. Now, as the early morning light crept into the room, she needed his touch. She kept telling herself the news over and over: they were going to have a baby. They'd arranged to meet her parents for brunch, before their next shift. He turned onto his back and pulled her closer. She could smell his sticky breath, the oil in his hair, the garlic on his tongue. Over the past few weeks, since going away together, they'd grown closer and at times it seemed to her as if their bodies were one: their pulse, their flesh, their blood. It hadn't been like this with Carl, they'd been a popular couple and had similar interests but she realised now the connection had been superficial. She wondered if her mother understood that by walking away from her life, Ceri had found herself.

'Fancy an early morning swim?' Pepe said, sitting up and leaning over her.

'You're kidding!'

'No.'

'You're wearing me out, you know that,' she said.

'Yep, that's the idea. I like you when you're sleepy and content.'

'And you don't like me when I'm not?'

'I like you any which way,' he said, and threw back the sheet. She laughed and they tumbled over into a hug, falling onto the floor, kissing, the sheet caught between them. She could feel his erection through the tangled cotton.

'It's autumn and in case you hadn't noticed, the sea is noticeably cooler. I might die of hypothermia.'

'I'll keep you warm, don't you worry. Besides, swimming is good for pregnant women.' He scooped her up into a hug. The idea of sex hovered but he seemed to change his mind and jumped up, uninhibited as he crossed the room, the muscles on his back pronounced, probably due to all the swimming they'd done while they were away. She threw the sheet back onto the bed, folding it under the pillows. Next came the throw, and the cushions. The flat had come furnished, but they'd added bits and bobs to make it feel like home, but what would happen now? She realised how ensconced they both were in their shared life. But, there was the issue of visas and with it, an impermanence that hovered like the blinking hazard lights of a temporarily parked car, and now there was the permanence of a new life.

'We need to make plans, start thinking about what we're going to do,' she said.

'And we will. After a swim.'

Ceri stopped him in his tracks. 'Seriously, we need to talk.'

He looked at her, held her face. 'I know.'

They stood on Bronte Beach watching the leatherbacks plough up and down the sea-water pool. The sun sparking the water so that it glistened and shone in the cool early morning light. There was a group of young adults kicking a ball around, a woman throwing a stick for her dog. It had been good to feel the water again after the trauma of the past few days. But the metallic taste in her mouth was making her feel sick, a constant reminder of the child inside her.

'Feels good to be back. As soon as I'm next to water, I feel connected with the world again,' Pepe said.

'There's a reason for that,' she said. 'It has more to do with being in touch with the earth's magnetic field than anything,' Ceri said.

'I thought you were going to start talking about amniotic fluid,' he said.

'Nope, although that's probably true as well.'

He pulled her closer. 'Happy?' she asked.

'I am,' he said. He looked out to sea and there was something in the way his eyes settled on the middle distance that told her he wasn't in the moment, that something was troubling him.

'What are you thinking?' she asked.

'About life, how momentous it is. About how my father will never meet my child.' He turned back to her and held her with his dark brown eyes, amber flecks shining in the sun. 'How simple and yet incredible that we're going to have a baby.'

'We need to talk about where we're going to live,' she said, sitting on the warm sand, feeling the comfort of it on her skin.

Pepe sat beside her, wrapping his arm around her shoulders. 'There's something I have to tell you,' he said.

Ceri felt her breath grow shallow; she pulled away from the security of Pepe's arms and looked at him, waiting for bad news.

'I've been offered a job. A proper job.'

She breathed deeply, tasting the salt of the Pacific on her tongue. 'When? I mean when did that even happen?'

'It happened on the day of the accident. I didn't want to tell you until we'd got stuff sorted out with your, well with Jude. It's in London. It's the same charity I worked for before but they want me to head a team in England. It's good money, I mean not loads, but it would mean a pretty big promotion.'

'Wow! Shit! That means we're going to have to go back to Europe.' She'd thought they could stay in Sydney. Apply for residency. She had enough money and she was qualified. 'When?'

'Soon. In a couple of months.'

'But you'll hate London. The weather is shit and there's no beach.'

'I know, but if we're going to have children, then we need to be close to family.'

Ceri sank back into the sand. 'But if we go back, we might not be happy,' she said.

'Baby, I need to give this a go. I spoke to my mother yesterday while you were at the hospital. She's so excited to have a grandchild. She'd be devastated if I stayed here for the rest of my life, and I think you'll need to be closer to your mother too. This is about families.'

She thought about her mother, how she'd assumed she'd be there when the baby was born, and then her siblings and how much she missed them. Pepe was right, it was time to go back. She threw a clump of sand and the granules arced into the water. 'But your mother hasn't even met me yet.'

'She's going to love you,' Pepe said. 'Because I do.'

Ceri smiled, remembering her mother's words: *I like him already*.

# FIFTY-TWO

## Anna

Ten days later, after Jude had been discharged, his leg still in plaster, Anna found him in his apartment packing up the last of his things, which didn't add up to much. Just a few beaten-up pairs of jeans, T-shirts and a collection of books. It wasn't a big room. It was one of those all-in-one flats which had the kitchen and living area in one room, the bedroom and shower unit in another. She'd agreed to see him after he'd texted her to tell her about the rehab clinic he was going to. She noticed he had his well-worn copy of *The Great Gatsby* on the coffee table. He'd always made a habit of reading it every couple of years and had refused to put it on Kindle. Looking around her the place was bare, just a couple of postcards stuck on the pin board and a few kitchen essentials on the surfaces. It looked tidy. He'd obviously gone to a great deal of effort to clean it up. There was a 1930s poster on the wall of an old liner painted in pastel colours. His suitcase was by the door, looking battered and covered in stickers. He had always liked to look well travelled, which he was. His job had taken him all over the world.

Jude was sitting on a chair opposite her, elbows wedged between his knees, head bent towards the floor, his hair still sticking up from a night's sleep. He looked crushed

348

in his worn-out trainers and joggers. She didn't imagine he'd gone running in a while.

'So, you're off?' she said, scanning the kitchen to see if there was any sign of a coffee maker.

'Yep.' He looked at her, his face immobile. She'd always loved his green eyes, but looking at them now they appeared empty and full of sorrow.

'The test result is back.'

Jude raised his eyebrows. 'It felt silly doing a test after all these years. I feel a fool for making such a fuss. It's not as if I can wind back time and be Ceri's father. Roland's done a pretty good job of that,' he said. 'I can't be a better husband either, or a better friend.'

'Well, Roland was better equipped, emotionally speaking,' she said. 'Shall I make us a coffee?'

'Sure. Percolator's in the cupboard above the hob.' He pointed in the direction of the kitchen. 'What do you mean, better equipped?'

'Well, if there's one thing therapy has taught me it's that we all have our reasons. Roland may not have had a good relationship with his father, but at least he knew who he was, had a solid family background and money, although you can be a good parent without money.'

'Yeah, well from my experience, if a mother has to scrape around on her own earning it, there isn't much space for that – it's about survival,' he said, picking at a scab on his hand.

'Your mum loved you, Jude. Many people love you.'

He looked up at her, his eyes filled with sadness and regret which wrenched at her insides and left her feeling responsible even though she wasn't.

'Is that so,' he said, his voice shaky.

She nodded, unsure if he was questioning her feelings towards him.

'I didn't choose to be the way that I am,' he said.

She took a deep breath. She needed every bit of resolve not to run into his arms and give him the reassurance he needed, but if she did that, she'd be back where they started, with him making assumptions and mistreating her. 'I think taking responsibility for our actions is probably the most liberating thing we can do. Sure, maybe your father was an alcoholic, I guess you'll never know.' She almost said we, but thought better of it. 'Although I've always believed in the nurture versus nature argument, I do know we inherit all kinds of aspects of our character genetically. But in the end, it's up to the individual to make the best of the package we have.'

Jude looked away, his gaze falling on something outside in the road. Anna had never seen Jude so low. He'd always made her a coffee, when he was around of course, which wasn't very often.

'What's wrong?' she said.

He sat up, held out his hands, which were shaking uncontrollably. Again she felt inclined to rush up to him but she held her ground, choosing instead to fill the percolator.

'That's what's wrong,' he said.

'Probably best not to have a coffee, then,' she said.

'I have a taxi booked to pick me up in half an hour. The rehab clinic is in the north of Sydney. It looks pretty cool, actually. There's a pool and the grounds are beautiful. In case you're worried, I've spoken to the team, told them everything. Filming has been postponed for a few months. I'll be home in time for Christmas, if you'll let me visit.'

Anna turned towards him, leaned against the kitchen counter, the milk bottle still in her hand. 'Oh, Jude. The problem is you'll be off again soon after that, and I'm not sure that's what I want any more.'

'Yeah, I get that, although I think this will be the last one.'

'You mean they're firing you?'

'No, I mean I'm going to retire, probably teach, maybe take up gardening. Christ knows, I might even write that novel I've been hammering on about. I need to get out of this business. I'm too old, for one thing. Everyone I deal with looks like they've just reached puberty. But more importantly, it's not been good for my mental health or my marriage. It took over my life.' He looked across the space between them. 'Even my relationship to my work was unhealthy.'

Anna was leaning on the kitchen work surface, arms folded. The percolator was bubbling behind her. She felt as if some part of her had fallen away. They'd lived like this for so long. She turned off the gas and went to kneel down in front of Jude, taking hold of his hands to still them.

'It's going to be all right, I promise. This is really positive.'

He looked down at her, his green eyes shining. 'They say alcohol is more difficult to come off than heroin. I had to have a drink just now, before you arrived, it's got that bad.' She'd never seen him this frightened before. This was a man who had mingled with drug lords, interviewed murderers, been wrongly imprisoned by child soldiers in Rwanda. He was fearless.

'I can't tell you how desperate I am for the next drink.'

'How much have you drinking?'

He looked down at his feet, gripping the seat with his hands. 'You've only got to look in the bin to see how bad it's got. I don't know at what point it happened, but here I am: a mess.'

She jumped up to make the coffee. She pressed the peddle of the bin and saw three empty bottles of Vodka bottles. 'Shit.'

'Yep, it ain't good.'

Anna sighed. She felt unsteady at the thought of him being in this state on his own. 'Jude, I'm not going to pretend you don't look like shit right now but this is a beginning. Milk?'

He nodded. 'Are you going to be here when I get out?'

Anna thought of her clients. 'How long is the programme?'

'Twenty-eight days is the minimum.'

She thought of Janet. She had an online session booked the next day. She could offer that to the rest of her clients until she got back. It was a long way to come without making the most of it, and besides she needed time to process everything.

'I'll try,' she said. 'Let's just see how it goes.'

'I'm not doing this because I might be Ceri's father, if that's what you think.' He looked away, squeezing his eyes shut. 'I'm doing this for you.'

Anna handed him his coffee and kissed his forehead. 'You need to do it for you,' she said.

# FIFTY-THREE

## Ceri

Ceri sat next to her mother in the downstairs lobby of St Vincent's Hospital, her hands wedged between her thighs, her body tense with anticipation, her water bottle at her feet, empty. She must have drunk a litre and a half already in preparation for the scan her mother had booked and she was desperate to visit the loo.

She could see her mother tapping away at her screen. The results of the DNA test were waiting for them all to open together, after her scan, and although none of it mattered, not really, it felt as if all of their lives were on hold while they waited. Her parents had booked a return flight for the following week. Ceri had finally handed her notice in to Bar South so that she could spend some time with them.

They had sat for the past twenty minutes engrossed in their own thoughts but the silence between them was a comfortable one. The life of the hospital buzzed around them, a sense of urgency ringing in the air. It was another world down on the ground floor, in the lobby, closer to the world outside. Ceri could see the queue of ambulances, the street beyond, cars passing, a deep blue sky and a few clouds blooming like bruises across it. People were jogging, walking their dogs, holding conversations on their phones – the real world.

They were waiting for Pepe so that they could all go up together. He'd been working out his notice, and had had a Zoom call with his new boss that morning. Life was shifting, slotting into place. They'd booked their return flight a month from now. Her mum had organised the scan and a visit to the gynaecologist. Ceri was grateful that she'd taken over, although she'd barely had time to think about what was going to happen next.

Ceri watched the comings and goings of the downstairs lobby with interest. The glossy cleanliness of the hospital, the polished white flooring, the way doctors and nurses bolted through with that sense of urgency. This great organ of a building with all its technology, highly trained medical staff saving lives on a daily basis, seeing death as well. It didn't bear thinking about. Now things were settled and Jude was ensconced in the rehab clinic, she had time to look at the world again. Pepe was a man of big horizons who wanted to seize every living moment, so the last week had been difficult. She hadn't even told him how sick she was feeling. How her breasts had grown into small melons, how she lived with the constant taste of lead in her mouth. Her mother had bought her some boiled sweets, which apparently had helped her, but Ceri was more health-conscious.

Her mobile pinged with a message from Pepe to say that he was outside the gynaecologist's office. Typical of him to make a small stab at freedom she thought, meeting them there rather than where they'd arranged.

'Who's that?' her mother said, engrossed in her own phone.

'Pepe. He's waiting for us upstairs.' Her stomach did a little somersault, nerves she supposed. It was too soon surely to be the baby. 'I think I might change my mind about those boiled sweets,' she said.

Pepe stood up as they pushed their way through the swing doors. He looked handsome with his black hair swept back off his face. His eyes warmed as she came towards him.

'You look glowing,' he said.

'Let's not count chickens,' she said. 'I won't be convinced until I see this with my own eyes.'

'Either way,' he said. 'It doesn't matter.'

He embraced her mother and then she felt her mother hovering behind her, giving them both space. The nurse invited them all into the room. Lori turned to her daughter.

'No, you go in. This is a special moment for you two.'

Ceri was asked to undress and given a gown to wear. All the while Pepe waited beside the table covered in white paper, ready for her to lie on. She went and placed herself on the tissue, taking hold of Pepe's hand immediately. The woman who was operating the scan introduced herself as Tracy.

'I'm going to rub some gel on your tummy.' She showed Ceri the gel, as if she were a child. 'It might feel a little cold.'

Tracy rolled the scanner over Ceri's stomach, watching the screen closely. Ceri could see smudges of black and grey and white fuzzy lines but there was nothing definite. She felt Pepe inch closer to her and she willed herself to keep focused on the screen even though her instinct was to turn away.

'There we go,' Tracy said. And that is when the shape of the head of their child became visible, then came its beating heart, and as Tracy rolled deeper into Ceri's middle, they could see the baby's legs and arms and hands. The baby was sucking its thumb.

Ceri felt the tears trickling down her cheeks. A little life happening right inside her, she still couldn't believe it.

Pepe stepped forward and wiped them away, giving her a kiss on her forehead.

'Our baby,' he said. 'Woohoo!' Pepe drew closer to her and the screen, his face open, his eyes wide.

'Can my mum come in?' Ceri asked.

'Sure,' Tracy said.

Pepe went to fetch Lori.

When Lori came in a minute later, she was already crying. Clearly Pepe had told her. Tracy smiled as they all looked at the screen in wonder while this new little being floated around oblivious – a little miracle! Tracy was concentrating on the screen, measuring the size of the baby's head. 'Well, I can tell you that you're almost four months pregnant, so it looks like your baby's due date will be just after Christmas.'

'Wow!' Ceri said. 'I'm a Christmas baby too.'

'Really, when's your birthday?' Tracy asked, still measuring and examining the screen.

'Christmas Day,' Ceri said.

'Aww, that sucks,' Tracy said.

'You get used to it. We try to celebrate my birthday on the night of Christmas Eve, don't we, Mum?'

'She was born just after midnight,' her mother said. 'Best Christmas present I've ever had.' She reached out and patted Ceri's leg.

Tracy was still peering closely at the screen. 'Do you want to know the sex of your child?' Tracy asked.

'No,' Ceri, Pepe and Lori all said in unison.

They'd all agreed to meet at their flat later that same afternoon. She realised neither of her parents had visited it yet and as she looked around at the art and sculptures they'd created together, she felt proud. Their little patio was still bursting with life.

'This is amazing, Ceri,' her mother said, walking straight towards the painting on the easel. 'You have real talent. I had no idea!'

Roland was sitting opposite her. His face was composed, but she knew him well enough to know the emotion was concealed. He needed to know he wasn't going to be replaced. Nothing could take away the love she felt for him. He was her father. Her mother went and sat next to Anna on the sofa while Pepe made tea for everyone. None of them were talking, they were all busying themselves with their telephones. It seemed the imminent results of the DNA test had left them all speechless. Odd to think the truth about her future – and her past if she thought about it – was contained in the slim envelope which she held in her hands. Everyone present except for one person. She had a feeling what the results would tell her – she'd always known. We all know really, she thought, but it's hard to listen to that knowledge when the truth remains unspoken.

Pepe handed everyone their tea. She held the envelope in her hands, waved it at the three adults staring at her and went back to sit beside her mum.

'Before I open this, I want you to know, Dad, that you will always be my dad. No amount of genetic coding can change that. But I'm only opening this on one condition; that you all promise to hang out together for the sake of our child. You were good friends once, and I think you could be again. This little one, whatever the results of the test, is something positive to bring us all together. It's not about the blood, it's about the feeling.'

Her mother hugged her.

Anna nodded. 'You have my word,' she said.

Her father gave a thumbs-up sign.

Ceri tore open the envelope.

# Epilogue

## Christmas Eve
## Dordogne

### Lori

Lori hadn't felt this complete in years and she hadn't baked a cake in as long either. It was a Victoria sponge, Ceri's favourite, and she was rather proud of the way it had risen. She dusted it with icing sugar and had managed to put all thirty-five candles on top. She'd placed it on the ugly plate that Roland's auntie Marie-Claude had given them for their second wedding anniversary – a Sèvres something or another – worth a bomb of course. She'd thought it odd, as china was supposed to mark the twentieth year of marriage, but it had remained in their life all this time. Perhaps Marie-Claude had guessed their relationship would last the course.

The sound of the family chattering away in the living room drifted into the kitchen. Anna and Jude had driven through France with their dachshund puppy, Max, who was sniffing around her feet looking for crumbs. Lori watched her mother talking to Anna and her father was in the armchair by the fire, talking to Roland, who had his arm around both Margot and Marie-Claude. He'd been sad when his father had remarried a woman half his age, but Lori had been grateful that at least they'd reconciled their differences after a few intensive sessions with the therapist. Anyway, Margot was far happier without him. She and Marie-Claude now shared the apartment in Paris. Her mother, who had grown wilder in her old age and died her hair pink, laughed at something Anna had said. As if sensing Lori's gaze, Anna looked up and they held each other's eyes for a second. It was always the four of them but it was Anna who had made this happen, Anna who had just enough emotional distance to act with everyone's interest at heart, including Ceri's. Lori couldn't undo the years she'd lost but at least there was a future to contemplate. Lori smiled, raised a glass. Anna knew her well enough to know this was a sign of her appreciation.

The kitchen was alive with the smells of Christmas preparations, red cabbage bubbling away and the smell of mince pies coming from the range. Roland had uncorked a bottle of champagne, and an alcohol-free one for Jude and Ceri. She could hear Jude teaching Ollie and Jake a riff on the guitar. It looked as if he was taking to his new role as father with his usual panache and generosity. Savannah and Will were clapping to the sound of the twins' awkward attempts at playing 'Hey Jude'. Pepe and Ceri were out in the garden showing Pepe's mother the vegetable patch. Lori remembered the daffodil incident. They weren't her favourite flowers but they signified the start of spring and they were sturdy. She looked out of the window at her daughter with her round stomach protruding out of her red stretchy trousers and a red cashmere jumper Pepe had bought her for her birthday. Because of Anna's Christmas gift to Ceri all those years ago in the hospital where she was born, it had been a tradition ever since that Ceri wore red on Christmas Eve *and* Christmas Day.

It was her day, after all.

# ACKNOWLEDGEMENTS

I have always believed that a novel is written by more than one person, and in my case this is definitely true. I would like to thank my agent, Rowan Lawton, who believed in me when I didn't. Also to my editor, Harriet Bourton, who shared her expertise with understated generosity, and to Suzy and Francine, who both offered their expert editorial eye, and to Lucy Brem. Also to the many people who have kept me sane along the way, including: my dearest friend Saskia Sarginson, who always offers unwavering support; Frances Merivale, whose editorial eye I cannot live without; David Simons and his eye for detail; Maria Lloret Gomez de Barrida for sharing her knowledge as a therapist and explaining the procedures, and Ceri Cliss, for the use of her beautiful name. And finally, as always, Alex.

# Credits

Sara James and Orion Fiction would like to thank everyone at Orion who worked on the publication of *Ever Since That Day* in the UK.

**Editorial**
Harriet Bourton
Rhea Kurien
Lucy Brem
Sanah Ahmed

**Copy editor**
Francine Brody

**Proofreader**
Clare Wallis

**Audio**
Paul Stark
Jake Alderson

**Contracts**
Anne Goddard
Humayra Ahmed
Ellie Bowker

**Design**
Rachael Lancaster
Joanna Ridley
Nick May

**Editorial Management**
Charlie Panayiotou
Jane Hughes
Bartley Shaw
Tamara Morriss

**Finance**
Jasdip Nandra
Afeera Ahmed
Ibukun Ademefun
Sue Baker

**Production**
Ruth Sharvell

**Marketing**
Katie Moss
Brittany Sankey

**Operations**
Jo Jacobs
Sharon Willis

**Publicity**
Alainna Hadjigeorgiou

**Sales**
Jen Wilson
Esther Waters
Victoria Laws
Rachael Hum
Ellie Kyrke-Smith
Frances Doyle
Georgina Cutler

**A heart-rending story about motherhood, forbidden love and long-buried secrets . . .**

Could one mother's secret
be another's second chance?

**Mothering Sunday**

**SARA JAMES**

**One crisp and bright Mothering Sunday, Alexandra Abbott's now elderly mother, Elizabeth, reveals a secret that she has kept buried for over 50 years. . .**

**April 1963:** Aspiring artist Kitty Campbell has recently given birth to her first child in a mother and baby home. Kitty is to give her baby away for adoption but, when the day comes, she can't bring herself to part with her tiny daughter.

In desperation, Kitty flees. She stops at a tea shop to feed her hungry baby and meets the owner, Bet – a mother with her own heartache to bear. But Bet is kind to Kitty, holding the baby and offering a listening ear.

Then Kitty makes a decision that will change all their lives for ever. Several decades later, can the truth from that day finally right the past and bring a mother and daughter together?

**"Full of insight and wisdom, Mothering Sunday is an inspirational story with uplifting messages about family love, belonging and second chances. . . the perfect gift for your own special mum"** *Lancashire Post*